Able Hands

Able Hands

MARK J. CANNON

IGUANA

Publisher: Meghan Behse
Editor: Holly Warren and Heather Bury
Front cover design: Ruth Dwight (designplayground.ca)

ISBN 978-1-77180-381-6 (paperback)
ISBN 978-1-77180-382-3 (epub)
ISBN 978-1-77180-383-0 (Kindle)

This is an original print edition of *Able Hands*.

To Marie

1

Light of Day

Parallel to the Blacklynn River was the old two-storey cider mill in the midst of restoration. An overgrown wood lot blinded Jacob's view as he approached along Riverside Drive. An intense dread flashed through him as he neared the building. An unmarked cruiser and an ambulance sat by the front doors, with another cruiser blocking the second entrance farther down. Police tape covered the main entrance guarded by two young officers whose imposing figures provided an added deterrence. People from the area and drivers-by alike were gathering and murmuring as the usual morbid curiosity developed.

In seconds the scene had Jacob shaking uncontrollably, his abdomen squeezed tight and his knees felt weak. The contents in his stomach curdled and immediately wanted out. *What in God's name happened?* he asked himself, as several horrifying scenarios played out in his mind. He jumped out of his truck and raced for the entrance when the two officers stopped him in his tracks. He began shouting beyond them to a detective by the front doors; his queries for the moment ignored. Just then the cruiser blocking the second entrance backed up to allow the coroner's car in. Jacob's body went limp, an agonizing fear weakening him completely.

Part 2
1984

Standing on his third-floor balcony, Jacob took in the panoramic view of the north shore of Lake Ontario, the water a combination of greys and blues with small whitecaps. The sound of those waves slowly slapping up against the posts of the old wooden dock, grey with age, quickly became a welcomed pacifier. He drew a deep breath of warm air into his lungs — in the nose, out the mouth, recalling his training in judo. That was his mother's compromise on the less violent of the martial arts. Just like so many kids who grew up in the early seventies, Jacob had wanted to emulate Bruce Lee.

He had grown into a solid young man. At twenty-one, his six-foot, one-hundred-ninety-pound frame helped with his chosen career in construction. He was one of the lucky few who loved his job and was eager about going to work every day. Being a part of a working-class family of five siblings from the small city of Saint John instilled in him a fine work ethic. On this promising day it was unseasonably warm for early May, and he thanked the day as a gift. It was a matter of seconds standing on the balcony, barefoot and in boxers, that provided confidence to wear a cotton button-up and leave the windbreaker behind. There were only a few brilliantly white, puffy clouds following a slow stream to the east — dots in the vast sky of tropical blue. The sun had a direct line with no interference for its skin-piercing UV rays to try and do their worst.

For so early in the morning, on the start to an otherwise average Monday, he was surprised at the heat penetrating his forearm hanging out the window driving to work. The current project he was working on, a condo-conversion in an old warehouse district, was a thirty-minute drive away. Behind the wheel with a heavy foot, to get what he referred to as his "a.m. nectar," he approached the same turn he took every morning. He could feel the piercing eyes of an elderly woman on the corner across the street locked in on him as he completed his turn. Oddly, her expression seemed almost happy, for the most part.

However, a circle of cold formed on the centre of Jacob's chest, penetrating inward. In that moment, he was overwhelmed by the feeling that she knew who he was, or she knew something personal about him. He looked over his shoulder, completing the turn, and squinting in an effort to focus in on her through the rear-view. A chill enveloped him, and for a second he experienced a pressing and almost uncontrollable desire to crawl out of his own skin. He drove some distance, his chest rose, and a pronounced sigh accompanied his exhale. He gently shook his head and looked to his destination of dark roast and normalcy. Not easily forgotten, the effects of the look were still resonating.

§

Sam Ellison came out from the back of his bright, clean, and newly expanded bakery added onto the rear of his café. Sweat had glued patches of flour to his face, neck, and arms. Jacob met his gaze and they nodded to each other warmly.

Good crowd, Jacob thought. *Looks like all the work paid off.* They exchanged smiles and asked after each other's weekends.

"It's a nice-looking start for a Monday out there."

"It is at that. Are you finally able to keep your head out of those ovens for more than five minutes at a time?"

"I would've been done an hour ago if I didn't have to bake so much banana bread. You know it's inhuman to eat that much banana bread, right?"

Jacob pointed his finger at Sam, and with a wink said, "It is mighty fine banana bread. I must admit. With the coffee, it's my sustenance, or life blood, or however you say it. And, it's almost as good as my mom's."

Looking down and rubbing his foot back and forth across a cracked floor tile, Jacob frowned, the vertical lines between his eyes becoming more pronounced as they squeezed together. The notebook came out from his back pocket and his pencil from behind his ear like a doctor pulling out a stethoscope.

"Almost as good as mom's, eh? Hey, Jacob. Relax buddy; put the pad away. It's not even seven o'clock. And on a Monday at that?!"

"Hey, this isn't the first time I called these guys about this."

"Jacob, it's not the end of the world." But then Sam relented, "Well, I suppose you're right. That is where everyone stands, in front of the till. I guess it doesn't look so good, does it?" He shifted gears. "So, am I gonna see you at the shop Wednesday night? I bought a set of Marples, the chisel guide, and an oilstone from Lee Valley. We can try them out."

Jacob grabbed his usual, a large Colombian dark roast and two one-inch-thick slices of banana bread. Just before reaching the door, he spun around to see Sam waiting with his hands on his hips.

"Absolutely," he exclaimed. "I'm looking forward to it. See you tomorrow morning, Sam. Keep that banana bread coming."

And Sam, shaking his head and smiling, raised his hand in farewell. He was Jacob's senior by almost seventeen years, but he saw Jacob as mature beyond his years; most did.

§

The coffee was safely stowed away, and a smile resurfaced when he looked at his watch; making the building department by opening was in sight. He pulled out of the parking lot of Sam's café and was easily flowing into traffic before the congestion began. He hit the power button and was surfing for something to listen to when he came across "Sweet City Woman" by The Stampeders. The song, the smell of banana bread, and there he was — five years old and back home with his mom. She was wearing *The Best Mom* apron standing in the kitchen baking a list of favourites, with the radio on as always. Of course, banana bread was at the top. He put away the sweet memory as quickly as it was found and changed the station. Aware that it was an odd preference at his age, he sought out jazz.

The warm air blew in through his rolled-up, long-sleeve shirt and tickled the hairs of his underarm and chest. Within seconds, he had undone his buttons. *It wasn't that long ago I was digging snow out from the job sites.* Rubbing his fingers together, he recalled the pain from split and often bleeding fingertips from throwing salt around the entrances and walkways. He took one more look at his watch as he arrived at the office.

Henderson Construction & Design's office was on the first floor of a thirty-storey building by the lake downtown. As he came in the entrance, Jacob saw elaborate furnishings, artwork, and plants wherever he turned his eyes. He always stopped to admire how everything flowed together — something new to him.

"Hi, Annie. Can't help but notice you're always the first one here in the mornings."

"That's right," she quickly replied, moving her stacks of papers around like an orchestrated dance. "But I also get to leave between three and four everyday. So, coming in early isn't so bad. Anyway, how are you coming along, Jacob? You're into your second year and still here; that's a good sign," she giggled.

"I'm doing okay. I love it, actually. The more I learn, the better it is," Jacob said, reaching across the desk to get the file and a cheque for the building permit.

"Well, it's not lost on the guys here how quick you're progressing. So, keep up the good work. Oh, speaking of work," she slapped the back of Jacob's hand, "you have a couple of new files here."

"This usually stays here. Don't I have to review it with Donny?"

"Like I said Jacob, it's not lost on them how well you're progressing. So apparently, Donny feels you're ready to take the file and get started on your own."

"Thanks, Annie. Take care," he said, unable to contain his expanding smile.

With exuberance, he hurried back to his vehicle, but it was an awkward-looking sprint across the parking lot in heavy steel-toed work boots. His heels hit first, and his toes loudly slammed down on the pavement like the clop of a horse. Prior to his second stop at the building department, he had a quick scan through the file. It was like a gift he couldn't wait to open. Before he pulled out of the lot, he looked to the building across the street and he saw the same elderly woman locked in another stare. *Impossible.* She wore a paisley summer dress in multiple shades of brown. A beige scarf adorned her silver and white hair with the balance of it wrapped around her neck. Jacob's eyes nervously darted back and forth a few times, while pulling on the steering wheel to make the turn, but then letting it swing back. He did this a few times. Looking down he paused with a deep breath, then he looked behind him, to his left, then right. Finally, he threw the gearshift into park. Once he'd summoned his courage, he turned his eyes toward this strange-looking woman but was met with an empty sidewalk and the grey stucco building behind it.

He swallowed a lump of air, felt the hair rise on his forearms and neck, and shook himself from side to side to rid the ebb and flow of goosebumps and cold tingling skin. He put the truck back in gear and slowly drove away to continue his day. He forced his eyes wide open to refocus and looked in the mirror several times. "What — the — hell — was — that?!?" he said aloud. "She looked like a gypsy woman or fortune teller, or … something. And where the hell did she go? Jesus, Jacob, you're losing it," he said, as his voice dropped several decibels. The last swallow of his dark roast painfully pushed another dry ball of air down his throat, followed by yet another glance to his watch. He swore at how much the ball of air hurt his throat. Then another look in the rear-view and another glance to his watch…

Part 3

Arriving at the building department, Jacob's knees started to feel a little shaky as he approached the tall maple and glass doors inside the vestibule. On the other side worked a lovely co-op student, Sara Millen. Marching in like on a mission, he lost his footing momentarily, slipping over a freshly washed terrazzo, and almost completed the splits. After an ugly recovery, he scowled at the floor behind him where he just slipped. *Well, can't blame the floor for my looking like an idiot*, he thought. *It would've been better if I tripped over the caution sign that's RIGHT THERE!* He quietly chuckled. Wondering if Sara had seen this, it didn't take too long before beads of perspiration started forming on his forehead, and his throat was getting dryer by the second. *Damn. I should've got another coffee.* He searched through his empty pockets for a candy or stick of gum, but that only resulted in quietly cursing himself for not restocking. He was grateful to see Sara wasn't at the counter yet to witness his ungraceful entrance. He was, however, surprised someone was already at the counter being served. *Did this guy sleep outside all night to be first in line?* he thought, looking at his watch: 8:36 a.m. *Hmm, five minutes after opening. Not bad.* Taking a seat, he couldn't help but snicker at a sign posting the department's hours straight across from his seat. The sign, which was covered in clear plexiglass, provided a reflection. He looked up to the counter, then quickly to his image to pull a tuft of hair away from his sweaty forehead. No one had seen anything, so a couple more times would suffice. He started shaking his legs and tapping his hands on his thighs; at the same time, he surveyed the place like he was watching a tennis match. He rubbed the sweat off his hands onto his jeans, and with his fingernail, he tapped the glass of his Timex. His classic timepiece, straps barely hanging on, with a scratched and cracked faux crystal covering a barely visible face. It was his eighteenth birthday present from his father.

"Isn't Sara working today?" Jacob blurted out.

The building inspector, Jonathon Vargas, mumbled in a barely audible yet patronizing tone.

"Just take a number and have a seat, Mr. O'Connell. Someone will be along to help you."

Jacob said nothing and kept his thoughts to himself. There were all sorts of design problems for his employer, with this particular building department. There were more inspection failures here than in any other municipality in a thirty-mile radius. Failures where there should be none.

This guy really is a dick. I can see why everybody gets so pissed off at him. Damn it, I wish Sara was here. I got things to do. Jacob rolled his eyes. *Yeah, right.* The shaking in his legs began to subside, then he slid his back down, pushing his bum forward on his chair, crossed his leg and began to drift. He closed his eyes and a smile returned thinking back to an encounter with Sara on site only a couple of months after he met her at the bar. He tried to ignore Vargas during his daydream. He was becoming an intrusive factor in this part of his life. The few times he was able to see Sara were exciting for him, providing Vargas didn't ruin them.

That day was etched into his memory. It was like a movie he could play over and over. Her fire-red hair, including the hair on her arms and eyebrows, all caught his attention. He was amazed how it all encompassed her; even the freckles crossing her cheeks and nose were the same colour. His attempt to stay cool was failing, having great difficulty hiding his bashful smile from her.

"Do you have the engineered drawings for the floor and truss systems?" she asked. Vargas was furiously writing in his inspection form, making furtive glances toward the pair. Jacob fumbled through his file, dropping and picking up papers. He used the back of his forearm to wipe the dripping sweat from his forehead. When he finally gathered his papers, he stood up with a helpless look and handed Sara a stack of drawings.

"Sorry, these aren't the right ones, Jacob." She held them out to be put back in his file. "It is hot in here," she whispered, looking at him, and gently tapping her index finger to her cheek.

"Yeah, it is." He used the side of his thumb to clear the little beads of perspiration from under his eyes. "Thanks," he said. His eyes softened and his smile accented his crow's feet and one dimple on his left cheek. Sara couldn't help but notice. When he handed the proper drawings over, their hands touched, yet neither of them flinched or pulled back. In his peripheral, Jacob could see Vargas quickly looking back down at his own report and shaking his head. It wasn't accompanied with an observational smile, it was something else — unclear, but definitely disconcerting.

As the inspection continued, Jacob held his hand out, indicating she go first up the stairs. When they returned, he purposely went first in front of her, which caught her attention. He remained quiet while she went through her checklist. He acted as a guide more than a nervous contractor waiting for the inspection to pass. There were the occasional questions back and forth, but no straying off topic. After a year into his job, Jacob had come to learn it was a common practice in the business to distract inspectors in hope they would overlook some of the incomplete items or minor infractions.

Finally, the inspection came to an end with Vargas dramatically tearing the top copy of the triplicate inspection form. Jacob held his hand out, and Vargas, completely lacking in affect, didn't even acknowledge him. He pulled a stapler from his back pocket and affixed the inspection failure to the wall by the entrance of the building. This was policy, but only when the contractor, or a representative wasn't present. He turned to Sara, inappropriately eyeing her up and down and pointed to his code book.

"This is what steers you, Miss Millen, not some attractive site superintendent, or *assistant*." He accentuated the word in a teenage-like insult. "From now on, make sure these guys have the work on the checklist ready for the next phase before we head out for an inspection. You're wasting valuable time and resources just because you think…" He stopped himself there, looking at Sara's face. Jacob ripped the inspection report off the wall.

"Take that outside, will ya?" Jacob said, feeling horrible for Sara. "For Christ's sake," he added, spinning around, and walked to the other side of the building so Sara wouldn't feel any more embarrassment than she was already experiencing. "Fucking prick!" Jacob said to himself.

Out the building Vargas went, his long legs tight together as he walked with odd short strides toward the municipal vehicle.

"Let's go, Millen," he barked out to Sara. "And get those violations cleaned up. Don't call for another inspection until you're ready next time," he snarled.

Sara was not only embarrassed, she was furious with Vargas. She felt that for now, being a co-op student, she had to take the insults. But she indicated to Jacob how she really felt. Jacob turned to see Vargas walk out, and Sara taking a moment to shuffle some papers and compose herself. He walked back over and looked at her with raised eyebrows and a small smile.

"Does he always walk like he's gotta take a shit?" Jacob said, expanding his smile. He hoped to ease her discomfort a little before she left.

She smiled back. "Yeah. Pretty much," she said, holding her hand at hip level, forming a fist, squeezing it as tight as she could. "Ooh!" And she walked out the door. Message delivered to a comrade in arms.

But when she turned back around, her long red hair, brightened by the sun, caught his eye. An overwhelming feeling of familiarity about her gnawed at him.

Jacob now recalled more awkward moments interacting with Sara when Vargas was present. And one in particular rarely left his thoughts. Everything is under a microscope when working for the government. The mid-eighties hadn't exactly experienced a profound revolution of enlightenment in the workplace. But Vargas's behaviour was more than growing inappropriate, it was beyond the pale when it came to Sara, especially when Jacob was there.

He ran up the stairs of another job site to catch up with Sara. While arriving, he slowed down his breathing with a couple of barely announced exhales.

"Sara, you forgot to take the engineer's report for the steel columns and beams."

"So, what exactly did they teach you in that school?" Vargas quipped. Jacob had become familiar with his condescending tone and look. "You're supposed to know these procedures by the end of your second year in school. What were you doing there? Or rather, who were you doing there that made you miss so much?" Jacob looked at him disgusted. Vargas continued, "Well? Did you spend all your time partying and whatever else?" Jacob was about to call him on the carpet for that one, but he didn't get a chance. Sara walked over to a workbench near Vargas and dropped the file folder down. Her eyes were a squint, but they still bore a hole straight through him. Considering the level of anger she was experiencing, she acted with poise and professionalism, and spoke calmly.

"Jonathon, I'll be waiting outside in the truck while you finish up here." She started walking away, but only a few steps in Vargas's voice became elevated.

"Where are you going? We're not done here. I'll let you know when we're finished. Just because you make mistakes doesn't mean you get to run away."

Sara didn't respond verbally. She walked until she thought she was out of earshot from Jacob, the client. After stopping, she slowly turned around and subtly motioned for him to come join her. Begrudgingly, he shuffled toward her, a clear look of anger quickly became apprehension seeing the look in her eyes. The look on her face was visceral as she stood her ground, and even though Jacob was slightly taken aback, he was also pleased to see it. He could sense her anger like it was a scent in the air to breath in.

"We are done here, Jonathon," she said, with her hands on her hips and leaning into him on her tiptoes within inches of his face. "You can finish this inspection yourself," still speaking quietly, but with a fire behind her words. Vargas attempted to interrupt, but she wasn't done yet.

"Don't you ever talk to me like that, let alone in front of a client. You may have gotten away with that kind of crap with other people, but it ain't gonna fly with me, mister. I'll report your ass so fast your head will spin. Are we clear!?! And I don't care if you're the boss or not. And if you want me to help you here, this stops now."

At this point, Vargas was diverting his eyes everywhere but at her. He only stopped long enough to focus on his words that were weakly whispered out like a scolded child.

"I apologize. It won't happen again," he said flatly, waving his free hand like an umpire calling safe.

Before the two of them turned around, Jacob struggled to constrain his smile. Watching and hearing bits of Sara taking a strip off Vargas like that earned her his respect and admiration. Jacob quickly looked back down at the blueprints like he hadn't seen or heard anything. However, when they returned, he couldn't resist giving Sara a shy smile of recognition. Witnessing Sara's character in her rebuttal of her boss's behaviour, he found it difficult not to stare at her.

Wow, that's my kind of woman, he thought. *No fear that one. Wow. Wow, and another wow.*

He lowered his head a bit; bringing his attention to study the blueprints. It wasn't working very well. His eyes were looking everywhere but at the details of the drawings in front of him. And his thoughts were even further away. *If it's true that everyone has a perfect match, I think I just found mine.*

Part 4

The floor cleaner smell in the building department reminded Jacob of grade school. He thought of the shrill of the principal's secretary paging kids to the office amplified by the intercom, its pitch creating a piercing feedback that felt like an ice pick being driven into his ears. He remembered it well. He would push his shoulders up as far as they would go, trying to squeeze off the sound, and it always made him shiver. But currently, it wasn't feedback that broke the solace of his daydream. It was the sound of screeching tires and some kind of impact from the other side of the doors he'd just come through. His head cocked to the side for a split second, discerning a sound that seemed familiar. His abdomen pulled in tight and a dreadful cold wave encompassed his body. *Please don't let it be...*

It shocked him out of his daydream, and with eyes wide and his entire body tense, he was in motion. He burst out through the doors, cleared the stairs and landed on the sidewalk. It reminded him of running hurdles. When the closer broke and the door slammed against the grey stone exterior of the heritage town hall, it had sounded like a gunshot. The street was four lanes wide, divided by a huge grass boulevard, but traffic on his side had stopped. His hand went up to block the brightness of the sun, then his eyes quickly adjusted. Jacob's stomach dropped, and his knees wobbled at what he saw in front of him — Sara lay on the ground. An unexplained memory from a similar event flashed through, but it was pushed away faster than it arrived. His focus centred in on Sara's body, lying on the asphalt, contorted and covered in blood and dirt from the street. He was ready to act, and at the same time, the look of shock and trepidation on his face was undeniable.

A quick study of her body revealed an obvious broken leg and a compound fracture to her arm. The more pressing issue was the injury to her head. He could see the blood coming out a large gash on the side of her head and from her ear. A courier quickly dismounted his bicycle, stepped off the sidewalk and looked to Jacob.

"I seen the whole thing. I know her — Sara from the building department. I deliver to them all the time. What can I do?" His words a rapid stream.

Kneeling beside Sara, Jacob reached up with his arms wide open and waved his hands in to receive the toss. "Give me your bag."

"What?" The courier had been wearing his light-blue canvas shoulder bag like a prized possession.

"Give me the bag. Now!" Jacob yelled.

The courier stripped his satchel off and reached it out. "Yeah … sure man. Here ya go." He passed it off to Jacob. Jacob tore off his white sleeveless undershirt and ripped it in two. One piece was used to try to get the bleeding to her head under control; the other was rolled around her fractured arm. Then he folded the messenger bag and placed it under her head. The sirens in the distance were a welcome sound. He began checking for vital signs after clearing her throat; her breathing and heartbeat were absent. He wasted no time — between counting compressions, he was breathing into her lungs.

"Sara! Wake up, Sara!" His own breathing was becoming pronounced and perspiration began to form on his forehead. "Come on now, Sara, wake up."

Tears started to drip down his cheeks. More people were gathering around. The usual questions came from throughout the crowd and morbid onlookers.

"What happened? Is that the guy who hit her? Is she dead?"

Jacob yelled at them to shut up and get away, and all the while, the compressions continued. The courier stepped in and did his best. "Back up, please. Let him do what he needs to. Please, step back." The crowd was barely shifting. "Back up, for Christ's sake." His voice rising to a near scream got some results. Jacob was yelling out Sara's name now, begging her to come around. He turned his head and put his ear to her chest, then to her mouth. He frantically continued making compressions and emptying his air into her. He could hear an ambulance or police car closing in now. He thought he'd make one last effort before the paramedics forced him out of the way and took over.

"Come on, Sara! Do it for me. Come on now, sweetheart, breathe, breathe, please, just breathe for me." His voice was getting weaker by the second, but he wasn't stopping; he wasn't giving up.

Jacob quickly glanced through a hole in the expanding crowd and saw the same woman from earlier. His eyes opened as wide as they could to make sure it was her. He was sure of. It was the same woman standing on the sidewalk. This time, however, Sara was next to her. He quickly looked back down at Sara and then back to the sidewalk. He squeezed his eyes shut, refusing to look back up when they reopened. "She's not there. She's not there," he kept repeating to himself. "Jesus, Jacob. Just don't look back up." He focused on the compressions. His face had grown red, his cheeks wet with tears. He did not deviate from his task.

Only minutes had passed since he had burst through the doors of the building department. He felt that time was running out and he could feel his energy leaving. Her broken and bloodied body lay below him, and because he was completely exhausted, he was unable to avoid looking up. "No, Jacob. Don't look. Ah, Jesus Christ!" It was incomprehensible to him, but there she was. "You're not seeing that. She's not there. Come on, Sara. You're not there, you're here — so wake up." Looking back up again, this mysterious woman next to Sara looked directly into his eyes. He couldn't turn away. The chills returned, with his body hair standing upright. He could hear her speaking to him, but her mouth wasn't moving; and she was too far away to hear anyway. Nonetheless, her words arrived directly inside his head.

"You will save her, Jacob." In that moment, what he was hearing in her voice was somehow familiar, calming, reassuring. "She will live. It's all right, Jacob. Everything is going to be okay. You've done this before, and you will do it again." She spoke with a soft voice, as if making a gentle introduction.

In those few seconds, he paused compressions, and again closed his eyes tightly. His chest heaved with a breath, and he brought his hands up to cover his face and eyes. Weary and with his head pounding, he slowly pulled his hands away. A yellowish orange light glowing about them, forcing him to squint. He thought it was the sun shining onto his hands. He tried — but failed — to ignore looking back at his hands out of the corner of his eye. His body was vibrating, his arms felt weak, and his hands started shaking uncontrollably. He resigned to giving up the compressions, his head lowered, bent over on his knees. Without reason or intent, he placed his hands on both sides of Sara's head, looking as if he was about to kiss her goodbye.

A completely surprising surge of warm energy rushed through his entire body. It went from his chest, through his arms, and out of his hands as he held Sara's head. He closed his eyes and mind to what he was seeing and experiencing. "This has to end. It has to. Please, let it end." When he looked back up to the sidewalk, Sara was gone, and to her side, with equal relief, the older woman was gone too. His head dropped, then he shook his head and belted out an awful sounding cry.

What in God's name just happened? What's happening to me? He couldn't understand why he had failed to save her. The paramedics finally arrived on foot and were within steps of them, when suddenly

Sara took a gasping draw of air and began to cough. Jacob's burst was a combined laugh and cry. His tears were still flowing, fluids came from his nose, and his undershirt was soaked in sweat. He was a mess, but it couldn't stop his growing smile. He put his hands over his face again. His large frame was bent over, nearly collapsed from his spent energy. More short gasps of laughter escaped as his cries began to subside. His adrenaline waning, he was still shaking and weak, watching over her as she kept fighting to keep her eyes open between breathing and sputtering coughs. He looked at her, and not caring what he looked like, he pulled the bottom of his shirt up and wiped his face. "Hey, what's say you never do that again, all right? The paramedics are here; they're going to help you. You're going to be okay, Sara. You're going to be okay." He saw a look in her that said she somehow knew everything that just happened. It was an affable look of gratitude, of recognition undeniable.

The paramedics gently pulled Jacob away and started their procedure of securing Sara's vitals. Once stabile, they placed her on the backboard and onto the gurney ready for transport. Jacob stood as close to her as he could throughout, and although he was happy, he was spent. In the time that passed on what he thought was a perfect day, Jacob stood up with an expression of an amazing epiphany. He was taking in a near three-hundred-and-sixty-degree survey of the surrounding area. He was elated, giddy. Sara was alive; she was going to be okay. All else was secondary.

The supervisor, and most experienced paramedic, recognized Jacob's gaze floating in every direction. He managed to get his attention and focus. Standing in front of him, he pulled his shoulders together and looked into his eyes. Jacob was almost limp, giving the medic full control.

"Sir, how are you feeling?" Jacob looked up at him, clearly shaken.

"I'm fine; I was just looking for someone. Ah, here he comes." He was still hanging onto the courier's bag. "Hey man, thanks so much for your help. I'm sorry, there's blood on your bag." The courier looked like he was ready for the Californian surf. He had on a bright tie-dyed

T-shirt with a yellow background. His long blonde hair was tied in a ponytail and he wore camouflage shorts with Dash running shoes. He extended one hand for his bag and the other to shake Jacob's hand.

"I'm Gary by the way, and the blood doesn't matter, buddy. And I didn't do anything; it was all you brother. You did a fine job today."

Jacob responded with his name, but barely acknowledged the compliment by the courier. He turned his gaze back to the sidewalk where the mystery woman had stood next to Sara. He looked lost, in need of direction.

The paramedic came back over to Jacob. "You did absolutely everything right for that young lady today. She's alive because of you. Where'd you learn first aid?"

"Oh, uh, through work ... St. John's course at the Y."

"Uh, that explains it. Well, it was a hell of a job. You sure you're okay?"

Jacob's words were coming out as a tired soul ready for slumber. "I'm good. Hey ... thanks, all right." Jacob could barely raise his arm, weak and worn from the compressions and expended adrenaline, but he managed to shake the paramedic's hand.

The medic was about to leave when he turned around to Jacob once more. "Oh, by the way, she'll be at South Central. In case you want to see her." With those words, he hopped into the supervisor's Suburban and was gone. Jacob pulled in the longest breath and exhaled like it was the sweetest air he ever tasted. He paused for a minute, standing still trying to get his bearings.

My God, Jacob. What happened back there? He held his palm against his temple. Before he made it back to his truck, he tried to replay everything. *I was giving her CPR, but it seemed too late. She seemed already... But then she started breathing again! How?* A massive piercing pain in his temple overtook him, and, leaning over, he vomited himself empty. He slowly stood up, still dizzy and spinning. When he finally got his bearings, he looked down at his hands, palms turned up and, with a blank look on his face, he thought, *Maybe I just need some rest before I can think straight and remember.*

2

Ardent Resolve

Part 1

Life on the Millen family farm on the outskirts of Saint John was an idyllic place to grow up. When Sara wasn't playing with the family dog or feeding her bunnies, she often swung on a swing, staring off with her head tilted into her arm. Her more solitary moments were spent filling in colouring books or drawing pictures with pencil crayons on coloured construction paper or drawing pads. She would often lay on the picnic table on her belly drawing pictures of her life on the farm. Occasionally, her father, Joe, would come in from the fields — soy, wheat, or corn — and find her there, drifted off to sleep. She found the sound of the farm equipment soothing.

However, one day in late summer when she was five, Joe came back from work to find her sleeping yet again, with some crayons spilled and papers blown about. Joe walked over to her and began gently shaking her. "How's my strong girl today? Did you fall asleep drawing pictures of clouds or bunnies this time?" There was no stir from Sara. "Sara, sweetie, time to wake up and come in for lunch." Joe, with his large hands felt that her back was unusually warm, so he turned her over, but she was still asleep. He put the inside of his wrist to her forehead, picked her up, listened to her little chest breathe and sprinted into the house.

"Shannon! Shannon!" he yelled out to his wife from the back breezeway. "Call the doctor. Sara has a fever and she's not waking up.

She's still sleeping after I picked her up," Joe said, his voice frantically rising. He began pacing back and forth through the kitchen. "Come on, sweetie, wake up now. You have to wake up, Sara. Shannon!" he screamed out.

When Shannon came running into the kitchen, she saw the look on Joe's face. "What is it? Oh my God, what's happened?" Shannon felt Sara's sticky forehead and looked up to her husband. "Let's go. We need to take her to the hospital." Shannon held her little girl in her arms, she grabbed a cloth, ran it under cold water, and out the door they went.

Relatives, friends, and even some neighbours would say Sara was a reincarnated fortune teller or gypsy, and some people found that kind of spooky, but in a good way. There was an odd reaction from most adults who would interact with her. Although she spoke with the same cute high-pitched voice as any other little girl, the way she said things made her sound like an adult. She was calm and direct in what she said. She always came across as logical, and well beyond her age. After her emergency run to the hospital, she stabilized but began to develop a host of symptoms; some were life-threatening.

She had an unknown disease at the time that attacked her immune system. She could become deathly ill just from coming into contact with the most insignificant, benign germ. Her illness mostly resulted in respiratory breakdowns, bronchitis, or sniffles that would turn into deadly pneumonia in a very short time. And one of the other symptoms was breaking out in rashes, some of which would blister.

The Millens were terrified a few times thinking they might lose her. She was confined to the hospital for months. Sara cried to go home every day. Her parents finally had a professionally designed clear plastic tent installed in their house around a hospital bed, which was supplied by the Optimist Club, and once Sara was stable enough, they moved her home.

One morning in late spring, Sara's mother entered her room to find her standing outside of her tent playing with her dollhouse and many stuffed toys. Shannon yelled out, "Oh my God, Sara, what are you doing out of your tent? Are you trying to get sick?"

Out came this little squeaky voice, "Mommy, I got out last night and look, no cough and my spots aren't sore and itchy." Sara was pointing to her arms and lifted her nightgown to reveal that her spots had shrunk in size and volume overnight. "I'm all better, Mommy."

"Come now, sweetheart, let's get you back in bed and you stay there, young lady. I'm going to get the doctor. How in God's name did you get out of this tent?" Shannon was talking to herself, looking at the zipper release on the outside of the tent.

"Jacob let me out. And we played with more of my toys. I like Jacob."

Ignoring Sara's statement as nonsense, Shannon flew down the stairs. "Joe, call the doctor," she shouted. And without hesitation, she turned to go back up the stairs, two steps at a time.

Sara called out from her room to ask her mother, "Is Jacob coming back tonight, Mommy? I want to go to school with him in grade one."

"I don't know, sweetie. We will have to see." She hurriedly went through the routine of washing her hands, putting on a fresh mask and gown and went to Sara to check her temperature. Sara's grandmother had stayed with her through most of that year, but not the previous night. The Millens had to work the farm as much as possible. They were blessed to have Joe's mother there to help.

In the next few weeks, Sara's spots disappeared, and her temperature remained normal. Shannon and Joe called the doctor to their house, and after two weeks of monitoring, blood tests, exams, and so on, all signs pointed to her being able to leave the tent and join other kids for the start of grade one.

Sylvia Millen, Sara's grandmother, lived in town, about a ten-minute drive from the farm and a block away from where Sara would be going to school for grade one. Sara was so excited to be able to visit Grammy in her own home again. She loved the inviting kitchen smells from her cooking and baking. Sara also loved the homemade comforters and afghans her grandmother made and draped over her when she would drift off to sleep. Sara's favourite spot was the fainting couch, especially on days when rays of sunlight came through the bay window.

And Sylvia always had a bouquet of lavender on the window bench, a scent that would stay with Sara over the years, a Millen women tradition.

Sara was also excited to see that boy, Jacob, who lived across the street from her. Sara only had a couple of short meetings with him before she became ill, but now she would be able to play with him and the other kids from the block. She noticed something special about how attentive he was to her, and how caring; it was unlike most boys. Sara eventually forgot about the night Jacob visited, playing with her in her bedroom. And for Jacob, that meeting had happened just in a dream, or so he thought.

§

One day during the summer break after his first year of kindergarten Jacob was returning home from Grimmer's General Store at the end of the block. He carried a bag full of penny candy, compliments of his grandmother. She would always reward him with a small plastic margarine container half full of coppers — this is how she referred to the mountain of pennies she had saved over the years.

The sun was rising bright and shone directly into his eyes as he walked toward home. He couldn't wait to tease his brother and sister, Kevin and Kate, with his bag of gold. Looking into the sun always made him sneeze; this moment was no different. The quick succession of sneezing from the blinding sunlight was interrupted by the horrible sound of tires screeching and then some kind of unholy thud from an impact.

Mr. Alex Grimmer, commonly referred to as just Grimmer, was a well-loved and respected man in town. He had a welcoming personality and look. Always in his work clothes and with dirty hands, he was a giving soul, even to strangers. Today, as he often did, he drove back from the market to stock his neighbourhood general store with fruit and vegetables. His 1947 Ford pick-up truck was dark blue once but was now faded to a combination of light blues and greys, like the sea on an overcast day threatening to storm. Grimmer always wore a thick pair of round wire-rimmed glasses, and for a moment he became blinded by the sun. Sara's bike had rolled down the sloped driveway just enough to run into his path. When he felt the impact, Grimmer slammed the brakes hard and didn't move another inch ahead. But the damage was done, and the knot in his stomach like a ball of lead.

The light blues and greys of the truck and the white oak rails affixed to its box, along with the red of Sara's bicycle and the white of the tires, all became part of a collage inside of Jacob's dreams for the next few years. It became a completely different and twisted version that would play out and would occasionally turn his dreams into nightmares.

That terrible day, when Jacob put his hand up to block the sun, with his eyes squinted, he tightly clenched his jaw to stave off a series of sneezes. Sometimes it worked. He then stood still in complete shock at this horrible scene in front of him, strangling his bag of candies.

He looked out to the street to see Sara lying on the ground, her hair soaked in blood. Frozen, he kept looking at her red bike and its white tires, and then the red blood on her white face. Grimmer was out of the truck, coming around to the front to see what he had done. Sara's grandmother came flying out of the house, screaming Sara's name. Grimmer was about to reach down to pick Sara up, but Sylvia arrived, and slapped his hand out of the way, cursing at him.

"Damn you, Grimmer. Why are you even driving when you know you're half blind? Look at what you've done!" Sylvia cried out.

Mr. Grimmer was shaking; his words came out in a stutter, "I … didn't see her, I c-c-couldn't … the sun … I didn't see from the sun. I'm so s-s-sorry Sylvia, please … let me help?" He swallowed hard to get the last words out.

Sylvia started screaming — the sound something young Jacob had never heard — and it frightened him. It was a scream so profoundly norm shattering, yet for some reason, instead of running away, he stepped off the sidewalk and instinctively walked toward it.

"Jacob, get back. You stay out of the way now. Go home. Do you hear me, Jacob?" Sylvia's tears streamed down her cheeks as she continued to wail.

Jacob ignored her instructions. He arrived at the gruesome scene and knelt next to them. Sylvia didn't bother with him anymore; she was inconsolable at that point. She had Sara's limp and seemingly lifeless body in between her folded knees laying on the pavement. Sara's hair was now matted down, almost completely dark with blood, and her grandmother was lost to grief. Grimmer had one knee on the pavement, the other bent, with his arm resting on the bumper of the truck and his head hanging down. At that moment, Jacob reached his hands out, and, barely visible in the light of day, there was a glow about them, a familiar hue. For a few seconds, and ever so gently, his hands touched both sides of Sara's head. Sylvia didn't know what she was seeing or how to react. With her free hand, she tried to push him out of the way, but something made her stop and she just let him be.

"You're going to be all right, Sara. Just wait. You're going to be okay. I know it," Jacob said, letting go of her head and standing up. He took one last look down, and as he turned around, Sara started to sputter a tiny cough. It was complete shock to both Grimmer and Sylvia. They both believed little Sara was gone, or on the way, slipping out of her hands so to speak. Now it was panic. He didn't know what to do or which way to go, and the neighbours were coming out one after the other with suggestions. Jacob heard someone say they called for an ambulance. That's when Sylvia had a neighbour drive Grimmer's truck, and they rushed Sara to the hospital, with Sylvia holding her the entire way. Grimmer seemed lost, standing on the sidewalk bewildered, his hand on top of Jacob's shoulder, keeping watch over him.

Mr. Grimmer let the neighbours buzz about talking about what happened and took Jacob by the hand to walk him home across the street. As he came through the door, his mother was coming up the stairs from the laundry room in the basement. She looked down to see blood stains all over him.

"What happened? Where are you hurt? Where did this blood come from? Oh my God, Jacob, what happened to you?" Irene was frantically pulling at his clothes, looking for the origin of any injury. Mr. Grimmer was standing behind Jacob, white as a ghost.

"I'm okay, Mom. It was Sara. Mr. Grimmer hit her with his truck … but she's okay. They're taking her to the hospital to make her better. Can I have some of my candy now, Mom?"

When Irene was satisfied Jacob wasn't hurt, she pulled him into her arms and squeezed hard in a longer-than-usual hug. She kissed his cheeks and forehead. "Go in the bathroom and put your clothes in the hamper; I'll be in shortly. Alex, please come in before you fall over." Irene brought Grimmer to the kitchen to make sure he was stable. "Let me get Michael to watch the kids and I'll take you home."

"Thank you, Mrs. O'Connell." Grimmer's words came out like a whisper. His head was still hanging down as he rubbed his hand over his stubbly face, with a look of disbelief.

Jacob set his bag of candy on the countertop, then he looked around and thought, *I can't let them find it.* He put it in the vanity drawer while he got undressed, then he went about being a six-year-old boy with a bag of treats. His conscious mind was safe for now.

Irene went to the bathroom to find Jacob with blue lips from sucking on his jawbreaker, looking in his bag of goodies. "What did I tell you about jawbreakers, young man?" she scolded him.

"Only have them when you're in the room with me. Sorry, Mom." Irene began to wash him up and gently asked him if he was all right after what just happened. Jacob passed it off as Sara got hurt, but she was going to the hospital to be okay. The reality of what happened, the horrible sight of it, hadn't registered, and going over to her hadn't registered in his mind. He had no memory of it.

Irene believed it would be better for him not to think about it. She finished cleaning him up and put a fresh shirt on him. "Oh my God, Jacob. You have a small grey patch of hair on the back of your head. When did that show up there?" Jacob was staring at the bag of candy, uninterested in questions of grey hair. To his dismay, she took the bag of candies from him.

"You can't have all these at once."

"Ah, Mom."

"Unless you plan on sharing with the others. Are you?"

"I guess so," he said, dejected.

Irene patted him on the behind of his overalls and sent him on his way.

Part 2

It was exceptionally cool for a June morning in Saint John when Joe Millen boarded the train bound for Montreal, with a transfer waiting onto Toronto. He went ahead of Shannon and Sara because they had a lot to transport, not including what the moving van would be bringing later. All of their expenses were covered by Mr. Grimmer's insurance, both business and auto, because of the circumstances. The Millens had to leave their home and a way of life they had known since they were kids themselves. And Joe was a proud man who always paid his way, but this was his little girl, and it seriously affected Shannon, so he accepted the insurance company's money to start over in Ontario. The doctors recommended that once Sara was stable enough for travel, with her mother by her side, she would be moved by ambulance to and from both airports and flown to Toronto to be cared for at the famous Hospital for Sick Children, affectionately called Sick Kids. There she would receive multiple surgeries to reconstruct her many broken bones. They had some of the best orthopedic surgeons, neurologists, and neurosurgeons in Canada. And there she would receive the best treatment necessary. If she were to regain normal range of motion in her legs, she would need ongoing physiotherapy, and the hospital was the best place for it. The recovery was a painful experience for little Sara. However, she was a resilient child, and the fight to get better only made her stronger. And maybe it was the head injury, but it didn't take long for the memory of her recovery and the accident that caused it to fade away like a puff of wind in the fog.

§

Sara's mother dropped her off at school and leaned over the seat of her olive-green Newport to wave goodbye. Sara always teased her mom that the car was the olive and the red seat covers were the pimiento inside.

"Have a good day at school, honey," Shannon said with her brilliant and contagious smile. Shannon's hair was more auburn than the fire-red Sara inherited from her father's ancestry, but the beauty was identical. They both had a warm inviting smile and aura about them that instantly put people at ease.

Sara stopped, turned around, and stuck her head back in the passenger side. "Thanks, Mom. I'm done track about a quarter past four today. Oh, and please don't forget my outfit for the play tonight?" she said, with a wry smile.

"Don't worry, honey; I'll make sure it's with me before I leave for work this time. I wish I could be at your track meet and see your play tonight. I hate these afternoon shifts." Shannon's smile dropped momentarily, and they both did the pouty lip thing.

"It's all right, Mom. Thanks. You'll just have to come when you're back on days is all."

The smiles started back up before the car did, and as Sara ran up the long walk to the front door of her school, she heard her mother yell out. "That's a promise, Sara." Shannon made sure not to call her daughter any of her usual terms of endearment so as not to embarrass her. She sat for a moment, watching Sara run up the steps, feeling overcome, her lips pursed and eyes welling up.

It was 1978, and Sara was nearing the end of grade ten. She had developed into quite the athlete, to everyone's pleasant surprise. She'd been a tomboy not too far back, but she shed that look and was turning into a feminine young lady, closing in on her sweet sixteen. When running track at school, her long red hair swung from side to side against her lower back. She ran often — at school, at home, or just about anywhere she went. Her parents thought the stronger she made her legs, the less she would dwell on the pain and the scars.

After track that day, Sara and the other girls ran into the school, dripping with sweat and ready for the showers. It was mid-April and cold enough for Sara that she was still in sweatpants. She stopped at her locker to grab a new towel and her shampoo before heading off. She froze her movements, looked straight ahead into the locker, then suddenly felt a chill run across her shoulders. Still looking straight ahead, she slowly backed up and quietly closed her locker door. To her right at the end of the hall the janitor was gawking at her in between swipes of his mop. He had on a grey uniform. A nametag that read Dave Rosa was sewn to the upper left of his button-up work shirt. The pants had a single black stripe up the outside of the legs, and he had on large, black steel-toe work boots, with the tongue laid over the toe — overkill for this job. His hair was curly black, unkempt, and in need of a wash and cut. He was younger than the other maintenance men, and he'd just started after the Christmas break. There were already other complaints about him staring a bit too much at the girls, but they were hard to prove.

"What exactly are you looking at?" she said, staring straight back at him. She wasn't using the typical teenage snooty attitude about it, she just delivered it like a reasonable question, which she received no reply to. "It's not nice to stare at people, you know," she continued to look straight at him as she secured the padlock to her locker. Sara was as fiery as her red hair and tall considering what she suffered as a child. At five-foot-eight, she was taller than a lot of boys, including this janitor. He put his head down and did his best to ignore her. She spun around, and her long hair snapped in the air as she sprinted down the hall toward the girls' showers. She could feel the cold chill growing, making her body shiver. She had never experienced it to this level. It disturbed her.

§

At the end of May, Sara and a dozen other girls were outside the school preparing for the long-distance track competitions, stretching to get the kinks out. The smell of flowers and the surrounding cedar trees were fresh in the air. The branches of the willow trees hung over the river that ran next to the high school. She loved the beauty of the cherry trees in full bloom surrounding the perimeter of the property. The building was built in the fifties, and its red-brick veneer changed hues with each new department that was added on over the years. The automotive shop and maintenance departments had their access to the rear that faced the track and field area. You could always find a small number of students congregated down by one particular willow tree at the far edge of the property smoking cigarettes. Sara could be found there with friends from time to time, but smoking wasn't her thing.

Nearing the end of her stretches, she felt that unnerving sensation return. She took to surveying the area, and across the track to the bleachers was the janitor changing out bags from the garbage bins. This time he was pulling the bags out and snapping the new ones open, all without diverting what appeared to be an angry stare pointed at her. Sara gave him a dirty look and took off running at an unusually fast pace. Once around the track, she slowed to her normal pace but pulled off to the side to speak with her gym teacher.

"Mrs. Gilbert, that creep keeps staring at me," she said, nodding in the janitor's direction. "He did it before when I was going into the showers. Can you do something about it?"

"Are you serious?" she asked, indignant. "When did this happen, exactly?"

Sara's breathing was slowing from the run. She held her chest and took a deep breath to finally calm herself. "It was last month, the first week after trials. Mrs. Gilbert ... please, I don't want him to know that I'm the one complaining about him."

Sara's teacher was in excellent shape and had an admirably forceful personality. She had short spiked hair, and of course, people at the time assumed she was a lesbian and made comments. Mrs. Gilbert was strong and didn't back down from teasing or bullying, though. The girls admired her for that, among other things.

Most strong, confident men had difficulty dealing with her in just about any confrontation. The janitor would be no different, but she had rules and protocol to follow.

She hadn't been surprised at Sara's news about this young man. She stood solid with arms crossed holding her clipboard, with a pencil behind her ear and a whistle around her neck, tied with yellow nylon rope. She looked the part, wearing a white and light blue vertical striped, short-sleeve, button-up shirt, and white Adidas gym shorts with blue stripes on the side.

She put one hand on Sara's shoulder. The look on her face was caring, yet cross.

"Don't worry about that. I'll take care of it. Don't let him get you upset, okay? Go on, sweetie, get back out there and keep those legs limber." And under her breath, Mrs. Gilbert said, "I'll deal with this little shithead." Obviously she hadn't buried the comment far enough, since Sara turned back from the track and gave her a smile to indicate she heard and agreed with the last comment.

At day's end, Sara was leaving the school with friends. Outside the entrance looking in the front foyer, she caught sight of an animated Mrs. Gilbert speaking to the principal. With another step forward, the janitor was revealed looking rather disheartened. There appeared to be some finger pointing, and it was directed at the janitor. The collective hope of the girls of the school and Mrs. Gilbert was that the janitor be fired, or at the very least, for the unwanted behaviour to stop. Before she turned back to her friends, Sara inadvertently locked eyes with the flushed janitor.

A knot immediately formed in her stomach as she wondered if her complaint had reached him. Had her request to her teacher fallen on deaf ears? Or would he simply figure out that it was her? A nervous-looking Sara bolted from the steps of the school. Her neck was heating up, and her face turned red. She held her stomach briefly and squeezed it in her hands.

"Wait up, guys, I'm coming," she said in a squeaky voice. Her legs grew weak and heavy with every step she made to catch up to her friends.

Part 3

It was an unusually warm night for the first Friday after the school year ended. The roller skating rink closed at 9 p.m. during the week and 10 p.m. on weekends. For Sara, thoughts of school, and certainly of that janitor, had mostly faded now. She was enjoying the night out, flashing a bit of her athletic prowess, which seemed to include her skills roller skating. Her long hair flowed behind her as she cruised around the rink, often hand in hand in a chain with three or four of her friends. The girls were quite familiar with the music's programming, which meant that "Y.M.C.A." indicated closing time. It also signalled to Sara, still fifteen, that she had to leave.

She had a curfew, so she passed on pizza at The Raven, a regular social haunt for the kids in the area, and started peddling her bike toward home. She took a short cut, as usual, through the rear loading area of the ice cream factory where her mother worked. The sun was just falling beyond the horizon far enough where the orange sky meets the teal. It would be completely dark any moment now. Looking up to the sky, her pace picked up; her feet were peddling in an increasing, yet smooth rhythm. Nearing the road at the end of the factory's property, she could see how dark it was as she came to a near dead stop for any traffic ahead.

It was a fair distance to the first streetlight that would illuminate any sense of security after exiting the factory's property. Across the street sat a one-storey commercial building, which had been boarded up and abandoned for several years. The equally small parking lot's asphalt was broken apart and overgrown with weeds that covered most of the property. And of course, there was a burnt-out streetlight near a barely noticeable driveway cut. The commercial area ended ahead with sporadic well-maintained businesses, transitioning into a residential neighbourhood. But getting there required Sara to cycle through a couple of blocks of no-man's land. Old ash trees, overgrown shrubs, and bushes did battle with the tall weeds that ran along this poorly maintained side of the ice cream factory, darkening the transition that much more.

Seeing the streetlights ahead, she relaxed her pace slightly. Her breathing slowed, along with her heart rate. The headlights of a car were shining on her from behind. She looked back but couldn't see any details on the car, getting no idea what type of car it was. She looked back again, then ahead, and pedalled faster, but the car kept pace with her. No matter how fast she went, she continued to see the same level of light, and the car wasn't passing her. She quickly cut to the left and pulled into a widened driveway of a commercial medical building. She knew this area well as her orthopedic surgeon had a physiotherapy office here. The parking lot had an exit to an alley behind it. She thought she could outmanoeuvre the car through the alley if for some reason it gave chase.

To her horror the headlights shone on the back of her arm and continued to follow her into the parking lot. Before making it to the alley, she felt a push from behind — the beginning of the impact. Her legs flew up off the pedals into the air and she struggled, hopelessly trying to hang onto the handlebars to steer the bike. The force of the impact threw her sideways. She slammed into the first bin so hard she slid right across it and crashed into the second. After that, Sara's body bounced onto the ground, her bike falling on top of her.

For a moment her thoughts were hysterical and uncontrollable. *Oh, my God! What's happening? Who is this maniac? Is he going to kill me?* Many frightening scenarios were playing out in her mind. She attempted to stand up, feeling the pain throughout her body and head. She staggered into the bin and slid back down to the ground. She tried to get up again and pick up her bike to get away. The shock and panic had her legs frozen and heavy like cement. Sara also didn't realize her bike wasn't rideable.

"Oh my God, oh my God!" she cried out. *Why can't I get up?* Her hands and arms were shaking uncontrollably as she looked down at her palms, covered with blood and dirt, burning like they'd been set in a hot pan. She heard the car door shut. The headlights blocked her from seeing anything. She yelled out, "Please don't hurt me ... please don't. Why are you doing this? What do you want?"

She couldn't see who was coming, but she was horrified. All she could see was a silhouette of what seemed like a towering figure slowly and purposely walking toward her. And now, he was standing over her.

"It's not very nice when people fuck with your life, is it? Maybe you should think about that before you go flapping your gums again ... RIGHT!?!"

This stranger's voice tore through her like the voice of the devil. She sobbed and feared what was going to happen to her next, believing whatever it was might end in her dying a horrible death.

"Please don't hurt me. I'm sorry, I don't know what I did."

Her head was spinning and pounding like it were about to explode. Sobbing and still on the ground, she suddenly found herself becoming angry like she never had before. The fear began to leave her, and her survival instincts started to kick in.

This figure turned and began walking back to the car. She watched him walk away with a familiar gait, one side of his hip significantly lower than the other. The headlight blocked by his legs just enough that Sara could see the back of his grease-stained grey work pants, with a vertical black stripe on the outside of the pant leg. He had heavy-duty black safety boots that looked like the tongue was glued to the top of the boot. She tried to focus enough to make absolutely sure it was who she suspected.

He stopped and stood still in front of the headlights. "Stupid fuckin' bitch. Little prima donna," he spat. "Next time I'll just run you over so you won't be able to walk again ... fuckin' bitch."

Sara raised her arm and blocked enough of the headlights to see the very same dirty grey shirt. She couldn't make out the name, but the patch was there. Rosa had gotten fired; he was let go the day she complained, but Sara certainly wasn't the only one to complain about his behaviour. And it wasn't just the students who had a problem with him staring at them. Sara was indignant.

Her fear quickly turned to unadulterated rage as she realized who had just hurt her and nearly scared the life from her. A moment earlier she had a profound experience thinking she was about to die.

The more that sunk in, the more the rage built. She was sliding into that dark place where anger turns to rage, and you start to see red — Sara stood right on the threshold.

Rosa got in the car, but before he went to back up, he held the door open and laughed.

"Scare the shit out of you all right? Did you piss your pants? Stupid bitch." He closed his door and backed the car up to turn it toward the entrance from where they came in. But in that final manoeuvre, as he pulled the gearshift into drive, he lost sight of Sara. The last he had seen her, she was lying on the ground next to the bins with her bike on her legs looking a mess, defeated. Her clothes were torn and dirty, with various spots covered in blood and grease from the bike chain. He turned back to the darkness of the alley, and a sickening laugh could be heard fading as he rolled up the driver's side window.

Just before he pulled away, he heard a loud smash and felt a blow to the side of his head. The pain was overwhelming. Pieces of glass embedded into the skin of his cheekbone and temple. The impact had come from a two-foot-long chain and padlock Sara used to lock her bike. She had swung it like a three-hundred-pound man tossing an Olympic hammer and with deadly accuracy.

Shocked and hurt from the unexpected impact, Rosa put his hand up to feel the side of his cheek and temple. When he put his hand in front of his face to see if there was any blood, he received a second blow. This time there was no glass to slow down the swing of her spikeless mace. The impact was enough to knock Rosa senseless. His leg spasmed and his foot pushed the gas pedal down, driving the car into the side of the building. There it sat, idling up against the reddish-brown brick veneer of the building that housed the physiotherapy offices, still high idling in gear. He started to come around and tried to shake off the concussive blow. His head was both pounding in agonizing pain and spinning in circles. He tried to look out his side of the car when he heard Sara's furious voice. "How do you like that? You sick bastard!"

The glass that wasn't in his lap was buried into the side of his face and temple. The blood and swelling in and around his eye blocked his vision. His weakened attempt to try and focus again was met with a primal scream preceding a third and final blow. The chain and padlock met the upper part of his cheek and part of his orbital bone, knocking him out and onto the passenger side seat. The raging scream reinforced her swing with all she had. She wanted to assure he couldn't get back up and come after her. After the blow, Rosa was out cold, blood running down his face, over his chin, and onto his neck; it ran into his ear, pooling in his ear canal. His left eye was badly damaged; he wouldn't see properly out of it for quite a long while. The car continued to idle. Sara had to pull herself back from acting on the homicidal rage inside her that truly scared her. She never thought she was capable of such an act.

She pulled the chain and padlock up and over her head, onto her shoulder, and under the opposite arm — a protective sash. She picked up her bike with the bent and broken front tire and limped her way back out of the alley and onto the street. Not far away she found a convenience store where she called her father first and then the police. The police arrived on the scene first. Upon discovering Sara covered in blood and in obvious shock, the police called for an ambulance. When they went to the back of the building, they found Rosa's car still idling and pushed up against the building. He had to have been out of it for at least ten minutes — Sara had delivered one hell of a blow.

The police went in with their guns drawn. One of the officers yelled out, but no reply came from in or around the car. When they finally got up to the driver's side window, they discovered a man on his side just starting to stir from their yells. They noticed the car seat and Rosa's head and face covered in blood and a strong smell of urine. Rosa was becoming alert as he was pulled out and handcuffed. The cuffs were moved to the rail on the outside of the ambulance where he was checked over by the medics. He was fading in and out, so they placed him on a gurney and handcuffed him to it. When the police heard Sara tell them everything that happened, including what Rosa had said to her, they found it fitting to leave him on the gurney outside the ambulance waiting to be loaded for possible transport. He had a list of serious charges against him, the first one being attempted murder.

One of the cops told the EMT staff to just patch him up — "just the basics" — because they were taking him to the precinct before the hospital. "This piece of shit deserves no special treatment after what he's done," he said. "If he's alive, that's good enough," spouted another officer. The medics said Rosa was well enough to go to the police station. So the handcuffs were tightened as far as they would go and in the back of the cruiser he went; with gauze wrapped around his head to hold the layered pieces in his eye.

Later, in the interrogation room, they left Rosa in his urine-soaked clothes the entire time. The first cop on the scene leaned into Rosa and loudly embellished his laugh. "She kicked your ass, eh, fuckhead!?! Oh, and by the way, you're the only one here tonight who pissed their pants, you piece of shit!"

When Sara's parents arrived at the hospital, she was getting checked over by the emergency room doctor. Except for some stitches and bandages for the scrapes and minor cuts, she was cleared to go home.

"Sara honey … Oh my God, baby, are you all right?" Shannon was a wreck.

"I'm okay, Mom," Sara said, hugging her.

"What in God's name happened? Who was that maniac who hurt you? Why did he do that? The police didn't say much." Looking at her daughter, Shannon broke out into cries that were only interrupted when she gasped for air. Sara was being the strong one in this exchange, pulling her mother in and holding her tight.

"He's the janitor from school, Mom. The one who got fired. Remember?" Sara continued to hold her mother, but stared blankly ahead. "I'm okay, Mom. I'm all right," she said, appearing stoic, yet her voice lacked emotion, and came out in a monotone. Then one single tear slowly dripped down her cheek, but no more followed.

Joe talked to the arresting officer and found out who Rosa was. He made sure not to say anything stupid in a vengeful way, but like any father would, he wanted to kill the man who hurt his child. He was impatient to get back to Sara, so he thanked the officer and went back in.

"How's my strong girl? Let me have a look at you."

Joe leaned back with his hands on the sides of Sara's arms and did a quick survey of her injuries. That lasted all of two seconds when Sara quickly wrapped her arms around his thick neck, and then she broke down. Joe wrapped his arms around his daughter and struggled to stop himself from bursting out into tears.

"It's going to be all right, sweetie. It's going to be all right. You are as tough as any man I've ever known and smarter than the rest of us," he said with a smile.

Leaning back again, he held her cheeks with his huge hands, wiped her tears away with his thumbs, and kept repeating, "that's my strong girl." Joe grabbed Shannon and all three hung on to one another.

Back at home, Joe stepped outside for some air. Comfortable for the moment now that his daughter was safe, he was reflecting on the police officer's parting words. "Mr. Millen, you have an exceptional daughter there. A lot of people would have given in after what she went through tonight. She has some courage, that one. She's a hero in our books. You must be very proud. Anything you need, anything at all, please don't hesitate. Give my best to your wife and daughter, sir." The officer shook Joe's hand and passed his card over with his free hand.

Joe came inside the house after finishing a double scotch and smoking his first cigarette in six months. He shut and locked the front door, then looked up the stairs toward where Shannon and Sara were. With his hand on the newel post at the bottom of the stairs, he bent over and rested his head on his bicep, and a barely audible cry slipped out. His chest heaved a couple times, then he stood straight up and took a deep breath. He wiped his eyes between forefinger and thumb, and after what was a long night for the Millens, his pace was slow as he started his trek up the stairs.

3

Snow Daze

It was exhilarating for the kids as they all paused their morning routine of getting ready for school and stood next to their mother, listening to the school closure reports on the radio. An impulsive chorus of "Yays" sounded from the trio of O'Connell kids who were getting the day off. Michael, however, who was finishing up grade twelve, was too cool to get excited about a school closure. He didn't have a full slate of classes as it was, much to the chagrin of his father, whose thoughts were often made known. "You could have just worked harder and been out after grade eleven and had a job already."

In grade two, this was Jacob's first real snow day, considering the school was only a block from home. When the buses weren't running, the school was usually still open, but not today, since the weather was horrendous the night before and had continued to be horrible into the morning. Overnight high winds caused drifts two- to three-feet high, making the roads impassable. Plows and graders worked all night, still going steady at 7 a.m., with several hours ahead of them. Hard, packed snow blocked many driveways, and like at most homes around them, the O'Connells' cars remained in the driveway encased in snow. And the jubilant children throughout the area were warm and safe inside. Under the overhead light of the garage to guide him, he had already started on the gigantic task of clearing the O'Connell cars and making a route to the street for them.

Jacob was the same as most kids his age — he sought out his own entertainment. In his case, he went down to the rec room in the basement to see what he could find. He went into the laundry room and looked at the shelves supporting clothes, laundry soap, fabric softener. On the other side of the basement were a few household tools and other items stored away. But he locked in on the blue, vinyl wrapped clothesline and decided to try some acrobatics. He managed to get his knees hooked over the line and began to swing upside down. There he was, back and forth and believing he was going along fine, so he called out to his brother and sister in the next room to come view his newfound skill; then the line broke. His brother and sister didn't get to see the show, but they heard it.

After he stood up and rubbed his head, which sounded like a coconut more than a scull, he realized he'd broken his mother's clothesline that she used during winter months. In stealth mode, he quickly dashed upstairs to his room, shut the door and went to his closet to grab some toys and make like all was normal. He rubbed the top of his scull repeatedly and felt the rather large bump developing on his head. He then went to the bathroom and looked at it in the mirror. Seeing the size of it, he realized he couldn't hide it from anyone, especially his mother. He went downstairs and straight to the coatrack in the front entryway, grabbing his toque and throwing it over the big bump, but he couldn't take the pressure of the unknown, so he went to the kitchen to tell his mother what happened, no matter how much trouble he got from it.

"Mom," Jacob almost whispered.

"Yes, honey, what's the matter?" Irene was working at the table writing in the calendar.

It was obvious her son was nervous about something. And without hesitation he spurted it out, "I broke your clothesline, Mom. The one downstairs. I'm really sorry."

"How on earth did you manage that, for Pete's sake?" she asked, not a hint of anger or disappointment in her voice.

"I was swinging on it…?" He didn't get a chance to say upside down. Irene looked at him and wondered why he had his toque on

MARK J. CANNON   39

inside the house. Removing it, she was flabbergasted by the size of the bump on his head.

"My God, Jacob! Look at the size of that goose egg. Are you okay, honey? Do you feel sick to your stomach at all?" She instinctively reached her hands out to hold both sides of his face. She looked into his eyes and then put her hand on his forehead. There was no more talk about a broken clothesline. She proceeded to prepare an ice pack for his knot. After clearing him for feeling dizzy or needing to throw up, she sent him off to the living room to watch television. She warned him not to fall asleep, but she would constantly monitor him anyway. A nurse at the local hospital, she returned to writing her shifts and the kids' events on the kitchen calendar. While in the kitchen, she was simultaneously baking ginger cookies and prepping for supper, which was hours away.

The smells of baking spread throughout the house. A half hour had passed with Jacob watching television, and Irene hadn't heard a peep from him. "Are you doing okay in there, Jacob?" she asked, but her query was met with silence. "Jacob, you aren't sleeping are you?" Into the living room she went to make sure he hadn't fallen asleep.

"No, Mom, I'm right here."

He was looking out to the driveway through one of the many eight-inch-square frosted windowpanes from the den. He watched his father tackling the mountain of snow on and around the cars in the driveway. Irene walked in and stood behind Jacob with both hands on his shoulders. She joined in on watching her husband in action for a moment. He had his car cleaned off and was halfway done clearing the snow off the family station wagon. Thomas slipped trying to reach across the roof racks and landed on his bottom, covered in snow. Irene gasped when she saw him slip, but she quickly joined Jacob in giggling, realizing he was okay. The only thing Thomas had hurt was his pride, and that wasn't so serious.

"Okay, my little care package, enough of that. Back into the living room with you," she said, steering Jacob to the living room. Before leaving the den, she looked out at her husband brushing the snow off his backside. The look of consternation on his face melted when he met Irene's bashful gaze. His look quickly turned into a sheepish smile. Thomas and Irene were the exception to the norm: five kids in and still very much in love.

The daylight hours of the snow day were concluding, and it was nearing time for supper. Thomas was now in the living room with his youngest, having a heart to heart. "That's quite a bump you have there, son. I suppose you won't try anything like that again, will you?" As Thomas asked the question, his hands were gently cutting through Jacob's hair around the bump on his head.

"No, Dad. Never again." Thomas continued examining him with an expression of love and concern. There was no question, like every child in their home, Jacob felt loved and cared for.

The dining room table was set, and everyone except James, who was the oldest and away in the navy, sat in their chairs waiting for dinner. They waited, as always, for Irene to sit down.

"Kate, it's your turn to say grace tonight. I would suggest you say something for Jacob not being seriously hurt today," Thomas said, giving an intentional look of seriousness to the kids. With grace behind them, and dinner underway, Irene looked over to Jacob.

"Jacob, honey, is something wrong. Don't you like your chicken?"

"My tummy feels bad, Mom."

Jacob couldn't say anything further as he began to vomit, and his eyes rolled back in his head as he fell onto the floor. Irene grabbed him within a second of him landing, and looked to Thomas immediately.

"Start the car," she said forcefully. "Jacob. Jacob!" She jumped into action, having Michael fetch Jacob's winter coat. She wrapped him up and ran out the door to the car. Thomas had the wagon started, somewhat warm from moving the cars around earlier. They drove as fast as they could in the conditions, knowing time was a priority. Jacob was breathing, but unconscious. Not too long after being in the hospital, Michael got a call from his father to grab the other kids and join them.

They all went down into the surgery waiting room to join Irene. Entering the room, Kevin and Kate ran over to their mother. Seeing their mother's cheeks stained from tears, they began to cry. She held them both. "It's going to be all right, kids; he's just got a nasty bump and they are going to make sure he's okay. So stop worrying and stop that crying you two, your brother is going to be fine."

Michael sat by his mother and took her hand in his. "Do they know what's happening with him, Mom?"

"They're pretty sure it's a subdural haematoma. Basically, it's a bleed on the outside of the brain..."

"I know what it is, Mom. Is he going to be okay, really?"

"They're going in to release the pressure it's causing. That's what caused him to go unconscious. And they will make sure it doesn't become a blood clot, so we'll find out soon."

For Irene, the wait for someone to fill her in on his progress seemed like an eternity. Dr. Miller, who Irene worked with on occasion, came out in pale green scrubs head to toe. He took his cap off and revealed a head full of curly black hair. He was a good-looking man with olive skin and sharp features, and he was well liked by all. "Irene, he's all right. We didn't find any blood clot. We couldn't find anything for that matter," he said, sounding perplexed. He was standing in front of Irene, holding her hands, but his words were drowned out when she bellowed out cries of joy. The only words she heard were, "He's all right." Having regained her composure, she looked to the doctor while drying the tears from her face.

"What do you mean you couldn't find anything? You said the X-ray showed a bleed on his brain. Where did it go? Is it going to turn into a blood clot? Oh my God, what if he ends up with a blood clot floating around his brain?"

"Irene, please, he's okay. Yes, the first scan definitively showed a bleed, it's there on the film. We went in and released the pressure, so that buildup of blood is gone. The second scan didn't indicate the source of the bleed. It's like it healed up that fast. Usually it will show the residue from that area, but it was clear." Dr. Miller grabbed both sides of Irene's shoulders and gently squeezed. "We looked all over to make sure it didn't pool up somewhere else on the brain, which it didn't, I can assure you."

"Thank God." The words came out of Irene in an exhausted breath.

"It was weird, though. We thought there might be a problem with the scanner because its images came out with a bit of colour in them — a kind of yellow, almost orange hue, which is odd since they should be black and white, but the tech said the images are fine."

Suddenly Irene stood still and looked out the window hearing that last sentence. She did her best to remain inanimate.

"Just to make sure, we're going to follow up with a few more tests before the night's out."

Irene was distracted. Dr. Miller found her reaction strange but concluded everyone reacts differently when it comes to a loved one being ill.

"He's in recovery now. You can go in and see him, Irene, Tom. He won't be awake for about a half an hour, but you can go stay with him. Just mom and dad for now, please?" he said looking at Kevin and Kate.

Michael put his arms around his brother and sister. "Go, Mom, Dad. Go in and see him, I've got things covered here." Thomas placed a firm grip on Michael's shoulder without saying a word, then escorted Irene into the recovery room. On the way in he turned toward Dr. Miller and thanked him with a handshake. The doctor simply smiled. Thomas gently held his hand against the small of Irene's back, and they went in to be with their youngest. Before leaving the room, Dr. Miller looked to the kids.

"Your brother was very lucky tonight."

§

Irene picked up Jacob from the hospital a couple of days later.

"Mom." Jacob's inquisitiveness was back to normal.

"Yes, honey."

"When I was in the room with the really big mirror on the ceiling, I saw the bird we saved and fixed so he could fly again. Do you remember that bird, Mom?"

"The bird that lived in the cigar box in your bedroom? That bird?" she asked apprehensively.

"Yeah. I dreamt he came to see me in the room. He was in the big mirror and told me I was going to be okay and I had a lot of work to do. Do I have to do some work, Mom?"

Irene had to muster up the strength not to reveal her emotions.

"Yes, you do honey. And you can start by cleaning up your room now that you're feeling better. Well, maybe tomorrow. You can rest today. Okay, my little care package?"

"Okay, Mom. When we get home, can I watch *Sesame Street*?"

"Oh, I suppose so."

"Yay," Jacob shouted out in happiness.

"I think maybe, for today only, you can watch whatever you want." She looked over at Jacob with a smile and ran her hand through his hair, noting that the swelling was gone.

Like it happened yesterday, Irene remembered what Jacob did for that bird in detail. She wondered what was to come for her special son. However, the last few days brought as many moments of fear as wonder. For Jacob, though, she hoped only for wonder.

4

Pride

After Thomas and Irene were married, they bought a good-sized post-war three-bedroom brick bungalow with a detached double garage in a nice area. As the family grew, they renovated the basement to include a rec room, and an additional bedroom, bathroom and laundry room. They lived a comfortable life there that went well into their retirement. They bought it just in time for the arrival of James, the first of their five children. When Jacob turned ten, James had already been in the navy for a little over three years, and Michael, his second oldest brother, had left for the west coast the year before. Members of the O'Connell family seemed to desire work, except for Kevin. He didn't lack desire, though, so much as direction, which was a bone of contention between his father and him. Even at ten years old, Jacob had a paper route through his neighbourhood, and his area seemed to expand every couple of months.

When he turned twelve, Jacob decided it was going to be his last year delivering papers, but he still took his responsibility seriously up until the end, as his parents had taught him. "Jacob, honey, come now, your father is willing to drive you today, so the least you could do is be ready when he is," Irene called out from the entry at the bottom of the stairs. She was looking back and forth from up the stairs toward her son's room to outside where Thomas was waiting in the idling station wagon. It was a cold, wet, damp-to-the-bone October morning. And, being Saturday, the papers were the last and heaviest of the week.

"Yeah, Mom, I'm coming already," Jacob chirped. He came stumbling loudly down the stairs and onto the landing.

"Did you just get short with me, young man?" Holding his raincoat, and her other hand on her hip, she looked down at him with consternation, tapping her foot on the floor. Jacob knew this familiar, telling look.

"No, Mom. I'm sorry," he said, lowering his head. "But I'm going as fast as I can. Dad's just faster than me."

"He is so, there's no denying that." Her stern look started to break with a smile. She helped young Jacob get his raincoat on over his heavy wool sweater.

"Your father already put the papers in the car, so you should thank him. Now out the door with you. Keep covered up and I'll see you both when you get back."

She stood on the covered porch in her favourite green terry cloth robe, which was in near tatters, her arms crossed trying to control her shaking. She pulled one arm out to wave to her brave men as they went into the trenches of the heavy Saturday morning paper deliveries. Jacob was in such a hurry to get out to the car that when he turned the corner around the back of the station wagon, his feet went flying up into the air and Irene lost sight of him. She took a step toward the edge of the porch and saw a glow between the car and the garage. It was something she had seen before but never this amplified. She flew down the steps, losing the slippers along the way, and raced over to Jacob. Thomas was out of the car and scurrying around the other side to see what happened. They arrived at the same time to see their son crouched on his knees, holding his elbow.

"Oh my God, Jacob, are you all right? What happened, honey? What did you do? What did you hurt?" Irene's flurry of questions came as she crouched beside Jacob and wrapped her arm around him. Her other hand was trying to hold his arm to inspect what damage had occurred.

"I'm okay, Mom. I just hurt my elbow, but it's okay. I just rubbed it like Dad showed me and it doesn't hurt anymore. See?"

Jacob straightened his arm out and flexed it a couple times. Thomas was on the other side of him. He came around and picked him up from his underarms.

"Are you sure you're okay, son? Really, it doesn't hurt? You're sure you didn't break it or something?" Thomas asked while pulling Jacob toward him and putting his arm around him.

"Yeah, I'm sure. It's okay. Really, Dad, Mom, it's really okay. We can go now," Jacob said as he looked to his mother and father with assuredness.

"If it starts to hurt, you come right home and we'll go and get an X-ray," Irene said, bent over with her hands on both sides of Jacob's shoulders and looking him in the eye. "Okay, Jacob?"

"Yes, Mom. But I'm okay, really. Can we go now, Dad?"

Thomas looked to Irene and they both slightly raised their eyes up in acknowledgement to each other of what they had seen, again. Not a word was spoken of it, though. "Okay, son, let's go. Honey, you should get inside. You're soaked. I'll keep an eye on him. We'll be back soon."

It was the beginning of the awkward and klutzy teenage years for Jacob, which Thomas had known all too well. Some memories of childhood always linger.

"I'm glad you didn't really hurt anything, other than your pride," Thomas said with his hand on Jacob's shoulder.

"My pride? What do you mean, Dad?"

"Never mind, son. Let's get those papers delivered before it gets too late. You know how some of your customers get when you're late, right?"

"Yeah, I do. Like Miss McArthur. She gets mad at me every time," Jacob replied, reaching into the back seat to grab a stack of papers. He proudly and confidently pulled out his Swiss army knife — a birthday gift from his father — and began to cut the binding away.

"Angry, Jacob, she gets angry, not mad." Thomas put the station wagon in gear and began to pull out of the driveway. "Probably more like upset." Then Thomas muttered, "Don't they teach English in school anymore?"

"Eh?" Jacob asked, looking confused.

"You're a good worker, son," Thomas said, with a smile on his face and his hand rubbing the top of Jacob's wet head.

"But what did you mean, Dad?"

"Never mind, son, let's get those papers out now, okay?"

"But, Dad!?"

"Angry, Jacob, not mad. Mad means insane, like a mad dog. It doesn't mean angry," Thomas said, with his eyes on the road, his smile wide now.

"Oh, okay. Hmm."

Thomas was a man of simple pleasures, and because of the rain, he looked forward to getting into his workshop in the garage. He wanted to clean up and organize his carpentry tools and lumber in preparation of the next project. But even while he was thinking of the shop, he watched his son running papers to the houses. He hustled a few houses at a time before racing back to the car for a retreat from the torrential downpour.

It mattered to Jacob if Miss McArthur didn't get her paper by a reasonable time, even though she often complained. Despite those complaints, she always gave him a tip and something special at Christmas. It also mattered to Jacob that old Mrs. Fraser had her paper put neatly into the mailbox mounted on the brick wall under her front porch. She was frail and didn't move so well anymore, so this would be an easy grab for her. She had gone from using a cane to a walker as her health declined. Jacob noticed this, and so in the winter he shovelled snow from her sidewalk, front walkway, and steps leading to her porch. He never asked for anything.

"How's Mrs. Fraser doing these days?" Thomas asked, checking his rear-view before driving a few more houses down the street.

"She's not moving too good. She broke her hip."

"She's not moving too well, Jacob."

"Eh?" Jacob uttered, confused again.

Thomas looked over at him and pulled him in under his arm, giving him a few squeezes. "We'll work on your English lessons later on sometime. Let's get you finished and home to get out of those wet clothes." Thomas drove away with a smile many parents would recognize — what meant so much to him was how his son respected his elders and sincerely cared for people.

5

In a Flash

It was lunchtime for seventh graders Jacob O'Connell and his best friend, Pat Keegan. The two lived on the same block and had been friends since they could walk. The smells of bologna, processed cheese slices, and white bread were freed from many lunchboxes and allowed to fill the classroom air. The milk cart rolled along the hall and up to the door of each classroom. The students whose parents could afford it rushed to get their daily allotment, chocolate being the popular choice.

Jacob tapped Pat's shoulder so he would turn around. "Hey, Pat, you coming up to our cottage this weekend?" Before Pat could answer, Jacob excitedly interrupted. "Kate's bringing Heather Harr-isss."

Pat's eyes had opened as big as saucers upon hearing the news. "Really? Oh … okay, yeah, I'm pretty sure I can come."

Pat's voice had changed several octaves, but it wasn't physiological. He was trying to play it cool by walking back his excitement at the thought of Heather being there. But Jacob, a true friend to Pat, didn't tease him about it.

That summer, Pat and Heather ended up down by the water a couple of times learning how to kiss. The kisses were long, wet, and sloppy, but knowing how to French kiss at that age brought you the seal of cool. As time went on, to Pat's delight, the two became an item.

Jacob made it through the winter and spring continuing to deliver papers. At the end of the school year, true to his convictions, he hung up his paper bag for good. His friend Rob had a job in a convenience store and always had money on him. And Pat cut grass, cleaned out gutters, raked leaves, shovelled snow, or did any other odd jobs to earn a buck. Jacob was going into grade eight, so he thought it was time for a real job with much better pay.

It was Sunday night before the last week of school and he was downstairs in the kitchen on the phone.

"Is Pat there?" Jacob asked with a shaky voice. Pat's older sister, Gwen, who Jacob thought was a beautiful older woman (at fifteen), had answered the phone.

"Just a minute," she said, between smacks of her gum.

Jacob had to hold the phone at arm's length to protect his ear from Gwen's screaming out to her brother. Pat was upstairs and hadn't heard the phone ring, so he ignored his sister calling out, thinking it was for chores. In the background, Jacob could hear Pat stomping the closer he was to the phone. Gwen held out the phone to her brother and then dropped it just short of his reach.

"Oh, thanks a lot, cheese feet!" Pat screamed at his sister.

"Cheese feet? Did I hear that right, Jacob? If I can hear that from here, he must be really screaming at whoever it was," Irene said in astonishment, sitting at the kitchen table with a look of disapproval. She shook her head and whispered to herself, "cheese feet?" She couldn't help but quietly chuckle while continuing to make the grocery list and accidentally adding the new item after *bread*. She caught herself immediately, but knowing that they were low on cheese, she decided to just scratch out the second word.

Jacob looked over at his mother and rolled his eyes upward. Then he slowly walked the extra long cord from the avocado-green rotary phone around the corner into the dining room for a chance at some privacy.

"Pat, last week of school. Are we still doing that thing on Friday?" Jacob asked in a whisper.

"Oh yeah, I went down to Thorton's with Rob. He got a whole box of stink bombs and itchy powder for a bunch of us. Those grade eighters ain't gonna know what hit 'em. Cool, eh? I can't wait."

More than a typical convenience store, Thorton's was a landmark store for model makers, attracting enthusiasts and collectors from all over. This was Rob Sipe's first job, and at student rates he earned two dollars and fifty cents an hour. And it helped make ends meet for his family. He worked four hours every night, with six hours Friday, and twelve on the weekend. He was a friend to Pat and Jacob since he moved to Saint John a few years back. He, his mother, and sister had left Grand Bay to escape an abusive father.

Jacob had difficulty not raising his voice in excitement. "Wow, this is going to be a bang, man! We shouldn't do too much. I don't want to get in trouble. Mr. Clark is a real jerk. I heard he gave Mark Stewart the strap so hard he cried."

"Ah, don't worry about the principal; he is a stupid jerk. I wouldn't cry if he gave me the strap."

Jacob didn't argue Pat's bravado. He heard his mother approaching so he said a quick goodbye.

"Jacob … what are you boys up to now? I hope it's not trouble. It's the last week of school, and I know how you boys can find mischief without looking."

"No, Mom, we're not going to get into trouble. We were talking about an overnighter here or at his place after school's done," Jacob said nervously.

His mother looked at him in a questionable disposition. "Is that right? Okay then, what are you so nervous for?"

"I'm not nervous," Jacob squeaked.

"All right, then," she said unconvincingly. "Your voice is really changing, Jacob." She gave him a wink and walked back to the kitchen.

§

Rob was a high-spirited kid with nervous energy to spare. This was how he coped after what he experienced with his father. Sometimes survivors of abuse hid in their shell, sometimes they made themselves big. Rob was so loud everybody always heard him coming. By Pat and

Jacob's standards, Rob was a wild man. He had wavy brown hair that hung past his shoulders, and he was so thin that when he wore tight jeans, he looked like a walking stick. Pat and Jacob thought he had a cool way about him, and he showed no fear.

Monday morning of the second week of June, and the last week of school was a glorious warm and sunny day. Rob, Pat, and Jacob met up just a couple of blocks from the school and began to prepare for the antics ahead of them. Rob and Pat were dividing up the stink bombs and packets of itchy powder. Unexpectedly, Rob pulled out a handful of large and very illegal firecrackers.

"Check these out. Cool, eh? We can set them off by Clark's office." Rob was holding them out in his hand as if he was showing off money.

"Are you crazy, man? I'm not doing that. That's nuts … right in front of the principal's office!" Jacob was becoming animated in his objections and Pat took notice.

"Yeah Rob, that's too crazy. We might get expelled or have to repeat grade seven. My parents would kill me. Well, my Dad would," Pat said, agreeing with Jacob. Then he pointed to Rob's hand with the deadly firecrackers. "Just forget it, Rob. Got it!?" Pat said sternly.

Not listening or caring, Rob had tied a half dozen firecrackers together with the intention of creating the loudest possible explosion. He was going to try lighting one of them to hear how loud it was. He had one single to light, but he was still holding the half dozen tied together.

"Don't, Rob! Don't, or you'll get us all in trouble," Jacob said, angry now. But before this last attempt of trying to convince him, the cold butane started filling in and around his cupped hands. Pat and Jacob started backing up. The lighter clicked, the butane exploded, then the single firecracker lit up, then the six tied together caught. It was a triple bang, first a concussive sound of the butane igniting, then the sound of the single firecracker followed by the loudest from all six. But when the butane in Rob's hand lit, it went back into the lighter and blew it up. The combination of the six firecrackers and the lighter going off at the same time sounded like a grenade and dwarfed the first two sounds.

Jacob landed face down on the front lawn of one of the many well-kept homes on the street. His ears were ringing so loud, he instinctively cupped his hands over them to help soften the pain. He could smell fresh cut grass, butane, and the gunpowder from the firecrackers. It was an odd combination to smell — one he would never forget. Any single one of those smells would forever after trigger that memory.

"Pat ... Pat, are you okay?" Jacob screamed upon seeing him laying on the boulevard next to a bloodied Rob. Again he yelled out, but he couldn't even hear his own voice. He could see that Pat was knocked out or worse. He crawled across the sidewalk and onto the boulevard to him. Thankfully, he saw him make some movement, so he hoped he would be all right. There was hardly anyone in the vicinity when this noise broke the calm of the morning. Jacob's eyes were watering heavily, and it was difficult to focus as he turned to Rob lying on his side in a near foetal position.

"Rob! Rob, get up. What are you doing?" Jacob said, frantic now. When he grabbed Rob's hips to turn him over, dark blood was pumping out of his neck. It started to slow down. He called out Rob's name again, and then Pat's, but nothing was happening. Pat was barely moving, still out of it. Jacob's watery eyes turned into a flow of tears at what seemed a hopeless situation. Part of the lighter that blew apart went into the side of Rob's neck and partially pierced his carotid artery. He was out from the concussive blast and was rapidly losing any vital signs.

"Rob, please Rob, wake up ... wake up. Rob!" Jacob cried, shaking his body and helplessly watching his friend slowly die in front of him. He became weak in the knees, his surroundings began to spin into a dizzying blur, and then falling on his back next to the other two, he passed out from the shock.

"Are you all right, son? I heard the noise. I was out in the backyard gardening, and I thought I better come out and see what made that noise. I thought it was a really loud backfire at first." The man who came out to see what was going on was an elderly retired gentleman in his early eighties. He was quite talkative.

He was kneeling over Jacob and still gently shaking him, as he was coming to, his ears still ringing. The man kept talking. Jacob was trying to focus on who was standing over top of him. First, he could make out Pat, then the man who stirred him awake, and finally, Rob.

"Hey buddy, are you okay?" Rob said. "That was pretty loud, eh? Are you going to get up now? Come on, we'd better get out of here," Rob said, as a matter of fact.

Jacob rose without a word, staring at Rob with his head cocked and his eyes squinted, looking like he was attempting to focus. Rob had a few stains of blood on his neck, but that was it. No one stopped to ask or offer a reason why the top portion and arm side of his shirt was covered in blood stains. Jacob thought he would find Rob lying on the ground, dead from blood loss. They helped Jacob to his feet, and he was obviously dazed, having difficulty getting his footing. He looked over the three of them, but he was still unable to say anything coherent.

"Okay then, are you boys going to be all right now? No more blowing things up, right?" The neighbour said, slowly walking back to his door. Jacob looked at him like he was an alien.

"Uh, yes sir. Thank you," Pat and Rob responded.

They waved to the neighbour and turned to walk away, but Jacob was already several yards ahead of them. His eyes looked dark, and his steps a little wobbly as he walked toward the school. He seemed content not to say a word to anyone at that moment. His head pounded intensely and he was on the verge of vomiting. He was also angry over the confusion. The more he tried to understand what just happened, the more his head pounded, and the more his stomach flipped. So, he let it go. The questions could wait.

6

Discoveries

Pat's father, Billy Keegan, was a good man, but he'd been scarred by World War II and was prone to alcohol-fuelled fits of rage and violence. There were many occasions when Billy's brother, John, a police officer in town, got called out to calm things down at the Keegan residence. And no matter that Billy was his brother and a fellow war vet, he wouldn't hesitate to throw him in the drunk tank for the night if he was becoming a danger to his wife, Martha, and to Pat. There were a few times that John had no choice but to arrest Billy for violent acts against his wife and son. Like so many domestic violence situations, Martha would always drop the charges, hoping things would get better. Once John, out of uniform and visiting for a party, took Billy out in the backyard and walloped him for slapping Martha. For quite some time after that, things were not the same between John and his brother, and John took it upon himself to take watch over the family. Although Pat had to grow up in a hurry as a result of his life at home, John often filled many roles for Pat's absent father.

These roles often involved taking Pat and his friends on fun fishing trips. So before departing on one of these excursions, there was a quick hug from Jacob for his dad, then Thomas slipped a few dollars into the top-left pocket of his button-up shirt. All of the supplies were loaded, the aluminum boat in tow on the trailer, and now the boys were in the car. At 6 a.m., it was a quiet goodbye with hands waving out of the car's windows. This was Jacob's first fishing trip to the Miramichi. He was going to be staying with Pat at his uncle John's cottage — a reward for the boys passing grade nine. Thomas looked apprehensive as he watched John Keegan's station wagon pull away with his youngest son in the back seat. John could see Thomas's look, so he gave him a nod and a wink of recognition as well as a final wave.

Irene stayed inside the kitchen while the male gathering unfolded, waving goodbye from the window. Thomas entered the kitchen from the side door. He could see the same concern on Irene's face that he was feeling.

"He'll be fine, sweetheart. Don't worry about him. He's a smart, strong boy. Besides, he's got a decorated cop as a chaperone. It doesn't get much better than that, right?"

"Oh I know he'll be fine, Tom. It's not him I worry about so much. It's what can happen with the older one's who will be drinking and racing those boats."

"You're right, but he will be fine. If anyone stirs anything up, John won't have any problem dealing with them," Thomas said, sitting at the kitchen table. He unfolded the Saturday morning newspaper, trying not to be noticed peeking at Irene.

"You're right, old man. Let's have some breakfast since we're wide awake now," Irene said, finally turning away from the window.

Thomas rose from his seat and walked over to her. She was facing the sink when he nuzzled up from behind. He wrapped his big arms around hers, kissed the side of her cheek, and held her tight.

"Have I told you how beautiful you look today and how much I love you?" Thomas said, spinning her around to face him, then kissing her.

"Does this mean you want French toast and bacon for breakfast?"

"No. Of course not. It means I think you're beautiful and I love you. French toast and bacon would be lovely, though, now that you've brought it up," Thomas said with a wry smile.

"Oh, you're a charmer, Mr. O'Connell. Go read your paper and leave me to it," Irene said with a loving smile. "It's a good thing you're a handsome man, or it would be scrambled eggs and dry toast for you, mister." There were a few more kisses and a long embrace before they went about their morning. There were still two more teenagers in bed who would be awake soon enough.

§

After arriving at the cottage, Jacob and Pat started unloading the station wagon. The view around was spectacular. The river was within sight, through woods dotted with black oaks, maples, and birch trees in between tall pines and poplars. They maintained a clear line of sight to the river by keeping the brush cleared, and all the branches cut up to eight feet high. Pat's Aunt Marlene, who arrived before them, was preparing salads and making hamburger patties for John to barbeque later that night for dinner. She came out onto the landing to meet John, holding a cup of coffee for him.

"Hi, boys. It's nice to see you again. After you're done unloading, there are some sandwiches in the fridge if you're hungry."

"Thanks, Aunt Marlene," Pat said, waiting for them to go back inside and close the door. "Jacob ... hey, Jacob, look over there." Pat nodded his head toward the cottage next to theirs. There where a couple of girls around their age who came out the front door and started a sprint toward the riverside beach. There was no vocal response from Jacob, but both of them couldn't resist watching intensely as the girls faded from site.

"Okay, Jacob, I said look, not stare ... jeez."

"Oh yeah, like you weren't staring too."

"I cannot tell a lie," Pat said. "I could look at those two all the livelong day."

John came out of the cottage and sat on the edge of the deck's landing. "Pat, why don't you take Jacob out and about to show him the place? There'll be a crowd starting to show up down at the river by now."

"Okay, Uncle John. Can we have a sandwich first?" Pat asked.

"As long as you don't go swimming right away. You know the rules. And make sure you're back before five o'clock for supper. It's barbeque tonight. And Marlene says we're going to the bonfire on the beach after dark. Maybe you'll get to see those two girls you were just gawking at," John said, slowly cracking a weak smile.

"We weren't gawking," Pat protested.

"Okay. Whatever you say. I just fell off the turnip truck, and I was never fourteen. Come on in and have something to eat before your weak knees crumble."

Pat and Jacob looked to one another, confused.

"Are your knees weak? Mine aren't."

"That's not what he meant. Let's go inside," Pat said, slapping Jacob on the back.

§

An old footpath not too far from the cottage led down to a popular spot to swim in the river. It was a bit of an inlet from the flow of the river. Along it sat an old elm tree with a rope and tire hanging from it over the water. The tall grass surrounded the area above the water on either side of the footpath. Near the swimming spot was a simple wood structure for privacy to change in. This spot seemed like a safe place for swimmers to stay far enough out of the way of the boats and water skiers.

Both Jacob and Pat had come prepared to swim, walking barefoot with beach towels draped around their shoulders. They'd intentionally left the flip-flops at the cottage. Pat was familiar with the area, so he wasted no time shouting a *Geronimo* and jumping into the water. Jacob looked over the small cliff, surrounded in pussy willows, cattails and tiger grass, and to his dismay, as he was about to jump in, he heard Marlene calling out to them.

"Boys, come back to the cottage. John has to go back to Saint John."

Pat was used to his uncle being called away on police business. Sometimes he would be gone for part of a day or he would be gone for days at a time. It was the nature of the business. He worked different parts of the province in multiple roles.

"Hey Pat, what's going on?" Jacob asked, waiting for him to come out of the water.

"Maybe there's been a murder," Pat said, shrugging his shoulders.

"A murder? Who got murdered?"

On their way back to the cottage, Pat assured him he was joking. The boys picked up their speed and hurried back up the path, curious to find out what was going on. Marlene was standing at the top of the redwood-stained deck leading into the cottage. She waved the boys inside.

"Come on, boys, there's been a change of plans. Your uncle John will explain."

Inside the cottage, Marlene stopped Pat in his tracks. "Hold it there, young man. Out on the deck and brush that sand off."

Jacob followed his friend back outside to make sure he wasn't dragging any sand with him. John took a bag out to the car then talked to the boys outside.

"Hey guys, I'm sorry, I won't be able to take you fishing tomorrow. I've been called back to work a case. I'll come back as soon as I can, but I won't know when until I get there. So, in the meantime, I trust you two will be good and help Marlene out with keeping the place tidy, right?"

The boys didn't hesitate to assure him they would be on their best behaviour. Pat was well aware protocol here was not to ask any inappropriate questions, so he only asked when John would return, if they'd have to go back home sooner, and the like. John hoped he wouldn't be gone for more than a couple of days. He was looking forward to being able to return to enjoy the rest of their holiday. The boys were relieved knowing they would be able to stay and have fun. And they didn't mind the sense of adult responsibility; in fact, they enthusiastically engaged in it.

"And don't be spending all of your time chasing girls."

"We haven't chased any yet, Uncle John," Pat said with a smirk.

"Okay, Casanova. Jacob, are you okay with this? Are you going to be able to handle this guy all week?"

"I'm okay, John. Thanks."

"Always the gabber, eh Jacob? I'm kidding. Okay, you guys, have fun, be safe, and listen to Marlene. I have to go."

It wasn't quite dark yet at this time of the year, just after at 9 p.m., as they headed down to the beach for the festivities around the bonfire. Marlene carried the marshmallows, and the boys each carried an armload of firewood. They were getting closer to the opening leading down to the riverside beach when Jacob picked up on a scent that put his mind in a whirl. He spun around on the spot with his arms full of firewood to see who walked by. The scent stayed strong as a beautiful, young red-haired girl with bright orange and red freckles walked past him. She looked to be the same age as Jacob. They looked straight at each other, but Jacob continued to do so while walking backwards. He was captivated, and seemed to have no concerns he might be looking a bit too long — neither did the girl, apparently.

Jacob looked at her like he knew her, finding it upsetting that he couldn't place her. When he attempted to turn back around, the load of firewood slipped out of his arms and he dropped to his knees. He held the side of his head as if he had just been wounded in the temple. Marlene spun around, set the marshmallow bags on the side of the trail, and rushed over to him. She called out for Pat several feet ahead, then bent down to tend to Jacob, but it was over in thirty seconds and he slowly stood up.

"I'm okay. I wasn't watching where I was walking," Jacob said dismissively.

"You're not all right, Jacob. What just happened to you?" Marlene asked, trying to hold him steady with an arm on his shoulder and looking in his eyes. "Have you had problems like this before? Are you going to be sick to your stomach?"

"He gets them once in a while, Aunt Marlene. His mom calls them cluster headaches. See, they usually stop pretty fast. He'll be okay, really," Pat said assuredly, yet he still watched his friend, waiting to see him steady on his feet.

"Are you sure you're all right, Jacob?" Marlene repeated.

"Yeah, I'm fine, thanks. It was just a small one. Maybe too much for one day. But yeah, I'm okay. We can keep going, honest, Marlene. We can go," Jacob said, almost impatiently.

"All right. But if you feel worse, tell me right away and we'll head back to the cottage."

Jacob waited until Marlene was a few strides ahead before he said anything.

"Did you see that girl, the redhead?" Jacob whispered to Pat.

"Yeah, she was hot, man!" Pat said as he looked over Jacob in her direction.

"Yeah, but she seemed … I don't know. I feel like I know her. Do you know her? Have you seen her here before?" Jacob asked excitedly.

"No. I've never seen her around before. There are people from all over the place here in the summer. What's got you all lit up, Jake?"

Jacob ran his hand through his hair with a puzzled look on his face.

"I thought I knew her from somewhere, but I can't figure out where."

"We've known each other since grade one, we wouldn't forget that girl from town. We would definitely know her man, I'm telling you that," Pat said, raising his eyes up and down.

"Yeah, I guess so. Just forget it. Let's go," Jacob said with a discouraged look and a tone in his voice to match. He did notice she didn't laugh when he fell; she looked concerned.

7

A Dark Side

It was Sunday morning, mid June, and the fog that started wafting in around midnight, had mostly dissipated by the time the police arrived at 9:37 a.m. — according to the official logbook. The victim was left tied around the base of a willow tree. A neighbourhood couple walking their dog made the discovery. Farther onto the property was a dilapidated shed with only one wood-framed window next to the spring-hinged door. Both had remnants of peeled white paint and the window consisted of four panes, which were near impossible to see through. The building was covered in vertical ribbed steel, with faded army green paint and a lean-to roof with moss covered, black, rolled asphalt roofing, which had rotted over time. The weeds and grass were at least two feet high all around the area, except for a trampled down trail leading to the building's door from the far side of the lot. The trail split and went farther beyond to Len's Creek, but it couldn't be seen and could barely be heard from where the investigators had congregated that morning.

The property, whose maintenance had clearly been abandoned, was often used as a shortcut to a convenience store around the block. There wasn't anything inside the shed that sat there to hold much interest for most kids, except privacy to sneak a cigarette or smoke a joint. Old man Murry Madge, who lived directly across from the property, constantly complained about it and would often chase the kids away. Sadly, he hadn't heard anything the night before. Had he noticed what was happening in time, he may have been able to help save young Rebecca Jacobsen's life.

John Keegan was a twenty-year veteran of the RCMP. He mostly worked robberies and assault cases, but he also handled some homicides. However, homicides were rare in Saint John, so he'd been assigned to several posts throughout the Maritimes over the years. When he was called away from his holiday in the Miramichi, he'd hopped into Marlene's 1970 Datsun fastback and was gone. When arriving on scene at the north end of town, his thoughts were *this is awfully close to home*. The area wasn't overly populated, being closer to the edge of town, where the population started to thin out.

He arrived to find three patrol cars, plus a canine unit already there. They purposely blocked the view of the lot from the street. John's partner, Martin Elves, had gotten to the crime scene before John. Martin was a serious-looking man, tall and thin, with a gaunt face and typical short black hair as well as an overgrown cop mustache. Only in his midforties, he looked like he'd had a decade added to him from working this job. He was standing at the edge of the wooded lot, a file folder in one hand and an evidence bag in the other, waiting to greet John, who had seniority. Martin had a look on his face that John had only seen once before from their time together as partners.

"Jesus, Martin, what have we got here? I didn't get much from dispatch other than a possible assault and that you needed me here pronto. So, what is this?"

"Yeah, sorry, John. I hated to pull you away from the holiday, buddy. This is a grim one. Come on, I'll walk you through it."

John and Martin were only a dozen feet inside the lot before John could see the trampled grass around the base of a willow tree. There was a tarp laying off to the side and a rope left partially tied around it where they had removed the body. Their forensic photographer had taken pictures of everything in the immediate area and had already left. Two patrol officers stood by with their heads down, saying nothing to each other. It was obvious to John that Martin was upset and struggling.

"It gets worse, John. There's more evidence in the shed over there at the back of the lot. I think this guy has done this before."

"What the fuck has he done, Martin? You haven't told me anything yet," John demanded angrily. "Sorry Martin, but what's got you so messed up?"

"An older couple from down the street saw it and called it in. She's thirteen, John. It's Lars Jacobsen's daughter, Rebecca."

John turned white and instantly lowered his head, holding it with his hand. His voice in attempting to speak was barely audible.

"Oh, Jesus Christ … was she?"

"We don't know yet, but it looks that way. She's at the morgue." Martin kept talking. "We won't know anything until later. The dogs got us to the fort from tracing some of her clothes … her underwear. After that, the trail disappears down by the creek."

John staggered back to one of the cruisers at the curb and almost fell while leaning up against it. John cocked his head sideways and yelled out to Martin. "She's dead?! You couldn't say that straight up? Why didn't dispatch tell me it was a homicide? Why in the Christ did you use her panties? You couldn't use any other piece of clothing? What the fuck is wrong with everyone? Jesus Christ, Martin, hasn't she been violated enough already?"

Martin gently grabbed John by his forearm. One of the neighbours was looking over, so Martin put his back to him and stood in front of John.

"John, lower your voice," he said in a near whisper. "Look, I'm sorry, but the call was put out to you before I got here. The call in hadn't confirmed anything yet. You know that, damn it." Martin continued to speak softly yet forcefully. "I know Lars is an old friend. We used her panties because, number one, they were found away from her, closer to the fort. Secondly, we thought that would be where the dogs would for sure pick up the guy's scent and give us a direction. I'm sorry John, but there was no disrespect intended here by anyone. We took care of her properly, followed procedure all the way."

John took a deep breath and put his shaking hand on Martin's shoulder. "You don't have anything to say sorry for, Martin. I'm the one who owes you an apology. I know you would do this right."

"Well, this piece of shit just threw an old canvas tarp over her and left her there. But there's some beer cans we can run prints on, and we'll bag the cigarette butts, see what that gets us. We gotta get this bastard, John!" Martin exclaimed.

"Well, Martin, that's what we do, isn't it." John replied as a matter of fact. "Yeah, this one isn't getting away. That can't happen. I'll get the guys out knocking on doors and I'll see you back at the precinct. I'm going to have to call Marlene, tell her I won't be back for a while. Then ... I'll go and see Lars."

"You want me to go with?"

"No, thanks. I gotta do this one."

"I'm sorry about the way this played out, John. And give my best to Mar when you see her, will you?" Martin said, shaken.

John simply nodded and went about taking control of the scene. Martin got in his black, unmarked cruiser and headed to see what information he could glean at the morgue. After the coroner's results, he and John would plot a course ahead in this grisly investigation.

8

Life Calls

It was late in the summer of 1979, and Pat and Jacob both worked as labourers for Alan Jones, a residential house framer and a friend of Thomas O'Connell. Jacob had started working for Alan in the middle of the summer between grade nine and grade ten, and Pat was added to the crew shortly after. They were now in their third summer and heading into their final year of high school in the fall. Pat missed work on Friday to take care of some personal business in acquiring a vehicle — a 1975 GMC half-ton pickup. Jacob had been home from work for a little over an hour that Friday when he looked out the kitchen window to see a truck pulling into his driveway. When he saw it was his best friend driving, he spilled his near full glass of water and went barrelling out of the house.

"Oh, nice man," Jacob shouted. "This is why you took off work today? Why didn't you tell me?" Excited in his queries, he had to take a breath and slow himself down.

"Yeah, eh?" Pat said, beaming with pride. "Uncle John helped me get it at the police auction. I couldn't believe it: he offered to buy it and let me pay him a bit at a time."

"Wow. You're so lucky, man." Jacob was as excited for Pat getting his first set of wheels as he would have been if it were his own. Their inspection of the truck quickly ended, and with unrestrained exuberance, they hopped in and were racing down the street in short time. They began what would be a tradition on paydays and headed to Dairy Queen for burgers and fries. The parking lot was full of teenagers who were driving their parents' cars, and others with their own muscle cars, many with the hoods open and under examination.

"So, Pat ... you taking Heather out tonight with the new wheels?" Jacob asked, raising his eyebrows repeatedly.

"I'll be picking her up later on. We're going to the quarry for a swim," Pat said, in a spiritless reply. "What are you doing tonight? And please don't tell me you're going to be hanging out at home again. You hardly ever go out, Jake. What's up with that?"

"I'm trying to save my money. You know that. But I'm actually taking Mandy Mathews out tonight. We're catching *Escape from Alcatraz* at the Strand."

"Ooh, Mandy Mathews ... I hear she—" Before Pat got another word out, Jacob stopped him.

"Shut up. I don't want to hear it. I like her, and I don't care about the rep."

Pat smiled, looking at his friend. "Okay, Jake. It's cool. Well, I hope you have a good time."

§

It was nearing the end of August when Jacob and Pat got together for one of their usual trips out for a burger on payday. They had both just finished work and were still dirty. The sweat was clinging to Pat's brow and his clothes were dirtier than usual. Jacob noticed his appearance was out of the usual. Jokingly he started waving his hand from side to side.

"Did you forget to shower this morning, bud?" Jacob teased.

"I didn't make it home last night. Heather was freaking out again about being pregnant and everything else."

"Well, it is pretty serious. So, yeah, I imagine she's uptight about it, and moving too."

"Yeah, well, it is serious. Serious enough I'm going to be moving with her to Clarington, two provinces away."

Even with the radio playing, a silence developed.

§

A few days before the Labour Day weekend, the O'Connell house was alit with raised voices from a heated conversation coming from every direction. It was a mash-up of emotions, with Irene and Kate calling out their nays and the boys exclaiming their yays. When Thomas and Irene were young, work had commonly been considered more important than education, for purely practical reasons. Irene, who once agreed with that notion, had changed her views on the subject in favour of education. When Jacob was five years old she returned to work as a nurse. However, she also went to school for two years to obtain her certificate.

"Mom, the course in Hamilton will give me upgrading for grade twelve equivalent and will be a two-year college certificate. I'm basically getting a year head start. Construction is what I want to do, Mom, and there are more jobs there than here," Jacob pleaded.

His brother Kevin interjected.

"You got that right. He's right about that, Mom. I can't find a good job here that pays a decent dollar."

"That's because you're stupid and lazy," Kate quipped.

"That's enough of that. This is important. It's not a joking matter," Irene barked, her voice growing shaky.

"Sorry, Mom, I was only teasing. I didn't mean to upset you," Kate said, putting her hand on Irene's shoulder.

"Come on, you two." Thomas motioned to the door. "Let's take a walk around the block and let your mom and Jacob finish this conversation. We've given our opinions."

Thomas had talked with Jacob's boss, Alan Jones, several times about Jacob's abilities and the possibilities of being a carpenter for a career. Thomas had taught Jacob throughout the years while creating building projects at home, so he knew Jacob's natural aptitude already. He also knew his son was capable of far more and believed he would likely strike out on his own one day.

"Are you sure this is the right choice for you, Jacob, or is it because Pat's going to be living in Clarington? It's a reasonable question, honey," Irene said, cupping her hand to Jacob's chin. "You don't have to answer me right away. You don't have to choose to go right away, either."

"I love you, Mom, you're the best. I wouldn't have made it this far without you and Dad, but I've already chosen," Jacob said, squeezing his mother's hand. "This is what's right for me, Mom. Are you going to be okay about this?"

"Of course, sweetie. I just don't want to."

"Really, Mom, do you want me to stay here that bad?"

"Oh, I was kidding, Jacob. You're so serious for a young man. But you've always been serious," Irene said with a crooked smile. Sad as any mother watching a child leave the nest.

"And I wonder where I get that from, mother dearest?"

"Don't call me that, or I won't let you go. I'll tie you to your bedpost if I have to, mister smarty-pants." Irene's smile was fully fledged now. "And just because you're taller than me doesn't mean I won't slap you. I'll get up on a chair if I have to."

Jacob leaned over and hugged his mother.

"Thanks, Mom. It really means a lot to me."

Pat got on with his new life with Heather and went to work as a framing carpenter. Jacob finished the usual busy season of the summer with Jones and received a glowing letter of reference to take with him. Excited about this new venture in his life, he then set about making preparations to attend his construction management course. One day near the end of his time working for Jones, he arrived home and popped out of his co-worker's truck. There, at the end of the driveway, stood his father, with his arms crossed and a serious look on his face.

"Hey, Dad. Is everything okay? You look pretty serious about something," Jacob said somewhat apprehensively.

"Come on, get in the car, son. We have an errand to run."

"Okay. Where are we going? Do we have to pick up stuff for the barbecue tonight?"

"Something like that. Let's go," Thomas replied dismissively.

A few blocks from home, Jacob noticed they weren't going toward the grocery store. He kept looking over at his dad, but he had such a serious look on his face that Jacob was hesitant to ask him where he was going. His patience failed.

"Hey, Dad, why are we going this way? The grocery store is the other way, so what's up?"

"I told you, we have an errand to run. Be patient, son. We won't be long."

A few more minutes went by and they were now going toward some industrial projects under construction. All that remained before the start of another residential area were a couple of car dealerships. As the Chevy dealership approached, Thomas started slowing down and then pulled in.

"Do you have to take the suburban in for maintenance again, Dad?"

"No, not exactly. See that Silverado over there? The blue one there. It's nice, eh? It's only a few years old."

"Yeah, it is nice," Jacob said, somewhat confused.

"Well, I set up a deal for financing on it," Thomas paused, looked over to his son to see any reaction. "The financing is in your name, Jacob. I paid for the deposit and co-signed for you. The payments need to be paid off over two years. What do you think?" Thomas could see Jacob's look of curiosity and jubilation combined. He didn't hesitate to say, "Don't worry, son, I've already set aside the money for the truck. The payments in your name will help you establish a good credit rating. The truck is yours, Jacob. You need a way to get back and forth to school, and when you get a job, too."

Jacob was frozen still in his seat, and then tears came out. Seeing Jacob's emotional reaction, Thomas attempted to stir him out of it. "You do realize, now that you have transportation, you will have to come home every time your mother requests it, right?" he joked, holding his hand on Jacob's shoulder. Thomas barely got the words out and Jacob gave his father a hug so tight he started turning red.

"Ah Dad, this is incredible," Jacob exclaimed. "I was thinking I could never get the money saved up to get anything except an old beater, if that. Wow, this is just … thanks, Dad. Really, this is amazing," Jacob said, with his voice shaking.

"You worked hard, son; you deserve it. Okay, let's go have a closer look at your truck and get inside and finish the paperwork up. You can use some of that money you saved up for expenses living in the city. I love you, Jacob, and I'm very proud of you."

Jacob's eyes began to well again.

9

Moving Shadows

Part 1

It seemed like winter was never going to end during Jacob's last year in college. And spring had so far been wet, damp, and miserably cold. The day had given a brief reprieve from the rain, but grey, overcast skies still hung around. It was the night before Jacob's graduation, and he was sitting in his new apartment unpacking the last of his clothes and putting his toiletries away. He walked into his living room and looked out past the balcony at the lake not too far away. A deep sigh came out, and then a look around his mostly empty bachelor pad. Tomorrow his best friend, Pat, and his now wife, Heather, would be coming to the graduation ceremony, along with Thomas and Irene. Once again, he scanned his apartment, pausing to look at each of the few items he'd moved in. He decided to hang his battery-operated wall clock on a nail left in the wall, painted the same colour. He stood back and looked at his new décor. "Oh hell. Enough of this shit." And grabbed his keys and out he went.

He grabbed himself a coffee on the go and took a drive downtown where his future employer's office was. He had been on a couple of job sites through his work placement with the same company hiring him, so he was familiar with the area. A huge addition and renovation to a commercial building was underway to accommodate an architect's firm — that was to be his first stop. From the driver's seat of his pickup, he was admiring the façade on the building facing the street. Someone was working on the scaffolding on the fourth storey around the side of the building. He thought it might be the assistant site supervisor, Terry Haskett. He'd worked with Terry for a few days on this job. They got along well and went for beers after work once.

It's a little late to still be working, he thought, looking at his watch — *7:30 p.m. Thursday. Is that Terry? The bricklayers are still on the second storey. Oh, what the hell, I'll see if it's him.* He walked around the side of the building under the scaffolding, everything still wet from all the rain they'd been having, despite the tarp above. The scaffold planks were covered in bricks above him, and the planks staggered so he couldn't see up to make out who it was. When he reached the side door, he thought for sure it would be locked, but, to his surprise, it wasn't. The doorknob was what they refer to as a construction lock, so it was used on multiple sites and completely beaten up and scratched. If the lock had been picked, he wouldn't know it.

The stairwell was under construction, with new drywall in the process of being taped. There were foldable ladders and planks used to support the workers for the long reaches. He weaved his way through, and after the third storey the rest of the way was clear. From in the stairwell he thought he could hear something coming on the fourth floor, so he stopped and stood still. Sure enough, he heard some shuffling and intermittent hits of a hammer against the metal scaffolding. "Hey, Terry," he shouted out. The noise stopped, but there was no reply of any kind. "Terry, it's Jacob. Is that you up there?" Still no response and not a sound. He thought of just making a run up the last set of steps to investigate, but suddenly he felt uncomfortable. He leaned his neck to the far left until it cracked, and he stood still with a pained look on his face. He took a couple of pronounced steps up and could hear movement at the same time. He stopped again, and so did the noise. "What the hell?" *Maybe it's some kids*, he thought. Another couple of steps and a clear shuffle across the floor this time. He stopped and cleared his throat, feeling the need to announce his presence again. He felt a wave of heat go through his chest and into his neck, and he could feel his skin become clammy. "The hell with this," he said out loud and ran the last few steps up and onto the landing.

He burst through the doorway and into the fourth floor, entering a sea of steel studs and corrugated metal wiring. A workstation stood in the centre of a large opening. He could see all the way through to the other side of the building and to the doorway that led to another set of stairs. No one was in sight, so he took a breath and slowly scanned the room. Suddenly out of his peripheral, he caught the back of a man running from the far side of the room and into the stairwell. His breathing stopped, his stomach tightened, and he could feel his heart racing. "Terry?" he yelled out, even though he knew it wasn't him. The man who ran into the stairwell was tall and thin, with black hair and a beard. Terry was stocky and average height, with sandy blonde hair and a mustache. Jacob turned and ran back down the stairs, dodging and weaving his way around the ladders and planks. He came flying out the side door and ran to the sidewalk. He stopped to look down the street to see who would come out the other side, but no one came. He sprinted a few steps, then walked a few back and forth like this until he reached the other side of the building. He looked down the narrow alley to the rear but gleaned nothing.

His jaw muscles flexed, and he grit his teeth together tight. He went racing down the alley to see who he could find. In the parking lot were a couple of vehicles and the contractor's trailer, but no one on foot. He surveyed the entire area from where he stood; he found no indication of anyone or anything out of the usual. Just before he went to turn around, a vehicle that was out of sight from the other side of the trailer went racing down the back alley. Jacob didn't know what to think. All he could make out from the logo on the side of the truck were the words *City of Toronto*. "That's weird," he grumbled to himself. He wasn't sure what to do. He thought about calling the police, but for what? He thought about this legally and realized even though he worked there as part of his co-op, he was still trespassing.

He turned around with a disappointed sigh and headed back to check the doors on the building before he left. *Who in hell would be in there? Well, if it was a thief, he didn't get away with any tools. The boxes are all locked.* He secured both side and rear doors.

Running across the street to his truck, he concluded he wouldn't be able to solve this one of life's mysteries. This uninvited excitement and unsatisfied conclusion left him feeling as though he'd lost something, and he just wanted to go back home for the rest of the night.

Part 2

Miles of black storm clouds encompassed the sky, blocking out the moon, and a torrential rain was pounding down in buckets when the truck slid into the shoulder of the road. Blinded by opposing high beams, Jacob's overzealous attempt at correcting the steering wheel flipped the vehicle over on its side. Unable to resist the momentum, it broke through the wooden guard posts and snapped the high-tension horizontal cables, making a sound like whips cracking. The truck rolled a half-dozen times down the hill before stopping, roof down, inside the ravine. Jacob would never forget the sound of metal and glass grinding into the sand and gravel, in what seemed like slow motion. The first sounds were soon followed up with those of the cab crunching and the windows smashing as the truck rolled down the hill. Experiencing this from inside the driver's seat, of what felt like unsustainable gravitational forces, was exceedingly disorienting.

Pat came to, lying face down, inhaling the musky smell of wet grass, the pain forcing him to register the reality of what had just happened. His face and forehead were cut up from being tossed out the passenger side window, and blood partially blurred his vision as a result. He wiped his forehead and eyes to see the pickup was on its roof, with most of the cab crushed. Farther away from the front of the truck was Jacob lying face up — no movement. Pat could see Heather's legs sticking out of the truck, so he crawled his way over.

"Heather!" he yelled out. At the same time, he called out to Jacob. "Jake, are you all right? Jacob, wake up. Jesus, Heather. I can't reach you. Heather!" Pat yelled even louder.

Jacob was just coming to as Pat crawled back out the overturned pickup. The smell of gasoline was evident, and Pat could see a small flame coming from the engine.

"Jesus, Jacob, help me get Heather out of the truck. Oh my God! Baby, are you okay? Are you bleeding? You are bleeding! Is there anything broken?" Pat asked, frantic now.

"Pat, I think my leg's broken," Heather calmly said.

Jacob's eyes were wide open now. He joined Pat, and the two prepared to pull Heather out of the truck. Jacob first noticed she was bleeding from her ear.

"Oh my God, baby, you're bleeding a lot," Pat said, looking her over.

"Pat, calm down. Let's get her out of here before—" as the words left Jacob's mouth, the front of the truck let out a small explosion, then came a hissing sound.

By the time they had pulled Heather a safe distance away, the truck was engulfed in flames, without the ceremonious explosion, though. Pat looked over to Jacob and saw dark red, almost black, blood slowly oozing from a gaping hole in his left hand.

"Jake, you need to wrap that up." Pat said, nodding his head to it.

"Don't worry about it. Pat, you need to climb up to the road, try and wave somebody down," Jacob said looking up the ravine they rolled into.

Before Pat headed up the hillside, he saw Heather pass out.

"Shit! Oh no. Heather. Baby, wake up. Heather!"

Jacob felt Heather's neck for a pulse and looked to Pat. "She's just passed out. It's probably from the pain. She's okay, Pat, now go. Go and try to get some help. I'll stay here with her to make sure she's okay. Don't worry, Pat. I know what I'm doing."

Pat went up the hill in a scramble, crawling at first, grabbing at the grass and weeds. Then from being half bent over, he started running almost upright in a panic to make it to the top. Jacob reached out one more time to check Heather's pulse, but they were too far apart. He listened to her chest and her mouth for signs of breathing, but it was barely present.

"Goddamn it, Heather, don't do this to me."

He reached down with both hands and began to shake her. "Heather! Heather, come on. You can't die! Goddamn it, Heather, wake up!"

Jacob only had training in basic first aid, having not finished the entire course yet, but he thought he knew enough about CPR to get by in a pinch. Pat reached the hill by the highway, soaked from the pouring rain. He was a sad, desperate-looking figure in polyester pants and loafers, with a white cotton button-up, transparent with the rain. A Jeep Cherokee was parked across the highway just down the road about a hundred feet, but no lights were on. Abandoned, he figured, so he chose to ignore it. Distraught, he began jumping up and down, waving to the oncoming traffic, even stepping onto the edge of the highway. And to his relief, a transport truck with no trailer attached pulled over.

Jacob and Heather were down below in the crown vetch and sumac–filled ravine, so Pat couldn't hear Jacob's panicked voice. At one point Jacob looked up to the top toward the highway, and he thought he saw Pat. *What's he doing just standing there? Is there no one on the highway?* He thought to himself, alarmed. "What the hell is he looking down here for? Pay attention to the road damn it," he quietly said. Then Jacob attempted to focus on whether it was actually Pat or not. And just then, whoever was standing on the edge of the hillside, turned and slowly walked out of sight. This unnerved Jacob, but he thought maybe Pat was in shock and had started wandering. All of these thoughts raced through his head, and he put them aside, concentrating on Heather.

Pat ran over to the side door of the big rig and opened it.

"Thanks for stopping. My wife and friend are at the bottom down there. We rolled the truck. Can you call an ambulance please? My wife is hurt bad." Pat's voice was cracking with emotion. The trucker didn't hesitate to grab the mic to his CB radio.

In the middle of the call the trucker released the bottom of his mic, holding it to his chest. "What kind of injuries?" the trucker asked. Then his next statement into his radio, "We have a lady here with a head injury and suspected broken leg ... over." The static-filled reply came through and the trucker looked down to Pat. "They're coming. You go back down, and I'll wait here for them."

"Thanks, buddy," Pat said, his torso and arms shaking violently from the cold.

At that moment, Jacob was clumsily trying to push on Heather's chest without the proper pressure and blowing air into her lungs. On his knees, he pulled his arms toward his chest, squeezed his fists, and with his face scrunched up he screamed as hard as he could. He put his hands up to cover his face, and, still bent over, he became wrought with emotion. He continued screaming hopelessly at Heather to wake up.

Pat wasted no time as he began to traverse the slippery hill back down. He lost his footing on the soaked ravine and slid into a group of sumacs below that stopped his tumble. He regained his footing and looked down to see Jacob kneeling over Heather. It looked like he had his hands on her head, and he thought he could see a light glowing around them. In the pouring rain, and from this distance, he couldn't figure out what it was. What wasn't covered by overcast, was darkened by the evening's arrival, so Pat thought this was maybe a flashlight or a glow from the truck burning and quickly forgot about it.

"Jacob, there's help on the way. A trucker stopped. He's up there now," Pat called out, carefully negotiating the wet humps of grass that made up his lateral trek across the hill to get to them. "Jacob? Jacob!" Pat called out again, raising his voice. He was relieved to see his wife's breath rising up into the cold air. When he came upon them, Pat could clearly see tears streaming down Jacob's face. He looked to Heather, but only saw a smile on hers.

"Heather, baby, you okay? Jake. What's wrong? Are you all right?" he asked them.

With the overwhelming amount of emotion in the air, Pat's eyes began to well up, too. He knelt down next to his friend, with one hand on the back of his shoulder and his other to Heather's face. He smiled to both of them.

"We're going to be okay, guys. There's help coming down to get you up the hill, baby. We're going to be okay."

Heather looked up to them both and smiled with a huge sense of relief. The blood on her face was slowly clearing away from the falling rain. Pat cocked his head in curiosity over the strange look on her face. She looked like she was experiencing euphoria, instead of writhing in pain.

"How do you feel, baby? Are you in a lot of pain? Can you feel everything okay?" Pat asked feverishly.

"I'm okay," she said, sounding slightly inebriated.

She attempted to raise herself up to her elbows and tried to focus better.

"Heather, please … put your head back down. You've got a serious head injury there, so let's not push it, okay?" Jacob said, taking off his sports coat and placing it on Heather to keep her warm.

"What did you do to me, Jacob?" Heather asked, calmly without accusation.

"What do you mean? I just kept checking your pulse, making sure you could breathe. I kept checking your breathing because you passed out a couple of times," Jacob said. Pat thought her behaviour was odd, but assumed it was a result of the accident. After Heather and Jacob were in the ambulance, Pat was about to hop in when he saw the lights of the Cherokee come on. He stopped for a second to watch it drive by, but the weather was making it hard to see. He was pretty sure he could make out a guy with a beard, but the driver avoided looking at Pat.

"That's weird," Pat said, and then hopped in the ambulance. He looked out the windows in the back doors of the ambulance and stared at the back of the Cherokee until its brake lights were out of sight.

"What's the matter, Pat?" asked Jacob. Pat was slow in turning away from the window, and Jacob recognized his annoyed look before he did.

"Nothing. Just looking at the traffic." Pat looked at Jacob and could tell he knew something was off.

§

Looking at his reflection in the hospital's mirror between washing the blood off his face, a jumbled memory attempted to come to the surface. Watching the blood swirl down the white porcelain sink, he could see a child's red bicycle with white tires. He shook his head to erase the vision from his mind. Failing that, he slipped into another trance and could clearly see Sylvia Millen's face looking up at him at Sara's accident scene when he was six. He didn't remember any of it.

Pat's voice echoed in the corridor calling out to Jacob. The sound got closer, and Jacob snapped out of this trance. He tried to shake it off and grabbed a handful of paper towels to dry his face when Pat entered the washroom.

"Hey Jake, how ya' doin', buddy? Are you feeling okay?" Pat asked in a sombre tone.

"Yeah, I'm fine. Did you get any news yet?" Jacob was distant in his response.

"No, they're working on her now, but she's stable, they told me that much."

As Jacob pulled the paper towels from his face, Patrick reached out and grabbed his left arm just above the wrist.

"Your hand, Jacob … your hand had a huge … it had a fucking hole in it. It was bleeding like crazy. What the hell!" Pat exclaimed in confusion and angst.

"I don't remember cutting my hand. I sat next to Heather and you were back in a few minutes. Why do you think I cut my hand?" Jacob said, convincingly. Pat stood looking dumbfounded, without a word.

"It was pretty handy that trucker coming by when he did, eh?" Jacob said. Pat was standing still, staring at Jacob.

"Pat. What, man? You're freaking me out," Jacob said, as he stopped drying his hands.

"Jacob … that took at least twenty minutes before he came along," Pat said, raising his eyebrows. "It's not the busiest stretch of highway there."

"Really, it seemed like it was all of five minutes, tops." Jacob's response was aloof.

"Why were you leaning over Heather like that when I came back down?"

"I was sitting beside her Pat, not leaning over her," Jacob said, rolling up his used paper towels and throwing them in the trash.

"Were you holding a flashlight? I don't remember you having one," Pat said.

"No, I didn't. Why?" Jacob replied, looking down at his watch. Then he looked past Pat toward the washroom door, wanting to get out. Pat's stance was seemingly confrontational, and his voice had become elevated.

"I thought I saw you pointing a flashlight down on Heather when you were leaning over her. Were you?"

"I wasn't leaning over her. I was sitting beside her," Jacob snapped.

"Okay, Jake. It's no big thing. It was scary for all of us." They smiled at one another, and out the door they went. Just before he left the room, Pat briefly looked in the mirror, raised his eyebrows and let out a sigh. "What the hell!? Well, maybe something rang his bell on the way down," he said to himself, unconvinced.

10

Eager Apprentice

Pat and Heather were back home in Clarington recovering from the car accident and Jacob was starting his new job in Toronto. As he was pulling into the parking lot at work for his first official day on the job, his boss, Donny Reynar, pulled in behind him.

"Mornin', Jacob. Excited to get started?" Donny walked toward Jacob with his hand out.

"Oh, yeah. It's good to finally get started."

"Hey, did you get a new truck? That's not the truck you were driving before, is it?"

"No. It's a rental. I rolled my truck last week," Jacob said, shaking Donny's hand.

"Oh no. You weren't drinking, were you? Are you going to lose your licence?"

"No, nothing like that. I was driving friends home and it was dark, rainy, and some asshole blinded me with his high beams on a curve. I went off the road and rolled down a hill."

"Jesus," Donny exclaimed. "I hope no one was hurt. You don't look any worse for wear."

"Nothing happened to me, but my friend's wife broke her leg and got a concussion, but not too bad. She's at home resting. And my friend's there, being her nurse." They both chuckled.

Once inside, Annie, the office receptionist, gave Jacob his pager and official hard hat with the company logo on it. His official title at work was Assistant Site Superintendent. To start with, he mostly ran around cleaning up after one tradesman, making the job site ready for the next one scheduled in. Donny constantly found Jacob asking the tradespeople questions. He would occasionally have to reign him in a bit, but he admired his resolve and desire to learn.

Jacob's first week at work was busy and distracting for several reasons, but when he overheard some of the guys in the office talk about needing to meet with Ontario Health and Safety on site at the architect's building, his heart sank. Then he heard part of the conversation between the project manager and the masonry contractor. They talked about the scaffold collapse and two men being in the hospital, the one who had it the worst had a broken back, fractured scull, and was in a coma. The contractor was asked if he had any guys he fired recently who would be pissed off enough to sabotage scaffolding, knowing what could happen. That's when Jacob had no choice but to go to his immediate boss and tell him what he had seen. He worried he was going to be fired for going onto the job site after hours, unaccompanied. After he told them everything, the response was quite the opposite.

He told them about the stranger, that he was sure it wasn't Terry. However, the description caught the attention of a few around the office. That's when Donny pulled Jacob into his office with his boss, the project manager. "Keep going, Jacob. It's just us now," Donny said, with raised eyebrows pointed at his boss. But when Jacob concluded his version of events with a City of Toronto truck driving through the back alley "pretty quick," as Jacob described it, they looked at each other, stunned.

The project manager was the only one to speak. "Well, that's just a frightening thought. Jacob, thanks. And whatever you do, don't repeat what you just told us to anyone. Okay?"

Jacob didn't ask why, he just replied, "my word." The information Jacob provided created implications that were controversial at best. But the information was moot because none of it could be proven.

Three months into his job, Jacob's boss invited him to go for a pint at his local pub on a Friday after work. He was happy, and relieved, to finally receive an invite. As time went on, Jacob and

Donny became good friends, which was a bit surprising considering the difference in age. O'Toole's pub was decorated like it was left over from the early seventies. It had a common Irish theme, pictures of the emerald isles, green clovers, and prints of several Irish-American boxers from Jack Dempsey up to Micky Ward, which was their newest poster. And of course, posters and memorabilia representing the three big local sports teams — the Maple Leafs, Blue Jays, and Argonauts — hung in various places throughout the pub. All the woodwork was stained dark and there was minimal lighting — a typical dimly lit, smoky bar. Jacob walked in a few feet behind Donny, looking the place over. The bartender greeted them.

"Hi, handsome, what can I get you? IPA, as usual, Donny?" The energetic bartender asked.

"That's correct, my dear. And this younger, more handsome version of me, Jacob here, will have a Guinness. Right?" He turned to Jacob.

"Yes, I'll have a pint of Guinness, please." He was trying not to stare, and it was not lost on the bartender. It took a few minutes, but she placed the pint in front of him. "Thanks, um, uh…"

"It's Sara. And you're Jacob. Hello, Jacob," She said with a bright smile, holding her hand out across the bar. Jacob was lost in her dark green eyes but managed to shake her hand.

"Nice to meet you, Sara."

"Yes … yes it is, Jacob." Sara's reply was intended to be slow and to the point.

He raised his glass to her.

"Good pour. Thank you."

"You're most welcome, Jacob." And that was it, the hook was in for Jacob, enamoured with Sara's exuberance, and, of course, her beauty.

Donny couldn't help but smile, looking at the instant attraction between the two. He placed his hand on Jacob's shoulder.

"Let's get a seat down by the pool tables. Maybe I can teach you a thing or two."

"Don't let him swindle you, Jacob, he's quite the shark," Sara said. Her smile held Jacob's attention completely.

"You play?" Donny asked, walking down the three steps to the lower level and toward the tables. "That is when you're not staring at pretty bartenders," Donny said, smiling. He could see Jacob was having difficulty not looking back at her. Finally, at the open table, Donny bent down to remove the balls out of the bottom feeder and looked to Jacob.

"Are you okay, Jacob? You seem a little sidetracked."

"Oh, yeah, just not feeling very well." Jacob said, still looking back to Sara.

Donny was laughing at the delay, the dazed look on his face. "I asked you that ten minutes ago, Jacob," he teased.

"Huh?"

A heavy laugh came out from Donny, but a timid and shyer one came from Jacob in return. But what Donny witnessed of the reaction between Sara and Jacob was undeniable. It was understood — Sara had Jacob befuddled. He wasn't concentrating on pool too much, looking back to the bar every few seconds.

"Yup, she's uh…" Jacob said, quietly and unsolicited.

"Yes, she's a stunner, that's for sure, and a sweet girl, too. So, no bad thoughts. She's almost young enough to be my daughter, which is kind of sad." Jacob wasn't picking up on what Donny said.

"No, nothing like that, that's for sure."

Surprising enough to Donny, he believed him. Jacob managed a clear line of sight through the usually crowded pub on a Friday after work. And at the end of his tunnel vision was a beautiful young woman with straight, long, brilliant red hair and hauntingly green eyes. They were both trying not to be caught looking too long at the other.

A time later, a new responsibility was added to Jacob's duties in his new job. He regularly dropped off blueprints for review and approval and picked up building permits. It was on a Friday when another trip to the building department was required. When Jacob was waiting at the counter, Jonathon Vargas was helping another customer when he called out, "Sara, can you bring the Langdon Child Care permit out, please? That's what you're after, right O'Connell?"

Jacob was surprised by the casual use of his name, or that he used his name at all. He usually called him "next."

Suddenly those familiar green eyes and fire-red hair came around the corner. To Jacob, just in a brief moment, everything around him slowed down to a near freeze. He could feel his breath stop, and under the lump in his throat was a belly dancing around in excitement. And once she saw Jacob, her beaming smile greeted him. Out of the corner of his eye, Jacob caught Vargas's noticeable reaction of displeasure seeing the connection between Sara and him. Being so happy to see Sara, he put Vargas's reaction aside for the time being.

"Jacob! Hi, how are you? It's great to see you," Sara said, excited. And Jacob had his own uncontrollable smile.

"You're working here now? Are you done with bartending?"

"No. This is my work placement through school, but I hope to. For now, I still need a job that pays," Sara said, looking Jacob in the eye. She intentionally kept her body still, and only her eyes moved in Vargas's direction. He picked up on the hint. Before Jacob could politely end their conversation and save her possible grief, he was interrupted by Vargas.

"You need to give him a receipt for the cheque," he barked to Sara, even before any papers were present. He pulled out a receipt book from under the counter and slammed it on top. "Then you can keep going on the Zimmerman plans. See if you can actually catch any mistakes this time." Vargas leaned over his glasses, looking Sara up and down, then locking in on her modestly exposed cleavage for too many uncomfortable seconds. Even when she went to retrieve the permit and receipt for Jacob, he watched her bum most of the way. Jacob stood still, staring at Vargas with a look that could kill, or at least maim. Sara returned to the counter with Jacob's permit package and receipt, but he kept a straight beam on Vargas. However, he realized it was getting uncomfortable for everyone, so he finally looked back to Sara.

"Thanks, Sara. So, are you working tonight?" he asked, stacking his papers and tapping their alignment on the countertop. "Maybe I'll see you later? The guys from work might be going for a beer after work," Jacob said with a wink.

"They might be, eh?" she said, smiling back a bit bashful. They giggled over their joke, and she returned the wink. "Yes, I'll be there. Who knows, if I get a full-time job here, maybe I'll retire my apron for an official municipal shirt. Pretty, isn't it?" she joked, pointing to the logo on her white collared cotton shirt.

"As long as you're in it, Sara, yes, it's pretty." Jacob smiled wide. All that was left was a farewell salutation. But Vargas pulled off his glasses, and with the same hand, put them down on the counter with emphasis, making sure the back of the frames made contact for full effect.

"Are you two quite done already? Sara," he said, looking at her and nodding his head toward the rear offices. "We have work to get back to." He put his glasses back on, and slowly turned his head to look over his bifocals and briefly peer at Jacob.

"Take care, Sara." Jacob turned toward the exit and raised his hand to wave goodbye.

Vargas turned back to the drawings and the customer in front of him like nothing was out of the ordinary. Once Jacob was on the other side of the door and out of Sara's view, he looked through the glass straight to Vargas one last time. They locked eyes for a few seconds, but Vargas was first to relent. As is his habit, he looked over the top of his bifocals and spewed a harrumph.

"You should watch out for that g—" he tried to say but stopped in his tracks when he realized Sara had already started to walk away.

The customer standing in front of him grumbled. "Can we get back to this, please? Or do you guys need a minute?"

"Right," Vargas said, in slow motion, turning back from watching Sara walking away, clearly staring at her behind like a hungry dog. He then noticed the look from Jacob on the other side of those vestibule doors. A look that spoke volumes.

11

The Good, the Bad

In short time, the confusion Jacob was experiencing all day and at the scene of Sarah's accident created an anxiety that crept up on him and then hit him hard. The bits of memories piercing their way into his conscious thoughts on top of the energy he just expended was too much. Individual images of family, friends, and strangers were running through his head in less time than it takes to blink. And time itself became obscured to him. He saw it slow down, speed up, and even stand still. Although he couldn't remember the moment he saved Sara or seeing the mystery lady speak to him at the scene of the crash, he remembered seeing the strange woman before the accident. What Jacob experienced in saving Sara's life that day took more out of him than he knew he was ever capable of. He started driving to O'Toole's for a drink, but his new habit of keeping his schedule had him looking at his watch: 10:20 a.m. "Jesus, Jacob, wake up." He rubbed his hand on his undershirt, then, pulling it up to see it covered in blood brought him back to reality. "Wow. Gotta get it together." He concluded he should have been heading straight home to begin with.

The first thing he did was pour a shot to calm his nerves. His entire body was vibrating to the point that his limbs were becoming numb. He threw his blood-stained clothes to the side of the hamper and got into the shower. The hot pulsating water from the shower massage was failing to penetrate his tense back muscles.

His hands pressed against the wall of the shower, and his head almost fell onto his bicep. Several deep breaths failed to return any strength. He reached out through the curtain and grabbed the tumbler of whisky off the vanity and drank the rest of it in one swig. The sound of the glass breaking on the ceramic tile floor when it slipped out of his shaking hands put him back behind those tall maple doors. He was replaying the sound from inside the building of the screeching tires and the impact. It was the sound of the impact that sickened him, and the whisky in his stomach came back up and washed down the drain.

Back under the shower head, he increased the massage setting to the max. It battered away at his head and the back of his neck, turning his skin red as the temperature continued to increase. When he turned around to face the water, he started seeing flashes of the woman beside Sara in the crowd and then Sara when she was under him. Her voice was sounding out, over and over again, like a recording he couldn't shut off. He felt his heart rate increase rapidly, his breathing accelerated, and he started to get pins and needles throughout his body. He was getting dizzy, lost his balance, and slipped back in the shower onto his bum. There he sat, choosing not to stand up too soon, legs crossed, and he rested his arms on top of his bent knees as the penetrating massage beat down on him. After waiting several minutes for this sensation to leave and for his breathing and heartbeat to go back to normal, he got out of the shower. With just his towel on, he flopped on the sofa, and when his head hit the back cushion, he was out within minutes.

What appears in between a breaking overcast in the evening sky is a muddy, golden-orange moon. It is held up in the sky by air so thick all movement becomes a slow crawl, and his breathing is like that of a panting animal. All of his thoughts and movements are being choked off from the stifling heat and humidity, beyond any conditions he's ever seen. Purgatory, he thinks. Then he sees an escape from a neon sign in the distance. Yes, Sara would be working in an air-conditioned bar, with the same inviting look. He feels like he is wading through a heavy, thick fog from the chest down where each dragging step is a concentrated effort. He's now walking down a sidewalk made of old chrome moon hubcaps with red sand in between. One scene blends into another. Time is irrelevant, when suddenly he finds himself sitting at the bar. He looks to the tables in the lower level to see this strange woman once again, wearing the same clothes, and the same headscarf. With a look of consternation, Jacob leans across the bar and begins whispering to Sara. He turned his gaze and nods toward her. "Who is that lady? It's the third … no, wait, it's the fourth time I've seen her today. She keeps staring at me. It's freaking me out." When he turns back to hear Sara's response, he finds himself sitting at the table with the mystery woman sitting across from him. Looking into his eyes, she leans her hand across the table and places it on his. And, as at the accident scene, her mouth doesn't open, but he hears her speak all the same, "I told you she would be okay."

Jacob snapped awake, sat up, and leaned forward on the edge of the sofa, breathing heavy with his head and chest covered in sweat. "What's going on with that woman? Who the hell is she?" he said to himself. He stood up, went to the fridge, pulled out a jug of apple juice, and poured himself a glass. He walked into his bedroom to get changed, but his hands started getting hot and then they started to glow. The glass fell from his hand, and he could see the shape of his fingers melted into the side of the broken glass. He turned his palms toward himself to see them glowing brighter and brighter. The heat became so extreme and the light was blinding him to the point he couldn't take it a second longer and bellowed aloud in agony. When it started to subside, he slowly opened his eyes to attempt a look at his hands, only to find himself back on the couch, snapping awake, still in his bath towel, still covered in sweat. It wasn't more than a minute after waking, when he dropped his head, and put his palm to his temple, pushing hard against it. His face cringed, and, moaning, he started leaning back and forth on the sofa, until he finally lay his head on the cushions, his body in the foetal position, and passed out. He slept still for over an hour, and just before he woke, he dreamt of being six years old, standing on the street and holding a bag of candy. He started walking to Sara lying in front of Grimmer's truck, and as he came upon her, he woke.

§

"Sara? Ms. Millen, can you hear me? Come on honey, time to wake up now. Let's get you up and see if you can give us a cough or two. We don't want you getting pneumonia now."

The nurse repeated most everything while hooking her up to all of the monitors in recovery, in preparation for transport to her room. Her leg was in a cast and hooked to a line keeping it elevated, and a pillow lay under her arm, which was also in a cast and sling.

"Sara, I need you to wake up now, honey. I need you to sit up a bit and try to cough, just a little. Come on, sweetie, you can do it. I know it's hard, but we need you to cough for us."

Sara began to stir, and the nurse continued.

"That's it, just take it easy. You were in a bad accident, but you're going to be okay now."

"You're going to be okay." Sara already heard these words in what seemed like a dream only a few seconds ago. Between the anaesthetic and the morphine, she was struggling to wake up.

"Jacob?" she moaned quietly.

"Who's Jacob, honey?" The nurse asked.

Sara fought to stay awake, but her eyes closed. All she remembered was a familiar and soothing voice in Jacob telling her she would be okay. The nurse finally managed to have her sit up and cough a little bit before the transfer to her room. Later, a different nurse came out of Sara's room and walked back to the nurse's station, finding a sombre-looking Jacob with a bouquet of flowers in hand.

"I'm here to see Sara Millen. She was hit by a car this morning. This is where the paramedics said she would be. The recovery nurse sent me up," he said to the woman monitoring the station.

Jacob felt a tug on the arm holding the flowers. He turned to meet the nurse who had just been tending to Sara. "Wow! You must be the guy who performed CPR on Miss Millen this morning, right? One of the paramedics told us about you … uh, they were right," the nurse said, flirtatiously.

"Right about what?" Jacob sounded uninterested.

"Right about you, honey! The EMT supervisor said there would be no mistaking you for a regular Joe."

"Okay? I guess I'll take that for a compliment," he said, puzzled and irritated, only interested in seeing Sara.

"You should, honey, trust me," the nurse said, looking him over.

"Sara is sleeping right now. She's had surgery to repair her arm and leg, but the MRI was clean — no brain injury, thank God," a return to a professional tone. Jacob lowered his shoulders and let out a pronounced exhale.

"That's great news," he said with tempered excitement. The nurse wrapped her arm around Jacob's and slowly walked him back toward Sara's room. She was tilting her head in Sara's direction beyond the window to her bed.

"I was told she called out your name when she woke, during post-op."

"Really?" Jacob sounded surprised.

"Is she your girlfriend?"

"No, I wish. Just a friend. She's someone I know through work. And a bartender at O'Toole's," he said it like everyone would know where the bar was.

"Well, the way she called your name out, maybe she wishes too? Anyway, she will most likely sleep for a few more hours at least. You can come back and visit her between seven and nine." She looked up at Jacob, seeing a mild look of disappointment. "Don't worry, I'll tell her you were here to see her."

"Thanks," Jacob said and handed the nurse the flowers. "Can you make sure she gets these?"

The nurse took the flowers and gave them the once over. "You wish, indeed."

Walking toward Emergency's automatic doors, Jacob saw Vargas coming from the opposite direction, carrying a small clay pot with a little philodendron sprouting out.

"Worried this is going to be a worker's comp claim, Vargas?" Jacob snapped.

Instead of his usual condescending remarks, he kept his focus moving straight ahead and got on the elevator. Jacob turned to see him inside, sliding along its floor, keeping time with the door as it closed, his eyes dark and trained in on him.

12

Familiar Warmth

By the time Christmas arrived, Sara had recovered well from her injuries. Muscles that had begun to soften were put back into shape with a few months of hard work. Jacob was happy to be a part of that process, and over several weeks of helping her get on her feet and back to work, they began dating. Jacob had fallen for Sara; however, he was shy about bringing his new girl home for the holidays so soon.

"It would be a lot of travelling in winter conditions."

"It will just have to wait until the next summer's vacation."

"And besides, she has her own family to visit."

And then he ran out of excuses. He hoped the ones he'd come up with might be enough to keep his siblings off his back over his "new love interest," as they liked to refer to Sara. They were all adults now, but they still loved ribbing one another, often behaving like children while doing it.

Much to Jacob's irritation, Kate suggested — in front of their mother, of course — that he bring her home for Easter to meet everyone. Irene loved the idea and started pushing for the plan right away. As he walked away from that thoughtful conversation, the girls were sure they could hear him saying, "Now is the winter of my discontent."

Irene was quick to ask, "What's that, honey?"

"Nothing, Mom. Just mumbling." At the first opportunity, Jacob tried to bore a hole through his sister with the old stink eye, but she just laughed — and so did he, eventually. The time finally arrived for the family to gather for breakfast — a spread for kings and queens alike. And there were still four days until Christmas. The pounds were waiting to attach.

Irene called out, "Thomas, breakfast is almost ready. Gather our family together, please."

"I'm just getting washed up," he bellowed through a handful of water.

The hum of the household with all the family home for Christmas was a wonderful homecoming for Jacob. With only a few years of city life under his belt, he still appreciated the quiet comfort of home. The smell of peameal and maple bacon being fried up reminded him of many a family weekend breakfast. The dining-room table was set with jams and jellies, platters of home fries, and bowls of fruit. Every setting had colourful serviettes, and the plates were adorned with the traditional orange slice and a sprig of parsley. Even though her favourite Christmas gift from her kids was well worn, Irene proudly wore *The Best Mom* apron. She merrily hummed a tune as she created a symphony of scrambling and frying eggs, boiling coddled eggs, popping up and buttering toast in sync, and tossing bacon into a lined basket — like a short-order cook. And everything was always placed in serving dishes — *always*.

"What's wrong with my little care package? I can see it on your brow, Jacob. I can always tell when you're thinking too hard on something. You can tell me after everyone's outside after breakfast," Irene spouted, with little air between sentences.

"It's nothing, Mom, really. Well, it's not that big a deal. Just … really, it's no big deal. It doesn't matter," said a fickle-sounding Jacob.

"*You will tell me*, but after breakfast." She still had a commanding voice, and it quickly reminded him of who the boss was.

"Have too much coffee this morning, Mom?"

"Jacob!"

"Okay, Mom. After breakfast, we'll talk. Well, after we're done playing some shinny."

"You need to get all your goalie equipment on, so that will give us a chance for a quick chat. We can finish up later, but right now my concern and curiosity must be served, my youngest," Irene said, ever the well-spoken, happy, and often overzealous dramatic actor.

"What concern over curiosity," Thomas interrupted, entering the kitchen.

He came in with James's daughter, four-year-old Jessie, wrapped around his leg and sitting on top of his foot, like a ride at the fair.

"Just you never mind, Grandpa; it's mother and son talk. You just concentrate on not crushing that grandchild of mine."

Jacob smiled, watching the interaction between his parents.

$

With breakfast behind them, and everyone readying themselves for the O'Connell's version of family Hockey Day in Canada, Jacob purposely lagged to get suited up. Once the house was near empty, he began with telling his mother how much his feelings for Sara had grown. It was clear to Irene that he was already in love. The family knew about Sara's accident, but Irene knew just how extreme the effect was on Jacob. She knew how strong her son was — physically and morally — but his sensitivity had tipped the scales in dramatic fashion before and it often worried her.

After he explained about the problems developing with Jonathan Vargas because of his relationship with Sara, Irene was quick to offer her advice. "I think I know where this is headed, sweetie. I need to tell you about Frank Jennings and your dad."

"Are you talking about the time dad hit that guy out in the front yard?"

"Oh, you remember that, do you?"

"Vaguely. It's more of a blip than a memory really."

"Yes, I did try to shield you from seeing that. Your dad and I were at the legion for the annual harvest celebration dance and there was an upset. Your dad had a few drinks and was getting frisky — you know, grabby. So, I jokingly slapped him, in a playful way. And of course, it was just as Frank Jennings looked over. Lousy timing, I tell you." Irene lifted her head for a quick survey to make sure everyone was out. "We've known each other forever, and he had a thing for me since junior high. I was never interested in him, and he knew that.

"Oh my, Frank thought he was coming to my rescue and tried to have it out with your dad. It ended up being a big kerfuffle and then it was over. No punches, just some shoving, and once I explained to Frank, it was over. I did my best to laugh it off as a joke, but this thing with Frank never ended. As time went on, I would occasionally run into him, and he would say inappropriate things. It didn't matter where I was, as long as I was alone of course. Oh, he would drive by and whistle or stare at me if I were out working in the garden — you know, things like that. Well, one day your dad heard a remark, had enough, and confronted him.

"Frank's a big guy, a lot bigger than your father. Sure enough, he stopped the car and got out. He went right at your father thinking he would intimidate him. That was his second mistake."

"What do you mean, his second mistake?" Jacob was enthralled.

"He should have never stopped to begin with," Irene said, almost whispering, Jacob smiling widely now.

"Anyway, once again your dad tried to calmly tell him to stop with the comments and the looks. Frank would have no part of it and took a swing at your dad. That was his last mistake."

Jacob was giggling at this point, but also brimming with male pride for his father.

"Your dad dodged his punch and wham. It only took that one hit and it knocked him out cold. That's when you had run up behind me to see what the noise was about."

"So, what happened after that?" Jacob asked like a curious child listening to an adventurous story.

"Well, your dad hit Frank pretty hard. He broke his jaw with that punch," she whispered.

"Wow, Dad, tough guy. I always knew he was a solid guy, but holy."

"When I talked to you kids about the war, that monster inside I was referring to? That's what can happen, at a minimum. Your dad was extremely upset that he had to go that far, but Frank had been out of line for a long time and wouldn't stop it. So, your dad stopped it."

"Did you guys ever have any more problems with him?"

"Not another word, look, or whistle. He actually moved six months later. You're probably too young to remember. He only lived a block down the street. It was a last resort for your dad. You know how he feels about this stuff. So, you keep your cool with this guy. Don't be getting into trouble over him, but don't let him push you or Sara around either."

"So, what you're saying is don't let the monster out unless I have no choice, right?"

"More or less. Jacob, you're meant for better things than that, and we both know that."

"Okay, Mom. Thanks."

Jacob waddled away with his goalie pads on, and he wondered what she meant by that last statement, "meant for better things," but as he had done before, he just as quickly let it slip away from his thoughts.

13

Run-In

Just over a year since Sara nearly lost her life on her way to work, she was marking another milestone with her last shift at O'Toole's — it was time to retire her apron. The same night, Jacob was planning to ask Sara to move in with him. A lot of excitement was in the air. The weekend before, Sara's family and friends celebrated her graduation with her. That night was particularly special for Jacob and Sara as well, but their fun started after everyone left the party. Sara aggressively pushed Jacob against the wall, and they started kissing passionately. She was maybe inspired by the few drinks she'd had earlier in the night. Sara and Jacob left a trail of clothes throughout the apartment leading to the bedroom. By the time they made it there, the clothes were all off, and the night became one of pleasure and discovery. They had had sex before, but this was different — more passionate and deeply intimate.

But as much as last week was fresh in his thoughts, this night at O'Toole's left Jacob in a nostalgic mood, thinking back to Sara in the hospital. Some moments or images are earmarked in a person's memory for all sorts of reasons. For Jacob, one such moment was entering Sara's hospital room and seeing her in bed with her red hair against the backdrop of a brilliant white pillow, with those weary green eyes looking up at him. It existed alongside another memory of her looking back at him through a crowded pub while she tended bar. And they were both immovable memories of her. He waited until the day after her accident to see her, when she would be awake for more than thirty minutes at a time, and reasonably alert. There she was, the woman who left Jacob weak in the knees and with butterflies in his stomach. Finally, the morphine was reduced to a point that they could have a coherent conversation.

"Hi … there you are … the man who saved my life. Thank you, Jacob." Her words came out slow through her dry mouth, but they were deliberate.

"You don't need to thank me for anything. I don't know if I helped. The paramedics were there in a couple minutes. It was just good timing," he said modestly.

"No, you saved my life. You did the CPR, you kept my heart beating, and you breathed life into me. You don't remember what happened?"

"Sure, I do, Sara, I was there, remember?" Jacob sounded trite, having difficulty with her "breathing life into me" comment.

"The light?" she said in a whisper. "I was standing next to my grandma watching you. You put your hands around my head and your light went into me." Sara was becoming animated, showing him with her hands. "It saved me, Jacob. The way I hit my head, that should have killed me. I was right on the edge of leaving, but you stopped me from going, with your hands." Her words slurred a bit.

"Wow! They're really pumping you with some good stuff," Jacob said with an uneasy smile, having difficulty keeping eye contact.

"Jacob! You don't remember me, do you?" It was the strange woman haunting him that day, and later arriving in his dreams. He was now starting to see a connection. In snapshots, small glimpses, he was seeing Sara as a child laying in her grandmother's arms, covered in blood. It wasn't making sense, and he quickly grabbed his temple and pushed hard, trying to pass it off like he was thinking.

"You're from Saint John, right?" she confidently enquired. "You seemed so familiar all this time, but my grandmother told me who you are. She was at the accident. She was standing next to me, remember? You are from Saint John, Jacob. Please don't tell me you're not." She waited for some kind of acknowledgement, but he remained blank, continuing to rub his temple as if he was scratching.

"I used to play with you and your sister Kate at my grandmother's house across the street from you. The three of us used to play on my grandma's porch, and she would give us vanilla cookies and orange juice as a treat."

Jacob was not only puzzled, he looked bewildered at this point. He sat back against the large window ledge, letting out an exhausted breath and looking at her with his hands crossed on his lap. He realized she was right, and saying Kate's name was no coincidence. He was realizing it was indeed her he was glimpsing. Sara began to shift a bit on her good elbow so she could sit up and look Jacob in the eye.

"We moved after my accident. I had to go through a bunch of surgeries and a lot of physiotherapy. Strange, right?" She pointed to her arm and leg. "It was a year of learning how to talk and walk all over again. We had to move to Toronto to be near Sick Kids. You don't know any of this?"

"No. I'm sorry. I didn't. Or I forgot it. But I think I'm starting to remember you being hurt. Not ever playing with you, or anything else for that matter. But then my memory of childhood is spotty at best."

The puzzled look started to leave Jacob's face. It was replaced with one of disbelief. He was growing uncomfortable as the seconds were passing. He wasn't pulling all the parts of this memory together just yet, and it was bothersome.

"You know, my grandmother said you saved my life when I was six and you would always watch over me," she said, looking him in the eye, wondering if this was too much.

"Sara, I really have to go. I've got a killer headache." He resumed rubbing his temple.

"Wait, do you remember Mr. Grimmer? I was run over by Mr. Grimmer. My grandma yelled at you to stay away, but you walked over to me where I was hit. You put your hands on my head and a kind of light went from you and into me and I came back. I was nearly dead, Jacob, just like this time," Sara said, collapsing back onto her pillow.

Jacob's head started to pound the more she told him. He was suddenly recalling standing on the sidewalk on a sunny day with a bag of candy. But now, after what she'd been saying, along with the dream the day before, he got another glimpse of Sara lying next to her bike. The more he saw, the more his head pounded.

"Okay, Sara, let's talk about this another time. Okay? I really have to go. I'll come back tomorrow to check in on you."

"Jacob, please?"

"No, I'm going to go now, but you get some rest and…" He didn't exactly run out of the room, but it was close. Sara turned her head away from him, frustrated that he couldn't remember. Meanwhile, out in the hallway just outside her room, Jacob grabbed his chest and bent over. He began perspiring heavily, and his breathing increased as if he had just run a marathon. He started getting weak in the knees, but this time it wasn't contributed to his crush on Sara. Something was obviously wrong, something familiar came out in Sara's words. He knew it, and it was hurting him.

Bits of memory from the day of the accident were seeping in through the cracks. They entered his mind's eye like a bad cable connection. Now the pain in his head turned into a cluster headache with a migraine right behind it.

"Damn it, I need a drink." He stood up, wiped his face with his hand, and started down the corridor to the elevators — away from this moment.

While sitting at the bar watching Sara buzzing around making drinks and keeping the bar clean, the trip down memory lane ended. He ran his hand over his face and head, slammed his shot back and took a huge swig of his Guinness. Remembering those two days had always stirred him deep inside. He chose to embrace the best part of the memory, and that was Sara. They had come a significant distance since that day. It would take years before they would piece together certain memories. Memories of seeing the accident at six years old, of going over to Sara, were a painful attempt to recall, so he steered clear, for now.

She was pleased that this would be her last night, but for the moment, she was happy because her favourite customer was in front of her. He just happened to be the man she was head over heels in love with. The only detractor was trying to keep Jonathon Vargas in place without threatening her job. It would prove to be a constant challenge.

"Oh, God! Look who's coming in," she whispered to Jacob. "Hi Jonathon, how are you doing? What can I get for you?"

Before he had a chance to answer, Jacob touched Sara's wrist. "Remind me to ask you something later in case I forget."

"I'll have a Black Label." Jonathon settled onto a bar stool.

"That's appropriate," Jacob mumbled about his choice.

"Sorry, did you say something, Mr. O'Connell?" Vargas asked, looking square at him and sounding like a teacher scolding a student.

"Ah, no," Jacob snipped, reaching down the bar and grabbing a copy of the *Toronto Sun*'s sports pages to disengage. "Does the kitchen have a pot of coffee on the go, sweetheart?"

As soon as the words left his mouth, he and Sara held their collective breath. They knew how it would go over with Vargas.

"There is. I'll get you a cup. Be right back." She nervously shuffled away.

Vargas obviously had had something else to drink before he came into the pub or he was a serious lightweight with only half his beer gone. "Oh, wow. It's 'sweetheart' now, is it? That didn't take long. I didn't even know you two were dating. Holy shit! I guess I should have known with all the flirting going on in front of everybody," Vargas blurted without hesitation.

"Well, Vargas, it's not a state secret. Not that it's any of your concern," Jacob snapped.

"Oh, right, you're the hero. Of course, it all makes sense now. Women always fall for the hero, don't they? Until they really find out what they're like."

Sara stood still with Jacob's coffee in her hand, listening to Vargas go on. "Okay, Jonathon, maybe you've had enough? I'll see you at work tomorrow, okay?" she said, with trepidation. Even though he was completely out of line, she figured she wouldn't have a job come tomorrow if this went the wrong way.

"Jesus, Sara, this is only my first beer. Relax, it's all good," he said, waving a hand. He ordered another beer, but this time he wanted a shot of vodka to go with it. Surprisingly, Jacob was calm and quiet, but his leg started shaking and the fingers of his left hand were individually tapping up and down his thumb. Then, his fist alternated between opening and clenching shut. He was thinking of every inappropriate comment he'd heard Vargas say to Sara — and to him — over the months. Sara was concerned by the look on Jacob's face. After a few more drinks, Vargas's words became sloppier with drunken slurring. No one was speaking with him when out of the blue he sloppily blurted out. "Yeah, I get it. The hero wins the day." He unceremoniously backed away from the stool, threw his cash down on the bar, and looked to Sara. The couple of other people at the bar looked at him like a drunk, laughing it off.

"See ya tomorrow. Hope I didn't say anything out of line." And with that remark, he looked at Jacob and suddenly appeared sober as a judge and sauntered off toward the exit.

"That was creepy," Jacob whispered, leaning over the bar. "Did he just fake being drunk?" Sara wasn't responding. She was waiting for Vargas to clear earshot. "Are you okay, sweetheart?" He could see Sara's nerves starting to fray, but she didn't get a chance to respond.

Vargas stopped cold, somehow hearing what was said. "Of course she's okay! She's got the big hero to save the day," he bellowed before continuing on his way.

Sara looked at Jacob and spoke in a whisper, "No, Jacob. Please, just let it go. It's no big deal, all right, honey? There's no problem here I can't handle."

"Hey, if you're okay, I'm okay. But you know this guy is going to keep being a problem, right? I'm sorry. Let's just forget it," he said assuredly, trying to alleviate Sara's stress.

"Well, my personal security guard, I'll deal with it when the time comes. And besides, this is my last night bartending, so let's enjoy the rest of our night. If you're lucky, I'll let you walk me home," she said playfully. "Although, I will say, that that's the first time I've ever seen him come in here. I thought he was too prissy for this kind of place."

"I wish I had your attitude and temperament, sweetheart."

"You do. You're just grumpier." Out came a hearty laugh.

She leaned over the bar and the two shared a long kiss. Seeing the body language between them, it was plain for anyone to see there was something special there.

Later, Jacob was in the men's room washing his hands just before heading back to the bar. Suddenly out from the stall comes none other than Jonathon Vargas. In the mirror, Jacob could see him standing right behind him — too close for comfort. He was surprised, thinking he'd already left. Just before Jacob attempted to acknowledge him, Vargas took a swing at the back of his head, but he was no match. Jacob reversed his arm to block the punch, ending his sneak attack with one decisive and crushing straight on punch to Vargas's nose. Vargas fell back into the stall, landing on the floor next to the toilet. With blood streaming out of his broken nose, down his face, and onto his shirt, he looked a mess.

"What the fuck is your problem, Vargas? Really, what's the matter with you?" Jacob said, pointing to the side of his head. "I don't care that you don't like me; that's just fine by me. You want to give me grief every time I go into your building, well, that's fine, too. But this shit is crazy, Vargas. You've got a problem, and you damn well know it!" His words came out in a flurry, as he suddenly started to shake with anger.

Jacob reached out a conciliatory hand to help lift Vargas out of the stall. He would never hit a man when he was down; he was his father's son. And he hoped this gesture would help neutralize the situation somewhat. But Vargas slapped Jacob's hand away.

"Fuck you, O'Connell, you fucking asshole. What is it with guys like you that think you have a right to everything in the world? That's going to end one day, you know," he said, wiping the blood from his mouth. He swung the door open so hard it bent beyond the closer's limit and broke it clean off.

Jacob looked at him in astonishment. "Wow." He pulled the door closed and walked back to Sara. As difficult as it was to calm himself and stop shaking, he thought it best to keep this from her, saying nothing for now.

14

Unexpected Evolution

Sara was quite comfortable in her pink and blue flannel pyjamas, sitting in the cushioned captain's chair at the kitchen table. Their new apartment actually had room for a table, compared to Jacob's old bachelor pad. To complete the look, she was wearing her favourite extra fuzzy bunny slippers Jacob got her for Christmas. And it certainly made her look as cozy as she felt. After several years of living together, they felt like an old married couple. And yet, they still desired — with much anticipation — what the next day would bring for each other. Saturday morning meant nothing pressing on the agenda, so they could relax. Sara leaned back in her chair with a belly full of bacon and French toast. A beam of sunlight shone through the window and highlighted Jacob's hair.

"Honey, is that another wisp of grey hair I see there?" she said, leaning over to run her fingers through his rumpled morning hair.

"Yup. Apparently, I'm old before my time. Do you want to trade me in for a younger model?" He looked at her, pulling himself away from the sports pages.

"Absolutely! You are near thirty after all. Maybe it's time," she joked.

She stood behind his chair, leaned over, wrapped her arms around him, and repeatedly kissed his cheek. And he leaned back, gladly accepting her affections.

"It makes you look even more handsome, distinguished looking."

"Oh, that's me for sure, distinguished."

"I've always seen that little spot on the back of your head, but I figured it was something you were born with," continuing to run her fingers through his hair.

"No, not exactly, it just showed up when I was a kid. My mom would mention it to me occasionally. She said I was born with an old soul and the grey patch was there to prove it," he laughed. "She also said it's why I get along with people older than me, especially seniors."

"When exactly did she say it showed up?" The query was nonchalant.

"I guess I was fairly young, like six or seven, maybe younger. I'm not exactly sure, why?"

"Oh, just curious. I don't remember any of your brothers having any grey hair. And your dad is in, what, his late fifties? He hardly has any."

"I guess I'm an odd one. Well, unique. How's that? I'm just unique." He leaned back in his chair, rubbing his hands up and down both sides of his chest in a pose of faux pride.

"Oh, you're unique all right. There's no doubting that. But really, I think you nailed it the first time, honey: oddball."

"Oh, my wounded heart."

"I suppose I'll have to trade you in on that younger model after all. Maybe a Chippendale dancer," she laughed.

"Okay, that just plain hurts. Let me just check my back for an exit wound." He pulled Sara onto his lap, sitting in the chair, and they both laughed and kissed.

Sara wondered if the events of his life had left their mark. She hoped it was just grey hair but continued to worry for the long road ahead. She let Jacob remember things on his own. She wouldn't provoke him into trying to remember anything; She'd only help him remember if he asked first. Besides, they had been working toward a quiet life of small-town living and raising a family. If all went well and nothing major popped up in their life to interfere, they were close to making their dreams come true.

Jacob was on a rotation of emergency contacts should anything arise on any of their projects on nights or weekends. And he had landed with that weekend, which had started out so enjoyably for Sara and Jacob.

Not long after breakfast, their time together was interrupted and he had to go to a fourteen-storey apartment-to-condo conversion. There'd been a leak into one of the units caused by a loose tarp on the balcony above — not exactly life-threatening, but it had to be rectified to stop any more damage from happening. Jacob kissed Sara goodbye and promised to return as soon as he could. The problem was resolved without a great deal of effort, and he was back in his truck in no time, heading home. The skies grew dark again with another fast-moving system approaching, threatening more rain at a minimum. He thought a perfect way to enjoy the remaining time that was left in the day was to hang out on the couch with his sweetie, watching a movie. He pulled into the Lakeside Market to get some flowers for Sara.

There was a large overpass almost directly above the market, and with the exception of a gas station a half block away, it was a desolate and dark area. Next to the market was an abandoned commercial building and a couple of boarded-up one-level post-war bungalows. The properties were overgrown, and the buildings were covered with graffiti. The look of this area and the undeveloped land directly across the road were hardly attractive. A rusty chain-link fence blocked off the large area of that unwanted land, which was equally overgrown.

Jacob was looking over the variety of flowers in the market trying to decide what to get. He called the store's attendant. As he waited, he stared out with a blank expression across the street. In front of the rusty fence, he could see the bike courier from the day of Sara's accident years back. He should have known something was wrong with this picture. The guy was wearing the same clothes, carrying the same satchel, and had the exact same bike. Today's weather definitely called for something warmer.

"Can I help you? Sir, have you picked out some flowers?" the clerk asked, noticing Jacob staring out to the road. "Uh, sir, are you all right? Do you need some help?"

Jacob turned around, clearly not paying attention. "Um ... I'm sorry. Yes, please. Those yellow and white daisies over there, thanks."

The clerk was wrapping up the flowers and couldn't help but see Jacob staring out to the same spot again. "Is there something going on over there? We get drunks and junkies a lot. It's turned into a ghost town around here. It's time to move." The clerk handed the bouquet over to Jacob.

"A ghost town, eh? It definitely looks like one. Or a forgotten end of town at least." He couldn't help but smile at the term *ghost town*, especially after what he had just seen outside. The courier was there and gone in the time it took for a second look. A cold shiver crawled down his body. It threw off his concentration completely.

"That's ten dollars, please. No tax for the flowers."

Jacob gave him a twenty-dollar bill. He tried to avoid looking outside again. He grabbed his change from the clerk and thanked him. Before he reached the door, the clerk told him to "be careful out there." Jacob smiled, nodded a farewell, and walked out to his truck.

He was in the last parking space next to a lane leading to the back of the building and an exit onto another street, away from what he had just seen. As he was coming around the front of the truck, he stopped for a second and looked over again. Still, there was no one to be seen. He put his hand up to his temple and held on while a blinding pain ripped through his scull. This one went from his forehead to back of the neck. He couldn't stop himself — he went down on one knee and stayed put waiting and praying for it to subside. While bent down, he could see the courier in his mind like he was standing in front of him the day of Sara's accident — it couldn't have been any clearer.

"What the hell is this?" he asked himself, getting angry. He slowly rose up from what was far worse than a cluster headache. He was at a loss to understand. He wasn't trying to remember, that much he understood now.

"That was him! That's the exact same guy from the accident. Damn it!" he blurted out, slamming his fist on the hood of the truck, then looking around in case anyone heard him. *It feels like I'm losing it all over again. Hell, I'm not sure what happened then, let alone now.* He kept his thoughts to himself this time, getting in the truck.

His frustrations building, Jacob slowly ran his hand through his hair, occasionally massaging his temple with his palm. He sat still for a moment with the radio on as a distraction, before he drove off. He chose to keep going east toward home, right past where the courier had been standing. Barely past the spot, he appeared again, this time standing on the other side of the fence. Jacob spun his head around to look back. He squeezed the steering wheel hard and slammed the brakes on. The courier was just standing there, behind his ten speed, the satchel resting on his hip and the strap looped over the opposite shoulder as per usual. Jacob stopped and stared, but the courier was standing still, eerily expressionless, returning his look.

There were approximately twenty feet from the road to the chain-link fence. It was hard to see for the tall grass and weeds, but there was a cut out in the curb for a future driveway. Jacob pulled into it, parked his truck parallel to the fence, and got out. Of course, before he came around the truck, the courier disappeared again. Jacob was bouncing from anger to fearful curiosity.

Looking intently, he walked up to the fence to see if there was anything around, but he couldn't see the courier, or anything else for that matter. The more he thought about him, the more his head would pound. He was trying to understand why now, and why here. In the far distance was the shore of Lake Ontario, so if not for the overpass, it would be prime real estate. That stretch of shoreline was built up with large pieces of armour stone and pieces of recycled concrete in rectangular-shaped wire wrapping.

He felt a fine mist slowly wetting his face as he put his hand over his brow and strained to see out as far as he could, but he couldn't find anything of significance. There were a few lonely ash trees randomly placed around, and everything else was a steady growth of grass and weeds three to four feet high. He turned back toward his truck and slowly walked along the fence, finding his curiosity had taken over any lingering fear. The only thing he noticed — and it was a strain to make out — was a hump in the ground that meant nothing to him. Back inside his truck, he rubbed his face with both hands, got his eyes in clear focus, and, bewildered, he headed home to Sara. Pulling away, he looked in his rear-view and there was the courier again. He was back on the street side of the fence, watching Jacob drive away. Jacob flipped the mirror away, turned the radio on, and stared straight ahead.

15

Exposure

The old holdover train station had high-domed ceilings with layers of paint peeling to expose a multitude of colours from different eras. The ceilings dropped to an archway where one area opened to another. Each of the archways were highlighted with large decorative cornice brackets, big enough you could swing on them. Behind the counter of the reception area for sending and picking up packages or lost luggage sat a huge cast iron weigh scale to apply the rates for packages being sent, and long solid oak benches could be found by the entrance, with one-inch white and black octagon mosaic floor tiles throughout. The rest of the building was used as a warehouse. Several overhead doors led to the large platform in front of the trains. The restoration project was preparing the space to become a museum of the railroad's past.

In less than three years, Jacob was a full-fledged construction superintendent, and Mike Shaw was his new, equally eager, assistant. Mike had substantial carpentry skills and was a quick study, similar to Jacob. They were preparing the site to rebuild a walkway over a storage area below. Mike, who was usually a safe and efficient worker, didn't realize how close he was to the foundation's edge and fell in. He caught his thigh on a jagged piece of metal form tie sticking out and tore a gaping hole in his leg.

Jacob was no more than twenty feet inside the building's entrance when he heard Mike scream. He ran out and quickly climbed down inside the concrete foundation. Mike was holding his thigh tightly with both hands. He looked up at Jacob with a fearful look on his face.

"I think I cut an artery, Jacob." He moved his hands to have a peek at the damage and the blood sprayed across the foundation wall six feet away. "Ah, yeah … it's an artery for sure. Fuck! Damn it!" he yelled.

"Mike, don't even try to move!" Jacob demanded. "Zander! Call an ambulance now!" His scream echoed through the empty building to the ears of another co-worker.

Inside the hole, the odour of creosote from old railway ties and diesel from clear stone lining the base of the foundation was nauseating in such an enclosed space. Mike was still wearing his carpenter's pouch, and it was getting soaked in blood, along with his pants. He had already raised a sweat from working, but now it was increasing.

Jacob took his belt off and pulled it tight around Mike's leg, managing to reduce the massive amount of blood loss.

"Ah, Goddamn it, Jacob, it hurts like a son of a bitch!"

"I know, Mike. Don't move. You've cut the artery for sure, and we gotta stop the bleeding until the paramedics get here. I need you to try and calm your breathing. Can you do that?"

"I'll try. Shit, Jacob, I don't want to die over something stupid like this. I'm sweaty, but I feel cold." he said, looking at Jacob. He was fighting now to keep his eyes open.

"Don't talk like that. Just concentrate on trying to relax your breathing."

His words were slow to come out now, and he slurred a bit, which Jacob knew wasn't a good sign. He tried to keep Mike alert and not let him pass out.

"Zander!" he screamed out. "Did you call that ambulance?"

"They're almost here. They were just around the corner when I made the call," he said, running back to the entrance to wave the EMTs in.

"Okay, Mike, did you hear that? They're almost here. Mike? Mike! Jesus, Mike wake up. Come on, bud, don't you fall asleep on me now," he said, shaking him. Mike's arm fell to the side of his body, revealing a large pool of blood underneath him.

At this point, Jacob had Mike's leg straight out and the belt tied as tight as possible. The blood that sprayed along the concrete wall made the scene look that much more frightening. The paramedics were there in short order. Despite the siren's blare, Jacob started to fall over. He passed out, lying on his side.

When he came to, he thought he'd just blinked. He had no concept of how long he was out. Mike was already on a stretcher and was being loaded into the ambulance. One of the paramedics was inside the foundation with Jacob, pointing a light in his eyes.

"Mr. O'Connell, are you hurt? Did you cut yourself anywhere? Mr. O'Connell?"

"No, no." Jacob was confused, trying to get his bearings. "Where's Mike? What happened to Mike? What the hell is going on?" He was upset that he passed out but more so because he lost a chunk of time. Then he thought to himself, *No, damn it! Not this again!*

He was dazed, and his aggravation quickly turned to anger. He tried to stand up, but he slipped to his side and his behind landed back on the gravel base.

"Relax, buddy, it's okay, I think you just passed out from all the excitement. You put that belt on your buddy's leg like that?" the medic asked, while helping him stand back up. "Well, you saved his life by thinking so fast there. Do you normally pass out at the sight of blood? Or just *that much* blood?" The question came out like routine.

"Um, no. I didn't have any breakfast. And … not much sleep."

"You probably just passed out from exhaustion."

"How's Mike?" Jacob asked, slowly climbing out of the hole.

"The guys gave him plasma and are already gone with him to the hospital. I just wanted to make sure you were okay," the medic said.

Jacob stood on the edge, looking inside the foundation and shaking his head. His eyebrows squeezed together with an expression of disbelief. He lowered his head and mumbled to himself, repeating what he said before coming out. At first he was more amazed than curious as to how Mike managed to survive from that amount of blood loss. Looking at the blood inside the foundation, including what was sprayed against the wall, a familiar dizzy, lost feeling was uncomfortably present. He realized he would have to get to the hospital and check on Mike, see that he was all right, and make the necessary phone calls.

§

Through the emergency room doors was a familiar smell of antiseptic and alcohol. Jacob instantly took a deep breath, trying to make it past triage. His back was straight and stiff, and his walk showed he was clearly uncomfortable. He started rubbing the side of his temple, feeling a dull pain. After a time, Mike was moved to recovery and Jacob sought out anyone who could tell him exactly how he was doing.

At the nursing station, he met a woman in green scrubs who turned out to be one of his surgeons. Hearing Jacob's enquiries, she reached out her hand. "Mr. O'Connell, yes?" she said in a French-Canadian accent.

"I'm Jacob O'Connell. How's Mike doing?" he replied, shaking the doctor's hand.

He could smell all the things that were making him queasy on her scrubs. He did his best not to look like he was completely nauseated, but his smile was plainly a concentrated effort. When she pulled her hairnet off, his nausea took a back seat while he admired her beauty. She was a stunning brunette with deep, dark blue eyes. He suddenly looked down and realized he was still shaking her hand. "Oh, I'm sorry," he said, letting go.

The doctor gave Jacob a lovely smile in recognition.

"Well, Mr. O'Connell, he's just been brought to recovery, so it will be an hour or so before you will be able to talk to him."

"Oh, that's okay. What kind of damage did he do? When will he be able to return to work? Sorry, never mind," Jacob said, feeling somewhat embarrassed.

"He had some significant damage to his thigh muscles and one tendon, but it was the femoral artery that was the threat. Fortunately, it was a tear and not a complete separation. I had Dr. Maltby join in the surgery to repair the artery. He's an excellent vascular surgeon," she said assuredly. "Michael is very lucky that you were there when this happened. You saved his life."

Jacob was captivated by her French accent. It brought him straight back to the east coast.

"I just did what I was trained to do from first aid," he said modestly.

"Well, not everyone reacts the same way. Eh, like most people panic when they see that much blood there. It's good you were there for Michael," she said, clipboard in hand, reviewing her paperwork. Jacob just nodded and turned back to the elevators.

With at least an hour to wait until he could talk to Mike, he headed down to the cafeteria for a coffee. Taking a breather, he started rubbing his temple the second he tried to figure out the lapse in memory.

Did I actually pass out from the sight of that much blood? He briefly considered this, but knew it wasn't close to the truth. *Ah Christ, being over tired and nothing in my stomach was bullshit — that wouldn't do it.* The cluster headache kicked in high gear. *Just leave it alone. Forget about it and think about Sara.*

§

Arriving to the recovery floor, Jacob had his face to the elevator doors, and he burst through when they opened. *Does he know I passed out,* he wondered. Then he slowed down, apprehensive of what he might discover from Mike.

"Hey buddy, how ya feeling? Is that morphine as good as they say it is?" Jacob quietly asked.

"Uh, yeah it is actually, or I think it is … I feel pretty good right now, that's for sure. How did you get here so quick?"

Mike could barely speak with a dry and pasty mouth. Jacob handed him one of the sponges with water to wet his lips.

"You were in surgery and recovery. So, it's actually been a while since you hurt yourself this morning," Jacob said.

"What time is it?" Mike asked, with his eyes rolling around.

"It's two-thirty. You've been out for a while. You look like you're going to be out of it pretty soon again here, buddy. Look, everything is okay, you're okay. I called Naomi and she's on her way to be with you," Jacob said reassuringly.

"You called Naomi?"

"Of course I called her. She's your wife. She needs to know you're okay."

"Right, right. Hey, Jacob, something happened in that hole today," Mike said, lifting his head.

Jacob held his breath, hoping he could interject before Mike said anything he didn't want to hear. "Yeah, I know, you lost a boatload of blood and almost died on me. You scared the hell out of me."

"I did die, Jacob, or I think I did. Maybe I was in between, I don't know. But I saw a lot of people there. Did you see all those people?" Mike asked, laying his head back on the pillow, his eyes closing more and his voice getting quieter. Before Jacob could answer, Mike was out. Jacob could feel the side of his temple pulsating a low-level pain. He put his head down, shaking it with what seemed like a sigh of relief, but when he lifted his head to look back at Mike, he became distraught. It was with a slow turn and a defeated walk that Jacob left the room.

16

Revelations

Part 1

The windows were open, and the sheers were giving way to a cool night's breeze to blow about the bedroom. Jacob could see the moonlight dancing on Sara's body and shining off the goosebumps on her skin. The curves, slopes, and valleys of her shape, those little fuzzy hairs standing up — all had his undivided attention. He propped himself up on his elbow and gently caressed her back, then, reaching down, he grabbed the sheet and pulled it up to cover her. His breath rose and fell with a sigh of contentment, while Sara slept through it with not a twitch. Waking up to make sure she was okay had simply become routine for him.

In 1995, they were doing well enough financially, so they decided it was time to get out of the city. They considered where Pat and Heather lived, but not just for the location. Clarington was far enough away, and they could afford it, but they had a plan to go out on their own when the time was right, and they agreed that the time was upon them. Combining both their skills into a new company and bringing Pat in all made perfect sense to them.

They wanted to raise a family in a small-town atmosphere, and this was close enough to any ideal location. Jacob wanted to create a residential and commercial construction company. He spent hours over the years imagining a life in the country, which included having his own woodworking shop. He would help get the company up and running, and if all went well, he would make custom pieces for both sides of the business. Sara would be the architect and designer and Pat would take care of construction and all on-site concerns, with Heather as the bookkeeper. This was their long-term goal, and Jacob couldn't wait to talk to Pat about their ideas.

Friday was a long day for Jacob at work, and he was grateful to get out of the city. It was an unusually humid day for early June when he and Sara drove out to Clarington. He had one arm out the driver's side window and his head half-cocked leaning in the same direction. Sara was happy to be finished with the work week and visit their friends for the weekend. She put on shorts and had her bare feet sitting up on the dash, pressing against the windshield. She realized in the last five minutes of the drive that there'd barely been an "uh huh" out of her man's usual chatty self.

"Jacob, honey, what's wrong?" she said, running her fingers through his hair.

He pulled his head back inside the car. "Long day today. I'm glad we're going away for the weekend."

"Come on, honey, there's something else bugging you. Are you nervous about what Pat and Heather will think of our idea?"

"Hell no," Jacob said confidently. "Pat and I have talked about going into business together a bunch of times over the years. Oh yeah, he'll be on board for sure."

"Okay, but there's something else eating at you. It's obvious. And you know I can always tell," she said confidently, poking at him and gently shaking his shoulder in jest.

"The company had first-aid course today for all the staff, and I had a massive cluster headache right after it started. I kept seeing something from a long time ago and it didn't make any sense to me."

"Oh my God. Maybe you're starting to remember. You get those headaches when that happens, we know this. So, this is good news, right? Or, should I shut up now? I'm sorry, I didn't mean to push," she began to pull back her rising excitement.

"That's okay. When it came … your accident, it was like it just happened — fresh. There's a moment that disappears. It just goes blank, and I can't get through it. But Goddamn it, it hurts!" He was shaking his head in frustration.

"Don't push it, honey. It will come. In good time. If it's meant to come, it'll show up when you least expect it."

They pulled into their regular stop along the way for fuel and coffee.

With coffees in hand, Sara decided to grab a seat to wait for Jacob while he was using the restroom. This was an old-style restaurant that served three squares and shut down shortly after supper. The place looked like it was out of a movie from the late fifties. It had red vinyl bench seats and a counter to sit at with chrome metal stools with the same red seat cover. The booths had those old radios that took a nickel to play a song. The restaurant smelled of a combination of bacon cooking and fresh baked bread.

It was the supper hour and the place had a near full house. The chatter was so loud that if any noise came from the washrooms, Sara wouldn't be able to hear it. A big burly man with a foot-long beard, who looked like the typical lumber jack, came out of the restroom. He saw Sara sitting at a two-person table by herself. "Excuse me, but are you waiting for your friend in the men's washroom by chance?"

"Yes, is he okay?" she replied, sitting straight up.

"I think you better go in there and check on him. He seems to be having a hard time. A migraine, maybe? I tried to ask him if he was okay, but he was bent over the sink and he just waved me away."

"Thank you," Sara said, rushing to the men's room. Jacob was still bent over the sink. She wrapped her arms around him.

"Jacob, honey, is it really bad?"

He slowly stood up as straight as he could. "I'm okay. Yeah, it was bad. A really bad one, actually. I'm sorry for making you wait. You didn't have to come in and get me, but thank you. Go ahead, and I'll finish washing up. I'll be right out." After Sara left the restroom, Jacob looked into the mirror, but his anger morphed into sadness, as he buried his face in his hands, fighting off any tears that might come.

When he sat straight up, he cocked his fist as if he were going to punch the mirror, but he just mimicked the motion.

They went outside and sat in the truck to drink their coffee and allow Jacob's head to stop pounding and get settled. He recalled the day in the hospital when she tried to tell him about the accident. He remembered what her grandmother told her about what he had done. And after that he no longer had to wonder who the mystery woman was.

Mostly, though, he remembered the instant onset of a massive headache as he left the room that day. Together they discussed that there was a part of his life he couldn't quite put together. The blank wasn't caused just by a poor memory. He knew that he would need Sara's help him to unravel it all.

"So, what happened today to make you start remembering?" she asked, holding his hand.

"I don't have the full picture yet, but when I was doing CPR, there was a bag full of equipment off to the side and it was red with white stripes. The next thing, I started remembering that day. I remembered your red bike with the white tires. The equipment bag was almost the same colour. Then the headache started, but instead of going into the full-blown migraine, I started to remember you at six years old before the accident. The strange thing is, the day of the accident I remember walking over to you after you were hit. That was a first. Your grandmother was holding you and then I was blinded by a light in my eyes, and boom, back on the sidewalk. That last part was like hitting rewind on a video without seeing any of it while backing up. So, whatever I did, or whatever happened when I went over to you, that's a blank."

"That's weird. And that's all you remember?" Sara asked.

"No, that was it. Oh, no, wait … I do remember my mom freaking out because she thought I was hurt. I had blood all over my shirt, from touching you, I guess. It's amazing I can remember anything that far back."

Sara could see the look on Jacob's face trying to recall that moment, but then the pain slowly started to rise again. He looked over to Sara, her bright red hair highlighted by the sun coming in through the truck's window and he froze, completely still. Something was happening to him while attempting to recall that specific moment. His eyes rolled back in his head and he fell over into Sara's lap.

In a matter of twenty to thirty seconds, in a dreamscape, he found himself back in 1969 and on the street in front of her accident again.

While slowly walking toward her, he can see the mangled bike just under the bumper of Mr. Grimmer's truck. Before he turns back to see Sara, through more of a haze, he barely makes out a teen standing on the sidewalk about twenty feet from the accident. He has a pair of stained and ripped jeans on and a dirty jean jacket with a worn and matted beige fur collar. Jacob thinks it's a strange choice for the warm weather. The teen's hair is black and greased back, and his clothes are equally dirty and greasy. The details of the person's face elude him as if they'd been erased from a drawing. The face is just a blank outline. Yet most bizarre, he still seems familiar.

The details of the scene's perimeter and anything beyond all fade away into a white fog, but for Sara. Now he is within steps of her and sees the rising sun hitting the few strands of her red hair not covered in blood. The light hits him directly in the eyes and causes him to raise his arm for a second to block its brightness — another familiar moment. Now being able to pull Sara back into focus, he takes another step forward and...

In a panic, Sara was shaking Jacob vigorously.

"Jacob! Wake up! You're scaring me."

Continuing to shake him, she was about to start yelling just before he came to. He lifted his head and looked over to Sara.

"Wow. That was just ... I don't know. What happened? Did I just pass out?"

Sara lowered her head, bewildered, and began to cry. He gently lifted her chin. "Hey. Sweetheart, it's okay. It's going to be all right. I'm all right. We'll figure this out. It's probably too much for one day.

We can crank the tunes for distraction. Anything will do, let's just enjoy the rest of the trip, okay?"

Jacob was doing his best to alleviate Sara's worry. She wiped her cheeks, and sat up, appearing stoic.

"All right, let's get going. But get in my spot. I'm driving!"

Jacob gladly relented, and they continued on to Clarington to spend the weekend with their best friends. On the way, Jacob revealed to Sara what he told his mother years back about her and the problems with Vargas. It was what his mother said at the end of the conversation that stuck out to him most.

"You know, I shook off what Mom said to me, just like I did with my memories. Thinking about it now, I remember her saying I was meant for better things, like I was supposed to know what that meant somehow. I wrote it off as mom being encouraging. After everything that's happened, I can't help but wonder. It was like some kind of unspoken agreement between us the way she said it. I think my mom knows a lot more about this than I thought."

Part 2

Jacob awoke feeling refreshed after a good night's sleep at Pat and Heather's, shaking off the unpleasantness from the day before. Both the startling and jumbled memories intruding their way into his everyday activities and the physical pain that came with them were exhausting. But this morning he was bouncing his way down the stairs, in a good mood and ready to tackle the day. Melissa, Pat and Heather's daughter, was the first one Jacob ran into.

"Hey pickle, how ya doing? Where's your dad hiding at?"

"Good morning, Uncle Jacob," she said with a smile. "He's in the shop or the office. When you go out, please tell him breakfast will be ready in a half hour, okay?"

"You can keep our stuff in the oven, please and thank you. We have to run out for a while."

Pat and Jacob went to the marina in Port Darlington to check out some of the boats and to see some projects Pat had completed over the years. Clarington and the surrounding area was large enough to sustain a construction company, yet close enough to the city to serve a wide clientele. The marina was a sign of prosperity, and more than three-quarters of the boats docked there were owned by people from the city. Many of those people came to Port Darlington to build summer cottages, and some made the move, becoming year-round residences, to be near the water. Business in the area was increasing at just the right time for them to start up their company. The last stop Pat wanted to make was at a property Heather's uncle Tony, a realtor, owned in town.

"So, what's this place you want to show me? Is it a secret boys-only clubhouse? Will we need to know a password to get in?" Jacob laughed.

"Good one," Pat said sarcastically. "It's a building Tony owns here in town. He used to use it as storage for his cars, and has a rental apartment above, so I thought about you guys."

"Seriously, Pat, it's a little early to be looking at buying a place here; we don't even have a business plan yet, let alone the financing. And we still have jobs we have to wrap up before coming here," Jacob said, trying to be easy on his best friend.

"Don't worry about that now. If you think it'll work to start out in, then we'll have a talk with Tony. Trust me, he'll make sure it's available for you when the time comes. I just want to make sure he doesn't put it on the market before you have a chance to consider it. Who knows, maybe he'll rent it to you if you don't want to commit to buying it right now." There was no denying the exuberance in Pat's voice.

"That might be the way to go on this one, Pat. Renting it, I mean."

Pulling in the driveway, they found a very short, beer-bellied Tony standing near the house. Ever the salesman, he wore a suit for this meeting, the sheen off of which hurt their eyes. It was bright baby blue polyester, with a pink speckled tie. And of course, he rounded out his fashion statement with a pair of brown cowboy boots — a powerful clash of clashes. Jacob had difficulty not staring for the first few minutes. It was a quick introduction and handshakes, then Tony opened the place up for them and let them look around for as long as they needed. And just as quick as the greeting was over, Tony said his farewell and left Pat to lock up.

The building looked to be in fair shape. It was a taller-than-normal two-storey commercial building with a barn-style roof. It had a faded vertical pine board-and-batten exterior. There were two ten-foot-wide commercial overhead doors, and off to the side was an entrance door leading to a small office and another leading to the apartment above. It was a nice unit. Pat had renovated it. Jacob was pleasantly surprised at what he found inside: a large space with two bedrooms and a bright kitchen with a peninsula counter and an island. Most pleasing to Jacob were the set of French doors Pat had had the foresight to put in leading from the master bedroom to a small deck out the rear of the building and the yard with lots of trees for privacy.

The utility of the place appealed to Jacob, and now he just had to see if Sara felt the same. Working in the city had taken a toll, and Jacob was ready for the simplicity of a place that could be his home and work area all in one.

"Well, what do you think? Do you think Sara will be okay with it? It's not exactly a home, but it has the shop space right there. I can get my hands on an old dust-control system from a guy I know. I can get it for a good—"

Jacob interrupted. "Slow down bud, you're going to pop a blood vessel."

"Ah, I'm just excited that you and Sara are moving here. The family's happy about it, too." Pat said, trying to lower his pace.

"Yeah, it will be nice to be here. And I'm okay with the building. It works for me. I'm sure Sara will be all right with it, too. It allows us to get started, and I'm sure she'll go along with that. I have to agree, I'm optimistic about this, buddy," Jacob said with confidence.

His mind started to wander already. He was excitedly speculating on how to set up the shop. Pat was happy to see his friend's enthusiasm, so he grabbed his shoulder and gave him a solid shake.

"I'll get as much as I can prepared here, so you can wrap things up in the city. How long do you figure it will take?" Pat asked with a smile.

"A year. Well, hopefully less than a year. It's hard to say right now."

"I was hoping we could start in three to six months." Pat sounded disappointed. "I thought you'd want to get away sooner rather than later, especially with the trouble you've had. Speaking of which, there been anymore from him?" Pat asked quietly.

Jacob's response was slow in return. "Nothing major, but yeah, a few things. Nothing really bad. It's certainly nothing Sara can't handle, but I'd like a chance to handle the prick, that's for sure," he snarled.

"Are the headaches still bad?"

"Oh yeah, same old shit. And they always show up whenever something triggers my memory, or I try to remember something. And it doesn't seem to matter what it is. Anything can trigger it. Sara seems to think it's caused by something other than just memory recall, but it's all a little too flighty for me to think about."

"Why, what does she think it is?"

"Oh, I don't know … some spiritual stuff," Jacob said dismissively.

§

When the guys returned, Heather and Sara could see them both smiling like they were kids again.

Jacob greeted Sara with a kiss. "Hey, Pat just showed me a place I think you're going to like. It's a place we can live and work out of. Pat did a reno on the apartment. It's really nice. It looks much better inside the apartment than the building does from the outside, honest." Jacob's enthusiasm and happiness were undeniable. "I'm happy. Are you happy with it? Heather showed you the pictures, right? Wow, I have to back off on the coffee. Sorry, I'm just excited." Jacob's words were coming out at an accelerated pace as he sat down at the kitchen table for breakfast.

Just then Melissa came downstairs after showering and walked by Jacob on her way to the kitchen sink. The lavender scent she was wearing smelled just like Sara's had many years back as a teen. Jacob was pulled back in time to when he was fourteen and, unbeknownst to him, passed by Sara on that trail in the Miramichi. His head dropped to the table, resting on one hand, the other holding his temple.

Sara used different lavender-scented products throughout her life, but none smelled the same as the one she had used that day in Miramichi. The odours of the river's water, the east coast air and the sand combined with her teenage body odour, making that scent unique. Over the years that combination was never present again for Jacob, until now. Sara reached over and wrapped her arms around his shoulders and leaned her head next to Jacob.

"Hang on, honey, it's going to be all right."

Jacob's response was one that Sara was quite familiar with. He wrapped his large and callused knuckles on the table. The room grew silent, and Melissa looked on with fear, being scared for her Uncle Jacob.

"Dad, what's wrong? Is Uncle Jacob gonna be all right? What happened?"

"It's okay, baby, he gets those headaches every once in a while … it'll be gone in a minute," Pat said, pulling Melissa into his arms to comfort her. Sara looked back at Melissa with a reassuring smile.

"Oh, he's going to be fine, Melissa. He's had these headaches since he was a little guy and they always pass. They just hurt like a bugger when they happen and this is a bad one, but it'll pass. Don't worry."

The breakfast would have to be enjoyed at another time.

Part 3

After a lovely weekend full of dreams and excited chatter about the future, Jacob and Sara headed back to the city, back to the life that over a dozen years had worn down the young couple in their early thirties. They concluded over time that there was a significant difference between people born in the city and those who moved there for a new life: after years of learning and negotiating the sprawling metropolis, it never became natural for the outsiders. The size of it, the amount of people and volume of traffic overwhelmed the pair, and it only became more burdensome.

Jacob was thinking of Pat, admiring how he held Melissa when she was scared for him. He recalled a difficult time in Pat's youth with his father that left him angry and confused for a few years, a time when he had acted antithetical to his nature.

Jacob took one last look at Sara before sliding on his side and propping his head up against the passenger side window of the truck.

"I'm just going to close my eyes for a bit, okay sweetheart?"

As Sara glanced over to say, "okay honey," he was out.

Deep into his sleep on the way home, he dreamt of the Rush concert he and Pat went to in Moncton when they were sixteen. It was their favourite band and a rare thrill they wouldn't normally be able to afford. The trip there and back was also beyond their means.

"That was incredible!" Pat, with an unstoppable smile, yells out inside the car.

"Oh yeah. Did you see Neil Peart throw those drumsticks up in the air right in the middle of that solo? That was unbelievable!" Jacob asks, equally thrilled.

Pat looks over to Jacob and, with a smile a mile wide, is busy reliving the moment, he asks, "What? Drumsticks? What about drumsticks?"

At this point, Pat's uncle John is laughing at them. "So, I gather you boys had a good time then?"

Neither one of them looks at John or acknowledges him in any way. He smiles, realizing they can't hear themselves think, let alone hold a conversation at a normal sound level. So, John keeps his eyes on the road back to Saint John, glancing from time to time at the excited boys and grinning at their animated bliss from what was obviously a high point for them.

As John drops the boys off at his brother's house, he asks, "You boys have your hearing back now? There's no need to keep talking like you're at opposite ends of the street, right?"

"Yeah, we're okay, Uncle John."

"My hearing is back to normal. It has been for a bit now," Jacob says, looking at the two.

"Good. Because I don't want to have to come back here because you pissed your father off, all right, Pat?" John says firmly.

"No, sir. That won't happen, I promise, Uncle John." He's swift to answer.

"It's okay, Pat, just be good tonight and call me if you need anything. I am glad you two had a good time. Life can't be all work and no fun. You know what I mean?"

"It was great, Mr. Keegan. It was an amazing show, thank you so much for everything," Jacob said.

"It was great, Uncle John. Thanks for the tickets and taking us there."

And in an uncharacteristic gesture for Pat, he leans into the car and hugs his uncle with a long, firm squeeze. John is taken aback for a moment, but realizes that despite his home life, Pat is developing into a solid young man with all sorts of potential.

"Okay, you two." John's voice cracks. *"Be good and we'll talk soon. Pat, say hello to your mom for me and the same goes for you young man, say hi to your parents."*

John points directly at Jacob, smiles and pulls away from the end of the next driveway, easing his way down the street as quietly as possible.

"Wow, man! Your uncle is one cool guy. I wish your dad was that way... I'm sorry, I didn't mean..."

"Don't worry about it, it's true," Pat says, appearing dismissive. *"If the old man knew where I went tonight, he would flip right out. Let's go, we'll use the side door. Be real quiet, okay?"* Pat's voice is down to a whisper as they begin their way up the driveway. Jacob tiptoes behind him.

While Jacob holds the aluminum screen door open, Pat opens the main door. With one step inside onto the landing, hands grab his collar and violently throw him down the basement stairs. Billy Keegan, half awake and still drunk, stands with a look that Jacob has become familiar with.

"Get out of here, Jacob!" orders Billy. He slams the inside entrance door in Jacob's face and screams at Pat.

"You little bastard. Think you can do whatever you want around here, eh!?!"

Before any discernable words come out from Pat, Jacob hears a loud smack. It sounds like a leather belt against skin, and Jacob hopes it isn't Pat's.

Jacob fears for his best friend, and without hesitation, he rams his shoulder into the locked door, bursting his way in. He stands atop the landing, looking to the basement, trying to focus. Instead of seeing what he expects — Billy standing over Pat with a belt in his hand — he sees Pat standing over his father's body on the floor. Pat looks up at Jacob with a look of fear and rage, breathing heavily and holding his partially broken hockey trophy in his hand.

At this point, Jacob's knees start to get weak because it looks like Pat has either knocked his father out or killed him. Billy isn't moving, neither is Pat. He stands still over his father, ready to put him back down should he rise. Jacob is frozen and completely at a loss for what to do next.

"You son of a bitch!" Pat screams at the top of his lungs at his unconscious father.

Looking down at Pat's father, Jacob can see a huge gash on the side of his head, and it's still bleeding. Just then Jacob can hear sounds coming from upstairs, getting closer; it's Pat's mother, Martha. She stands on the upper landing, looking down at Jacob. She notices the jamb splintered from the door being forced in.

"My God, what happened, Jacob?" And standing there silently, all he can do is point down the stairs.

Part 4

"NO!" Jacob screamed out, forcefully crashing out of his dream. His body lunged forward in his seat and he stared straight ahead. Tying to calm his accelerated breathing, he placed one hand on the dash of the truck and the other on his chest.

"My God, Jacob. Are you all right?" Sara asked. Startled, she pulled over to the side of the road. Jacob's blank look remained, and he wasn't responding.

"Are you all right, honey? What were you dreaming about?" she asked, turning to look at Jacob. "Sorry, honey, just breathe, catch your breath. And you can tell me if you want to."

Jacob stayed in the same position for a few more minutes, all the while his mind was running, *I remember. I remember. But then I can't remember. What the hell is this!?! This is driving me nuts.*

Without saying a word, he leaned back into the same spot, and within seconds he was back out again. Sara just watched him and listened to his breathing go back to normal. She put her hand over her mouth and fell back into her seat for a few minutes before pulling back out on to the highway. She rushed to get home. While turning out the dome light, she glanced over and was shocked to see that his grey hair seemed to multiply during that drive.

Jacob had gone right back into the dream in Pat's basement.

By now Pat's mother is by her son's side. Pat had been hit too, so she checks his bleeding cheekbone by his eye. And to Jacob's complete surprise, she leaves Billy lying on the floor without a word. She takes Pat by the arm and walks him upstairs to tend to his cut. Jacob slowly walks closer to Mr. Keegan but is startled by Martha's voice calling him to come upstairs.

"Jacob, dear, could you stay here with William please? I need to take Patrick to the hospital for stitches."

Mrs. Keegan speaks like she's running out to do grocery shopping.

"Well, what about Mr. Keegan? Shouldn't he go to the hospital, too?" Jacob asks, incredulous.

"Oh, don't worry about him. This isn't the first time he's passed out. He'll be fine. Just keep an eye on him, make sure he doesn't roll over onto his back. Okay, Jacob? We won't be too long."

"Sure ... okay, I'll stay here, Mrs. Keegan," he says, dumbfounded.

He turns to look at Billy again and is disturbed that he's completely motionless. When he turns toward the upstairs landing and yells out another question to Martha, he hears the front door slam. They're gone.

This dream was playing out in vivid detail, and Sara could see the perspiration building on Jacob's forehead. His body was starting to twitch.

Jacob walks over to Billy, leans over and stares at his chest, but he doesn't see it rise. He kneels down and calls out his name before placing his hand on his chest to check if he can feel any movement; he feels none. He begins to panic, fearing Mr. Keegan is dead. He doesn't like the drunk Mr. Keegan for all the horrible things he's done, but this was unimaginable. His thoughts jump to his friend, and how it would be a guilt-ridden hardship if he knew he was responsible for his father's death.

His last moments in the dream are of him pacing back and forth, running up to the top of the landing and back down again and continuing to pace.

His dream now shifted to the market where he bought Sara flowers that one night.

He sees Gary, the bike courier, standing in the exact same spot as the night he had the vision. Gary looks directly at Jacob and waves him over, but Jacob's frozen, unable to move his legs anchored to the ground.

"Come on, get over here. There's nothing to be afraid of. Come on, Jacob, I need you to come over here." Gary says, as friendly as the day they met. Suddenly, he finds himself standing back inside the market, with an eerily silent clerk behind him. He steps right behind him to where Jacob can feel his breath on his neck, and he whispers, "be careful out there." Jacob's skin is crawling, and he frantically starts looking outside, but he can't see through the fog of the dream to focus in on Gary again. He hears his words as clearly as if he were standing right beside him.

"What do you want from me? I already went over there. I even went over to the other side of the fence, too. So, what do you expect me to see now?" Jacob snaps.

"You already saw me, Jacob. You looked right at me." Gary is in focus now. He points to a mound of dirt on the property behind the fence.

"You met me before, through Sara. You don't remember, do you? It was Christmas Eve and I was late getting there. You defended me when Vargas gave me hell. I ended up telling him to go fuck himself. Still not clicking in?"

"Okay, this is just fucked up, period. Yes, I'm pretty sure I remember you. Although right now I don't want to. I just want to go home." Jacob starts to sound panicked.

"Very funny. Look, just come and have a look and you'll know what to do later on," Gary says as a matter of fact.

Jacob's legs feel like they're made of concrete, and the dream tips on the edge of becoming a nightmare. "Why do I need to do this again? I have no idea why you're bothering me with this. Why are you doing this, anyway?" Jacob pleads, nearly breaking down.

The courier stands uncomfortably close. "Vargas put me here," he says quietly.

"Jacob … Jacob." Sara was gently calling him. It took her some time to bring him around. He seemed stuck in his dreams, tossing from side to side: Finally awake, Jacob sat up, still silent.

"We're home, honey. You must have had some more wild dreams. You slept the entire way. This time you were talking to Pat, his parents, and even Gary, the bike courier. You were talking quite a bit. I'm worried about you," Sara said, gently grabbing Jacob's arm. He looked like a zombie, and few words came out. He proceeded right to bed once they got inside their apartment, and he was again out in seconds. In angst, Sara sat up beside him half the night. Finally, after several bouts of holding back tears, she went out into the living room, picked up the phone and, disregarding the time, she called Irene.

17

Conscience

It was just after three-thirty on the last day of Sara's employment at the building department. She worked her way up to being second in line next to the chief building inspector, Jonathon Vargas. The monotony of reviewing drawings for fire separations and structural designs for the government had come to an end, now she could head off with a wealth of experience and knowledge and create whatever she wished.

Jacob had finished at Henderson the week before, so he drove Sara back and forth for those remaining days. After he finally squeezed his extended cab pickup into Sara's parking space, he looked across the parkade and was upset to see Vargas there. Vargas looked at Jacob briefly, opened the back door of his Jeep Cherokee, set his briefcase on the back seat, and got in to leave. Getting out of the truck, Jacob couldn't help himself, "Hey, Vargas," Jacob said, enunciating his last name.

"Hello, Jacob. Big day. I bet you'll be glad to see Sara leave here, right?"

Jacob didn't answer. He stood staring, flipping his keys in his hand. "I couldn't help but notice that I never see Gary the bike courier anymore. That's odd he never said anything to Sara about quitting. She quite liked him. They were friends, kind of. Hmm … strange."

"Who knows what life brings," Vargas said from his seat, but before he could get his window closed, Jacob got in his dig.

"Or what it takes, right Vargas?"

Vargas spun his head around and gave Jacob a look to kill. He pulled out of his space and peeled away. But in his rear-view mirror, he could see Jacob, still standing there, flipping his keys and staring at him the entire time.

The brake lights came on and the tires on Vargas's car screeched to a stop. Then a louder squeal sounded as he backed up toward Jacob. He was coming at a fair clip, but Jacob stood perfectly still, flipping his keys in his hands. Vargas stopped short of him and steered around to his side to be face to face. Jacob's stomach tightened, and his fist was squeezing the keys so hard, they were hurting his hand, leaving marks.

"What's wrong, Vargas?" Jacob asked in a patronizing tone.

"Are you trying to say something specific to me, O'Connell?" Vargas squinted his eyes slightly, failing to posture a tough look.

Jacob leaned over and looked Vargas in the eye, waiting a few seconds before answering him. "If I wanted to say something specific to you, you would hear it. If I want to call you a cocksucker, for example, you would hear that too. And if you have something further to say that would require you getting out of that car, well, I'd say I'll gladly oblige you."

"Well, Jacob, don't forget, it's easy to be a tough guy when you're dumb enough to think you have nothing to lose." Before Jacob could take another step toward the car, the tires squealed, and he sped away, hearing Jacob's last word, "cocksucker."

That evening, shortly after dinner, Jacob uncomfortably delivered Sara an excuse to go to one of the job sites for something he'd forgotten. He promised he'd return directly. He drove back to the market where he first had the vision of Gary. After buying flowers for Sara, for good cause, and penance for lying about where he was going, he went out and stood by his truck. He was repeating his moves, and with a nervous energy, his hands were shaking, and his stomach churned. He stared out to the same spot, wondering if Gary would reappear. Leaning on the box of his pickup, he waited another minute, and, seeing nothing, he spun around and got in the driver's seat. Over he went to the same exact spot as last time and parked the truck close to the fence. He wiped his sweaty hands on his jeans, and he could feel his heartbeat speeding up, skipping the odd beat. Looking at himself in the mirror, he gently shook his head, and quietly said, "What are you doing, Jacob? This is crazy."

With a fast rat-a-tat-tat-tat, using his hands as drumsticks on the steering wheel, he finally jumped out. From atop the box of the pickup, he took one last look to the street. From that height, only three feet remained for the leap over the eight-foot fence. With his jaw clenched, and face squished together in anticipation of the landing, he hit the soil hard on the other side. Instantly, the pain shot through from the jarring of his knees, and as he slowly rose up, it radiated into his hips and lower back. His hands were fiercely rubbing his low back, as he was cursing his decision to jump, calling himself stupid. He stood still for a moment, continuing to survey the area and make sure no one had seen him. It was nighttime, but he was close enough to the market to be spotted. With each nervous step toward the area where he thought Gary might be buried, his knees were aching, and his anxiety rising. The mound of dirt was as covered in tall grass and weeds as the rest of the area, making it hard to spot. But Jacob found it, and as he looked down at it, he wondered, *but to what end ... even if this is Gary's unwanted grave.*

Putting the rumbling of his stomach aside, he leaned forward, and, squinting, began pulling back handfuls of grass to see what, if anything could be found. After a short time of failing to see in the dark, he pulled a lighter from his pocket, lit it and covered the flame with his other hand for fear of being detected. Just before deciding to give up, there was a small piece of a blue canvas strap.

Jacob dropped the rest of the way onto his knees. Running his fingers across the strap so as not to disturb it, he suddenly jumped up, took a few steps, and vomited. It was the same canvas bag he placed under Sara's head after she'd been hit by a car. He was shaking even more now, sick to his stomach and feeling weak throughout. He knelt back down, surrounded by grass, and closely examined the piece of strap. When he felt the material between his fingers, it brought back the moment of shaking Gary's hand, just like he was standing in front of

Jacob now. Then he could see Vargas in the parkade, and the look on his face — as sickening as it was — told him what he needed to know.

It was time to get back home. He stood up to look around again and made sure no one spotted him. He felt a sensation he'd never before experienced in knowing Gary was walking beside him even though he couldn't see him. It scared him, and at the same time, he felt comfort in doing what he thought Gary truly needed. He stopped for a moment, worrying that if his truck was identified as being at the scene, he might become a suspect. As soon as he was clear, he scaled the fence like it was a jailbreak and hopped into the box of his truck, remaining down low for another look around. He moved like a special ops soldier on a covert mission, and in seconds was behind the wheel and down the road toward home. He was exhilarated, sickened, and frightened all at once. He looked in the mirror. "Jesus, Gary! What happened?" he said aloud. Then he lifted the flowers from the passenger seat and held them up to his nose in an effort to take his thoughts in a different direction.

"Nice try, Jacob," he said aloud, tossing the flowers back down on the seat. His face was pained, and he couldn't hold back his emotions. He held his hand to his brow. "I can't believe this. Everything just keeps getting stranger by the day. If that's him ... oh hell, it's him! The cops will find out ... I hope. What's happening here, Jacob?" he asked himself, but he was unable to find an answer. "What am I going to say to Sara? This is too much. It's just too much. I can't do this now." He made his choice to keep it to himself for now, turned the radio up near maximum volume, and concentrated on getting home to Sara.

§

Overall it took a few months to complete the move to Clarington. Jacob and Pat had already set up the shop, and Jacob and Sara's furnishings were all moved into the apartment above. The last trip for the happy couple was in a loaded pickup pulling a small U-Haul loaded with the personal odds and ends they'd collected throughout their life together.

They made one last stop along the road at the usual restaurant. It was a welcome sight to the tired couple. Sara went for coffee, leaving Jacob pumping gas. A family came out of the store and headed toward their car. The parents each had a child by the hand and a third child followed close behind. This little girl was a dead ringer for a six-year-old Sara — the freckles, green eyes and long fire-red hair.

When Jacob spotted her, his hand unintentionally let go of the pump handle. He was frozen, locked in a trance. All he could do was watch. He was amazed at what he was seeing, and then his memory took over and brought him right back to Sara's accident scene yet again. This time, however, when he turned to look back down at the sidewalk, he could clearly make out all the features of the teen who was standing there — his greasy black hair and jean jacket with the arms turned up, revealing a tattoo on his arm of a cross with a snake wrapped around it. Of course, Jacob had no idea who this young teenager was. Nonetheless, the memory caused him to grab his head and endure another onset of a fierce cluster headache.

Jacob slowly lifted his pounding head to see the little girl staring at him. She had turned to look behind her when she walked by, just like she knew him. She gave him a little wave and got into the minivan with the rest of her family. Jacob waved in response, cocking his head to try and dull the pain by clenching the muscles of his jaw.

Sara returned with coffee and some biscuits in hand. While handing a coffee to Jacob, she saw evidence of a headache on his face — swollen and red, his eyes bloodshot.

"Oh, Jacob, honey. Another one? What triggered this one?" she asked, gently caressing the side of his face.

"I just saw your six-year-old doppelgänger, and it brought me right back to your accident again, damn it. I don't know why, but I feel it may not have been an accident after all," Jacob said, looking unsettled.

"Honey, there's no reason to think that. Mr. Grimmer was getting old. He had really bad eyesight. He would have never purposely hurt me."

"That's just it, I don't think the accident was caused by Grimmer at all. I think something or someone else distracted him before he hit you. I have no idea why that thought came to mind. It's kind of jumbled still."

"Well, I hope you're wrong, because it would mean something else altogether," she said, lifting her eyebrows.

They got back in the truck and turned to each other for a kiss, then, looking into each other's eyes, they squeezed their hands together.

"Ready?" Jacob asked.

"Ready." Sara smiled. Off they went with their belongings in tow, down the highway toward their new life.

18

The Cost of Friendship

Able Hands had been in business for just over a year, things were going exceptionally well, and the group couldn't be happier. Pat was established in the area as a qualified contractor, so this was an easy transition. He had his friends, acquaintances, and customers help him promote the company well before his partners arrived. Still a long way off from expanding, which was the plan, there wasn't really time for any holidays. They would try and have some long weekend getaways, but that was the extent of it.

Pat and Jacob were going north that weekend, beyond cottage country, for some canoeing and fishing. They had been looking forward to this for a while now. The days of old when these two friends would stop into a bar for some beers and a few games of pool, was a seldom occurrence now. Between work and personal responsibilities, their time was mostly eaten up. Around three in the afternoon on a Thursday of the Labour Day long weekend, Pat pulled up to Jacob's, with a canoe tied to the roof racks on his truck and a huge smile on his face.

Jacob had a huge duffle bag and a backpack slung over his shoulder. Before loading his fishing poles and tackle box into the truck, he peeked in before lifting the cap's door.

"Hey Pat, where's the film crew … and the other ten fishermen? You got enough crap in here to supply three camps, including the beer."

"So? I believe in being prepared," Pat said, wearing a goofy smile to go along with his truly ugly fishing hat.

"I see that," Jacob exclaimed. "But we're going fishing, not big-game hunting." Jacob ran back to the house to give Sara a kiss before he left. "Thanks, sweetheart. Are you sure you're going to be okay for the weekend? I don't have to go. I can stay."

"Oh, no. You have to go." She pointed to the truck with a smile. "This is the part where we survive as a couple without killing each other. This time away is well-deserved and much needed for both of us." She put her hands to Jacob's cheeks and kissed him goodbye.

"Okay, I'm just going to let that one go, and do some fishing. See you Sunday afternoon."

And with that, the boys were down the road.

§

On the second night after at least fourteen hours of canoeing and fishing, the guys chose their spot to set up camp for the night. It was barely dusk at nine o'clock, but the fire was burning high after their pike was cooked and their bellies full. Northern Ontario seemed to them like a land of never-ending lakes and forests. They were next to the outlet of a river that flowed into the lake. It was beautiful territory. Above the river was an opening before the woods became dense with different species of pine and spruce trees.

A narrowing section of the river provided a lot of dead growth for firewood, and the area closest to the river was surrounded in amazingly tall poplars. It was peaceful, with the odd owl and a couple of miserable blue jays calling out between the rhythm of the crickets, but for the most part, their site was quiet. The fire and running water were the loudest sounds to be heard. They had a full moon and a clear sky showing the constellations like a light show, Orion taking centre stage.

Pat was reminded of the many trips he made with his uncle John as a kid. He walked over to join Jacob in their folding chairs and handed him a beer. "There ya go, buddy, it's good and cold, just like my men." Pat barely got the words out before they both burst into laughter, Jacob choking slightly on his sip of beer.

"I have a gay niece and nephew, and there's your cousin Doug, but they've never noticed. Have you told Heather of this new development?" Jacob extended his can of beer in a salute. "Slàinte, my Irish friend. I'm sure the community will welcome you with open arms."

Pat was dribbling his beer trying not to choke from laughing.

After a few more beers, Pat pulled out a mickey of Jameson and offered up a swig to Jacob, which he accepted.

"So, Jake, buddy," Pat started to talk in a familiar tone.

"Oh, I see. Fill me up with some whiskey and then ask the favour, right? You're a devious friend, Patrick Keegan. Kidding, what's up, bud?"

"It's not really a favour, well, kind of. My uncle John wants us to help set him up to get a contractor to renovate their house back home. Not do the work, just prepare the materials and labour estimate so he can know what he has to do in getting a local guy. He needs to know he's not getting ripped off, basically. He's good with guns, not tools."

"Your uncle John and aunt Marlene are good people. What kind of renovation is it? Just a remodel or addition?"

"Their making it wheelchair accessible. Marlene has severe spinal stenosis and she is slowly losing the ability to walk," Pat said, but he kept looking out to the lake instead of at Jacob. "They need a ramp, front and back, and doorways widened, bathrooms changed. The typical stuff that comes with it."

"That's horrible," Jacob said softly, leaning forward in his chair to look Pat in the eye. "I really like Marlene. She's a great lady. Yeah, sure. When do they need it by?" Jacob asked, leaning back. He was curious why Pat was acting so distant and uneasy. "Sara can do the drawings, and we can do the material and labour takeoff. It'll give them a good idea of what they're up against." Jacob glanced over to Pat again, waiting for his focus to return.

"That's great," Pat said, looking a million miles away. "I'm going down, so I'll be sending back proper measurements. Plus, it gives me a bit of time for a short visit. Another shot?" Pat said, holding the bottle up.

"Oh, hell, why not, sure: hit me. We're on holidays after all. Even if it's only for three days. And I can fish with a hangover."

It suddenly became quiet, and Pat looked at Jacob with an odd expression.

"What?" Jacob said.

"I didn't say anything," Pat innocently replied.

"Why are you looking at me like that? I feel like you're about to tell me my dog just got run over."

"No. It's all good, Jake. I'm just grateful you're my friend."

It became quiet again.

19

Subtleties

Part 1

An unrelenting downpour, cold and damp to the bone, fell one November night two months following the fishing trip. Tapping his fingers on the window frame, Jacob stared out to the street waiting on John Keegan to arrive. As always, with Remembrance Day approaching, Jacob's thoughts were of his father — and John, also a vet. It was nearing seven at night and had been dark for over an hour, when he watched for a set of headlights to make the turn into his driveway. He was back and forth from staring out the window to sitting on the edge of the couch next to Sara.

"What are you so antsy for? John said you could expect him shortly after seven. It's not even seven yet." Sara put her hand on Jacob's arm. "Look, you're going to spend the night and do what you need to tomorrow. It won't take you that long to measure up and get their thoughts on what kind of finishing they want. You'll be back home tomorrow night. What's the worst case? You have to come home the next day. It's okay, honey. Besides, you like John and Marlene, so it'll be a nice visit. Right?"

"Oh, I do, absolutely. He and Marlene were really good to us when we were kids. John took us to that Rush concert — remember me telling you? Yeah, he got a check mark in the cool box from both of us that night. That was a weird night. Anyway, he'll be here soon. I'll go downstairs and wait for him there." Jacob was undeniably hyper.

"What was weird?" Sara asked but quickly dismissed it. "Jacob, honey, relax. He can wait for you to make it down the stairs," she said as she stood behind him, wrapping her arms around his large frame and kissing him several times on the neck.

"What you're doing for Pat with this is what a good friend does. And I'm sure John appreciates it as much as Pat does. So, relax and enjoy the trip."

Within a couple of minutes after the hour, and true to form, John pulled up in the rental car. He wasn't the type to sit back and honk for someone. However, he didn't have a chance to get out because Jacob was already at the car. Both Jacob and John waved to Sara standing at the bottom of the stairs. She was wearing grey jogging pants with her favourite bunny slippers. With her long red hair tied up in a single ponytail while folding her arms together to keep warm, she was a site Jacob adored.

"That's a wonderful woman you have there, Jacob. She's a sweetheart," John said as they pulled away on their way to the airport.

"That's exactly what I call her. She is amazing. And I wouldn't hesitate to say I'd be lost without her." Jacob was still stretched around, looking back as the apartment faded from sight. "Yeah, I got lucky there."

"It makes your life a hell of a lot easier when you find the right one. When it happens, a person just knows, like I did with Marlene." John looked right at Jacob, nodding his head. There was an awkward silence following, and then Jacob realized.

"Forgive my manners, John, how is Marlene?"

"That's all right, son. Thanks for asking. She was diagnosed with breast cancer six months ago now. She's just got through another round of chemo, so, she's really weak right now. But she doesn't like to talk about it, so we've kept it quiet."

"Damn, I'm sorry, John. I thought you were doing the renovations because she had to be in a wheelchair. I had no idea, and Pat didn't say anything. He just told me about the renovation."

"That's okay, we haven't told anyone, really — Marlene's choice. But we still have to do the work. She's still in a wheelchair, just for a different reason."

Jacob looked at John, nodding his understanding. "Right." He never thought John would lie to him, but he sounded uncharacteristically off from usual. He couldn't help but wonder whether or not the reality of needing any work done would depend on how sick Marlene was. Either way, it was a sombre moment for him, to see John under these circumstances. Seeing him older, somewhat frail and worn down, was an eye opener for Jacob. He couldn't help but think back to the vibrant couple who were so nice to him and Pat throughout some tough years. The conversation for the rest of the drive to the airport was sparse and consisted mostly of small talk. And on the flight, Jacob grew uncomfortably quiet, staring out the window while John drifted off. He was tired after visiting with Marlene's best friend from childhood, Nadine Gibbons. She lived between the city and Clarington and was still an active GP and a palliative care specialist. His visit wasn't announced to anyone, as he only had one reason to see her. He was preparing for the eventuality of end-of-life care for his wife, including assisted death. He would do anything to ease his wife's pain, legal or not.

Jacob thought consulting John and Marlene through the costs and procedures of the work needed for their home was going to be the easy part. John's behaviour made it seem like that was only part of the story. Jacob couldn't help but wonder what else was on John's mind.

In the car on the way to the Keegans' home, it was evident John was struggling to start this conversation.

"John, is there something wrong, something bothering you?" Jacob waited through another awkward pause for him to answer.

"I have something I need to tell you, Jacob."

Part 2

John Keegan was an imposing figure, in and out of uniform. All he had to do was look at a person a certain way, and it was a sign trouble could be close at hand. Jacob admitted to Pat that his uncle still intimidated him at certain times. In this moment, as a passenger in John's car, Jacob was in an uncomfortable position. He knew there would be no escape from what John wanted to talk about. To Jacob, this was one of those moments where everything around slows to a crawl and a dark haze descends, leaving only a single spotlight on the conversation about to commence. It was like the moment he had to give a speech on sharks for a grade eight book report — slowed down world, dark haze, spotlight, and two minutes of *ums* and *ahs*. Naturally, he tensed up and squeezed his eyes closed for a second, waiting for whatever was coming — for the bomb to drop, so to speak.

"I know what happened the night I took you boys to that concert in Moncton."

Jacob was expressionless for a minute. Then his mind started to whirl. *Oh God. What did I do? What's this all about?* He wondered. It was painfully clear to John he was becoming flushed with anxiety.

"Jacob, are you all right, son? You seem pretty fidgety there."

"Oh no, I'm fine. Just too much coffee today — kinda wound." His reply was rather dismissive. He was rattled and not good at lying, not even with little white ones. *That worked. No it didn't.* He was having difficulty reasoning with himself over the etiquette of this situation; *Respect your elders* — his parents' voices ever-present. And the more John talked, the more his head started to pound, which made it that much harder to stay focused. But even with pain and trepidation, he continued to listen and hear all he was saying.

"He was a changed man after that night, Jacob. And it was whatever you did that saved Billy. You saved my brother's life, Jacob — your best friend's father." John gestured with his palm up and gently poking his thumb into Jacob's side to make the point. He began to choke up briefly, but took a breath and continued. "And inadvertently, you ended up saving him from himself. He was on a spiral, son, I'll tell you that."

Jacob was caught off guard by what John just said. "Yeah, I remember a lot of that. I'm glad it changed. I'm glad for Pat, and for Martha." He tried to sum up quickly, seeing how emotional John was becoming. "But that wasn't me, John. He did that. Billy found the will to change."

"I don't know, Jacob. But anyway, he swore he felt the warmth of a light about him. He said it was comforting. It was hard for him to explain it exactly, but it brought him back to a time when he was happy, before the war, he said. And he's been that way ever since. Thank God!" John made the sign of the cross.

Jacob had understood what John was asking without his saying the words. "I have to say, this scares the shit out of me, John. From what I know — and that's not a lot — this has only ever happened when someone was fatally injured — you know, on the brink, I guess. So, I have no idea what will come of this, John. I can't make any promises ... well ... because I don't know what I'm doing, to be completely honest."

"Whatever happens, Jacob, either way, I'm beyond grateful," John said, a bit shaky with emotion.

"It's okay, John. I agreed to come here to help you guys because you're good people. You've always watched out for Pat and me, so, whatever I can do..."

The two arrived at the house, and Jacob went straight inside to greet Marlene. He was introduced to her sister Amy, who had stayed the long day with her until John returned. The pleasantries were over, and after a brief chat with John, Amy left for home. Jacob was sincerely saddened over what was happening, and he turned his attention to Marlene. She was near seventy years old, and the radiation and chemo had left her thin and pale. He had difficulty hiding his shock by the toll this disease had taken on her. However, the meeting was a short one, as she needed to go to her room and retire for the night.

The night settled down, and Jacob hoped he would get to take in some stories of the past. John was a great storyteller, and an animated one. And to Jacob's delight, some of those stories usually included his own father's experiences during the war — things that were never told in his own home.

"A long time ago your father told me how you got your name. It's a pretty good story, too. He must've told you it, Jacob?" John put two empty glasses on the table and poured out two doubles of a single malt.

"No, Mom said he kept that stuff close to the chest — the war, I mean. She would have told me, so he obviously didn't tell her either. She did tell me what you guys carried around from the war." Jacob paused for a second and spun the scotch in his tumbler. "She called it the monster inside. Actually, she told me that because of a fight my dad had with Frank Jennings. I was just a little guy when it happened, so I don't really remember, except for what Mom told me."

"That wasn't a fight, Jacob, that was your father teaching him a lesson. If I remember correctly, that lesson took only one punch. Your old man is a tough son of a bitch, but he never talks about it, never shoots his mouth off. There's a lot to be said for a man like that." John raised his glass and they shared a silent toast. The glasses didn't ting; they were thick and heavy with Glenlivet. "Anyway, your name came from a priest, Jacob Edelman, from up north in Dalhousie. He saved your dad's skin when they were under heavy fire, three times in the same day, same battle. So, he called him his guardian angel, and your dad named you after him. Don't you find this all, oh, I don't know … cosmic? Seems like more than coincidence to me, son. And that's all I'll say about that."

An uncomfortable silence returned after John's story, and Jacob began tensing up again.

"I'm sorry, Jacob, but I owe you an apology for this," John said, sweeping his hand back and forth across the kitchen table.

"You owe me nothing, John, and that's the way it'll stand." Jacob accepted a refill but put it back shamefully fast for such a classic Scotch.

"I'm going to call it a night, John. Tomorrow comes early, and I'm beat. I'm sure you are too. That's a lot of driving." Jacob paused to study his face, keeping his hands on the table and elbows propped up ready to lift himself.

"You're right … on both counts. You're a good man, Jacob. And that's not because of tonight. I mean it. I've known you right beside my nephew, all the way along. You're both good men." Jacob couldn't help notice a slight slur to his words. He already poured himself his third. Jacob put his arms down and indulged him a bit longer. "Yup, Tom and Irene did a fine job raising you kids. And no matter the outcome, Jacob … you will always have my respect and gratitude."

"Your respect is more than enough. Goodnight, John." Jacob stood up, reached his hand out, and received a firm handshake in return. Later that night, he walked by the living room where John was asleep on his La-Z-Boy with the TV left on, just like Jacob's father. The familiarity of it lit a smile on his face. His pause was brief, convinced the alcohol was an effective sedative. He carried on with soft steps toward Marlene. Manners told him to attempt to wake her, so he lightly tapped on the inside of the door frame. He was thankful the morphine was doing its job. He sat on the side of her bed, and with the dim lamplight left on, he was saddened by such a large assortment of pill bottles. Beside them was a pitcher of water, and a full glass, ready to wash them down with. The adjacent long, dark cherry bureau had three neatly centred jewellery boxes. Surrounding them was an assortment of family pictures proudly displayed. Jacob held Marlene's hand briefly.

"I don't know what I'm doing, Marlene, but let's hope it helps. So, here it goes," he said, nervously reaching his hands up to both sides of her head. He closed his eyes like he was praying, and upon opening them, there was no light of any kind. But a smile of contentment showed up on Marlene's face, who continued to sleep completely undisturbed. He grabbed her hand and gave it a quick kiss. Jacob was not prone to reciting these words, but they felt appropriate in the moment: "God bless, Marlene."

§

When Jacob returned to work, the look on his face was clear and Pat immediately started to apologize, but Jacob stopped him. "Don't worry about it, Pat. I would have tried anything to help my family … and friends. You know that. We're good, as always, buddy."

"Thanks, Jake … for everything," Pat said. He shook Jacob's hand and pulled him in close for a hug.

§

Marlene passed away approximately six weeks later. During the viewing at the funeral home, John took Jacob and Pat outside away from everybody else.

"Listen up you two, first off, thanks for coming. And take this to heart, if you ever need anything, I mean it, *anything*, you call me. And that's anytime, day or night. Jacob, I can never thank you enough."

"But I didn't do anything, John. It didn't help." Jacob was both sad and confused.

"You helped, son, just by coming down. And you helped me, too. I asked you to do the impossible and put you in an extremely difficult position, and you stayed the day with us," he said with surprise and joy. "Marlene enjoyed that day immensely. It really raised her spirits. And as it turned out, her last weeks were a lot less painful compared to what she had been experiencing." John lowered his voice to a near whisper, leaning into Jacob. "Maybe that was a result of you, what was meant to be, Jacob. You just don't know what life will deliver us from any given moment to the next," he said with his voice returning to normal.

John placed his hands on Jacob and Pat's shoulders.

"Boys … excuse me, I shouldn't say that. Men, I love you both. You have a great life where you are and there's more for the taking. And Jacob, whatever's going on with you, don't run away from it, embrace it. Pat … you two have been friends since you were in diapers. You both keep watch for each other, do you hear me?" John's question came with some emotion, but no tears.

"Yes, Uncle John."

"Of course, John." They were both shocked at John being so open with his feelings and emotions. Neither of them had heard him talk or behave like that before.

John pulled them both in at once for a hug with strength that surprised, but it shouldn't have been that surprising, considering the hug came from a large man who was both ex-army and ex-cop — John would be strong to the end. The two boys were reminded of John's many roles as he went back to sit by his wife's side. They could see that among the many titles that applied to John, the most important to him was *husband*.

20

Dyed in the Wool

Not long after setting up shop, Jacob built a set of custom kitchen cabinets for the Spreits. Maggie Spreit was a local real estate agent and Willy Spreit worked their farm just southwest of Clarington. It didn't take long for Jacob and Sara to become good friends with the couple. Their next-door neighbour, Edmond Zacharius, had grown tobacco since he bought the farm thirty years before. After the tobacco market took a drastic hit in sales and Mr. Zacharius finally gave up on trying to make quotas profitable, he decided to retire and leave town.

When Mr. Zacharius put his farm up for sale, Willy automatically thought of Jacob and Sara. He knew their business was growing beyond what the garage and apartment above it could accommodate. He'd heard Jacob complain often that his shop was bursting at the seams, so this place seemed perfect.

Willy went to Jacob's shop and asked him if he would take a drive with him to help with something at home. As expected, Jacob was accommodating. He blew the sawdust off himself with the air hose, and out the door they went. The conversation between them was casual as expected — talk about this year's Blue Jays team, about their chances and how nice it would be to see a game. All was as usual until they drove past Willy's place and kept heading west.

"Hey, Willy, are you daydreaming? You just drove past the farm."

"Oh, yeah. Well, I didn't really want to go there right now anyway." Willy was acting aloof. A half-mile down the road was the

Zacharius farm, with a For Sale sign out front. Bold red letters S-O-L-D appeared across the sign, with Maggie Spreit's name and company logo underneath. Willy slowed down and pulled into the long uphill lane leading to the property's house and barn.

"What's up, Willy? Is Maggie getting this place ready for transfer or something?"

"She just put the For Sale sign out a couple days back. Then I told her to put the Sold sign on it."

"You buying it?" Jacob politely enquired.

"No, I'm not buying it. I had Maggie reserve it so a friend of mine could check it out before it hit the open market."

"Oh. Okay. So, who's gonna look at it?"

"You, buddy. What do you think of that?" Willy asked with a wry smile, waiting for his response.

The look was exactly what Willy had expected. He was as excited as Thomas O'Connell was the day he surprised his son with a pickup truck before heading off to college.

"So? Don't just sit there with your mouth hanging open. What do you think, young man? Isn't it about time for you two to start raising a family?" Willy asked, having had this conversation before with Jacob. "The barn is really big. You could fit three shops in there."

Jacob's eyes were wide open and he looked around in awe and joy, like he was witnessing a child being born.

After they got out of the truck, Jacob was lost for a few seconds. He was trying to take it in on a panoramic scale, as it was an impressive property and had been well maintained. The scene was turning around in front of him so fast, he started to feel dizzy with excitement. There was a tire swing hanging from the century-old elm tree in the side yard. The surrounding grass was deep green and neatly cut. The red-brick farmhouse with brilliant white moulding and a recently installed cedar shake roof, completed the idyllic picture of farm life.

Willy looked at Jacob and was about to prod a response of some kind out of him until he saw emotions rising in his young friend. Willy was fifteen years his senior.

"You okay there, Jacob?"

Startled, Jacob had to compose himself. "Might as well dive in with both feet, right?" Jacob said, still looking stunned and continuing to stare between the house and barn.

"Think you're ready for something like this?" Willy asked, putting his hand on Jacob's shoulder.

"I think so, Willy, It's about time. No, it's definitely time."

They had a good look around the place and headed back down the laneway. There were 150 acres of land that Willy would lease for his needs, which would help the young couple financially. Jacob loved the place the second he laid eyes on it, and he knew Sara would love it too. He was in awe of the potential this farm held, thinking it would be a perfect place to raise a family. And it had more than enough room for his shop inside the barn's main level. It had a second floor with a loft above that. Sara loved antiques, and he could see plenty of space where she could restore what she wished and at her own pace.

As they were leaving, Willy shared some news with Jacob, not knowing he was already painfully aware of it. "Hey, I don't want to bring you down right now, but it's important you know before you decide to buy a house here. Did you hear Vargas is the chief building inspector in Clarington now?"

"Jesus, don't remind me. I just found out not too long ago. I'm still in shock. We both are." Jacob's tone shifted darkly.

"I have to deal with that asshole every time I go in. It doesn't matter who's in the office. I walk in, and boom, he's right there in my face every time! The guy just doesn't know how to let things go, and I am one hundred percent sure he moved here just for that reason."

"Or worse," Willy said. "Jesus, Jacob. After everything you told me, I would be worried."

And at the same moment they both uttered the same name, "Sara."

"Yeah, I worry about that often. I'm just not sure how far he would go with that." Jacob's look of childish admiration of the farm had completely diminished now. It was replaced with a firm brow of concern and frustration that was turning into anger.

"Well, Jacob, it wouldn't be a bad idea to keep as much space from the guy as possible. Don't need a repeat of what happened in the city. You've got too much to risk for that happening again."

"You got that right, Willy."

Returning home to get his truck after viewing the farm, Jacob headed to Port Darlington to stop in and see Pat. The Compass Rose Restaurant and Inn was one of their projects in progress. He expected Pat's truck, not a truck from the local building department, to be out front. Jacob's brewing anger followed him right into the restaurant.

"What the hell is going on here, Pat? What the fuck is that prick doing here?"

Pat had a look of concern instead of the shared anger Jacob was clearly expressing.

"Hi, Pat. How are things going? Hi, Jacob. Oh, things are fine, thanks for asking, Jacob … buddy … best friend … uh…" Pat made his point.

"Okay, I get it. Sorry, man." Jacob calmed down.

"Just so you know, he's holding up the guys from boarding the drywall because he hasn't received the final report from the mechanical engineer, so he's issued a Stop Work Order."

"Pat, I dropped off that report to the building department yesterday, and I faxed a copy to you last night." Pat could see his friend's anger right there at the surface.

"I'm sorry, bud, I wasn't home, was out at Heather's parent's anniversary party. I'll go get the copy and tell Vargas what's going on. You go, and I'll meet up with you later. We don't need any more hassles here from this guy," Pat said, giving Jacob a playful jab to the stomach.

"Yeah, okay Pat, thanks. Give me a call when you're free."

"Okay, man. Be cool," Pat said.

"Oh yeah. I'm always cool; you know that," Jacob said, as he walked toward the door. Both of them laughed at the irony at what he just said. Jacob was far from cool when it came to anything to do with Jonathan Vargas. To demonstrate the fact, he hadn't quite made it out the door, when he stopped in his tracks. "Pat … I dropped off that report at the building department yesterday. What the fuck?!? It shouldn't matter if you have a copy. Oh ... right ... it's not posted. That's bullshit, and you know it!"

"Never mind, Jacob. I'll talk to you about it later," Pat said firmly. Jacob stared at Pat, his brows squeezing together. "Jacob ... I said I'll see you later." Jacob was not used to hearing this tone of voice from Pat, especially not directed at him. It was effective, though. Jacob turned and walked away. Whatever was happening between Jacob and Vargas, Pat knew it was wise that Jacob leave. The volatile dynamic between the two could turn dangerous any minute, and that wasn't good for business.

Neither Pat nor Jacob were in the habit of being violent, but they could handle themselves in a fight. Pat had grown up with a violent, alcoholic father and had developed his tough side out of necessity. Jacob's toughness came from being the youngest in his family. He'd been the recipient of many a tussle with each of his three older brothers. Both Pat and Jacob were known to stand up for what they believed in and had slightly quick fuses and rough edges.

As things stood today between the two friends, they relied on one another to excel where the other fell short. In the case of dealing with Vargas, the responsibility fell on Pat's shoulders, which was in everyone's best interest and safety, especially that of Jonathon Vargas.

21

Intrusions

Part 1

On a lovely and bright midsummer day — 20 degrees Celsius, minimal humidity and few clouds in the sky — Jacob drove over to the Spreit farm to have a quick visit with Maggie and to get permission to drive onto the Zacharius farm with Sara later that night. He had sworn Willy and Maggie to secrecy about the property because he wanted to surprise his wife to be. He intended on showing her the same night he planned on performing a long-awaited marriage proposal. And he thought the perfect time for that would be during the annual garden party that night.

The long gravel driveway was lined on both sides with four-foot high wooden posts and three horizontal rows of rough-sawn fence boards, all painted white. The Spreits' home was a traditional light red — almost orange brick — two-storey farmhouse with high pitch gables and dormers on both sides. It had powder-yellow brick corbel on the outside corners and large cornice brackets under the original wooden soffits, all painted white. It was obvious that the century-old home had been restored to its original shape. The recently replaced cedar shake roof hadn't turned entirely grey from the sun yet. Even the copper step and pan flashings on the wraparound porch's roof still had its shine.

The porch was also recently completely rebuilt. The turned posts, handrails, and gingerbread, along with remaining mouldings on the house were all painted white. The stairs leading up to the porch went the entire length of the side of the house. The whole house looked warm and inviting.

When Jacob jumped up the four steps to the porch, he noticed a blue sedan parked in front of Willy's pickup truck. He didn't recognize the car. He also caught sight of Willy's tractor parked by the back door. *That's odd*, he thought. This time of year, Willy was usually out in the fields spraying fertilizer, nearly round the clock, always eating lunch on the go.

Jacob knocked and walked through the side door into the kitchen, as he had many times before. The old-fashioned squeaky spring-loaded hinges forced the wooden screen door to slam shut, announcing his entry.

"Maggie? Hi, Maggie, it's Jacob," he called out into an empty room. His steps were pronounced as he walked to the kitchen table for a seat. Sandwiches sat on the table, still under construction. Maggie came rushing from the hall.

"Jacob, hi, how are you? You frightened me. I forgot you were stopping by today. Just give me a minute and I'll be right with you. Take a seat and have one of those sandwiches. Be right back." The words flew out of Maggie's mouth. She briskly turned about-face and scurried back to the dining room. He'd clearly interrupted something.

He started to worry that he might have interrupted an afternoon delight, which threw him off. He then started tapping his index finger to his forehead. *That's a disturbing thought. Let's get that out of there right now!* And suddenly he forgot the awkward feeling from having possibly interrupted them and became completely preoccupied with trying to get that image out of his head.

He heard voices coming from the dining room, but the room was far enough away that it kept the conversation muffled. He leaned over to sneak a peek, but all he could see was a pair of black dress shoes straddling one of the chairs. He gave up speculating, grabbed the newspaper on the table, and pulled it open to the sports section.

It wasn't more than five minutes when Maggie came around the edge of the kitchen's archway. Maggie was a naturally beautiful brunette, thin and with eyes so dark brown they were almost black. She was usually high strung — a nervous talker — but that day she seemed jittery, and Jacob could see her body involuntarily jerking a bit. He noticed her trying to hide her shaking hands.

"There, well that's over. So, Jacob … how are you, my dear?" She appeared distracted and her question sounded more rehearsed than natural.

"I'm okay, and you?" Jacob leaned over to look behind Maggie. "Is Willy coming?"

"Um, he's…" Before she could finish, the roar of the tractor's diesel engine fired up. "He's going back to work." The next second, Willy went by, heading to the fields. Jacob could see him from the window, and he didn't look happy.

"Is everything all right, Maggie?"

She hurriedly grabbed the seat next to Jacob and leaned in like a teen leaning over a desk in school about to tell a secret to a friend.

"It was the RCMP from Toronto. Willy's brother owns a bike courier business in the city, and one of his couriers was murdered," Maggie whispered.

Jacob sat back in his chair, taking a pronounced breath in and out. She didn't catch it, but she did manage to see the look on his face like he'd just been gut punched. He wondered if this was another unlikely coincidence or if Gary had worked for Willy's brother.

"Would you like a coffee?" she asked, quickly tapping his forearm.

"Yes, please. I think I need one about now. The RCMP guy, did he say the name of who was killed?" Jacob quietly asked, like he was making small talk, barely interested.

"Yes, they did. They showed us a picture. Actually, he left it." She ran out to the dining room, and briskly returned with some papers and a picture. "Here's the picture. His name was—" She didn't get a chance to say it.

"It's Gary," Jacob said, dropping his hand holding the picture down on the table. His face cringed and his right eye started to close, as he clenched his jaw.

"That's right," she exclaimed. "You know who he is? What are the chances of that?"

"I don't know his last name, but he delivered to where Sara worked."

"Small world, eh? It's Benson. Gary Benson," she said, handing the sheet of paper over with his info on it.

"What would make them think you guys would know anything? Hell, when was the last time you two went to the city for anything?"

"I couldn't tell you. But they were asking about Henry, Willy's brother. They just wanted background info. You know, cross the t's and dot the i's."

"Willy's brother owns that courier business? Well, Jesus, everything just goes full circle, doesn't it?" Jacob's question was rhetorical, and Maggie looked confused when she heard it. "Is Willy okay? He looked upset."

"Oh, he's okay. It's his brother, Henry. He's had trouble follow him his whole life, wherever he goes. Willy is usually the one to bail him out. I've lost track of how many times now. We thought he was doing better. The business seemed to be doing well. Oh, who really knows about people, Jacob? It did upset Willy though. It's family; what do you do?"

Jacob guzzled his coffee, thanked Maggie for the hospitality, and hastily headed out the door and back toward Clarington.

Part 2

The late-night tour of the farm property was approved, so his thoughts shifted to the night ahead with Sara. He wasn't too far down the road, looking aimlessly around the truck when he glanced across the rear-view mirror. Suddenly, the truck tires screeched and they took a dramatic, near ninety-degree turn across the opposing lane. The truck cleared the first part of the ditch and came to a bouncing stop in a field of soy. The truck was enveloped in a cloud of dust, and Jacob still had both hands squeezed, white-knuckle tight, on the steering wheel.

He spun around, looking to the backseat of the crew cab, but found nothing. He turned back in his seat, and, sitting sideways, he stared out the passenger window, his eyes wide. He allowed his breathing to slow and his shaking to subside, but he couldn't stop himself from looking at the back seat a few more times. Whatever it was that created such a reaction was gone. He slowly turned his body back to face the wheel and, without being able to help himself, looked back to the mirror.

"Jesus!" he yelled out, spinning around once again, confirming he saw Gary's reflection now for the second time.

He kept his head down, concentrating on returning his breathing back to normal. "Gary," he said loudly. "Gary?" He slowly lifted his head to peek to the back but again found nothing. And just as slowly, he looked back to the mirror, and there was Gary Benson. As large as life to Jacob's eyes, but when he turned to the back again, he wasn't there. Jacob started squeezing his fist and slammed the side of it against the steering wheel. "Come on, Jacob. This can't happen," he said aloud again. "Great, I'm talking to myself now."

A tingling sensation in his neck made Jacob cringe, when suddenly he heard a voice say, "Don't get angry, Jacob. Remember? Angry, not mad."

Jacob jerked his head toward the mirror. "That's not funny. Where did you hear that? And don't fuck with me." Again, Jacob lowered his head, shaking it. "I can't believe this shit is happening."

"Relax, buddy, I'm not here to haunt you," Gary said with a pleasant tone. "Sorry about repeating your dad. He's a nice man, I shouldn't do that. I really am sorry, Jacob."

"Okay, that's enough," Jacob snapped. "What do you want? Seeing as I'm having a conversation with a *dead man* in a field where anyone going by can see me, could you hurry the fuck up, please?" Jacob asked Gary, not removing his eyes from the mirror.

"Always polite, ever the well-mannered man, eh, Jacob? Even when you're angry. Sorry, but being dead gives you new perspectives, and I know this is freaking you out. Listen, Willy's brother knows nothing about my death. Except for Vargas and me, you're the only one who knows. And no, I don't know why you see and hear me. The cops will come with questions for you and Sara. I need you to steer them in the right direction, Jacob."

"Forget it. I say anything and I get pulled in. Vargas is here now, so I don't need it," Jacob said firmly.

"Yeah, I know. Sorry to see that happen. That psycho has a bead on you two. Anyway, just give them a hint. Don't involve yourself. That's all I'm asking Jacob. You can do that, can't you?"

Jacob lowered his head again, and with a sigh, he relented, "Yeah, I'll try. I can't promise anything, though." When he attempted to look back to the mirror, his head suddenly started to pound. He brought his hand up to feel the right side of his forehead at his hairline. Pulling his hand away revealed a small amount of blood from a minor cut on top of a fresh bump he hadn't felt a minute before. He turned both his palms up. His hands were shaking. He looked back to find the mirror bent on a forty-five-degree angle, with the glass facing the roof of the truck toward the passenger side. With his head still pounding, he felt a dizziness he realized had been there all along. When he turned the mirror back to its usual position, he discovered it was shattered in a dozen or more pieces that were still glued to its surface. He slumped back in his seat, and with a dazed expression, he stared out the front of the truck. He was ignoring his pounding head and shaking hands. He just sat there, still and quiet. His hands came up to cover his face, and then, with a grunt, he pushed his fingers through his hair.

Again, he lowered his head for a second and brought it back up, put the truck in gear, and floored the gas pedal. With tires spinning, the truck quickly spun in a circle, the dust rising like a cyclone. He went flying through the ditch, and the front wheels came off the ground before slamming back down on the pavement. The tires squealed, leaving their mark, as the truck fishtailed a few times before straightening out, speeding back into his lane and toward home.

Part 3

When Jacob got to his shop, he saw a dark blue sedan with tinted windows and an antenna in the middle of its roof parked out front.

"Hmm, wonder who that could be?" Jacob said to himself sarcastically. After what just happened on the drive home, he decided to do his best to keep those investigators away from Sara. An attempt to go into the apartment was met with a locked door. To his relief, Sara was out.

In the shop, two of his workers were busy running off some custom mouldings for various projects. One was sweeping the floor, obviously uninterested in talking to the police, and the other pointed to Jacob when he entered.

"Gentlemen, what can I do for you?" Before an answer came back, Jacob gestured to them to leave the shop. "Let's do this outside, please? I already know what you're here for."

The two homicide detectives were put off by Jacob's last statement and looked to one another and then back to Jacob.

"Relax, guys, I know about Gary. I just came from the Spreit farm. They're good friends of ours. I was there just before you left. Maggie filled me in a bit." The two officers seemed puzzled. "The truck..." Jacob pointed. "You had to have seen my truck before you left, right?" Jacob didn't wait for a response. "Anyway, you're here because Sara worked at one of his regular stops. I actually met him once..."

The detectives' attire reminded Jacob of Heather's uncle Tony. Together, they looked like Abbott and Costello.

The tall, thin Abbott of the duo spoke first. "That's right, we want to talk to anyone who has interacted with Mr. Benson ... Gary." He seemed serious but amiable. Jacob leaned his back against the front of his truck and could see the shop workers behind the detectives mocking their gestures like two silent actors. When the officers looked away, Jacob waved to the guys to knock it off.

Costello took his turn. His seriousness was a strained effort that fell short. "So how … exactly how do you know the deceased anyway … ah … Mr….?" He frantically flipped back and forth through his notepad, as disorganized as his appearance suggested.

"O'Connell. It's O'Connell. Jacob O'Connell." He was already losing patience with these two, thinking about Sara and tonight. "And you are?" Abbott introduced himself as constable Evans and told Jacob his partner's name was constable Harris.

As the interview continued, Harris failed miserably in his attempt as the bad cop, but as it went on, Jacob realized he was being questioned as a possible suspect.

"Look, guys, I met Gary once, and I just said that. Maybe you should write that down in your notepad." That remark only got him a dirty look. "Anyway, I met him when I went to pick up Sara up at work once. So, enough with the tone and the look already," Jacob said sternly. "Sara knew Gary professionally, as any other person trying to make a living. The only time she ever dealt with him or had any interactions with him was at work, so she might be able to help you, but not today and not tonight."

"What do you mean by *interactions*?" Harris asked.

Jacob snapped back. "What part of *professionally* didn't you understand?"

The officer ignored Jacob's consternation.

"It's important we talk with Miss Millen. Have her call us at this number, please," said Evans, as he handed his card over. Jacob handed him one of his own cards in return.

"If you need to call, make it here. The business is ours." Jacob nodded his head toward the big sign over the garage door that read *Able Hands Construction & Design Ltd.*

"Is the design part hers, the furniture and all that frilly stuff?" asked Harris. And without a breath, he kept rambling, "My wife does that. The curtains, wallpaper, all the knick-knacks and stuff. It drives me crazy…"

Jacob couldn't stand the ignorance. "Ah, no … she's an architect. Design doesn't always mean what you're talking about. However, I'll be sure to let her know you thought she fluffs pillows for a living. Wow!"

While Harris continued to flip back and forth with his notepad, Evans could clearly see Jacob had moved past annoyed and was now angry.

"You always have an attitude when you talk to the police?" asked Evans.

"I have a good friend who's a cop, and he doesn't talk to people like that. You get the same respect as you give. You're cops, not gods. I'm sorry, I wasn't going to say anything, but you come in here … you know what, never mind. Is there anything else you need from me?"

"No, that's it. Just have your wife give us a call, please," Evans said, turning around and walking back to their car.

"Have a nice day," Jacob mumbled as the two got in their unmarked car and drove away. Jacob shook off the unpleasant interaction and went about preparing for the night ahead.

§

It was turning into a lovely evening for the festivities that were underway at the annual garden party. The air was charged for the crew of Able Hands. Jacob and Sara were already in the parking lot at the Oasis Hotel when Pat and Heather pulled in. They all gathered around Pat's truck along with the few employees that had already arrived, then as more came, they made a company posse there. The entire group totalled a dozen. Judging by their energy and behaviour, they were more than primed for the night to unfold. It was a first for the company, as the Mayor of Clarington had made mention of them as one of the new successful businesses to join the area, and they were recognized for partnering up directly with local people like Pat and

Heather Keegan and for hiring local carpenters, labourers, and other skilled tradespeople from the surrounding area. The business becoming so successful brought them a certain amount of notoriety.

§

Sara could see the obvious discomfort on her man's face after dinner. She politely excused herself from the table and took Jacob by the hand. "Would you be so kind as to take your stunningly beautiful partner for a stroll down by the water?"

"Didn't I already call you stunningly beautiful tonight?" Jacob whispered in her ear.

"Yes, you did. I'm just repeating your compliment, so you don't forget it. Besides, you keep saying things like that, and you might have company on the ride home tonight."

"Well, then, let's go, my stunningly beautiful partner."

Standing on the small beach area next to the pier, Sara squeezed Jacob's hand. "I have something I need to talk to you about." Then she placed her hands to both sides of his face and gently kissed him.

"Really? So do I," he replied.

Sara jumped in with, "Well, this is our night, so let's break with tradition and you go first."

Jacob took her offer and pulled out a small ivory velvet box from his pocket, grabbed Sara's hand, and dropped to one knee. "We've always considered each other husband and wife, and I love you more than life itself. I think it's about time we make it official. Sara Millen, will you marry me?"

22

From All Sides

Part 1

The Oasis Hotel offered its guests a pleasant snapshot of the lake and the town's history. A turn-of-the-century building, it was originally a mansion, which had been completely restored inside and out. With yellow ochre clapboard siding and powder-white mouldings, it had a bed and breakfast appeal. Eye-catching flower gardens followed the twists and turns of a flagstone footpath that wound through the property. The three storeys of this lovely old building had wraparound balconies, all accessible through French doors out from each room. And while lounging there, guests could take in the view of the lake. As the sun patiently floated above the horizon, it waited on the few remaining sailboats and windsurfers who could be found on the fading ripples, catching the dying winds of the day.

From spring to fall, guests from near and far filled the rooms of the Oasis. A white arched trellis, woven with deep green ivy, welcomed people onto the grounds. The spirit of summer was alive with strings of coloured patio lanterns that hung in a drooping sway above the deck where the diners lingered. And the lap of the waves rolling in with an uneven pace provided enough continuity to pacify guests into pleasant slumber. Without question, it was comfortable, inviting, and a perfect place for tonight's event, including Jacob's intentions.

Pat wrapped his arm around Heather, and from the raised deck he pointed out to the beach near the water's edge.

"Hey, hey, look at that. He's really going through with it. Finally!"

"What are you pointing at?" Heather was trying to follow his finger.

"There. Jake and Sara. Just watch. Watch to see if he does it. He's getting closer."

Heather focused in on what was happening between their closest friends. "Pat, did you maybe think it's a romantic moment they're having? Don't stare, it's rude. You do remember those, right … romantic moments?" she teased, poking a finger into his ribs.

"Funny." Pat continued to watch and waited for his best friend to propose.

"Oh my God! Are you serious!?" Heather's face expressed awe, then anger, when she realized what was happening. "They've been talking about this for how long now, and you couldn't tell me about this earlier?" she griped.

"I didn't know he was going to go through with it. Christ, he didn't know for sure if he was going to go through with it. So…"

Before Pat could finish, it happened. Heather squeezed the arm he'd draped over her shoulder and didn't let go until it was over. There they watched as Jacob bent down to one knee, and from that moment, their best friends knew all that remained was a wedding.

"Get up off your knees and kiss me you fool," Sara said, giggling. "Of course, we're going to make it official."

Off to the side of the pier was an elevated area of well-manicured grass, and in the centre was a big, old willow tree with its branches hanging a few feet off the ground. Along the edge, facing the water was a line of hostas and bunches of light green and blonde tiger grass. With the evening sun behind Sara's silhouette, Jacob took a wisp of her hair and pulled it back over her ear. Looking into her eyes, as if hypnotized, he wrapped one hand around her waist and gently pulled her in close.

"Did I tell you how much I love you? I know how important all of this is for us. I just wanted to be sure that I…" He stopped midsentence, swallowed a lump of air, and put his head down. Sara placed both hands to his face and lifted under his chin to see tears beginning to fall. They embraced and a few cries turned to laughter.

He leaned in for a kiss, and Sara gently put her fingers to his lips. "I do know you love me, without an *ounce* of doubt, ever. And my life would have a great big hole without you there. And anytime would have been all right, but getting married now makes perfect sense." She began kissing his cheek and then moved around to his lips for a long soft kiss. Sara wasn't one to speak in a mousy tone, but in this moment, she became quiet and demure. "I suppose this makes it the right time to tell you." There was a nervous look about her, seeing Jacob looking at her with anticipation. "I just found out this morning ... I'm pregnant, Jacob."

Jacob, in shock, failed to produce any words. Finally, he grabbed her by the hand and start walking. "Come on, I want to show you something. Let's go for a drive."

"Jacob, I just told you I'm pregnant. Aren't you going to say something?"

His look of shock was quickly replaced with a big, goofy smile. "I heard you loud and clear, and it's absolutely wonderful, honest. I couldn't be happier. But I need to show you something and now is the perfect time, believe me. Come on, let's go."

"Is it about being pregnant or the company?" Sara asked, holding Jacob's hand and trying to keep pace with his speed walking to the parking lot.

"I couldn't care less about the company right now, or anything else other than you."

Suddenly Sara was struck with an anxiety attack. "Oh my God, honey, we're going to have a baby." Sara didn't cry often, but she couldn't hold it back. "Do you think we're ready? The garage is kind of small for a kid, don't you think?" she spoke rapidly through her tears, and the pitch of her voice was rising.

"It's okay, sweetheart. Just take a breath ... calm. We're going to be more than all right. I believe that with all my heart. You are a strong, wonderful woman, and don't forget totally hot too." He stopped their march to the truck, smiled, and held her close. "And without question, you will be a great mom!" he joyfully exclaimed. "Of that, I have no doubt, never did, never will. So, don't worry, because after this, after having a child, it will only make things in life that much better."

Part 2

The air was charged with excitement for Jacob, and his eagerness to get Sara to the Zacharius property added an agility to his steps. Holding the side door open for Sara, he inadvertently looked back to the Oasis and the group on the deck, only to find Jonathon Vargas's eyes locked in on them. The hair on his neck rose along with his ire. He was sitting with the mayor, who had earlier praised Able Hands's accomplishments in the community, which now repulsed Jacob. He did his best to keep his reaction from Sara; however, his demeanour changed from relaxed to guarded in a second. Every movement from that moment was one of hyper vigilance and was exceedingly difficult for him to conceal. In his seat and ready to start the truck, he and Vargas had their eyes locked in on each other again.

"What's the matter, honey? Are you feeling all right?" Sara turned herself sideways to better look at Jacob.

"I think it was the champagne. It's not really agreeing with me. I only had a half a glass ... I'll be okay." He raced out of the lot and onto the road before Sara had a chance to notice what was going on. Still looking at Jacob, she grabbed his hand and squeezed it tight, holding it to her chest. Before turning west toward the farm, she held her left hand up to the fading sunset, admiring her new ring.

"All right, I can't take it. Where are you taking me, Mr. O'Connell? Are we going parking?" Her laughter thrilled Jacob.

His look to her was filled with intimate affection. "You are, without a shadow of a doubt, the most beautiful creature on God's green earth. And I am the luckiest man in the world. I love every single ounce of you, Mrs. O'Connell." Then he shifted to a playful tone. "The parking, well, we'll just save that for later. Maybe after the dance. How's that sound, young lady?" His comments made Sara blush.

"Well, Mr. O'Connell, I think I might just allow that to happen. If … and only if, you remain a gentleman. So, my husband in waiting, where are you taking me to?" But still she could pry no answer from him.

Jacob was starting to squirm in his seat. He was pulling himself toward the steering wheel the closer they came to the farm. Sara's eyes opened wide and she leaned forward as he began to slow down. He pulled onto the long, rising gravel lane with a skirt of pines and poplars facing the road of this well-maintained property. A sign read Zacharius & Sons with tobacco leaves painted on both sides of the name. As they started up the lane, Sara could see the farmhouse, the barn, and the surrounding fields. She noticed the house had a wraparound porch to the front and sides that had faded white paint on all the woodwork. The deck of the porch was battleship grey, but at this time of night it seemed a dark navy blue just like the sky to the west.

The trim of the large red barn to the left of the house was painted white — a classic look. The lane expanded to a large turnaround space the closer you got to the house. There was a light on inside on the main floor and a dim outdoor light next to the entrance. Farther into the property nearing the fields were large individual piles of lumber and debris from what had been the old tobacco kilns. There was only one low kiln remaining, and Jacob pointed to it indicating it might be used for storage.

"What are we doing here, Jacob?"

"Did you see Maggie's real estate sign under the Zacharius sign out front?" Jacob asked with a coy look on his face.

"Barely. Doesn't it say 'sold'? So why are we here? Oh, do the new owners want you to renovate the farmhouse? That would be a wonderful job."

"Yeah, kind of. I put an offer in on it last week. Willy brought me out to look at it, and I thought … well, I thought we could raise a family here. What do you think, sweetheart?" The silence in the truck was making Jacob squirm.

"It's only an offer. Maggie only put the sold sign up to hold it for us."

The silence continued, and Sara stared out blankly. No signs of emotion had surfaced yet, and Jacob's swallow sounded uncomfortably amplified to him. He placed his arm on the steering wheel and lowered his head with a small sigh. "I'm sorry, I can rescind it if you feel we're not ready. I just wanted to surprise you. I thought you might like it. Do you like it? I thought it might be like the place you had when you were a kid, remember?" The silence had him feeling that unwanted heat rising in his neck and under the skin on his face.

Suddenly, Sara placed her hands over her face, but failed to stop the flow of tears streaming over her freckled cheeks. Much to Jacob's relief, they were tears of joy on this night of nights — the pregnancy, the ring and marriage, and now a house, a house in the country at that. Overwhelmed, she cried out in an overabundance of happiness. She cried and cried, still holding her hands over her face. She at least looked at Jacob briefly for him to catch a small smile in the midst of crying.

Finally, she turned to grasp his cheeks within her tear-soaked hands and, in between repeated kisses, she said, "It's amazing, Jacob. Next to the day we met, this is the happiest day of my life."

Jacob collapsed back into his seat and took a long draw of breath.

"Phew! I thought you were upset with me."

She wiped away her tears and took a deep breath.

"Of course I'm not upset with you. I know you wouldn't do anything like this if it didn't come from the heart. This is a wonderful way to start our family."

They couldn't wait to share the good news with their best friends, and then all the family members. They turned the truck around and headed back to the garden party at the Oasis to finish the night off in celebration. Then suddenly Jacob thought back to what had happened in the parking lot. He grit his teeth and steadied himself for what may come when they got back.

23

A New Clarity

A small chapel on the edge of town could scarcely hold a dozen guests; however, for this impromptu gathering, it worked just fine. For Jacob and Sara this event was mostly ceremonial. They considered themselves man and wife long ago. They had a small window of opportunity to enjoy a honeymoon, so they took it — some hard-earned and well-deserved time away from it all. And to help them relax and enjoy their trip, the business couldn't be in better hands than those of their partners and best friends.

Neither Sara nor Jacob desired cooking in the sun — as Jacob always referred to sunbathing. It wasn't their idea of relaxation or enjoyment. A friendlier environment for Sara's fair-skinned complexion was the west of Canada. They flew to Calgary and rented a car to drive through Banff, Lake Louise, and ended up in Kelowna. A friend of Jacob's told him about his excursions through the west as a young man, saying he thought Kelowna was the California of Canada. So their itinerary was set.

Their first stop was Canada's "Castle in the Rockies," Fairmont Banff Springs. The hotel would provide the luxury and the Rockies would take care of the sightseeing in spectacular fashion. It was time away they needed as a couple and the rest required after a great deal of hard work.

With a few days left of their honeymoon, they stopped in Canmore for a coffee and a tour of a passenger rail dining car from an era long gone. Both sides of the cars had large windows to take in the view while dining. And as well to either side of the aisle were tables for four, completely set with brilliant white cloth napkins, crystal glasses, and a full placement of silverware. It was truly a beautiful setting for dining while travelling through the breathtaking mountains of the west.

The honeymooners were still in a state of bliss for finally reaching this point in their lives. The next stop was Calgary and a night out on the town, but that plan was interrupted. Sara suddenly had an uncomfortable feeling about being so far away from home, but before she expressed anything to Jacob, he spoke up with a look of concern. "We should go home now instead of going out tonight. What do you think?"

"I think you're right, but it's freaking me out because I was about to say the same thing."

"Really, why?"

"I don't know, just a feeling we should go home. We've had a lovely time away, so going back a few days early won't hurt. Right?"

Jacob looked at Sara with a loving smile, kissed her, and wrapped his arm around her waist. They walked back to the car without another word needed.

§

Barely a week after the honeymoon, Sara was well into preliminary drawings on one of the company's upcoming projects. Still at the apartment over the shop, her office in the spare room was overflowing. The medication she'd taken for her nausea that morning had made her drowsy and dizzy, which quickly advanced into vertigo. Never having experienced this sensation, she didn't panic; instead, she sat still, waiting for it to pass. She rubbed her stomach, lay down on the sofa, and drifted off.

Within minutes, she began dreaming of Jacob working in the shop late at night. She saw him working on a small wooden rocking horse even before she entered the building.

A hard rain falls outside as she goes downstairs to check in on her newly celebrated husband. Before opening the door, she pauses, feeling eyes upon her. A feeling of electrical shocks runs through her body. She quickly spins around to see if someone is there. On the other side of the street, and several yards away, someone is partially revealed standing next to a light post. With the heavy rain obscuring her vision, she strains her eyes to try and make out the tall, thin figure. And with no clear picture, she somehow knows who it is. And from the depths of her soul, she believes completely he is evil and full of rage. He might as well be a fire-breathing monster. It evokes a cold chill that runs through her body, along with the electrical charge she is experiencing. It forces her to leap the short distance through the door and into the shop. Her skin continues to tingle all over, and her ice-cold shoulders push up around her neck, creating an unnatural shiver. With the sense of darkness about to pounce on her, she frantically slams the door shut. Soaking wet, and shaking uncontrollably, she thinks it's strange that Jacob isn't reacting; he isn't coming to her.

The moment she stands inside the entrance, he cuts his hand open with a chisel. A sense of panic overtakes her, and she shouts out to him, but again, no reaction. A great deal of blood shoots out before he quickly grabs his hand, and, wincing in pain he yells out a few obscenities. And to her dismay, he still isn't aware of her presence. Unaware of her own movements, she is suddenly within feet of him, seeing a light emanating in front of his hunched over frame. He doesn't smoke, *she thinks.* So it can't be a lighter. *Although the light has a familiar hue, she holds her hands to her face, prepared to cover her eyes. She is unwilling to advance any farther. Eventually her courage surfaces. With little trepidation and heavy steps, she finally advances upon him, tapping his shoulder.*

"Jacob honey, are you all right? Did you hurt yourself?"

His turn is slow and ominous, his face about to show...

Sara woke with a scream. Bolting upright, she spun around and buried her fingernails deep into the cushions with such a grip her knuckles turned white.

"My God! What was that?" she bellowed. She wiped away tiny beads of perspiration that were forming on her forehead and the nape of her neck. Sitting on the edge of the sofa, she attempted to clear her head. More unsettled than frightened, she felt the need to evaluate the dream before it disappeared. Getting up to make some coffee, she heard the phone ring. She looked at the call display, which said *Victoria St. Medical Centre.*

"Hi, sweetheart."

He didn't get another word out. "Jacob, why are you at the clinic?"

"Oh, I did a good number cutting the side of my hand, so I needed a half-dozen stitches. I'm okay, but I'm coming home to take it easy for the rest of the day."

"Did you cut your hand with a chisel by chance?"

"Yeah, I did. That was a lucky guess. Anyway, it's no big deal. I'm fine. Did you want anything before I come home?"

"No, no. I'm fine, thank you, though. Just come home. We can have some time for ourselves. No work."

"That sounds inviting. I'll see you soon." Jacob handed the receiver back to the receptionist in the clinic. "Well, that was weird," he said. The receptionist queried why. "Oh, nothing. I think my wife is becoming psychic," he responded with an off-kilter smile.

"That could mean trouble for you," she said wryly. Jacob replied with a single nod and left for home.

Sara hung up the phone, and with a dazed look, she sat down at the kitchen table. Loudly tapping her fingernails on the arborite tabletop, she gazed momentarily out the window with nothing more to see than a few treetops and sky. She suddenly pushed away from the table and marched back to her drawings. "Coincidence. Has to be," she said en route.

Jacob came home with Sara's favourite ice cream. Happily, they coiled together on the sofa to share some maple walnut and a rare moment of peace and quiet in their hectic lives. They had the television on, but neither of them payed attention to it. They lay on the couch facing each other with one of the many afghans Sara's grandmother left to her, and before long, they drifted off together. Later in the evening, they took to the deck outside their bedroom for some fresh air and to watch the setting sun. Sara nervously revealed to Jacob the dream from earlier in the day, complete with every disturbing detail.

"The very minute I cut my hand — after saying a few choice words, of course — I instantly saw you in my mind, as clear as day. I saw you lying on the sofa, wearing the same clothes you were when I came home." Jacob was becoming animated, and his voice elevated. "Your eyes opened so wide…" A pause came, a few difficult swallows, and his eyes were tearing up. "It was like something scared the hell out of you. All I thought about on my way to get stitches was calling you. But honestly … it really gave me a chill. I didn't know … I didn't know what to think or say … or do, for that matter." He flopped back in his deck chair and ran his hands over his face and fingers through his hair.

"There's a stronger-than-normal connection between us," he continued. "Of that I have no doubt. There's something going on, and it's beyond me. My stuff is bad enough, and now this. It's a bit much right now," he said calmly and sincerely, taking a swig of his beer.

"Yes, our life has become strange for sure. But I'm relieved to hear you say that because it scared the hell out of me. I was afraid to say anything to you about it," Sara said, sharing his unease.

"You know I've never bought into this kind of stuff. This was different, though. My mom once said I was meant for better things, remember? But being with you is what makes me better." Jacob reached over and held Sara's hand. "Now that we're having this conversation, however, there's something I need to tell you about Gary."

He went on to reveal his dream about Gary and where his body was. And after it was said, he sat back in his chair and saw a look on Sara's face of what he believed was fear and disillusionment.

24

Progression

Part 1

Lying in bed with the remote in one hand and Sara's hand in the other, Jacob was intently watching the eleven o'clock news. Sara was buried deep in an article from an *Architectural Digest* magazine propped up between her knees and pregnant belly. A week passed since Jacob took the stitches out of his hand, and life had been uneventful from then — neither of them gave it another thought. Sara was gently caressing Jacob's hand, expecting to run her fingers over a ridge from the scar. She was curious as to why she wasn't feeling anything. She grabbed the bedside table lamp and pulled it close to examine his hand. Upon closer inspection, she could see the scar was no longer there. The look of shock on her face was stuck, mouth agape and eyes wide.

"Uh ... Jacob, honey." She pushed his shoulder, still staring at his hand. "Jacob!" Not getting a response, she sighed and pulled him by the chin to face her. "Will you look at this, please?"

"What?!" he growled. "Sorry. What's the matter?" He quickly dialled back the tone.

"Look," she demanded, lifting his hand, pointing to where the scar should have been. Jacob looked at his hand, and then to Sara, frozen and staring without a word. It was as if he had never been cut at all. They couldn't comprehend.

"Jacob … your scar is gone," she said, bewildered.

"What's going on with me, Sara?" he asked, with a sincere look of fear. "What's going on with us? None of this is normal." He squeezed her hand, then pulled her in tight and locked his arms around her. "I'm tired, Sara."

"I know you are, honey. I don't understand this either," she answered, trying to remain calm. "But I don't think … I don't believe it's something we need to fear." She pulled away and tried to inject some light into what seemed to be inexplicable. "What is it you say — it's up there on the strange-o-meter?"

They laughed off what remained of many unanswered questions the best they could. They ended the night in an embrace and fell asleep facing each other with the TV still on.

§

After the first week of December, Jacob and Sara welcomed their first child, Mary, into the world. She was aptly referred to as their early Christmas gift. She had the same green eyes and fire-red hair as her mother. As time ticked on, she became an amazingly perceptive and compassionate child. Her reactions were visceral, instant, and sustained if anyone close to her was hurt or feeling poorly. An endless need for discovery had her climbing into every box, cabinet or closet — accessible or not. Jacob predicted she would become a scientist or a lawyer, something that required an inquisitive mind, endlessly investigating and relentlessly demanding answers.

Easily perceived as Sara's clone, Mary had many eerily similar traits to her mother as a child, including talking articulately before she was two years old.

Mary's cry late at night had Sara scurrying to her room.

"Mary, sweetie, are you okay?" She switched the light on and approached Mary's bedside, swiftly yet gently. "Did you have a bad dream, baby?" Rubbing the tears from her eyes, Mary wasn't crying out loud, just sniffling. Sara briefly held her close before changing her nighttime diaper, but still Mary was silent. "Mary, sweetie, are you going to tell me about your dream?" Sara laid her back, ready to wipe her clean.

"Mommy, who's Jonathon?" Mary asked innocently. Sara paused before answering, choking slightly and clearing her throat.

"Jonathon? Well sweetie, I don't think I know Jonathon. Is he a new boy at daycare? Did you play with him today?"

"No. He's a bad man. He wouldn't let me play with Jacob." Mary kept talking while holding her favourite stuffed dinosaur. A horrible chill ran through Sara.

"Is Jacob a new friend at daycare?" Sara asked with trepidation.

"No. Me and Jacob played in my room. But the bad man scared him away and yelled at me, mommy." Mary's bottom lip began to quiver ever so slightly, looking like a cry might follow.

"That's okay, sweetie. Look, there's no more bad man. See?" Sara gestured around the room to show no one there except her toys. "That was just a bad dream. You go back to sleep, and you can play with your friends all you want. I'll tell the bad man to never come back. Okay, sweetie?" Sara hugged and kissed her daughter, left her room, and returned to Jacob, who was in deep slumber. She didn't wake him; she curled up as tight as she could to him, considering she was now pregnant with their second child. She stared out into the room, unable to sleep for some time wondering what could affect their next child. For the moment, though, it was Mary and her disturbing dreams that were her main focus.

Mary was the young parents' pride and joy. Once in a while she would spout out things about their past she couldn't possibly know. These events would inexplicably become a part of Mary's dialogue when she played alone with her toys. Imaginary friends would often seem familiar to Sara, more so than Jacob. And in short time, Mary's grandparents from both sides of the family quickly caught on to her delightfully capricious behaviour that mimicked Sara and Jacob as children. Her physical and verbal expressions were uncanny in their likeness to her parents. Irene thought the similarity was beyond the norm. Mary was well received within the family and close friends as a special soul uniquely aware of the world around her, well beyond her years.

Sara was ready to give birth to their second child. They'd already named him, slightly inadvertently. When the ultrasound technician asked if they wanted to know if it was a boy or girl, Jacob leaned over and tapped the screen before either could answer the question. "Look, is that a little bend there?" It was an honest question from a curious father, but to their dismay, the technician didn't hear Jacob clearly.

"So, you can tell it's a boy? Ben is the name you chose for a boy?"

"No," Jacob said with exasperation. "I asked if that was a little *bend* there. See?" He frowned at the technician. "I wondered if it was a penis. I didn't know it was a boy." Disappointed, Jacob lowered his head, upset that the cat was out of the bag.

A forced grin came when he looked over at Sara. He wasn't sure what to say. The young couple concluded that now they knew it was a boy, it was really welcomed news after having Mary.

The technician told Sara if she continued to laugh, she wouldn't be able to print off the image for them. She bemoaned about the screen on the monitor having a yellowish, almost orange tinge to it, almost like the glow of the sun, which was odd given it was a black and white screen. She said it must just be the aging equipment. Sara quickly stopped laughing and, grabbing Jacob's hand, looked at the monitor for an unusually long time.

"Ben sounds like a fine name. There must be a reason for it to have come out," she said as a matter of fact, still staring into the monitor. "What do you think, honey?"

Jacob looked at her, squinted his eyes slightly, and followed her line of sight toward the monitor for a moment, then back again. "It is a good name. Ben it is." The technician watched their reaction. Jacob, looking at Sara, cocked his head slightly, eyes opened wide and brows rising. But he decided not to call her out on her distraction.

Part 2

Benjamin Joseph Thomas O'Connell was born at eleven minutes after eleven at night, on the eleventh of November, and weighed in at a healthy seven pounds, twelve ounces. Both Sara and Ben were happy and healthy resting at home after a couple of days in the hospital. Pat and Heather brought Mary home after giving Sara the better part of the day to rest with little Ben. Jacob and Pat left the girls in the house to do the traditional lighting of the cigars. They sat in Jacob's office in the front of the shop and each enjoyed a stiff glass of smooth Irish whiskey. Jacob asked Pat how things were progressing with their municipal project at the library in Clarington.

"Am I going to be sorry to ask how the footings getting poured went? All of the conduits and town services inspected and passed? We've been lucky with the weather. It would be nice to pour before we get a real cold snap." There was a hint of distress in his voice.

Pat simply smiled and raised his glass. "To Ben," he said, winking at Jacob. "You gotta lighten up, Jake. For Christ's sake, you and Sara just had a son delivered to you. Breathe, man," he exclaimed.

"Yes, to Ben. My son. Wow ... a son," Jacob said humbly. "All right, Pat, I get it ... loud and clear: I have been wound for a bit."

"A bit?" Pat huffed with a smile. "How long have we known each other now?"

"I know, I know," Jacob said, and a long pause followed. He looked down to the floor, sweeping the fine sawdust with his foot. He looked back up, straight at his business partner and best friend. "I have to say I'm a lucky man. Everything went really well, with both Ben and Mary. Sara has more strength and courage than ten men. You should have seen her. No, wait ... you shouldn't have." They both laughed. And then Pat became somewhat serious and filled their glasses with another shot, just a single this time.

"Look, I know how hard this is with Vargas on the scene, and we'll deal with him somehow. But you have to stop and appreciate what you have in this life, my friend. We both started out banging nails framing houses and now we have a successful business — like really successful — and in short time. Our families are in the same area, and we're still in our thirties … barely. There's a lot more ahead of us is what I'm saying, you know?"

"I do get it, Pat. I do, seriously. It's because of what we have, and who we have that reminds me there's so much on the line. Plus, I have an overabundance of the protection gene. It causes me to have my guard up all the time with this guy. It's not just me anymore, it's all of us."

Jacob raised his glass for the second time, and Pat did so in kind.

"I know, Jacob, but let's both take care of it and cut the worry in half. If it was me, I wouldn't want to go up against the two of us any day of the week. And besides, we've got a strong crew of people in our life, professionally and personally, so try and relax a bit."

They clinked their glasses, and the smooth whiskey went down. They extinguished their cigars and both returned to their respective families and on with what the day held in store for them.

Part 3

The following summer, Jacob wrapped up his early morning work in the shop and went inside the house to clean up. He entered to find Mary playing in the living room with her toys and Ben bouncing up and down in the jumper hanging in the kitchen doorway. Sara was looking over the company's schedule when Jacob stopped on his way to the sink to give her a kiss on the cheek.

"You must be seriously wrapped up in that scheduling, sweetheart. You didn't even acknowledge my kiss." Jacob was being jovial. Sara remained quiet, not lifting her head from the paperwork in front of her.

"She had the dream again last night." Sara's voice was flat. "That's three times in as many months. I'm worried about her, Jacob." Sara looked over to Mary, her chin showing a sign of tremor. Jacob became dejected.

"I know, Sara. You became different in that way, the minute you got pregnant with Mary." Jacob pulled out a chair and joined her at the table. "But you haven't had any dreams or premonitions since then. So, maybe it'll pass for Mary too." Jacob didn't sound entirely convinced of his own words.

"That I've told you about," Sara spouted.

"Sorry, what's that?" Jacob didn't wait for a reply. "Why didn't you tell me? Don't you think it's important to let me know about these things, after everything we've been through?" His tone was more hurt than angry.

"I'm sorry, honey, but you deal with enough as it is. I didn't want to add to it. Besides, if I told you every time it happens, you would be inundated with it. So, that's why." Sara was sincerely amiable in her response to Jacob.

He rose from the table, pushed the chair in, and went to kiss Ben.

"Let's talk tonight. I have to go into town now," Jacob said, coming around the table to kiss Sara goodbye first, then he went over to Mary and picked her up in his arms.

"Goodbye, my little Dora the Explorer," he said, while her favourite show of the same name played in the background. He kissed her cheeks repeatedly and, while hugging her tight, he looked to Sara, anguished. "I love you, Mrs. O'Connell." The same came back from Sara as he rushed out the door and headed straight to his truck. His breathing was suddenly interrupted by small gasps. His skin began to tingle and his body shook like he had just fought off an attacking invasion of insects. The expression of distress on his face equalled the tremble in his voice while talking to himself. He'd heard it all his life: he wore his heart on his sleeve.

Part 4

Jacob had a stop in Port Darlington for the Glencross boathouse project, which included a second-floor suite and a loft above. These kinds of jobs kept Pat busy, even in lean times. As he was nearing the site, his cell phone started ringing. It was Charlie Dennis, his framer, calling. Jacob didn't need to have the conversation, since he was now closing in on the towering flames and could hear the sirens outside as well as through the phone. Sure enough, the boathouse walls and second floor were now a massive bonfire, and the structure was crumbling in on itself. A thought back to a conversation in a parkade had brought a sharp pain to Jacob's temple, flashing through possible scenarios. When he arrived and looked on this unbelievable scene, his stomach muscles began tightening to fight off a rising nausea. He clenched his jaw muscles to stop the piercing pain just under the soft part of his jawbone. He was salivating, as he always did when he was about to vomit, but he managed to fight it off this time. He walked to the operator of the fire truck to check if there were any injuries, or worse.

He saw Charlie standing, staring blankly, mesmerized by the destruction of what was left aflame. Jacob went over to him. As he approached, a loud explosion went off, scaring everyone into a guarded reaction, with arms raised in front of their faces. The gas tank of the site generator had blown, as the jerrycan was discarded yards away from the building — a clear indication that the fire was intentionally set.

"You okay, Charlie?"

Charlie's hands and face were black from handling some of the burnt pieces that had landed out on the street. He turned his head and looked to Jacob.

"I'm good. No one was hurt. I need to start looking for another job, though," Charlie said, returning his gaze to what was left of the boathouse.

"What makes you say that?" Jacob said, pointing to the boathouse. "Because of that? You didn't burn it down. That's not your fault, Charlie. And no, you're not losing your job," Jacob sounded adamant.

"This job was my responsibility and look what happened."

Jacob put his hand on Charlie's shoulder.

"The work is your responsibility, Charlie. You're not a full-time security guard, so relax buddy, that's what insurance is for."

"Jesus, Jacob, watching how quick it burned, it couldn't have started more than ten — maybe fifteen — minutes before I got here." Charlie became angry pointing to the lead fireman. "That fuckhead there asked me if I spilled gas from the generator. He said it like I was dumb enough to set the fire."

"That guy can go pound salt. Let's put up some caution tape around the site after these guys are done. First, though, let's get a coffee and maybe calm down a bit."

To Charlie's relief, his job was still secure, and when they'd finished their coffees, Jacob left him knowing that except for the fire, everything was fine. Jacob's next stop was at the town library to meet up with Pat to go over their projects' status and scheduling. When he showed up, he was as disappointed as he'd expected he would be.

"I just heard. Everyone okay? Do they know how it started?" Pat asked.

"No, they couldn't figure out how to light a pack of matches," Jacob said, shaking his head.

"Okay, then. You're obviously pissed. What happened?"

"Ah, nothing really. They just pissed Charlie off with some stupid questions. And I don't blame him for getting angry. I would be too. Well, I am, actually. But anyway… So, what the hell is this prick doing to us now?" Jacob asked in reference to Vargas slowing down the project with inspection failures.

"We're okay now. He just passed it and the steel is going in this afternoon. Everything will be ready for the hollow core in a couple weeks."

"And time for another inspection to fail. Son of a bitch!"

"Ah, relax Jacob. It's the Rangar crew. The brothers, not their subs. Alvin Rangar has a huge company and his inspections don't fail. I doubt even Vargas is stupid enough to piss off Rangar."

"Good, we need a break going forward on this one. We shouldn't have taken it, really, knowing the time it takes to get paid," Jacob said, with his irritation obvious, rubbing his brow with thumb and index finger.

"Jake, what's going on with you? We're okay, buddy." Pat motioned toward the site trailer with his rolled-up blueprints. "Come on inside. We have enough money and the other jobs are going well, with the exception of the boathouse burning down, but that was a fluke and the insurance will cover it." Inside the trailer, Jacob was quiet and still looked distracted. "Is that what's got you so riled up? Or is it something else? Everything okay with Sara and the kids?"

"Sara and the kids are great. And no, it's not the boathouse — although to me, that fire is suspicious at best. It's Vargas. It's about him fucking with me my whole working life and now through our livelihood. Fuck! Just last week he held up the tapers so he could count drywall screws. Believe that!?" Jacob's voice was not only rising, it was shaky. "If he would just come after me, then I could deal with it once and for all. But messing with our jobs, whether it's permits or inspections, it slows us down, slows down our income too. And not to mention the shit with Sara. Fucking prick!"

"Whoa. Jacob, this is really getting to you. Listen, we can deal with him together. We'll go to the town council or the MP, whatever it takes. But you need to calm down or you're going to stroke out on me, buddy. Look, you're starting to twitch."

Pat laughed hard enough that Jacob couldn't help but relent and laugh along.

"Seriously, though, if you let this get to you to that point, you'll just end up hurting the guy. And if that comes about, well, you know what happens then."

Jacob took a moment to digest what his partner and friend was saying. "Yeah, you're right. I'll head back to the shop and keep going on the furniture for this place. That always calms me down."

"You might want to consider taking some more time with Sara and the kids. We're all right. I got it under control here," Pat said, squeezing and gently shaking Jacob's shoulder.

"I know that. I just want to make sure we keep ahead of the schedule as much as possible. Besides, the house is right there. I can go in and see them any time. Christ, Sara's getting more work done with a newborn and Mary than I am, so we'll be all right." Jacob's mood began to lift.

"Tell you what, Jake, I'll talk to Uncle John and ask him what he thinks about this shit with Vargas. See if there are any ways to bust him, maybe enough to lose his job. And who knows, maybe he'll move if he has to get another job." Pat's words helped calm Jacob that much more.

"I suppose it doesn't hurt to try. Thanks, Pat man."

"How many times do I have to say ... it's Superman, not Patman!" They shared a laugh and said their goodbyes.

Jacob headed back to work at the woodshed. As he often did, he stopped along the way to get Sara some flowers. In the store, he came across a bouquet that looked similar to what he got her at the market where he had the vision of Gary. He never did say anything to the police about Vargas; he believed they would think he was crazy. And the two detectives who dressed like Don Cherry hadn't gained any results from their investigation. Jacob did his level best to try and distance himself from Vargas, but he bumped up against his creeping presence almost everywhere now.

The dreams Sara began to experience after becoming pregnant with Mary had morphed into her seeing things from Jacob's perspective, but only in those she had at night though. She couldn't understand how the ones during the day contrasted so starkly from those at night. And eerily, the ones during the day were in real time, with Sara standing just behind him. When she became pregnant with Ben, the intensity of those dreams increased. She started to feel it was a curse, but when she considered what Jacob was going through, she decided to accept this curse with little complaint.

25

Small World

Part 1

The stories John Keegan told Jacob over the years about some of his cases were chilling, and they all stayed with Jacob. Stories from a cop, especially one who served a good portion of his career as a homicide detective, gave him an appreciation of what the world was really like beyond his own door. John not only worked all over his province, he worked some hard cases in other parts of Canada as well; however, Saint John was home base.

John and Jacob agreed there are seriously evil people in the world — not the people who just do bad things, but those who don't have the same moral hardwiring as most. They believed that type of evil — antithetical to love, compassion and remorse — was in the deviant's every breath. Jacob was shocked to hear some of John's experiences, but it helped him know what to watch for. Both Pat and Jacob looked up to John when they were kids, and they still did. He'd taught them many needed lessons.

The Rebecca Jacobsen case had resulted in John's ardent belief of evil as something from a dark place, a place not of this world. Evil was something that was injected into our lives, he'd say, like black tar heroin into a vein. He believed there was no redemption whatsoever for any kind of sexual abuse, regardless of degree. And he once confided to Jacob and Pat that he could just as easily put a bullet through a priest's head for abusing a child as any other person — if the law allowed it, of course. However, he remained at odds over the fact that with murder, there are often mitigating circumstances that resulted in certain considerations.

What happened to young Rebecca sadly checked all the boxes of evil, which added to his rage. Although he'd been retired from the force for well over a decade now, the Jacobsen case continued to haunt him. He walked out of the precinct on his last day with the only copy of the original case file. With Marlene gone now, he spent his evenings examining and re-examining the file. During his morning coffee, he spread the file over the kitchen table, keeping the crime scene photos in a pile that he didn't look at. Page by page, again and again, he pulled the folder apart and reassembled it.

Eventually, he made a break in the case, albeit a small one, over twenty-five years after the case went cold. Stopping in at his old precinct one day, he went through the evidence box and file for what must have been the hundredth or more time. This time, though, he grabbed a single-page report with a small arc on the bottom corner of the page — a coffee stain. Shocked by his discovery, he stomped over to the records clerk and showed the paper to him. "What's this? When did this go in the file? There's no record of it in the log on the inside of the folder." He couldn't believe a report of a patrolman's interview with a witness from the neighbourhood would have been forgotten. He didn't have a copy of it.

"What the…? How could I have missed this? How could anyone miss this?" John's voice started to crack. He asked the clerk if he knew of anyone adding this, and a quick search through the computer showed nothing.

"John, if someone put that report in there, it wasn't logged in. Sorry," said a disappointed clerk. "You would think it would've been brought up to you." Everyone in the station knew of John's obsession over the case, and given that he was well-liked and respected, they were sure to update him on anything related to the file.

The report indicated that a local homeowner had seen a young man who was unfamiliar to the area in the convenience store close to the crime scene when Rebecca went missing. And the witness saw him close enough to identify a tattoo of a crucifix with a snake wrapped around it on his forearm. Now John would have someone from his old precinct try to match that tattoo with someone in the database, and maybe it would lead him to a viable suspect. He was back on the case, on the hunt. He found purpose again with a hope to give Rebecca Jacobsen justice, and peace of mind for her father and her other remaining relatives. This news quickly made it to Jacob by way of his best friend.

No visions of any kind — after seeing Gary in his rear-view — had surfaced for Jacob. However, recalling what happened in the flower shop, then and now, combined with this latest news about Rebecca Jacobsen, caused him to get his guard up, and the headaches came back. The news about the Jacobsen case brought back the many memories of those conversations with John. After past experiences, and adding to that Sara's and Mary's dreams, it pushed him to try and fill in some of those blank moments from his past. With Sara's help in piecing his past together, he figured out what happened each time he blacked out, but that was still only part of the puzzle. Sara worried that this endeavour could irreversibly hurt him, or possibly kill him. She had to be careful how she went about revealing information to him surrounding those lost memories. However, that time came, and with Sara's blessings, he headed home for a visit with unusual intentions.

The return to his hometown was usually exciting for Jacob. Driving past his high school always elicited fond memories. On this occasion, the memories sharply disappeared. He slowed his rental car to a crawl as he approached the property where Rebecca was murdered. The land was expropriated, the shack razed, and it had become a small public park dedicated to Rebecca Jacobsen, which was a nice tribute to a wonderful girl, but also a hard reminder of a brutal crime. After her death, the path to the small creek was cleared, widened, and lined with light posts.

And as he looked across the property, it happened again: Jacob saw Rebecca standing at the edge of the property. He knew her as a teen — not intimately, but enough to say a passing "hi" in school or about town. Now she stood with her back up against some mountain maples and hemlock bushes that lined the small wooded area at the rear of the park. She was difficult to make out through the swings and see-saw horses that somewhat obscured her presence. She almost blended in — camouflaged, part of the foliage.

He stopped the car and twisted around to take a good look. His whole body instantly felt weakened, like the life had been drained out of him. The onset of a painful cluster headache pierced his temple, and he flashed to Sara's accident scene as a child. As he slowly walked toward Sara, the pain in his temple increased its intensity. He turned to look down the sidewalk to see that teenage boy again, and — *snap* — he was back. Rubbing his temple, and briefly squeezing the folds of his abdomen, he regained his composure. Looking back to the park, he could barely make her out, seeing her phase in and out of sight, merging with the trees and bushes and reappearing again. He gathered the strength back from his rubbery limbs, jumped out of the car, and raced over. Just a few feet past the sidewalk and onto the property, he abruptly slowed his run to a slow step and stopped. Feeling his heart pounding in his chest, he stopped only to see her in full figure for what seemed a mere second. She smiled, then permanently faded back into the surrounding bushes. He backed up several steps and called out, "I'm not up for hide and seek today." Hoping he wasn't seen or heard, he was swiftly back in his car and speeding down the road. *Why is this happening to me?* he thought. *I can't do this again. I don't want to do this again.*

Part 2

For Thomas and Irene, having Jacob visit for an indeterminate amount of time at this point in his life was out of the ordinary, but they welcomed it all the same. After parking on the street, their son was barely onto the driveway when they could see the signs of distress on his face and in his body language. "He probably just needs a break, honey. We've both been there," Irene said, protective of her youngest.

"He looks worn out. He's been working too much," came the predictable reply for Thomas. The level of his voice tapered off as Jacob drew closer. His father's hearing was poor enough to cause his voice to elevate, and Jacob heard what he said. He didn't want either of his parents to worry about him. *They don't need the strain*, he thought. They were standing on the front porch ready to receive their son, wearing big, happy smiles. His smile beamed equally bright the instant he saw his folks.

He noticed immediately that they seemed much older now, which made sense since they were both in their seventies. Still, it was jarring for Jacob to see his parents had aged when he wasn't looking. Irene's hair was short and silver with streaks of white and she remained thin and in great shape. She looked as beautiful as ever in one of her flowery summer dresses and cork sandals. She took good care of herself, and her attention to detail about her appearance remained impeccable. Jacob did notice her head shaking a little bit, which concerned him. *Parkinson's?* he worried. His father's salt and pepper hair — more salt of late — kept him looking robust as always. He looked his old familiar self, standing next to his mother in his usual khaki shorts and a thin, short-sleeved, plaid shirt for the summer. He still had the frame of a well-built man, but Jacob noticed that the parts were sagging. Jacob already knew, from time spent with seniors, that nearing the end of life draws all parts of you in a downward direction. The seniors in his life were very comfortable with him. He learned early on that the mind changes very little over a lifetime — you still think of yourself as young as you age — but your shell indicates otherwise.

Like most evenings, Thomas fell asleep in what had become *his* La-Z-Boy. And like most evenings in the summer and early fall, he enjoyed his second-favourite pastime — watching a Blue Jays game — hockey holding the number one spot.

It was on the swinging sofa on the rear deck that Jacob decided to engage his mother with what he believed would be a difficult conversation. However, he didn't even get to finish his opening sentence. "Mom, I need to know something about me from—"

"I know what you want to ask about, Jacob. I've been waiting a long time for this day to come. You're missing memories and trying to remember causes those headaches. I'm sorry, sweetie, Sara and I have been talking … for a long time. To be honest, I didn't want to provoke anything else before by telling you. Not that we could control any of it anyway. Your father and I didn't understand what was happening to you, and honestly, we were frightened for you."

"So, you've known about this the whole time? I'll have to have a talk with Sara about that," Jacob said, with a wink. "I have to tell you, Mom, it's been a plague to me my whole life. The headaches are starting to back off a little. That is, if I avoid trying to recall certain memories too intensely."

"I'm so glad to hear that. Our reason for not talking to you about this wasn't just the headaches. We worried that you weren't ready to understand, for one; and, most importantly, we didn't want people to find out," Irene paused to gauge her son's reactions before she continued, pleased he didn't show any signs of disappointment or having taken offense.

"They're starting to subside because you're becoming aware of your gift. And it *is* a gift, Jacob, an amazing gift," she said, reaching down, laying her hand on top of his. "And we had to make sure no one else found out or you might have been taken away from us. We were so very worried about you … always."

Jacob hung his head and expelled a long sigh. "Yeah, I get that, Mom. I'm not even sure I want to know any of this." Then he leaned back and rested his head on his mother's shoulder. He felt like a child, momentarily, and wished his mother could make his troubles and fears disappear. "Ah, I'm wasted, Mom. This has made me incredibly worn out."

Irene patted her son's head, smiling. "We didn't know what to do about it other than try and protect you the best we could."

"Oh, I don't doubt that for a second, Mom. I'm not angry or upset toward you or Dad about any of this. How could I be? And I'm not actually angry. Confused, frustrated ... confused." He let out a weak giggle.

"You always were a sensitive child — compassionate, caring, empathetic — and you always tried to help others. Why do you think I always called you my little care package? But you were tough too, and together, those are all good traits, sweetie," Irene proudly said.

"You need to understand this, Jacob," Irene said sternly. "We don't know how this happens. When or why it happens, nor the reason behind it. And we're not entirely sure that you're supposed to know either ... or anyone, for that matter. Anyway, my point is we were, and still are, scared for you about all of this." Irene was becoming a little shaky with emotion.

"Are you okay, Mom? We don't need to talk about this."

"No, it's okay. But thanks, though," she said, tapping the back of his hand. "The first time we saw it happen you were only four ... or five. I'm not sure exactly. Anyway, a finch flew into the living room window so hard it killed him. You saw it happen and ran out to its rescue, convinced he was only knocked out. You insisted that if you could put it in a box with some grass and worms, you could save it.

"So, we decided to let you try to save the bird. You were so serious, we had to. Your dad got an old shoebox and you both went out in the backyard for grass and to dig up some worms for the bird to eat. We thought after you fell asleep, we would take the bird out and tell you it flew away in the middle of the night.

"It broke our hearts watching you tend to this bird, waiting for it to respond somehow. We went in your room to check on you near your bedtime, and there you were, in the middle of the room, sitting on the floor with the bird in your hands. Your back was to us. And then a light glowed in front of you. We thought you had a flashlight. When we bent down to see what you were doing, the light stopped. There was no flashlight. The bird took off and started flying around the room. Needless to say, we were shocked."

Jacob's emotions were rising to the surface. He began to shed a tear. "What's wrong with me, Mom?" His face was showing the strain now.

"Wrong? There's nothing wrong with you, sweetie," Irene said, turning to face Jacob straight on and holding his hand. "You seem to be blessed with an ability to heal people who are seriously injured, so it seems. I don't think it's like you can run around healing the sick … I'm pretty sure. But nothing about this makes you wrong in any way, shape, or form," she said with conviction, then looked him in the eye. "This is not something you can control, Jacob. I think you have to learn to accept that. What you can control is how you live your life for you and your family. The question you're left with is, what do you do about this now that you know? Promise me always that you'll be so very careful — for you, Sara, and the kids."

26

Awakening

Part 1

It was a slow and difficult process for Jacob to absorb what he discovered in segments of time with Sara, and then so much at once from his mother. For some time, the mood that seemed to surround him was one of melancholy, and at times he became despondent from the weight of it. Little happened over the next few years to bring up past events any more than usual. And avoiding that subject altogether suited Jacob just fine. Sara, however, remained guarded. Jacob had spent many long days in the shop, with a few workers and signed contracts waiting in line.

The doldrums of what felt like a never-ending winter, constantly enclosed with overcast skies, hit most people that year. And the relentless, bitterly cold, face-numbing stretches with little relief, placed a different pressure on Pat and Heather. Eighteen years ago, they'd had a small wedding followed by a short honeymoon in Niagara Falls consisting of only two days and one night. They endured a steady drizzle of rain the entire time. Now, in the depths of February, they were immured, and moaned an incurable desire for escape. If there were to remain any optimism for the beginning of 2005, they needed to take this long overdue holiday — a well-deserved Barbados honeymoon.

With their suitcases on the sidewalk in the airport's parkade, Jacob bid them farewell. "All right, you guys, have a great time and don't even think about work. Just enjoy." Jacob smiled, waved and turned around, walking back to his truck. Suddenly he was pelted in the back of the head from a perfectly thrown snowball of fresh packing snow. He stopped and stooped over to brush the snow away from around his neck. When he was first hit, he was annoyed, his expression clear. But when he turned around to see Heather laughing, and Pat armed with another childhood projectile, ready and willing to fire, he started laughing like he was a kid again.

Seeing Pat's arm rising again, he made a mad dash for cover. He grabbed a scoop of snow from the three-foot-high concrete guardrail while in motion, but before he could turn, he was hit with two more snowballs. *Was Pat two-fisted?* When he made cover on the other side of the box of his truck, he saw Heather and Pat, suitcases and carry-on bags tossed to the side, digging their bare hands into the fresh snowfall for more ammunition. They were all laughing while continuing the barrage of heavily packed white ammo, being gunned back and forth.

"You're children!" Jacob yelled out. "You're going to be soaked by the time you board the plane."

"Does it look like we care?" Pat shot back to his best friend.

"Jacob, we're going to be on a beach in the next eight hours. Who cares?" Heather shouted out in a voice of childish joy.

"Okay, okay ... cease fire," Pat said, clearing himself off, and reaching a hand to help clear the snow from Heather's hair and neck. Their laughter was slowly subsiding when Jacob walked back over to his friends. He squeezed them both with a rare hug.

"Thanks, guys. I needed that," he said, his smile turning with emotion.

"Yeah you did, Jake," Pat said softly. "Give our best to Sara and the little ones." He and Heather proudly took on the role of godparents. They loved Mary and Ben as their own.

They gathered their belongings and carried on toward the departure area inside of the airport. Jacob watched them walking away, thankful for what just transpired. "We love you, Jacob," Heather yelled out with a wave. Jacob was caught off guard.

"I love you guys, too," he said with difficulty. It was not usual for him to convey such sentiments aloud.

He was back behind the wheel, the key inserted in the ignition, but paused suddenly. He let go of the keys and folded his arms to rest on top of the steering wheel, laying his head on top of them. His chest started to heave, and a bellowing cry came from somewhere deep inside, surprising himself. It went on for a couple of minutes, with at least a couple more to compose himself before starting the engine. Looking out beyond the parkade to see the snow continuing to accumulate made his thoughts go back to his father clearing snow from the cars and the driveway at home when he was seven. And he remembered his head injury that same day and a dream in surgery of a bird he'd saved at four years of age. He'd identified the bird rescue as the origin of this distressing part of his life. His mother told him of that bird, and his study of the events that followed painted an oblique picture of what he thought his direction was. This time the headache rose weakly, and, unexpectedly, it quickly faded with the memory — shorter and so much less painful than what he would normally endure.

Pat and Heather had flown out on a Wednesday, and when Jacob returned to the shop shortly before noon after dropping them off, he gave his crew the rest of the week off with pay — no reason, he told them to "just go and enjoy some time with family and friends" and not to come back until the following Tuesday. "Valentine's Day is Monday," he reminded them.

Jacob was off to check in with their latest project, The Cider Mill, on the outskirts of town. Sara's blueprints had been submitted several months back and were finally approved and ready for pickup. Before the next phase could continue, a demolition inspection was needed, much to Jacob's chagrin, never having seen such a requirement before. Yet another delay to one of their projects, as always because of Vargas, he was sure. There hadn't been any major occurrences with Vargas, but there had been some heated arguments in the office and on site. Jacob would occasionally run into him, and although the looks were deadly, he always managed to maintain control.

On this day, there was apprehension in Sara's steps walking into the building department to pick up the permit. Having to deal with Vargas was highly probable. Just inside the municipal building, she started feeling cold chills. She stopped, closed her eyes, and took a long, deep breath. During the exhale, she suddenly thought of what followed being hit by a car from behind while riding her bike home all those years ago. The same feelings were rising again at the thought of being anywhere near Vargas, after all the time dealing with his aggression at work. The hit she laid on that janitor for what he did was vividly replaying in her mind. *That's what this bastard needs*, she thought, putting a boost in her energy getting up the last of the steps.

"Hi, Shelley. How are you?" Sara said with a smile, entering the office. "I'm here to pick up The Cider Mill permit." She was grateful to see her friend come to the counter, alone.

"Sara, honey. I'm fine. How are you? It's so nice to see you. The kids must keep you running off your feet?" Shelley was equally pleased to see her friend. Shelley was a rare, overly energetic character — so Sara thought — with bright, fake orange hair always tied up with a leather and wooden stick barrette. She had big lips with glossy ruby-red lipstick, and during summer days, she was often seen wearing a red polka-dotted white dress to highlight a gorgeous full figure. She would complete a picture if she smacked her gum and spoke with a nasally New York accent. Sara found her exuberant attitude contagious. But her glee quickly disappeared as she saw Vargas's head pop up from beyond the glass wall surrounding the top half of his office.

"I gather everything is okay with Jacob and the kids?"

"Oh yeah, they're all fine. Thanks for asking. They keep me—"

"Ready for phase two, Sara?" Vargas interrupted, without looking her in the eye, as he waddled over to her in his signature short uptight strides.

"Yes, we are," was Sara's short and cold reply.

"I sent Jeff down yesterday to complete the demo inspection."

"I know that, Jonathon, that's why I'm here ... for the permit." Sara was becoming increasingly irritated. Vargas was usually dismissive to anything she had to say.

"I hear your man's partner in crime is on holiday," he said, shuffling papers on the counter and averting his eyes downward. The room became silent and Sara started tapping her fingernails on top of the countertop. *Tick, tick, tick.* She stared straight at him, but he wouldn't look back. It appeared he had great difficulty with confronting strong-willed women like Sara. Other than in situations that common sense told her she could be in danger, she feared no one.

"Yes, so I understand," she responded.

There would be no elaborating or small talk. Inside, she was vibrating in anger and hoping for Shelley to return and take over. He finally looked down at Sara over the top of his bifocals. It was clear to all that he was doing just that, looking down on her. And once again, he stopped to gawk at her cleavage. This enraged Sara even more, but she closed her eyes a few seconds and a deep breath kept her composure intact.

"Well, you would know. I mean he's your business partner, and your man's best friend." His comment came in a tired breath, like a disappointed teacher.

"Jacob, Jonathon. His name is Jacob. And I don't keep tabs on Pat. I'm just the designer," she said abruptly.

In a completely inappropriate, low and suggestive tone of voice, as he slid his bifocals up and rested them atop his head, he said, "Oh, you're a lot more than that, Sara." He leaned his elbows on the surface of the counter and propped up his chin. Sara's face was becoming increasingly red, and her look at that moment would have intimidated most anyone.

"The permit ... please?" she delivered through gritted teeth.

Shelley returned and was obviously uncomfortable on Sara's behalf. She had been doing her best to ignore her boss's totally unprofessional behaviour. She leaned across the counter and pulled the paperwork from his hand, pushing him aside.

"Here's your permit package and receipt, honey. You take care now and make sure you give my best to Jacob and the kids. How time flies, eh? I forgot to ask, how's Ben enjoying the new toys we rounded up for the daycare?" Shelley hoped the conversation would drive her boss away and back to his office. Sara relented her anger to resume her polite engagement with Shelley.

"He loves them. I hear they all love them. We did pretty good on that toy drive. Anyway, thanks again, Shelley. Gotta go now," said Sara, looking at Vargas with a vicious smile. She grabbed the permit and receipt and did an about-face toward the door.

Vargas's head could be seen literally vibrating from clenching his jaw so hard. His reaction was to Shelley's intimate friendship with Sara and familiarity with Jacob and the kids. He was a dark, negative force to it all, a pariah. "You're welcome," he said to no response. "Do you believe that shit? What a bitch."

Shelley gave Vargas a clear look of disapproval and disgust. "That's inappropriate, Jonathon. No matter how you feel, it's wrong in this, or any, office." Her eyes were a squint. Clearly ignorant to, and lacking any social graces, Vargas shuffled back to his glass kingdom of power.

Part 2

"Prick!" Sara screamed out at the top of her lungs from inside the Suburban, gripping the steering wheel and shaking it, imagining it was Vargas's neck. She looked over at the building permit sitting on the passenger seat, slammed the gearshift into drive and screamed the tires over the salt and ice, sliding out of the parking lot. Shuddering from the experience with her ex-boss and *general plague*, as she often referred to him, she felt the need to take a shower. She had too many years of his entirely inappropriate behaviour from having to work under him. Her complaints to the union went mostly unanswered and his behaviour remained unchecked. She decided to put most of it aside, thinking only of a future for her and Jacob. She knew she would never have found that kind of pay, benefits or pension fund anywhere else, and that's the only reason she'd stayed so long at her job in the city. It was a sacrifice she endured and now they were reaping the benefits.

Now, however, was something entirely different, and again her fear was turning to anger and both were justified. The wind had brought the plague to their town. Pat's usual responsibility of getting permits fell to Sara this time. At this point, though, her feelings were more alert and heightened from the strange connection she now had with Jacob. And she now felt that this man was a danger to her and Jacob, and to her horror, possibly to her children as well. Like Jacob, she believed Vargas's move to Clarington wasn't a coincidence.

She decided to go to the daycare to pick up Ben, then together they would go get Mary from school and head home. Jacob was back working in the office out in the woodshed when she arrived with the kids. She was earlier than usual and had Mary with her, too, which got Jacob's attention. He nervously went out to greet them.

Crossing the wide lane, little Ben came running over and jumped up into his father's arms. Ben had chocolate stains all over his hands and face and the cute little overalls he was wearing. Mary wasn't far behind, still daintily working on her giant chocolate chip cookie.

"Look, Daddy, mommy got us a treat, and it's not even Saturday."

"I see that, honey. It looks good, too. Can daddy have a bite?"

Jacob had Ben in one arm and Mary holding his free hand. Together they trudged through the snow back over to Sara and he greeted her with a kiss, as always. He immediately noticed the look on her face, which, though uncommon for her, was telling. He knew she had to pick up the permit today, and her face confirmed the presumption of who she had to deal with.

"So, was it bad?" Jacob said while walking the kids toward the front porch.

"We'll talk about it later. Let's get the kids inside and cleaned up." Sara, holding both kids' winter coats, leaned over to wipe Mary's school uniform, which was a white button-up shirt, and a green-and-black plaid pleated skirt, with black leotards. She attended a Catholic school only because of school jurisdictions; neither parent was religious. It didn't bother Sara, but it irked Jacob.

"You can go back to the shop after we're done here. You'll have a couple of hours before supper time." Sara held the door open for the kids.

"Call me a half hour early, and I'll come and help get it ready, okay?" Jacob said, leaning in to give Sara another kiss. After the children were washed and changed, and out of their school clothes, Jacob walked across the yard, and gave a final wave. As he turned and headed toward the shop, the smile dropped from his face like a weight had pulled it down. He was thinking of what Sara must have endured earlier that day. The stress of thinking about it was wearing on him, so he did what he does best — he went to create in his workshop.

Later that night, after Mary and Ben were tucked safely into bed, the tired couple took to the loveseat in front of the fireplace. They snuggled up to each other with a glass of wine to discuss the day's events. Sara was sick of Vargas, so that conversation was shelved for now.

She wanted to talk about Jacob's gift-curse. She knew his memories had developed quite a bit, but the elusive moment of putting his hands on someone remained blank, a white blinding, needle-piercing pain of a blank. After his talk with his mother, however, he was left knowing more.

"I never did tell you everything my grandmother said, and you've never told me what your mom said to you about this. Who goes first?" Sara said, slow to turn and look at Jacob.

"I'll go. She told me everything, I hope. Apparently, she's known all along, but couldn't tell me." Jacob lifted his head in a faux air of righteousness. "But apparently ... you two together knew more than I did."

"I'm sorry, honey. I was worried about you. I had to find out if she knew something about it." Sara feigned a sheepish look, batting her eyes to reduce any possible animosity. "Are you angry with me? Are you going to tell me what she said?"

"Of course I'm not angry. But I'll tell you what. Why don't you tell me what your grandmother said first? Then I'll tell you my mom's version of events. Maybe together we might be able to understand what exactly this is." Jacob opened up his hands, palms facing him. "These hands, and what they can do."

After they finished their talk, Jacob faced a long, difficult night. He endured the horrible experience of being in a state of semi-consciousness while perceiving his dreams and nightmares in what felt like real time. A cascade of memories, varying from the raw and tragic to ones of intense emotional release, tumbled before him. He lay on his back while all of this rolled down on a giant screen in front of him, like he was watching a movie at a cinema. Unlike in Sara's dreams where she stood behind Jacob without being able to see everything that happened, this dream showed it all — the good, bad, indifferent, and evil. The memories rolled from top to bottom, starting with him as a child to him now. Nothing was missing, except his ability to recall it all when he woke the next morning.

Jacob's neck was stiff, his head and pillow were soaked in sweat, and his every joint hurt like he had a bad flu. He slowly rose in bed, and sat there, staring straight ahead, appearing totally lost. Sara was equally exhausted, feeling like she had been fighting all night. It was an early rise at 5 a.m., still pitch-black out. Sara looked over to Jacob and shook his arm to get his attention. When she reached up to run her fingers through his wet hair, she couldn't ignore the significant amount of grey hair in addition to what he had the night before. She knew the toll that trying to understand all of this was taking on him.

27

Profile

It was mid-June, and Pat was on site at The Cider Mill, going over the status for scheduling trades to come. He was so deep into the calendar, not just for scheduling trades, but also costs, payments, and the next draw from the bank — it was a balancing act — that he didn't hear Hector Stewart, the website designer for Able Hands, calling out his name. He'd stopped in on the off-chance Jacob was there with Pat. He wanted to pass on what he had gleaned from Pat's uncle John about Vargas.

The project still had more work to be done before calling for any inspections. This meant there was no reason for anyone from the building department to be on site. And it was still too early in the morning for the trades to get started. Hector walked in and stuck his head through the plastic barrier in the building's entrance.

"Yo, Pat! How's life?"

"Oh, you know … still above ground. How you doin', Heck? What's up? Are you here to take some pictures for the website?"

"I could do that, but that's not why I stopped in. I wasn't sure if Jacob was here with you or not, so I thought I'd take a shot."

"Jacob? He doesn't usually get involved with that. What do you need him for?"

"I have that information he asked me about, didn't he tell you?" Hector was surprised Pat was unaware of what Jacob was up to. What Hector actually did for him would be no surprise at all to Pat.

"No, Heck. Why, what is it?"

Hector informed Pat that John was running Vargas's name for him on Jacob's behalf. John had done this for Hector several times over the years when Hector was a reporter for the *Sun*. It was a tit-for-tat arrangement common among police and reporters.

"You're not going to believe this," Hector said, opening up a large file folder.

"Believe what, Heck. What's the big scoop?"

"His name isn't Vargas."

Pat kept looking at Hector, frozen in curiosity; no words were coming out. He worried that something had happened to force Jacob's hand to involve Hector and his uncle John.

"Did something happen between Jacob and Vargas recently?"

"Not that I know about," Hector continued without a cue from Pat. "So, his name was originally Vargascelli. And…" Hector flipped through the pages. "Your man, Vargascelli, is originally from Saint John … right in your own backyard, buddy. And … to your uncle's shock, coincidentally, he has just become a suspect in a cold case, the murder of Rebecca Jacobsen." Hector looked to Pat, waiting for some kind of reaction but none came. Hector couldn't tell if Pat was intently listening or shocked silent. "Okay … apparently your uncle kept the case going on his own, after retirement. He managed to match him by a witness description of a tattoo on a guy near there around the time Rebecca … went … missing." Again, Hector stopped to look at Pat. "Hey, Pat, you okay?"

"Son of a bitch!" Pat tossed his notepad down on a scaffold plank. "I remember that from when I was a kid. Holy shit! Wait until Jake hears this!" he said, holding his hand to his forehead in obvious dismay.

"Well, there's more here. Out in BC, he got off a sexual assault charge, which should have been rape, by the way, because someone in forensics screwed up and lost the evidence."

"When did this happen?"

"Ah, hang on a sec. I need new glasses … ah, here we go, seventy-eight." Hector flipped back and forth through the pages. "Wow! This happened like a year after the Jacobsen murder. Maybe he was just starting out then, huh?" Hector was sounding more like the reporter he used to be.

"And he never got charged ... with anything?" Pat asked in astonishment.

"Nope. He went off the radar after that. No, nothing anywhere. Why? Who is this guy to Jacob? How do you guys know him?"

Pat ignored the question and asked his own, "What about the name Vargas?"

"Well, his mother's maiden name was Maxine Anderson. She married a guy, Vargascelli, who took everything she had and left town. Out of embarrassment, she kept the name and said he died in a car accident, or something like that. She rents a place from an Alex Grimmer, and there ya go. It says she and Grimmer had Jonathon, but this was all very hush-hush," Hector summed up.

"Holy shit! This keeps getting more fucked up as you go. He was Grimmer's boy!" Pat exclaimed. "No wonder no one ever knew about it."

"Well, this is what John tells me. But he has all this as a side note. It's not part of the file. He has Sylvia and Gertie Millen written at the top of his notes, whoever they are," Hector said, not raising his head from looking into the file. He continued, "Says here that after getting out of the drunk tank for tossing his mother's place apart, Grimmer paid for him to get out of dodge. That's obviously when he moved out west and changed his name from Vargascelli to Vargas. Well, he was charged in New Westminster, BC, I guess after that he started a whole new life. Pat ... you didn't tell me how you and Jacob know this guy. What's up, man?"

Pat still ignored Hector's question. "Man, oh man, I can't believe all this," Pat said, taking a seat on a pile of lumber.

"Look Pat, you don't need to tell me what's going on. Just tell Jacob I have his file. I don't want to call him at home, in case his wife doesn't know anything about it. You know what I mean?" Hector wrapped up the folder, gave Pat a friendly gentle slap on the back of the shoulder and headed for the door.

Pat raised his head and said, "Yeah, sure Heck, I'll let him know. Hey, I'm sorry Heck. I'll talk to you about this another time. It's kind of messing me up right now."

"It's all good. No worries. I'll catch up with you later. Take it easy."

Pat left within minutes of Hector. As he walked out to his truck, he saw the municipality's building department truck pulling out of the far end of the parking lot. He couldn't tell if it was Vargas driving or not. A cold chill went through him as he thought about how Vargas might react if he'd overheard their conversation.

28

Another Run-In

Early Saturday morning, Jacob and Pat took a trip to their local building supply to pick up some finishing materials. They hadn't gone on a material run together in a few years, so this was enjoyably nostalgic. But Pat was feeling anxious carrying around the alarming information he'd received from Hector the day before. He felt it was urgent enough that he needed to tell him what Vargas's real name was, but the rest would have to wait until they left the supply. Jacob was trying to come to terms with the news Pat had just shared, and he was restless inside wondering what else was in that file. He kept himself preoccupied by loading the mouldings into the truck while Pat was inside signing off on their invoice. When he turned around to grab another handful, there was Vargas, standing within a foot of his face. His eyes were the size of saucers, looking vacant but with rage visible from his body language.

"Do you know what you did, Jacob O'Connell?" Vargas's voice was elevating with each word that came out of his mouth. "The hero! Little Sara's saviour!" His voice levelled.

"What the hell is wrong with you, Vargas?" Jacob said, looking to see who might be nearby. So far he had held his anger in check, but he'd had enough. He shoved Vargas hard enough his back slammed into the racks behind him. "You think I don't know who you are, Vargascelli, what you are?"

"Well, Jacob, you should know, you looked right at me," Vargas said, becoming highly animated now. "It worked perfect! Old man

Grimmer, you know … my secret pop, right. It was easy. He was half-blind already. A flash of sun in his eyes with little Sara right in his path. It was perfect, except for you!"

Jacob's head tilted and his right eye began to twitch. He hadn't seen Hector's report yet, so everything Vargas had just said hadn't registered. But he was worried about how Vargas could know he was aware of Grimmer being his father. He pushed it aside, however, and he heard the part about Sara loud and clear, with images of her popping into his head. Then he remembered that teenager not far down the sidewalk. Until now he wondered why he kept looking back to him, not knowing the importance of it in his memory. The headache started, but it was mild this time. He had control.

Jacob took another quick scan around, his rising anger ready to let loose, then he leaned into Vargas, nose to nose, with his eyes on fire.

"That was you?" he grunted, sounding like he was chewing the words as they came out. "What did she ever do to you? She was six. You're a fucking psychopath, pure and simple. And you've gone as far as you're going to go with this." Jacob felt his anger turning into rage — he was beginning to see red.

"Oh, Jacob, I'm just getting started," Vargas answered, like a child playing a game. And, backed up with Jacob inches from him, he laughed.

"I mean it, Vargas, if you go near Sara or my family—" Jacob didn't get a chance to finish.

"I know what you want to do, Jacob. You're just itching, aren't you? Well, I'm going to give you that chance. But … we both know what will happen if you go through with it. Don't we, Jacob, *little care package*?" he said, holding his fingers up in quotations.

"What the fuck are you talking about? Where did you hear that?" Jacob growled, standing back with an expression of astonished dismay and disgust. This entered a whole new realm for Jacob.

"I saw what you did back then, then I got to see it again, if you can believe that — twice in a lifetime!" Vargas sounded astonished. "It took me a while to find out what you are, but I did. And you'll pay for taking that life away from me." Vargas's tone became malicious.

Jacob's anger was turning into something he'd never felt before. He believed in that moment that he could kill. He chose to start de-escalating.

"What life, what the hell are you rambling about? You've completely—"

In mid-sentence Vargas, turning red now, screamed out, "Sara's life! She was mine, until you brought her back. She was mine and you took that away from me," he bellowed, in a rising octave.

Jacob snapped out, "Okay, that's enough. You're fucking insane."

With one hand, he grabbed Vargas by the throat, with the other fist clenched tight, he slammed him back into the rack of lumber again. His hand around Vargas's throat squeezed so hard his knuckles were turning white, and Vargas's face was turning blue. As quickly as his rage grew, the hand he had around Vargas's throat started to burn. The pain was enough for him to let go. Every digit had left its mark. He heard his mother's voice saying he was meant for better things, like she was standing next to him. He backed away.

Vargas hardly forgot about Jacob breaking his nose at O'Toole's. That anger had its chance to brew from exhibiting raccoon eyes into work for two weeks following, which Sara had seen every day.

His own twisted version of reality had built up all those years of Jacob with Sara looking down on him, funnelling it into demented rage, along with what he was feeling now, after being slammed against the lumber racks. He had the urge to take a swing, and he tried, but Jacob easily stepped back and blocked his arm, like he had at O'Toole's washroom all those years ago, except he was facing him this time. And although Jacob still had his hand clenched in a fist and was ready to respond, he didn't swing; he maintained control.

"Well, have at it, Jacob. Be careful, though, you have a lot more to lose than I do, guardian." Jacob just squeezed his eyebrows together and shook his head, at a loss to understand him. As messed up as he'd always believed Vargas was, this behaviour was something he hadn't seen before — not at O'Toole's nor the many way-beyond-inappropriate moments when he had seen Jacob and Sara together, not even in the underground parking where no one was around to see him. Every time over the years when no one was around to witness anything, Vargas wouldn't engage.

"This is truly wonderful. You don't have a clue what I'm talking about, do you? Well, big hero, the guardian, it's now or later. Because if not now, Jacob, it's definitely coming later." Vargas's laugh was vile. He kept going like he had injected a hundred units of liquid speed directly into his veins. But his next words were dangerous, especially for him.

"And when you least expect it, I'm going to take everything from you."

In less than a second, Jacob had both hands back around Vargas's neck and he was ready to crush it, no matter what pain arrived or what voices he heard.

"Whoa, whoa Jacob. Witnesses," Vargas squeaked out, sounding like he'd just inhaled a balloon full of helium, turning his eyes in the direction of the door leading inside the store. Pat was walking through at that moment with a couple of customers directly behind him. Jacob relaxed his grip, slowly letting one hand down by his side, but still had the other one on his neck when he turned to see Pat coming out.

"Last warning, Vargas, you go near my family or anyone I know, and I'll put an end to this, permanently!"

"Careful, Jake," Vargas used Pat's nickname for him to enrage him more. "That sounds like a threat, and in public, too. Anyway, I look forward to it."

Jacob's entire body was vibrating. He let Vargas go, still shaking his head in disbelief. He'd had scraps before, but this was something entirely different.

When Pat finally caught focus of what was happening, he ran straight over. He bellowed, "Hey, Hey! What the hell is this?"

Pat was incredulous, and protective of his best friend like he would be with family. Being true to himself, Vargas volunteered an unsolicited response to Pat as he brushed himself off, straightening the front of his shirt. "Just a little misunderstanding, Mr. Keegan. That's all it was … right, Jacob?"

His lame attempt of trying to make it sound like what just happened was nothing of consequence was pathetically obvious. He was continuing to push all the buttons, enjoying every bit of it.

"Yeah, a misunderstanding," Jacob said without conviction.

Before walking away, Vargas whispered to him, "I'll be seeing you, little Jake. Oh, and those headlights that blinded you the night you rolled the truck, that's right, buddy. I've been watching you for a very long time."

Jacob seemed to choke a little, standing still looking shocked and fearful; those feelings were overruling his rage.

"Jesus, Jake!" Pat exclaimed. You pick here to confront that fuckhead? What the hell?" Pat stopped drilling Jacob, realizing just how upset he really was. "Sorry man, you okay?"

"Yeah … I'm fine. Let's get a drink." Jacob didn't take his eye off Vargas as he walked out of the building. Pat was astonished at his friend's near-flippant reply.

"Jacob … when have you not confided in me about this guy?"

"More than you know, buddy. There are things you're better off not knowing."

Jacob got in the truck and waited, but Pat stood for a few seconds with his mouth agape. Jacob knew if he told Pat what Vargas just said, Vargas would not have left that building standing straight up, possibly not alive.

"It's ten in the morning, are you sure a drink is what you need right now?" Pat said, getting in the truck.

"Well, it's either that or a gun."

Pat laughed and grabbed Jacob around his neck and shoulder with one hand and gave him a gentle shake. "Let's go have that drink. If I remember correctly, there's still the rest of that Jameson in your shop from Christmas, right?"

Jacob looked over at his friend, exhausted.

"Yeah, it's there. Let's go."

29

Reconcile

From inside the front of the barn that Jacob converted to a space for the office, he could see the house and a fair distance down the laneway. Pat was standing next to Jacob's desk looking out one of the side-by-side double-hung windows with his hands folded behind his back, looking like a principal considering what punishment to dole out. Jacob was fighting to get the squeaky bottom drawer of the antique oak desk open so he could get at the bottle of Irish whiskey. Even in the protection of a closed desk drawer, the bottle was still covered in fine sawdust. It was the same for the glasses Jacob pulled out. It took a deep breath to blow out the quantity of dust from the bottom of the not-so-fine glassware. When raising their drinks to make a toast, the scratched glass was almost as cloudy as the whiskey itself. It was just how they liked it, and they laughed over the wild west reference that was made.

They took their much-needed respite from the unsettling event that took place earlier at the building supply. Pat couldn't wait any longer to fill Jacob in on the rest of what Hector had revealed to him at The Cider Mill. But his news was followed by a stern warning about his behaviour with Vargas. After that, Pat asked outright to hear everything that happened between him and Vargas, leading up to today. Jacob couldn't tell Pat everything, but he did his best to tell him what he considered relevant. What Vargas whispered into his ear as he left had to be held back to protect Pat — from himself.

The following morning, a large tan envelope was resting in between the front entrance and screen doors of the O'Connell's residence. It was addressed to Jacob specifically and not to Able Hands. The return address was Stewart Web Designs. Standing in his multicoloured, vertical-striped robe with morning coffee in hand, Jacob went for the morning paper, as per routine, and discovered the envelope lying next to it. *What's this? Oh shit, Hector dropped off the file.* He stuffed the envelope inside his robe so Sara wouldn't see it just yet.

Fresh in his mind was Vargas's behaviour with Sara when she picked up the latest building permit. On top of this was the altercation from the day before, and he was clearly shaken by all of it. Vargas was skirting the line between inflicting psychological harm and threatening death. As Pat and Jacob concluded the day before, this was at a point where the law couldn't help him. Jacob knew things were coming to point of action, and he had to figure out the right moment to have this conversation with Sara. What was said to him yesterday also left him with more questions. Jacob met Sara at the bottom of the stairs. Sitting on the bottom step, he patted the top of his thigh, inviting her to sit next to him. When she did, he kissed her cheek and whispered in her ear.

"Let's get the kids off to school because there's something I need to show you."

"Well that statement leaves a lot to the imagination," she laughed, then saw his serious look. "Is everything all right, honey?"

"Oh yeah, just some stuff we have to go over, but after the kids are gone to school, okay?"

"Okay. So, no sex then?" Not waiting for a response, she smiled and kissed his cheek as she rose.

Once alone, Jacob pulled the file from behind him on the countertop, and Sara thought it was just another work folder.

"Did you know that Grimmer had a kid? Because it's news to me."

"Okay … where did that come from?" Sara asked, somewhat bewildered. "Hang on, I forgot all about that. I remember my grandmother telling me that he had an illegitimate kid with

Mrs. Vargascelli. But no one ever knew about it. Not even the kid, apparently."

Jacob stood still, mouth purposely hung open, looking at her. "You don't think that would be something you would tell me?" he said, looking disappointed.

"I'm sorry, honey, but honestly that had completely left my mind. I was such a wreck watching grandma dying like that, and it was a long time ago. She was so full of morphine on her deathbed when she told me that, I couldn't tell if it was reality or not. She had so many stories that were way out there. Are you going to stop looking at me like that? Overreactor." She exclaimed with a grin. "What's this all about anyway?"

"That's funny... Yeah, I'm done ... overreacting." Jacob's faint smile disappeared in his serious expression. "Well, it turns out the kid did know who his father was. *When* he figured that out, though, I don't know. Just have a look at who Grimmer's illegitimate boy is."

Jacob gently placed the folder down in front of Sara and opened it up to the right spot. He walked over to the coffee pot and poured out two more cups. He could see the look of shock on Sara's face as she was reading. At one point, her hand came up to cover her mouth, gasping. The more she read, the more she trembled. When Jacob returned and set her coffee next to her, she reached out and clamped onto his hand, not letting him go as she continued to read.

"Oh my God, Jacob, is this true? Where did this come from? Where'd you get this?" Her face was becoming increasingly red from her rising blood pressure. She let go of Jacob, and firmly placed her arms on the edge of the counter, pushing herself back but not letting go.

"It was Heck I asked, but the info came from John Keegan. I didn't want to get into it with John, and I knew they knew each other from when he was a reporter."

"You got Hector to get this? Why? And why wouldn't you just go to John to begin with? More importantly, why didn't you talk to me about this first?"

"Sara, slow down, jeez. I didn't want you or Pat to know unless it turned up something important. I didn't want you guys worrying."

"You could say this is important!" she said loudly.

"Sara, please. I'm telling you."

"Sorry, honey. Wow! Vargas is Vargascelli…" she blurted out in astonishment. "He's Grimmer's boy!? Well, that must've been a real source of shame for him."

"He's not just Grimmer's boy, John thinks he's a possible suspect in Rebecca Jacobsen's murder."

The shock and fear on Sara's face was evident and Jacob instantly wanted to comfort her, but they looked at one another and continued going through the file.

"Oh my God, honey, I remember you telling me about her. You knew her from school, right? It really bothered you for a long time. Jacob … if this is real … what are we going to do?"

"Well, you're gonna be pissed at me, but I had a run-in with him yesterday at the building supply. He actually came at me." Jacob lowered his head slightly, pursing his lips.

"Jacob … what did you do?" Sara asked with alarm.

"He told me he's the one who caused the accident, where Mr. Grimmer hit you. Remember what I said at that restaurant?" Jacob didn't wait for confirmation before continuing. "He also said he was the one who turned the high beams on me the night I rolled the truck — you know, with Heather and Pat."

"Why would he do those things? My God, he's really insane, isn't he?"

"He's aware that I know about him now," he said, pointing to the file on the counter.

"Aware, how?"

"Well, the file. Pat actually heard it first from Hector, and he told me. I actually called him Vargascelli, among a few other choice words."

"So … what … he's coming after us now, Jacob?" Sara's voice began to crack with the escalating fear.

"No. It's me he's after."

"Ah, no honey, that's not even close to being true. It's obvious now, he's been stalking both of us all our lives. We just never saw all this before. So, it's us, not just you." As she said it, Sara realized the truth of it, her thoughts turning to dread. "Jesus, honey, the kids, what if he hurts the kids?" As her fear rose, so did her anger.

"That's not going to happen!" Jacob quickly replied, with his fists clenched. "I've already talked to Pat about this. Not to mention that John's now aware. He may be retired, but he knows people on the force. He'll know how to go about this, so try not to worry too much." He realized his tone was harsh, so he brought it back down. "Nothing is going to happen, sweetheart. I won't let him get close to us. I told him I'd kill him if he ever came near any one of us, and he knows that's true."

"That's not good to even say, let alone consider it. You can never do something like that … you understand that … right, honey? You can't ever do that!"

"All right, all right. Well, it's not like I'd want to take *anyone's* life. But if it comes to protecting you and the kids…" He just cocked his head.

He sat next to Sara and wrapped his arm around her, pulling her close to him.

"It's going to be okay," he said, squeezing her tight. It seemed that for the moment, those familiar words brought her comfort.

30

Providence Lost

A young and beautiful Maxine Anderson was invited to the Saturday night dance by a young and handsome Angelo Vargascelli, known to everyone as Gino. Maxine's beau had been killed during the war and now, in 1947, she had been in mourning for well over two years. She'd become a homebody. When she wasn't working as a telephone switchboard operator, she helped her mother around the house. She was truly heartbroken over losing her intended, but nearing the end of the second year, she met Gino at Al's Diner, where she went for lunch regularly when at work.

Al's was a small, narrow restaurant on the main street of town, squeezed in between Woolworth's and Laine's Bowling Alley. The decor was nicotine-stained yellow paint everywhere, and a huge blackboard with the complete menu on it sat on the wall dividing the dining area from the kitchen. The main room had six two-foot-square tables and six stools at the counter, all with black tops and chrome borders. When Gino accidentally backed into Maxine while hanging up his coat in the entry's tight quarters, he apologized and offered to buy her a coffee to make up for it. It was a bold move for a normally shy Maxine to accept, but she was instantly smitten, which was evident to all of Al's patrons and staff during a packed lunch hour.

Gino had light olive skin and dark-brown hair, and he kept it slicked back, with a small wave, like Gary Cooper. Although he worked as a labourer at the pulp and paper mill, on this day he was well dressed. He wore a black suit coat, pleated pinstripe pants and a pair of Oxfords, his fedora already on the rack. Maxine had long curly strawberry blonde hair, eyes like a clear blue sea in the tropics, and a head-turning figure. She had a wide smile, with big, beautiful lips highlighted by the contrast of her dark red lipstick up against her lily-white skin. They made quite a pair, looking like they had just walked out of a Vogue photo shoot.

It wasn't long before she was pregnant, after a hot and steamy romance. In order to save face during a time when having children out of wedlock was seriously frowned upon, they had a quick and informal marriage performed by the justice of the peace. Their honeymoon was a long-weekend trip to a wood cabin at a nearby resort, where the passionate lovemaking continued. The fiancé she'd lost to the war was a quiet, button-down type, and Gino was anything but. Maxine believed she had the best husband, and for about three months after the honeymoon, she wasn't proven wrong. Only a couple years after the war, with the economy booming, getting together for drinks was more popular than ever. Gino's taste for alcohol and women had already overtaken him, and things quickly soured between the couple. Halfway through her ninth month of pregnancy, she woke up to an empty bed, an empty jewellery box, and an equally empty bank account. He even took her family's antique silverware.

That experience left Maxine a bitter and lonely lady. When she lost her child by stillbirth, she felt it was an added measure of insult to injury. She told people Gino had gone back to Italy to care for his ailing father. Eventually, the fabricated story of Gino ended with him dying in a car crash on a dangerous mountain road in the Italian Alps — tragic. Everyone knew the truth, and when that became obvious to Maxine, she holed up. Her life consisted only of work and home, little else. She eventually started having her groceries and prescriptions delivered to her home, inside the screened-in back porch with the money for payment waiting in an envelope. She rarely had any contact with anyone. Even her doctor made house calls. This was her way of life for quite some time.

Several years passed when, to everyone's surprise, especially to her mother, Maxine was showing an expanding stomach. The only men who went into her house were her doctor and her landlord, so, who the father was, was a coin toss. She would name her son after her grandfather, Jonathon Allan (Vargascelli). The only thing Angelo Vargascelli ever gave Maxine, other than grief and humiliation, was his name. And for obvious reasons, being 1953, she kept it. However, the arrival of this baby made for a great deal of gossip in town. Nonetheless, she raised her son by herself, and this, of course, inspired more gossip — *how she could afford it?* As a result of it all, she continued living alone to spare her mother the shame. She was called horrible names: whore, with a bastard child, welfare case, and so on. However, Maxine endured and she began to raise her child as a single mother in the 1950s.

§

Ten years had passed, and Grimmer was now a widower, with a substantial amount of money, which was mostly from his wife's estate. He didn't care much about money — he considered it a necessary evil. After his wife passed on, he was lonely and heartbroken, and he required a lot of time to find a purpose again. When he wasn't running supplies to his general store, which was run by a handful of loyal employees, he was taking care of his rental properties. It was through these properties that Grimmer started to come back into the fold of society, where he could be found around people once again. There was always one repair or another required at one of his buildings. He always enjoyed completing repairs himself, but he eventually ran out of time.

He hired Lars Jacobsen, a local handyman, to do some work for him. Lars was a tenant at one of his properties, a fellow widower raising his daughter, Rebecca, on his own. Grimmer admired Lars for his character and knew him as a hard worker. He had a truck with his name on the side that read, "Jacobsen Handyman Service." Lars did all right for himself. He was never late for the rent, and any repairs required at his house he took care of himself, with no charge for labour. This alone endeared him to Grimmer, so he sold the house to Lars at a reduced rate, who made regular monthly payments. Grimmer put a clause in the contract for the mortgage that if he died, the balance would be paid by Grimmer's estate and the house would legally belong to Lars.

Considering everything in and about Maxine's life, it never dawned on Grimmer that Lars would see her as a possible wife and mother. So, he sent Lars to her Stanley Street address to repair a leaky roof and then fix up the damaged plaster and paint inside. He knocked on the door of this little bungalow with red insulbrick siding, an open porch to the front and a screened-in one at the rear. Lars was impressed with how well the yard was maintained, along with the picturesque raised flower beds and a small vegetable garden to the rear.

"Hello ... Mrs. Vargascelli?" Lars said, removing his cap, placing it in his hand.

§

As the years went on, it was evident the toll surviving on his own had taken on Grimmer. He found himself going to the church and its functions on a regular basis. It was at church that he was befriended by Sylvia Millen, a devoted churchgoer herself. The two became close, and when Mr. Grimmer found out he was dying from lung cancer, he chose to confide in Sylvia. He told her about the affair he had with Maxine, and in his suffering of pain and guilt, he revealed who his child was.

He told her that he provided financial support for her and the boy, but he never once called him son. As agreed with the boy's mother, he would never tell anyone he was the father. He told Sylvia about giving Jonathan a job at the general store in his early teens, and how he was caught stealing. But that was minor compared to the other things that occurred. In particular was his bizarre behaviour toward the other women who worked in the store. He constantly made passes at them, and followed a couple girls home from work, eventually stalking and spying on them.

It all came to a boiling point and Grimmer had no choice but to fire him. His known behaviour as well as what was just hearsay — several accusations were made that he'd killed some neighbourhood pets — became intolerable. He had been seen burning down a couple of dog houses and sheds in people's backyards. The police were involved several times, but they could never prove anything.

Grimmer broke down in front of Sylvia, carrying on about what an evil child he was. He was in obvious despair that he had created such a child, and he worried constantly for Maxine. The tears rolled down his face, feeling such remorse for having this illegitimate child through an affair. In his breakdown, he told Sylvia the guilt he carried for Sara, and that it was Jonathon who blinded him that day. Ultimately, he paid for the family to move to Ontario so Sara would receive proper medical treatment. He also provided a fund for her education when the time came.

Sylvia was overwhelmed by his generosity; however, she assured him that he shouldn't carry such guilt for the actions of his son. She hoped he would understand, believe and ultimately accept that some children turn out bad with no fault of the parents. When they last spoke about Jonathon, Grimmer felt the need to tell Sylvia everything about his behaviour and bad deeds. Alex Grimmer was once a rugged and strong man, but near his death, he was a thin, frail and frightened man. He always wore a flannel plaid shirt with suspenders holding up his baggy, green work pants — they had once fit tight. His walk became a shuffle with a cane to help keep him up, and his once perfect posture was destroyed. By the time he left this world, he was permanently stooped over.

31

Malevolence

Part 1

With his eyes fixed, looking straight ahead, Lars was completely mesmerized by the lovely figure standing in front of him, wearing a tightly fitting yellow sundress. He backed up to the first step down from the patio to give her some space. The sunlight behind her highlighted her shape, and he was clearly struggling not to stare. He recognized that it was about time for him to speak, but as he tried to introduce himself, he tripped over his tongue. "Excuse me … ma'am … um, ah, I'm Lars Jacobum … Jacobsen." *Jesus Christ, Lars, get a grip!* He fumbled his own name out like he had a mouth full of marbles.

"Are you sure?" Maxine quipped.

He ignored what she said and continued. "Um … Mr. Grimmer hired me to fix the roof, and you have some water damage inside that needs repair, right?" Lars was heating up under his collar, his face becoming red, and he'd started talking in hyperspeed.

"I'm Mrs. Vargascelli. Hello. You must be Lars." She sounded like a teacher correcting a student while she reached her hand out to shake his. He happily responded, but it had been quite a long time since Lars felt anything as soft as her hand.

He finally realized he was shaking her hand too long. "Oh, sorry," he squeaked, finally letting go and clearing his throat. He felt he was starting out on shaky ground, but Maxine softened to the well-mannered way about him. All that was left from Maxine was a warning about her son getting in the way and to make sure to let her know straight away if he was causing trouble. Then Lars went about his work.

The sticky start between the two was quickly forgotten, making way for some casual conversations. They were both impressed with the look of each other. At the end of one morning working to repair the water damage in the laundry room, Maxine brought Lars a sandwich and a cup of tea — she'd learned his preference for tea over coffee. When the work was complete, they had developed a connection through their mutual attraction and amiable conversation. And they were both single parents, although Maxine didn't say too much about her son.

Lars somehow found the courage and asked her to a picnic, but shied off a bit, saying it would be good for the kids.

On the day of the picnic, it didn't take too long for Lars to notice something off about young Jonathon. He knew about him getting fired from Grimmer's and had heard other rumours. Lars believed in the goodness of people, and he believed Jonathon just needed the guidance of a father figure. Lars hadn't heard any rumours about Maxine or about Gino running off on her, so he believed what she told her — Jonathon was Gino's son, and Gino had died on that dangerous mountain road in the Italian Alps. He saw no reason not to pursue her and was determined to join their families together.

Once Maxine decided that Lars was a good man and the opposite of Gino, her guard came down and she fell in love with the ruggedly handsome man of many skills. Lars was also a war vet and had received many commendations fighting the Wehrmacht just inside the border of Holland next to Germany.

They took the better part of a year before they decided to blend their small families. Lars rented his home out and moved in with Maxine. Considering it was 1968, Lars and Maxine bravely shook things up by moving in together without getting married. Blended families are a challenge at the best of times, but this one proved most difficult.

Jonathon was the kind of kid who didn't play well with others. He was fifteen now, and having a five-year-old constantly bothering him angered him. And he quickly came to resent her, thinking Lars spoiled her. And it didn't take long before little Rebecca became sullen and withdrawn. This was a reversal to her usually happy behaviour before living with her new family. Lars was disturbed by this, but he kept on supporting her with love and encouragement, assuming it was an adjustment period.

A while later, Maxine received a call from Rebecca's kindergarten teacher, asking for her and Lars to come in for a meeting. The following day at the school, not knowing what it was about, Lars was shocked when the teacher came right out and asked how often they used corporal punishment on Rebecca. He sat straight up in his chair, and with anger, he snapped back, "Never! And why are you asking this?"

"Well, Mr. Jacobsen, she fell and hurt her hip and the nurse checked it out, wiped some antiseptic on the scrape, and discovered several bruises and, frankly, it was a concern to us."

Lars thanked her for notifying them and reassured her that Rebecca was just clumsy and a tomboy. On the ride home, Lars was silent; his normal calm demeanour was replaced with anger. When they arrived, he got Rebecca out of the car and he suggested she go play in the backyard. Lars and Maxine went inside to find Jonathon lying on the living room floor, propped against the sofa watching TV. Lars walked over to Jonathon, and in one move, he picked him up by the scruff of the neck with one hand and slammed him up against the wall.

"Did you put your hands on my daughter?" Jonathon's face was expressionless, when it should have been wrought with fear. Not a word came from him.

"Lars!" Maxine screamed. "Put him down right now. What's the matter with you? Do you really think he's responsible for this?"

Lars, with his eyes afire, turned to look at Maxine. He was still holding Jonathon against the wall, his feet dangling a foot off the floor.

"Yes, I do." He let Jonathon drop and walked over to Maxine in an intense posture that scared her.

"Come with me," he demanded. And Maxine went, without hesitation, straight into their bedroom.

"Maxine." Lars was restraining himself best he could. "The teacher stopped me by the door when you were already outside and told me Rebecca has bruises on the inside of her thighs, and she might have been hurt down there." The knuckles on his clenched fists were pure white.

"Lars, she could have hurt herself playing or riding her bike. It could be a number of things, so don't attack my son. He said he didn't touch her."

"No, Maxine. He didn't say *anything*. He didn't even look scared when I grabbed him. I'm sorry, but there's something seriously wrong with that boy and I've had enough of it."

Maxine remained in the bedroom in tears. Lars walked toward the kitchen's back door to the rear porch, grabbing his coat on the way out. He picked up Rebecca, got in his truck, and left. The next day, Lars and a couple of friends, including John Keegan, and two pickup trucks loaded his belongings and left.

Maxine would never lay eyes on him again. She was broken-hearted, but she had no choice but to stand by her son. As Jonathon's behaviour became more bizarre and violent over time, she wondered if Lars was right, and she shuddered at the thought. After that realization, she once again insulated herself from the world — a world she had re-engaged in, with Lars by her side, a world in which she had again become happy. In short time, Maxine had lost all control over her son's behaviour, which had become perverse, violent, and highly unpredictable. She became so disconnected from him, it felt like a death of a loved one. And in her grief, she concluded he was pure evil and she let him go.

Part 2

The fridge was stocked with enough food to cook a decent meal, but there was nothing prepared, and nary a treat to be had. The cupboard didn't hold potato chips, cookies, or peanuts, and there weren't any baked goods on the counter, as once was the norm. On this night Maxine hadn't prepared a meal for dinner because she never knew when her eighteen-year-old son would be home. Depression had overtaken her, and she'd remained alone after the break-up with Lars. So now, if she wasn't on the couch with an expressionless stare and a glass of vodka, she was in bed with the glass in hand, reading a *Woman's Weekly*.

It was ten thirty at night when Jonathon strolled in, demanding something to eat. That night, Maxine was curled up on the sofa wearing her tattered housecoat, with a drink in one hand and a Rothmans cigarette in the other. She was blankly staring beyond the black-and-white RCA television, which was airing a weekly episode of *Dragnet*. Whatever he wanted to consume, it came with an urge for instant gratification, not unlike many of his other urges — disturbing and frightening urges.

He stormed into the living room and demanded she get up and cook him some hamburgers, to which he received a mild chuckle in response, not turning her stare from the direction of the TV. Once he saw the smirk on the side of her face, and the shaking of her head in disgust, he snapped. Not a sound came out of him as he took two giant steps toward her, grabbed her robe mid-chest and threw her off the sofa and onto the floor. He then picked her up and repeatedly slammed her into every piece of furniture in the living room before the punches started. By then he had her leaned against the kitchen table, pummelling her in a savage attack. She ended up in a pile on the kitchen floor, unconscious, robe torn apart, covered in blood.

When she finally came to, Jonathon was long gone, to her relief. Inches at a time she dragged herself across the kitchen floor, with one eye filled with blood from the gash above it. Her head was pounding, and she could barely focus or move, but she found the strength to rise up to the wall-mounted phone and called the police. When they arrived and saw how badly Maxine was hurt, an ambulance was immediately called for and she was brought to emergency. After she was examined, stitched up, and her broken arm set and wrapped in a cast, she was admitted and remained in the hospital for ten days. When she was first brought in, she slipped in and out of consciousness, and was barely coherent. She had a severe concussion, and a partially detached retina, but the psychological damage was worse. She became near catatonic for awhile, and her depression worsened. When Grimmer went to see her in the hospital, he was enraged, but he put that aside to tend to Maxine's needs.

That night would be the last time she would see her son. His attack on her, in his psychotic rage, breaking her arm, and leaving her bloodied and bruised, demonstrated what he was capable of. Many teary days and nights were ahead for Maxine from that point on, until one day, her heart finally gave out. Her death had no effect on her son, and he didn't return home for her funeral.

He was arrested for assault causing bodily harm — a serious offence that could land him serious time. The judge had asked the crown to raise the charge up to attempted murder, but it was declined. Jonathon was held in jail, and, with no surety or money, there would be no bail, even if bail had been an option, which wasn't obvious considering the severity of the assault. Grimmer believed that at the time Jonathon only knew him as a friend of his mother's family, but that wasn't entirely accurate. He went to see him in jail and proposed he leave, to the other side of the country, and never return. He offered to pay more than his way there, and Jonathon accepted — it was either that or stay in jail and take his chances in court. Grimmer wanted this kid gone so badly, he didn't care about him skipping bail, or the resulting warrant, and certainly not the cost. Grimmer made stipulations for Jonathan to receive ongoing funds from the bank. He had to have a current address and bank account in any city or town in British Columbia. The funds could only be withdrawn by him in person at two-week intervals. It was the only way Grimmer could think of to monitor him. It turned out, to his relief, Jonathon never returned home while Maxine was alive.

§

A few years after leaving for BC, Jonathon found his own way financially, cutting ties with the bank and Grimmer. Then to complete the separation, he changed his last name to Vargas. It was necessary for Jonathon to believe he had power over Grimmer and his mother, so they would never know when or if he might show up. He kept residence in New Westminster, a suburb of Vancouver, and received a community college certification as a civil technologist. He worked for a few different companies in urban development and municipal services management, before landing a job working for the government.

He never lasted too long with any one company in the beginning because he couldn't control his psychotic behaviour. Normal social interactions weren't natural for him. Over time, he was able to learn some social skills for his own survival in society and to get what he needed. Working for the government provided a type of safe haven for his personality type. Whatever his twisted urges were, it was an agonizing battle with himself to try and keep them hidden in the workplace. And outside of work, he wouldn't go anywhere near his co-workers or projects he was in charge of — he was learning, adapting.

Not too long after he started working for the government, however, his urges cost him a charge of sexual assault. They cost the victim much more. The evidence lacked a rape charge because the young woman didn't report it soon enough. His victim was a young devout Catholic woman who was working her way through school waitressing at a local family restaurant. Vargas would go there regularly for lunch during the week, and he ordered the same turkey club sandwich every time. After sitting down, he would always asked for a coffee, a glass of water, and a menu, even though he never deviated from the turkey club.

He gave this young woman, Michelle, the creeps — the same effect he had on all the waitresses who served him. She didn't have much choice — he was in her section, and she had to serve him. The constant staring got to her, but she was so shy she wouldn't complain to her boss. During one lunch hour, she brought him his club sandwich, as per usual, and then he raised his head up from the newspaper and locked his eyes in on her.

"Are you having your period today?"

She was startled, but her dignity would not let this go unchallenged. And her manager, Grace, could hear her from the kitchen.

"I beg your pardon. What kind of sick … you're disgusting!"

She slammed the plate on the table and rushed to the back of the kitchen in tears. The manager went to Michelle and put her arm around her shoulder.

"Don't worry, honey, that's the last time that creep will be coming in here."

The manager marched out from the kitchen and straight to Vargas. She stood so close to him, she was almost in his lap. She picked up the plate of food with only a bite taken out of his club sandwich and looked down at him with a look to kill.

"You can leave right now, or I'll call the cops. GET OUT!" she yelled, pointing her finger toward the door. The regular crowd of lunch goers all turned to look at the commotion and there was a red-faced Vargas. He wasn't embarrassed, he was furious that he was challenged, let alone by a woman. But oddly, he seemed to have developed difficulty confronting women. He didn't say a word. He stood up, threw a five-dollar bill on the table, but before he made it a single step, the manager grabbed the bill and stuffed it in his shirt pocket.

"It's on the house. Now get the hell out of here, you sick son of a bitch," she growled. The regulars, who were all aware of his treatment of the waitresses, applauded the manager, which enraged Vargas that much more.

"You got that part right. I am a son of a bitch." His reply was quiet and sinister. He turned to look at Michelle standing by the archway to the kitchen and blew her a kiss. She stood her ground, and slowly, he sauntered out the door, to everyone's delight and relief. The manager's shoulders sunk, she exhaled a long breath and lowered her head, shaking it in disbelief, grateful the moment was over.

Michelle had thrown out her torn and bloodied clothes from the attack. The attack that was precipitated from that day. The police managed to retrieve them from the garbage before it was hauled away. But it was all for naught, as the evidence was somehow lost or thrown out by mistake, as were Vargas's charges. Young Michelle had her life thrown into turmoil, and it nearly destroyed her. However, being the deeply religious person she was, she regretfully decided to keep the child.

Her boss, Grace, helped her during her pregnancy so she didn't overdo it at work. She became like a second mom to her. When she was in the hospital after giving birth, Michelle asked one of the two co-workers who were visiting her why Grace hadn't been in to see her. They looked to one another, then apprehensively to Michelle. "She's been missing for three days now. The police are looking for her all over the place. We didn't want to worry you with the baby and all." Michelle held back the cries, but tears fell down her cheek.

Michelle would become part of a long list of Jonathon Vargas's victims. Vargas may not have murdered young Michelle, but he did manage to kill a big part of her.

32

Visions

The O'Connell children were bouncing off the walls in excitement at being on holiday at their grandparents' cottage. It was summer in the Northumberland Strait, where the lobster, muscles, and scallops were plentiful and adventures endless. It was perfect weather for Canada Day, with temperatures in the mid- to high twenties and low humidity. This was Ben's second year of swimming under the watchful eye and teaching of Mom and Dad. Thomas bought their cottage in the fifties, and with hard work and skilled labour, he was able to keep it in top shape. He rebuilt the roof, raising the peak in order to accommodate a loft for their increasing family. And as time marched on, and the kids grew, so did their list of chores around the cottage every summer. There was always something that needed repair or a fresh coat of paint.

To Jacob and Sara's delight, no such tasks were necessary on this trip. July 1st landed on a Friday, so the weekend kicked off with a bang, thanks to the local fireworks show. With two weeks ahead of them, Jacob prayed for rest and a chance at peace and quiet more than anything — *a tall order*, he thought. For an overworked and highly stressed O'Connell family, this was just what they needed. It had just been a couple weeks since Jacob had had his run-in with Vargas, so he and Sara were on edge. They knew the police were looking at Vargas for Rebecca Jacobsen's murder, but that didn't comfort them, as he seemed a long way off from prison. The police didn't have any evidence other than an old witness statement, but the witness was dead now. As a result, the police couldn't get a warrant, so they'd been following him trying to obtain a DNA sample for a couple weeks now. Vargas had been proving a challenge for them, which really jarred John Keegan.

Being back at the cottage was near enough like home for Jacob. Unlike all those years ago, he would be without his best friend and partner this time. This was a long overdue gathering for the entire O'Connell family, so Sara and Jacob did their best to enjoy their time. Sara and Irene were still inside helping Mary finish up a homemade gift for Grandpa's birthday coming up. Michael, single now, was soaking up the sun on the front deck and waiting for, well, *any* woman to walk by. James was absent for good reason. He was still in the navy, a captain overseeing manoeuvres somewhere in the Atlantic.

So, this was a perfect chance for father and son to head down to the beach. Ben had come to love the water. Jacob couldn't handle the Water Babies course Sara put their children through. Blowing air into Ben's mouth and dropping him into the water was something he just couldn't bring himself to do, but swimming with him at the lake or in the ocean was just fine. Inside the little red wagon Jacob was pulling were all the needed items for some time at the beach. The bright yellow and blue sun umbrella, large beach towels, radio, air pump, and deflated beach ball, as well as sunscreen, of course. The pair would have fit well in a Norman Rockwell painting, with Jacob pulling the wagon with one hand and steadying Ben atop his shoulders with the other.

As Jacob was setting up the umbrella and an impatient Ben was attempting to blow up the beach ball, he noticed a young man pass only a few feet away. He instantly froze, lost in a state of shock and dismay and unable to stop staring at this everyday, average person. Jacob's hand went to the side of his head in a familiar action, holding back the pain.

He was vaulted back in time once again, looking out to the street where Sara, at six years of age, lay bleeding. The scene was slowed almost frame by frame just before he went to her. He saw the teen, who he'd just recently discovered was Vargas, holding a round pocket mirror. The look in his eye was far beyond that of a mischievous teen. Jacob now recognized it as pure evil with malicious intent.

This sensation of being pushed back in time was painful as always. He could see this young man on the beach, who was maybe in his mid- to late twenties, was a near identical twin to Vargas. *It's possible, but what are the chances?* Jacob was dumbfounded. But different from any other moments of forced recall, this felt like a warning to Jacob. The hair stood up on the back of his neck, and he immediately picked Ben up, like he was protecting him from something, even though nothing was there. His breathing became erratic, as did his uncontrollable thoughts of impending doom. He was experiencing a severe panic attack. In seconds, he and Ben, with the little red wagon, were on their way back to the cottage.

Based on his recent run-in at the building supply, Jacob had come to believe the words and the ultimate threat Vargas spewed out in his rage — he'd purposely blinded Mr. Grimmer for one terrifying conclusion. Knowing this was enough to put Jacob on constant guard. Not long after meeting Vargas, Jacob had thought, *This wack job would be a Freudian delight.* It had elevated far beyond that now.

This would be the final collection of memories for that day. With the exception of why light emanated from his hands, Jacob understood the scene in its entirety. And with this onset of recall, he felt another familiar sensation — a cold, disturbing shiver that drove throughout his body like a shockwave.

Ben was full of questions as expected.

"Why are we going back now, Dad? Why can't we go swimming? What's wrong, Dad?"

This was like any other never-ending query when any parent disrupts a kid's fun and adventure. Jacob felt horrible for cutting their beach day short.

"The beach is too crowded, Ben. We'll go back later. And I forgot, Grandpa wants to have all of the grandkids around for his birthday coming up."

When they got back to the cottage, Sara and Irene could see Jacob was upset about something. He did his best not to reveal anything in front of the kids. He just whispered in Sara's ear, as he leaned in to kiss her, that something was wrong and he had a bad feeling about something. And as soon as he had the chance, Jacob wasted no time in telling Sara what just happened on the beach.

"I think we should see if Mom and Dad can have Ben and Mary stay here for the rest of the week without us. I don't want to bring them back home right now," Jacob said, pacing inside a three-foot radius.

"Jacob, what are you talking about … going home for what? What's got you so worried? What's going on with you?" Sara said, grabbing hold of his cheeks, trying to slow him down.

"I don't know. I just have a bad feeling, a real bad feeling. I have to go back. We can come back and get the kids after I know everything is all right. You can stay here if you think that's better. I'll fly back by myself."

"No. I'm not letting you go back alone, not feeling like this. Besides, you're right, your parents and the kids always love to spend time together; they hardly see each other as it is."

"Okay, that's what we'll do then. I hope Mom and Dad are going to be all right with this. I don't like to spring things on them," Jacob said, letting out a long exhale, clearly shaken.

Jacob waited after the day's events came to an end before he spoke to his parents. All the adults were out back between the bonfire and the back deck when Jacob made the proposal to his parents. They happily agreed. Jacob was never very good at lying, so he made sure he could justify what he was about to tell them. He said there was some serious problems on one of their jobs and they had no choice but to go back and rectify it. He excused himself and took his mother by the arm for a slow walk down the laneway.

"Mom, other than the obvious, what does the word guardian mean to you? I mean I know who and what I am, we discussed that. But does this label mean something I don't know about?"

"Where did you hear about that?" Irene sounded upset.

"It doesn't matter, Mom. I just want to know why anyone would refer to me as a guardian?" He was becoming irritated now.

MARK J. CANNON   239

"I didn't know anything about it until Sara's grandmother, Sylvia, talked to me. And just who called you by this name anyway?"

"Mom!" was becoming impatient. He wanted answers, not questions.

"All right, sweetie. Calm down. I'll tell you what I know, but I still want to know what happened. Okay?"

"Yes, Mom … okay." Jacob's hands were gesturing for her to *get on with it, already!* But he would never say those words to his mother, no matter the reason. If his brothers weren't there to take him out by the woodshed, metaphorically speaking, Irene would.

"You have to keep in mind that as much as I liked and respected Sylvia, God bless her," Irene made the sign of the cross, "she was known for her flights of fancy. I think she wanted to remain a part of the sixties.

"Anyway … and this is according to her — it's not a known fact — well, her version is from some religious mythology. She believed certain people on earth are the living manifestations of what we normally call guardian angels. And, she figured what you did to Sara the day of the accident, was a result of you being one of these guardians."

Irene paused to gauge a reaction from her son, but none came.

"It's like being a guardian angel, but you're never aware of what you are, what your abilities are. Which … is kind of true in your case. I do … I really have a hard time with the guardian angel part. I honestly believe we are surrounded by them. But living people, and not knowing? I have to say that's a bit of a reach for me."

To Jacob Irene spoke as if the subject matter was prosaic. And it had thrown him off a little. She seemed unaware of how this was affecting him, but the truth was she knew exactly what was at stake. She also had to keep Jacob as far away from this truth as possible. This weighed heavily on her from the time she learned this information from Sylvia. It added a different dimension to the normal worry every parent has for their child.

They sat down on the large armour stone at the end of the lane.

Irene asked, "What's really going on with you, Jacob?"

"Well, Mom, is it okay if we leave that alone for now?"

"Of course. I don't want to see you like this, Jacob. This is worrying me. Have you talked to your father at all?"

"No. It's not something we really ever talk about. We both know what we know and that's that."

"Good. Your father does understand, but he doesn't quite know how to deal with it, so that's best," she said, patting the back of Jacob's hand, she rose to start walking away as if the conversation was over, and Jacob rose a step behind her.

"Mom, is there anything else you want to tell me about all of this?"

"Oh, I'm sorry, sweetie, I forgot. Um, no, I don't think so." Irene's tone was tentative and aloof.

He walked his mother back up the lane, stopped her before she went in, and gave her a big, long hug. She fought off showing any serious emotion, appearing stoic. And for Jacob, he worried about the stress he placed on her with this. He was aware of the effects aging was having on his mother, but in that moment, he noticed something about her more than before — her frailty, her struggle to remember, and the increased shaking.

33

Omens

Thomas drove Jacob and Sara to the airport so they could deal with the problem that had popped up at one of their projects. They said they would try to return as soon as they could. Thomas and Irene accepted the story they were told and were worried for their son and daughter-in-law. They knew the two didn't want their parents to worry for them, but they also knew that Sara and Jacob, being young parents still, didn't understand that worry for your kids never ends. While Sara went to the counter to retrieve their tickets and boarding passes, Thomas and Jacob talked.

"I noticed you had a talk with your mother last night, son. Is everything all right? Other than the problem at work?" Thomas asked gently, not wanting to push. He tried to hide his feelings from showing on his face when he looked at his son.

"Yeah, Dad. It's all good, really."

"So, there are no real problems at home other than work then? Anything I can help with … son?"

"No, Dad. I'm okay. Nothing else. Thanks for asking, though."

"I really hope the kids won't be too much for you and Irene," Sara said, being a typical mom, feeling a bit guilty.

"You don't need to worry about that, it's our pleasure. You just take care of yourselves, and we'll watch over the little ones."

"I appreciate it, Dad, I really do. Any problems at all, just give a call and we'll head right back."

"Okay, you two, better get going before you miss your flight." It was hugs all around. Heading down the ramp to board the plane, Jacob suddenly turned around and went back several steps to hug his father once more.

"I love you, Dad."

Thomas began to well up. His son hadn't done that in a long time.

"I love you, son. Be careful." Just before Jacob turned to go back, his father grabbed his forearm. "Don't forget you have a friend in John Keegan if you ever need him, okay?" He let go of his son, and Jacob's eyes bugged out for a second.

"Bye, Dad."

"Bye, son." Jacob slowly backed up, then turned and trotted back down the ramp to Sara.

They arrived back home in the early hours of the morning — too late for calls. Jacob was trying to deal with this guardian story. He told Sara about it, and that he was having a hard time believing any of it — whether it came from Vargas, Sara's grandmother, or even his own mother. "It all sounds like a bunch of old wives' tales," he spouted, but Sara was sure he was simply trying to convince himself not to believe.

The next morning Sara was already up, and the smell of Jacob's favourite dark roast was in the air as he came flying down the stairs. He prepared a cup to go, thanked and kissed Sara, and headed for the door.

"Jacob," Sara called out to him. He stopped and stood still for a second, closed his eyes briefly, and slowly turned his head, the door slightly opened, with his hand on the knob.

"I know, sweetheart, I know," he said, trying to exude a confident and comforting look.

"Be careful, anyway," she said in reply, her emotions gave way to a couple tears fighting their way out. He took a fast walk back to her and held her tight. He repeated his words, and out the door he went.

Jacob couldn't reach Pat on his phone, which was definitely not the norm. That feeling he had at the beach that something had gone wrong or was going to, was flaring inside him. The cream in his coffee he sipped on the way into town instantly curdled in his stomach.

Normally he would see Pat on site for an update on their projects, but he just wanted to see his friend — he needed to. He was nearing The Cider Mill when his phone started ringing. Once again, the hair on his neck began to rise, accompanied with another chill. He didn't want to look at it, but the bright glow in his peripheral annoyingly scratched at his vision. The call display was an unknown caller, so he ignored it. It dawned on him that the display could mean a hospital or any government agency, including the police, which only added anger to his fear.

Jacob knew the senior police officer, Paul Kelly, was close with Pat. Paul had worked with his uncle John years ago when he was a rookie. He was also made aware of Jonathon Vargas's status as a suspect. He, along with his fellow officers — regardless of rank — took turns following Vargas, trying to obtain an unsolicited DNA sample. And that had just become harder, as Vargas had three weeks vacation time, which he'd started a week ago. He wasn't travelling back and forth to work, so he wasn't as accessible. In fact, his vehicle never moved.

Jacob was at the entrance to the mill, being held back by the young officers, when he started coming unglued and yelling at Officer Kelly.

"What's going on, Paul? Why won't your guys let me through? Who's been hurt? And where the fuck is Pat?" His queries came in rapid succession.

Paul just finished talking to his forensics guy, with one smaller camera around his neck and a rather large one in his hand, propped against his knee to lighten its weight. A young woman stood next to him, carrying a large black case, and holding onto some evidence bags with her free hand. They both had on black, short-sleeved, collared shirts with the CPD logo on the chest. They walked away to their vehicle, and Paul hung his head down, wiped his brow, and walked over to a screaming Jacob O'Connell.

"I'm so sorry, Jacob, it's Pat. A scaffold collapsed with some drywall on it. It looks like it caused a pretty bad head injury. I'm really sorry, Jacob, Pat didn't survive."

"What the fuck are you talking about, Paul? Where's Pat? I want to see him right fucking now!" Jacob yelled out, his body vibrating, trying to push his way through the two uniformed cops.

"I'm sorry, Jacob, but he's gone," Paul said, placing his hand on Jacob's shoulder. The words that Paul Kelly spoke after "Pat didn't survive," fell silent to Jacob. He lost it completely and fell weak to his knees.

"NO! NO, NO, NO!" he screamed out. "What the … fuck! What are you talking about? Let me see Pat. You're a fucking liar… Jesus… No." The last syllable came out slow and weak and turned directly into a wail. He was inconsolable.

Again, he stood up and tried to push his way through the police. "Pat. Pat!" Jacob called out to his best friend. His voice hoarse now and tears streaming down his face. He fell to his knees again and bent over crying and screaming all at once. It was a horrible sound, and it had one of the officers crying in reaction to the level of Jacob's sorrow.

"Get those fucking people out of here!" Paul ordered one of his constables. He knelt beside Jacob and placed his hand on his heaving back. He was crying hard, and he began to vomit, which eventually, when nothing was left, turned into dry heaves.

"I'm sorry, Jacob, but we need to investigate. We need to find out exactly what happened here. For now, we're going to have to treat it like a crime scene until we have all the facts. We need to shut down the project and keep everyone out. Jacob, I'm truly sorry."

Hardly composed, he stood up and looked at Paul. "I want to see him, Paul. I want to see him now."

"We can't, Jacob. The coroner has to go in and claim the body."

"The body? What the fuck is wrong with you. He's not a body; he's my best friend," Jacob yelled out, nearly hysterical. Paul's reaction was to grab him and hang onto him, making sure he didn't pass out or fall. He walked him over to one of the cruisers and sat him down. Slowly, Jacob seemed to be calming himself down.

"You don't want to see him, Jacob, trust me. I know how much he meant to you, so I'll call you in a while. You can come down to the hospital and see him there, okay? Jacob, are you going to be okay, son?"

Paul helped him out of the cruiser and walked with him back to his truck.

"You're going to need to make some calls here, Jacob. Take a few minutes and catch your breath. Now, do you want us to call Mrs. Keegan or is that something you want to do?"

"No, I'll do it," he said, with an exhausted and hoarse voice, wiping his tears away with the back of his hands. "She hasn't heard anything yet?" Not even looking at Paul, Jacob asked the question staring straight ahead, clearly still in shock.

"No. He was found by your electrician when he came to work this morning."

"All right. I'll go see Heather. I'll talk to you later then. Thanks, Paul."

Jacob raised his arm to put the truck in gear, with an effort like he'd just fought fifteen rounds with a heavyweight. He pulled his truck to the farthest end of The Cider Mill's parking lot to face away from everything that was going on and he crumbled into tears again. Completely devastated in this news that made no sense to him. His suspicions were justifiably pointed in only one direction. *Would he go this far just to hurt me?* he wondered.

In the midst of his twisting emotions and jumbled thoughts, a sudden realization followed that ripped through his very core — *Sara*.

34

In Motion

Part 1

The truck fishtailed its way out of the gravel parking lot until its wheels found the pavement. Tires squealed for several feet as Jacob frantically sped away. *Home* was illuminated on the phone's display. He was pounding his fist on the steering wheel, because for him right now, waiting for the second ring to come to end, and Sara's voice to calm his panic induced fear, was an eternity.

"Hi, honey, how's the day—?" Her question was cut off.

"Thank God!" He bellowed, erratically pulling over to a full stop. For several seconds he couldn't breathe another word out while his head flopped between his arms holding the wheel.

Sara's voice through the phone's speaker asked repeatedly, "What's wrong?"

He fought with all his might to keep his composure until he got the words out, "Pat is dead."

After the shock and the cries over the phone from both ends finally subsided, he asked her to meet him at Heather's as fast as she could. This was news he didn't want to break alone.

When Heather saw Jacob pull into their huge horseshoe driveway, she thought nothing of it, since he often used the office there. But just a few minutes later when Sara's Suburban came bouncing in behind him, she knew something was wrong. Jacob slowly poured out of his truck with red, swollen cheeks stained from barely dried tears, and eyes completely bloodshot. All evidence to Heather, once close enough to see, that at a minimum her man was in trouble. She came out to the driveway to find out what was happening. The news crumpled her to the ground in a profound state of shock and sorrow. Pat was always the man she'd loved, from the very minute they met. An unbearable wailing came out of her, as Jacob and Sara carried her into the house.

Questions of where, why, and how screamed out from the house. Jacob did his best to try and explain what happened, concealing his own doubts and fears. They did what they could for her — making sure she was stable was the priority. The three of them remained together for a while, Jacob and Sara on either side of her on the sofa. Jacob promised to get all the answers for her as to how this could have happened. He pulled himself together and called a couple of men from work to come be with Heather and Sara, to make sure they weren't alone. Wanting those answers and needing to escape Heather's extreme sorrow, he left her with Sara and the others. With emotions and his intense resolve to carry out his duties of dealing with the police and coroner driving him, he was gone. The task of calling family members would need to fall on Sara and the others as the day went on.

Not quite to Paul Kelly's office, Jacob spotted him coming around the corner and walked straight to him. Paul gently grabbed him by the arm to lead him straight out the back door, and he lit up a smoke.

"Jacob, I was thinking, I have to clear the building for Health and Safety to come in and do their own investigation after we're done. But who knows construction better than you? If you can handle it, I'd like you to come to The Cider Mill and look at the scene. Pat has been taken to the hospital. Don't worry, they're treating him with respect. I made sure they wouldn't start an autopsy until he's been properly identified — procedure." Paul took a long haul off his cigarette, looking at the ground, kicking at a few pebbles.

His words meant a lot to Jacob at that moment. Paul had respected Pat in life, and now he was showing the same respect in death. It was clear that he also respected how they ran their business. Jacob still had to contemplate Paul's request.

"Look, before we get started, does it have to be Heather to identify Pat, because I don't think she can do it, not today, anyway."

"Oh … no. It can wait 'til tomorrow. But family, yes, unless there's none. Rules, you know," Paul lowered his voice to a whisper. "Before you answer, you should know I'm not legally supposed to do this. If it's found out, a defence lawyer would jump on it saying evidence was tainted. Not that we know that scenario is going to happen, but I would be remiss if I didn't tell you. We have to keep this between us, and no one else can hear of it — you understand that, right, Jacob?" Paul was leaning into Jacob like one spy talking to another. Jacob choked slightly on the smell of Old Spice and Export A.

"Yeah, I get it. Drop me off a block back, and I can get in from the river side. No one will see. So, yeah. Let's get this over with now," Jacob said with determined clarity.

"Honestly, I trust your judgement over theirs — government lackies. You sure you can you handle this, Jacob?" Paul asked, placing his hand on his shoulder.

"Yeah. I can handle it." Jacob shook off the irony over the government lackies comment not coming close to registering on Paul.

"Okay, then. Let's go see if this was an accident or not. Shall we?" Paul motioned toward his car.

"This wasn't an accident, Paul." Jacob spouted, getting inside the unmarked car.

"You can't say that, Jacob. We don't have anything to go on yet to make that determination, only assumption, really."

"Yeah, you're right. I'm just upset," Jacob said, staring out the passenger window, knocking on it with the back of his knuckles.

As he approached the mill, Jacob took a few deep breaths in and out like he was getting ready for a deep-sea dive, and in through the door he went. When he made it to where Pat died at the other end of the building, he discovered three partially assembled sets of scaffolding tipped over, with their planks off to the side. To get a quick grasp of this scene, Jacob stood back momentarily and surveyed it all. The fourth scaffold was down between bent-up braces and was partially covered by a dozen or more sheets of fireguard drywall. Next to that scaffold was another set of scaffolding that was still standing, both sets on lockable wheels. Beside the drywall was a paper tape dispenser, taping tools, and a five-gallon pail of pre-mixed taping mud spilled across the floor. And next to that were two eighteen-inch square by eight-inch thick galvanized and lead fire dampers, both covered in blood. The accident happened between the store and the restaurant, a clear and bright area.

Except the blood, none of what was there meant anything to Paul, not knowing anything about construction. Even though he was six-feet tall, two-hundred pounds, and well-built didn't mean he knew how to swing a hammer — he knew how, just not very well. His wife joked about how he was more dangerous to himself — and anyone nearby — with a drill than with a gun. And in telling Jacob this, he at least hoped it might distract him from his sorrow, if only for a minute. Just a few feet farther away from the debris was a large pool of Pat's blood from his head wound. This was the blood of Jacob's now-dead lifelong best friend, so Paul kept an eye on him, knowing all too well how it could affect even the toughest individual. He'd seen all sorts of people fall apart from a lot less trauma than this, but Jacob wasn't showing signs of losing it, and Paul was impressed with Jacob's bronze. Jacob squatted down and looked at the bracket on the bottom scaffold, where the diagonal brace locks in. He looked up at Paul.

"This release pin has been cut clean off, the other one too. There's four of them here," Jacob said, spinning around. He carefully picked up one of the pieces by its edges and showed it to Paul.

"Well, that makes sense, doesn't it?" Paul asked, looking puzzled.

"Two things Paul: cut not broken. You know ... like bent, twisted, or snapped," Jacob said, raising his eyebrows. "Okay," he said in reserved astonishment before continuing. "And two: if this happened from the scaffold collapsing, then how did it collapse to begin with? You see ... it can't, unless you purposely move the release on the pin. Or in this case, purposely cut one, both or all four and pull the other fucking brace off!" Jacob shouted out his angry conclusion. "The blood on those dampers look painted on, don't you think?" He didn't wait for a response. "This is so stupid, Paul. Pat wouldn't be so blind not to see, or so deaf not to hear this coming, behind him or not. FUCK!" The more he looked around, the more impassioned he was becoming.

"Okay, Jacob. I'm sorry. Let's get you out of here. You've answered all I need to know. The team already printed what they could, so, I'll see if I can get one off these pieces." Paul could see that Jacob was sliding back down into anger and sorrow, his emotions raw. He placed the pieces of metal in individual evidence bags and walked Jacob to the riverside door and made sure he was walking all right. Paul met up with him around the corner and they headed back toward the station.

Part 2

Things were quiet on the way back to town, with the exception of the annoying static and muffled voices coming from dispatch through the radio.

"You did a good thing for your friend, Jacob. I mean it, and I won't forget it. I'm sorry for upsetting you. I can't imagine how you must be feeling." Once far enough away from the crime scene, Paul pulled around to a side street and parked.

"Whatever it takes, Paul, whatever it takes," Jacob said tacitly.

Paul put his head down, rolled the window down, and lit another cigarette. "I hate this part of the job, and I'm sorry Jacob, but I need to ask, and I don't want to ask Heather if I don't have to. You know Pat, hell, better than anyone, except for maybe his mom and his wife. Did he have any enemies that you knew of? You were in business together. Were either of you having money problems that would land him in trouble? Was he having any affairs you knew of?"

"You're kidding, right?" Jacob asked, incensed. "Look, Pat was no different than me. Has anyone ever seen us getting shit-faced and scrapping it out in the bars, or going to the casino? You're on the wrong track here, Paul." Jacob calmed himself down. "Sorry, man, I'm being an asshole about this. It's just too raw and I'm right on the edge," he said, slamming the edge of his hand on the passenger door.

"That's perfectly understandable, but I have to ask these things, you know what I mean. I really am sorry."

"Ah, we're good, Paul. And in regard to money, we were doing really well, better than we ever dreamt of. Business was increasing every year and what loans we had are all paid off now. I mean, yeah, we finance some projects, but not very often. For the most part, we work on progress draws. We don't normally get too far in without payment, it's just good business. So, no, there are no liens on the business or loan sharks hiding in the shadows, and Pat was never a gambling man." Just saying Pat's name, Jacob started breathing heavily to ward off breaking out into tears again. "And as far as enemies, we've had a couple of run-ins with some bad trades along the way, nothing close to serious, though. There was the time that Neal Bishop hit on Heather at the annual garden party. It never went beyond a couple of punches thrown. And it was Heather who threw them. I have to say no on that score."

"I remember that." Paul let out a small giggle. "Yeah, well, Neal Bishop's an asshole at his best, everyone knows that." Paul looked over to Jacob and smiled.

"Okay ... Jacob, John told me about you and Sara with this Vargas piece of shit. Don't react, just listen. We've been trying to get the fucker's DNA, but he's a snaky bastard. So, I'll be going to question him, but whatever you're thinking, stay away." Paul's advice was friendly.

"I can get you his DNA with a couple of hard shots to his face," Jacob said keeping his head down.

"Jacob! Look, I'm serious here. If he comes around you or Sara for any reason, call me right away. Here's my card with my cell number. Don't call the precinct!" Paul looked Jacob in the eye. "You understand?"

"I understand, Paul. And thanks," Jacob replied, shaking Paul's hand.

The responsibilities in front of him were completely overwhelming. Paul dropped him off next to his vehicle. Once inside his truck, he took a moment to think about his friend and try and compose himself again. A call to Sara's cell phone went straight to voicemail, then the truck tore out of the parking lot. The next call was to the Keegans', and to his surprise, one of the guys from work answered, and not Sara. He assumed that watching over Heather would include Sara taking the calls, not the guys.

"Can I speak to Sara, please? Her cell went to voicemail."

"She's not here, Jacob. She went to the drugstore to pick up a prescription for Heather." Jacob hung up and his heart fell to his stomach — the sick feeling he'd felt at the cottage returned, but with far more intensity than he'd felt then or any moment since. His thoughts were scrambled in a panic again, because his gut had been accurate before, with dreadful results. He headed straight over to the drugstore not far from Heather's. His truck came bouncing in over the speed bumps inside the mini-mall where the pharmacy was. Sara's Suburban was nowhere to be found, she wasn't in the store, and the employees inside said they hadn't seen her.

Jacob drove at high-speed, running red lights and stop signs straight back to Heather's to see if Sara had returned. None of his employees knew about the history between Vargas and Jacob, not in that detail, and Heather didn't know that Pat was privy to the information Hector had provided. And she certainly had no clue that Vargas could be responsible for her husband's death.

Everything inside of Jacob told him Vargas had Sara. He had never asked God for anything in his life, but he repeatedly prayed out loud for her safety. He had the phone in his hand, but what Vargas said about taking everything from him, stopped him from calling Paul. Vargas made clear that's what this was all about, to cause him as much pain as possible. And what just happened with Pat, indicated to him this was indeed the beginning of Vargas's endgame. Not seeing Sara's car at Heather's made his instinct to get home right away almost impossible not to follow, but in that split second, he remembered Pat's guns in the office. He parked on the side street so no one inside the house would see him.

Pat, who was an avid hunter, had a .22 rifle for small game and a .30-06 for deer and caribou, plus a 12-gauge shotgun for ducks and a .410 for pheasants. He frantically fumbled through the top desk drawer to find the key for the gun case. He didn't bother with the rifles, since he was inexperienced with bolt-action guns. He made it known what he would sacrifice to protect Sara and their children. He had no idea what he was going up against today, so he would reluctantly bring the shotgun as back up, just in case.

When rustling through the rest of the drawers for the shells, he came across Pat's old World War II .45 calibre semiautomatic handgun, in mint condition. He forgot all about Pat getting it as a gift from his uncle John. He busted the lock off the case and took the gun, along with some shotgun shells. He checked to make sure the clip was full and placed the gun into his back waistband under his shirt. As he was about to leave the office, his cell phone rang. He quickly grabbed it to silence the ringer, and answered, praying it was Sara.

"Jacob, Jesus Christ, I just heard what happened to Pat. I'm so sorry, buddy, is there anything I can do?" Hector's words were always in a hurry — a professional habit.

Jacob sighed in desperation. "Ah…" Jacob was heading to his truck with the phone between his ear and shoulder, and his pause gave space for Hector to jump in — another bad habit.

"Hey, the last day I saw him at The Cider Mill, I'm pretty sure I saw Vargas leaving there just after talking to him. Creepy, eh? I wonder—?"

Jacob ended the call and hopped in the truck. What his gut was telling him was just confirmed. He had nothing but tunnel-vision now, as he barrelled down the road to the farmhouse. Home is where Vargas would do the most damage. Jacob was more than confident this is where he would take Sara. No time for calls, no time for cops, just get there. He followed his instincts, and there was no second-guessing it. There was no time.

35

Endgame

Part 1

Sara pulled into a parking spot at the mall that housed Heather's drugstore. She stopped briefly to fix herself up a bit in the mirror after so much crying. Heather had occasional bouts of anxiety, so Sara had the empty bottle of Ativan to refill. The drugs were desperately needed now. She stepped out of her car, closed the door, and turned with her purse in one hand and the empty bottle in the other. The Suburban was near a foot higher than her, so no one saw Vargas sneak up behind her when she was walking to the rear of the store. One hand was around her mouth, the other plunged a syringe in her neck. But she was too fast, knocking his hand away, pulling the needle out and ripping the skin on her neck in the process. Struggling for her life, she screamed out, but it was no use — he managed to pull her down to the ground, keeping her mouth covered. Her legs kicked wildly in every direction, trying to strike anywhere and everywhere. It was a courageous effort, but he wrapped his legs around her and pulled out another syringe to subdue her. In seconds, she was unconscious.

He loaded Sara on the floor behind the Suburban's passenger seat, taped her mouth shut, and zip-tied her hands behind her back. In his frantic search for the keys he'd dropped between the two seats, precious seconds ticked away. In that panic, he forgot to tie her legs. He pulled out of the parking lot no different than anyone else out shopping, except for the repulsive smile on his face when he looked in the rear-view at his prize catch. He wasted little time getting out to the O'Connell farm. When they arrived, Sara was just starting to stir a bit, only able to moan at that point. Vargas threw her small, light frame over his shoulder like she were a sack of potatoes.

Foggy patches of vision were slowly becoming exposed, her eyes fighting to open, yet what little she could see were incoherent images that she was unable to process. She was dizzied to a near vertigo and feeling nauseous. She also started becoming aware of her difficulty breathing, with the tape still on her mouth. A familiar picture was forming now — her room, the stained-glass lamp, her grandmother's comforter, and the recently added white-and-silver striped wallpaper on the exterior wall. A collage still out of focus, but slowly clearing to form shapes. She had the taste of metal in her mouth, but all she could smell was a disgusting and familiar perfume-like cologne. What she was feeling was akin to waking from anaesthetic and morphine, but without the euphoria. The outline of a figure was slowly coming into focus, and to her horror, it was Vargas, sitting on her cedar hope chest. She was terrified, which made her angry.

She screamed under the duct tape, and despite being muffled, what she was saying was fairly clear for Vargas, having a lot of experience with women screaming at him through taped lips. "What are you doing?! You prick! You fucking cocksucker! Let me go, you sick bastard!" She was raging, kicking her legs frantically on her bed to the point of falling off. Vargas's laugh was repugnant. If he wanted a fight, she was more than willing to oblige him.

"Sara, my dear. Such language for a lady." He picked her up off the floor and slammed her back on the bed. He reached into a small backpack and pulled out a Walther PPK. He cocked it, holding it in his hand and showing it off, pointing it to the ceiling. He placed the gun on the windowsill, and with his legs still on the ground, he lay on top of her and very slowly licked the side of her face, from chin to temple. Sara screamed through the tape, and in her battle and violent kicking and bucking up, her head hit Vargas hard enough it made his nose bleed. She had to stop herself from vomiting in reaction to his scratchy beard, the stink of his cologne, and his repulsive tongue on her face.

Losing control of Sara long enough for her to get a shot at him was an unacceptable feeling for him. He recalled the night Jacob broke his nose, and the trip to the hospital the following night when he couldn't breathe and how much pain and grief that caused him. It was several nights of holding his head over a hot pot of water so the steam could clear his nasal passages from the caked-on blood. Having that memory evoked every sensation that coincides with a psychotic rage. He started choking Sara until her face was red, her eyes were bulging, and the fear on her face was food for his compulsion. He had an empty look to his face, his eyes seemed to go black and pupils dilated. Once he reached that point of vengeful satisfaction, he let go, and sat her upright. He picked up the gun again.

"Now, Sara ... be a good girl or you won't live long enough to see me kill your man." Sara screamed and squirmed violently, but this time he just pushed her on her back and laughed. "When you calm down, I'll sit you up straight again so you can watch the show. Now, be quiet." He leaned over a bit and looked in her eyes. "Or do you want another kiss?" Her eyes bugged out in opposition. "That's what I thought. And this ... I didn't bring this beauty for you," he said, slowly rubbing his gun in a sexual caress. This is for Jacob, but if you don't shut up with your screaming under that tape and flailing about, well." His point was made.

He went about pulling the cedar chest around so the length of it would face the bedroom door. He put his gun back on the windowsill and sat on the chest, taking turns between watching Sara and looking out the window for Jacob to come up the laneway. Now the tears were rolling down Sara's face, and as the minutes seem to fly by, her fear for Jacob became overwhelming.

Part 2

Sara's Suburban was parked right in front of the steps of the porch leading to the front door of the house. The driver's side door and both passenger doors were left open, so Jacob concluded his suspicions didn't require any further validation. "I wonder how long this sick prick's been planning this? Hang on, Sara." He was quietly speaking to himself, then leaning over and pounding the dash. As he closed in on Sara's vehicle, he slowed to a crawl, his heart and head pounding from all that was happening. The steering wheel slipped in his sweaty hands as he pulled off the gravel lane and onto the grass. He went to the side of the house opposite their bedroom, attempting to gain some cover while entering the house. He knew Vargas was aware of his arrival.

Once on the porch, he found pictures stapled to the wall, the posts, and railings and randomly spread across the floor. There were shots of Sara at different times throughout her life at different locations, always from a distance. Some were with Jacob and some were with the kids. Jacob was shocked at the level of his obsession and wondered what kind of nightmarish ending Vargas had in mind for his family. But he wasn't going to stand out in the open to make it easy for him. No, this was a rescue mission pure and simple, and his only concern was to get Sara out unharmed, by whatever means. With the shotgun in hand, he turned the corner on the veranda and approached the front door.

"Sara, are you okay?" he yelled out.

Vargas had her sitting on the chest in front of him facing the door. He pulled back the tape on her mouth. A nerve-shattering scream came out of her, yelling out his name before being cut off, and it was unlike anything Jacob had heard before from Sara. The fear and terror in her voice was painful for him to hear, but he also heard her anger, which, he hoped, was a good sign she might not be hurt. He squeezed his eyes shut firmly for a second and felt every emotion ranging from fear to rage. His throat was dry, making it difficult to swallow, and despite the humidity, his lips were chapped, and every part of him felt unnatural, making him want to jump out of his own body. But he knew he had to control himself, to control the strong instinct to run straight up to Sara, as he was unsure of what exactly was waiting. A sickening voice came out of Vargas.

"Come on in, Jacob, we're just hangin' out, having some fun. Come on and join in." He poorly imitated a southern drawl as he pushed the muzzle of his gun into Sara's temple. Jacob, taking care with each step ahead, knew that Vargas had the upper hand. He recalled how Vargas's emotions and reactions were all over the map at the building supply, and with little provocation.

"You know what's going to happen if you hurt her, Vargas. You know that, right? So, just let her go. The cops are on their way." Jacob's words didn't ring loud with confidence.

"Of course I'm aware. And this is where we find that out Jacob. It's just a matter of whether you're going to be able to keep sweet Sara alive by getting to me first — if you manage to get to me." Vargas lowered his voice for a second to whisper in Sara's ear. "This is so exciting, Sara. A little impromptu, but that makes it more fun. Oh, and Jacob," he said more loudly, "nice try with the cops being on their way bit. It's an A for effort, though." He sounded out of breath, partially fading in and out. Sara's strength in constantly struggling to get away was wearing him down. After the head-butt, he tied a scarf around her kicking legs, but when he wasn't looking, she easily pulled one leg out. She wasn't going to give up.

Jacob slowly peeked in through the entrance door, which was also left open. He laid the cumbersome shotgun down, sliding it under the living room chair, and pulled the .45 from the back of his pants. He quickly stepped across the floor to the stairs and started up. Beads of sweat started to roll in full drops down his forehead into his eyes, stinging and blurring his vision. He used his forearms to wipe the excess sweat away, with adrenaline steering him now.

There was a sense of faith he hadn't experienced before taking him to Sara, and his memories were walking with him. He was seeing pictures just like the blink of an eye, several with each step. The light in his hands when he reached out to touch Sara's head at six years old. Then Sylvia looking at him from the sidewalk at work, then in front of the building department. Standing beside Sara in the hospital and helping her get her footing in physiotherapy. As each memory came, so did his confidence and desire to protect her.

"Come on, Jacob, we're in the bedroom, where the action happens ... mmm. We're just getting to know each other, on a personal level, you know," Vargas said, sounding angry.

Jacob squeezed his eyes closed, repulsed by what he was hearing. Part way up the stairs, he could hear Sara's muffled efforts trying to break free. Strangely, Jacob's resolve took on an unusual calm, considering the urgency.

"Sara? Sara, are you okay? Has he hurt you?"

"She can't talk right at this moment, Jacob. But if you come a little closer, maybe you can make out what she's trying to say. I bet it's something like, 'HELP ME, JACOB! Please help me.'" His shrill voice cut through the silence of what was usually their peaceful home.

Sara's muffled cries were based in anger. She was angry that Vargas had managed to sneak up on her with a syringe. Her anger only increased her desire to break free of her restraints. The ties were cutting the skin on her wrists, but she ignored the pain. Her instincts to protect Jacob were rising to the surface with a fervour. Vargas pulled himself a little too close, so she head-butted him again, in reverse this time. It bloodied his nose and stunned him for a second or two, but her attempt to get away failed. He held the gun to her head again, but this time he cocked it next to her ear and threatened to kill her. He rubbed the blood from his nose on the back of her shirt.

After having regained control, he pulled the tape back for her to yell out, "He's got a gun, Jacob, get out!" She screamed, but the tape was put back so whatever else she said was muffled. Vargas continued to speak loud enough for Jacob's benefit.

"Oh, Sara, come on now. Jacob and I are here to settle an old score. He's not going anywhere. Are ya, Jake?" He started rubbing the barrel of the gun around the side of Sara's head and temple. Jacob stopped for a second, his face cringing, teeth gritting as he was reminded of Pat's murder. Feeling his frustration building, he calmed himself by thinking of how he could gain any advantage over the situation. He would prefer to take Vargas apart with his hands, but he sensed he knew what he was walking into.

Part 3

Vargas recalled a cold rainy night many years ago, standing on the roadside looking down a hill at a smashed-up truck slowly burning away. Seeing Pat slipping and sliding his way back down the ravine to get to his wife and best friend, soaked to the bone and shaking uncontrollably, was a delight to him.

"You know something, Jacob, you got in my way a long time ago. I tried to make you pay for that. I watched from the top of the road, you know, and saw your hands light up on her. I mean Heather, of course. How is she doing anyway?"

"You didn't have to go after Pat. You don't need to go after anyone other than me. If I'm the big problem in your life, then grow a pair and just take me on face to face and leave everyone else out of it."

"I didn't have to go after Rebecca, either, but that's what I do Jacob, it's where the fun is. Hell, I had a great time taking a tire iron to Mr. Mouthy Bike Courier's head, over and over and … well, you get the picture. It's too bad I couldn't take out my old pops before cancer got him, but you can't win them all. There's more like me out there, you know. Like the kid who set fire to the boathouse for me — if you know what to look for, they're out there for sure."

"What's the matter, Vargas? You can't get anyone of your own, so you have to stalk someone else's life? Why me? Why us? Because you fucked up as a kid, you blame us? Why can't you just leave us alone for Christ's sake?" Jacob screamed at him, then lowered his voice again. "Do us all a favour — go find your own life. Or end it."

"That's very funny, Jacob. But honestly, where would the fun be in that? Besides, Keegan is on my ass, so, time to move on. There's no turning back now. I have no idea how the hell he found that out ... hmm, well, what can a person do?"

"You call this fun? You sick bastard!"

"Okay, Jacob, enough!" Vargas said, holding the gun to Sara's head again, his arm tiring. "I can hear you're getting closer. This goes down my way this time. If you want Sara to live, walk in here slowly, and show me you have no weapons. Even a Boy Scout like you knows how to use a gun. Come on, Jake, that's the deal." He put his mouth up to Sara's ear and whispered, "When this is over, you and I are going to have some real fun. Maybe we'll go and pick up Mary and Ben and have them join in." He giggled. But Sara went berserk, and, trying to hold her became near impossible. Vargas was getting worn out. He cracked her on the side of the head with the gun, then pushed it harder against her scull to calm her down, which it did.

He was putting on a torturous show for them, and he loved the sound of his own voice. He couldn't help himself. In the hallway with approximately eight feet to go to the bedroom door, Jacob had both hands on the .45, tapping the barrel on his forehead. He knew he was running out of time trying to think of how he could get Sara out of that room. He was next to the bathroom, which entered the master bedroom as an en suite. He tried the bathroom doorknob, but it was locked — no surprise there. Vargas continued to ramble.

"Come on, already!" he bellowed. "Jacob the hero, the rescuer, the guardian. Come do your best. I can hear you out there. Let's see what you can really do for poor Sara here. Or what you're willing to do — there's the rub." He kept trying to taunt Jacob. "So, tell me Jacob, what would happen if everyone knew what you could do? Do you think they would still think you the stand-up citizen or would they look at you as some sort of circus freak?" There was no reply coming. "ANSWER ME, DAMN IT!" Vargas screamed, quickly becoming enraged again.

"I don't know, Jonathon. I suppose they would look at me like a freak. I don't know much about any of this. Why are you so interested?"

"Oh, it's Jonathon now, is it? Really, are you actually trying to manipulate me with kindness? That's a game you don't play very well, Jacob. It must be all those years of being a respectable man that's infected your head." He laughed. "You're certainly not very adept when it comes to lying."

Jacob knew his rambling wasn't going to last much longer, and that he had a few minutes, if that, to try whatever he could come up with to get Sara out. On top of the humidity, which was causing constant perspiration, he was holding a gun, which he'd never done before and his body wouldn't stop shaking. He moved down the hall far enough he could see Sara in the mirror from Mary's room across the hall. His stomach bottomed out seeing her with duct tape on her mouth, looking angry and scared at the same time. He could see Vargas sitting up, then scrunching down on the chest to stay behind her when the time came. But most terrifying was watching him raising his gun up and down to her head and back to his lap.

"I guess not, but there's no talking to you, is there Vargas, because you're completely fucking insane!" Jacob tried to keep him off-kilter, angry and distracted. "So, why don't you just let Sara go and you and I can deal with this out in the yard like men. How does that sound to you? You complete and total piece of shit." He finally made eye contact with Sara, being careful not to let Vargas see him. He raised his index finger in front of his lips, and Sara's eyes said it all — *You're kidding, right?* She motioned her eyes to the bed, and in that moment something extraordinary happened — they could hear each other's thoughts. Not a conversation, but thoughts of meaning and direction. They knew what to do. They were ill-equipped in the moment to understand what was happening to them. It astonished and scared them at the same time. She prayed Vargas wouldn't notice as she indicated the direction again.

All the while, Vargas continued. "You sound angry, Jacob. Does losing a friend upset you?"

"Yeah, well, what do you expect? You're just a piece of shit … a coward. Pat would have ripped you to pieces." With Jacob buying what little time he could, he looked to Sara again, and they knew what they were going to do. She would have to move out of the way to provide him that one perfect opportunity. She was filled with dread, her stomach empty, but still nauseous, but she was ready. And his heart started racing faster, his sweaty hands making it difficult to maintain his grip on the gun. This was no scrap in the yard over inappropriate words or looks toward your wife. When he thought of his dad at that moment, Jacob wondered if he had the same courage his father did.

Jacob decided he would deliver the last taunt before he and Sara braved the moment that would determine the balance of their lives.

"What is your real problem, Vargas? Are you frustrated because your boyfriend wouldn't paint your toenails? Or did he want to play the man all the time? Or maybe it's little kids you like. You can't be a human being in real life, can you Vargas? Come on … admit it. No? Then why don't you let Sara go and we'll finish this thing right now? Last chance."

Again, they looked to each other and she motioned her eyes one last time. Knowing the direction she would be going in, Jacob closed his eyes for a second and pulled the gun up to his chin, then looked Sara in the eye one last time, and made his move.

36

Reckoning

Part 1

Sara could feel and see herself completing her jump away from Vargas before it happened. Time had slowed, nearly standing still for both of them. The breath in her lungs holding, waiting for an exhale when she heard his voice. *Ready, sweetheart? It's one, two, and go, okay? I love you, Sara O'Connell. It's going to be okay.* And when she heard that last number, Sara lunged off the cedar chest toward the bed, and Jacob spun into the doorway. They'd waited for a moment when Vargas was resting the gun on his lap, and he had it pointed it in the direction opposite to where she landed. In two seconds, Jacob looked at Vargas. He had the drop on him. He knew that if he did anything other than let go of his gun, Jacob would end him. In unison, Jacob and Sara moved so fast, Vargas didn't stand a chance. Vargas smiled in such a way as to say, *you got me*; yet, he attempted to turn his gun.

Jacob fired four shots in rapid succession, causing a deafening sound that left their ears ringing. And the room filled with smoke. With his complete lack of experience, he didn't realize how much of a hair trigger was on the .45. It was hard to distinguish through the noise of gunfire, but Vargas did manage to get one round off. Along with that noise was the sound of glass smashing. One of the bullets had gone through Vargas's chest and out the bedroom window. He looked surprised after Jacob fired, but he managed one last smile before he crumpled into a pile on the floor.

Jacob dropped his gun and rushed to Sara, carrying her out into the hall and standing her up. The smell of gunpowder followed them from the bedroom, smoke slowly dissipating in the air. He wasn't exactly a sharp shooter by any means, but four bullets from a .45 calibre centre mass at short range will stop anyone. It helped put an end to the terror of this day, and all the years Vargas had infected their lives.

Jacob cut the zip ties from Sara's wrists, revealing the damage they'd done. She didn't care; she leapt into Jacob's arms, wrapping her own above his shoulders, squeezing like she would never let go. She wailed out loud for the deliverance of the moment, and to be in each other's arms, safe once again. They both cried and kissed and hugged repeatedly. The whole event hadn't taken that long to play out in real time, but it felt like an eternity to them as they had to listen to Vargas ingratiate himself. Jacob started to examine Sara, asking if she was hurt anywhere other than her wrists. She happily responded "no." Both in shock, they headed toward the stairs and down toward the kitchen, where calling the police was top of the list.

They were on the last step when Jacob suddenly felt all the energy leave his body, collapsing onto the kitchen floor, and taking Sara down along with him.

"Jacob? Jacob, honey, where are you hurt? Oh my God, did you get shot?" She started pulling on his shirt, frantically inspecting his body for any injuries.

"I don't think so," he said, his voice barely audible. He looked up to her, his face growing pale. "You know how much I love you and Mary and Ben, right? All of you."

"Of course I do, but don't talk like that. You're scaring me." She was drowning in fear, briefly staring into his eyes. He smiled, and pulled her hand to his heart, pressing her palm down on his chest. His eyelids grew heavier, and he fought to keep them open, but they finally closed, and his hands slipped away from hers.

"No, no, no, Jacob, what's happening? I don't see a hole. I don't see any blood. Jacob, wake up now, honey, please wake up." She was completely overwrought, slapping his face, shaking him and screaming. "No, Jacob. Please, no," she pleaded, over and over again, but it was no use, Jacob wasn't responding. She knew he hadn't simply passed out and he wasn't wounded.

He died in Sara's arms. All of the screaming and shaking couldn't stop this stark reality from unfolding in front of her. After calling 911, she collapsed, crying uncontrollably, unwilling to accept this. She lay down and curled up next to his body and put his arm around her, the way they'd slept together a thousand other times.

Jacob was gone. He found himself back at the park in his hometown where he played as a child countless times. There he could see the finch he saved and a few other animals he tended to over the years all in the park together, surrounding him. He continued to walk through a veil of light from one scene to the next. Across the street was six-year-old Sara. He could see himself on the porch with her and his sister, Kate, all enjoying vanilla cookies and orange juice.

When he turned his gaze, he watched himself cross the road to where Sara lay after being struck by Mr. Grimmer and touching her head with the light coming from his hands. *There it is*, he thought, with a big smile, never having seen that light before today. He went into the ravine with Heather when Pat was on the side of the highway flagging down traffic. He saw the look on Heather's face as she came to. The moment had turned fear to elation, and he could see her peace and contentment as she thanked him.

He was getting a living visual tour of the moments in his life that had previously been beyond his reach. It wasn't quite like his dream, where he watched these moments roll down on a giant screen. It was as though he was walking through all that had been hidden from him for so long — the final pieces were being filled in. He stopped in this tour and knelt next to Sara in front of the building department after her accident. He adored her and simply wanted to look upon her.

He didn't need to go further. It was all there for him to see and understand who he was and what he was. His final and most important act had been to save Sara's life for the last time. He was comfortable now that she was safe, and even though he couldn't understand how, he knew she would remain so until her natural end. He had comfort in knowing his children couldn't be in better hands.

The price he had to pay was of no concern to him. His beliefs guided him, and his heart spoke to his only purpose — to be with Sara, Mary, and Ben for whatever time was needed. It was to love them and protect them to the best of his ability, and for that, he received what he considered the greatest gift of all: their love in return.

Part 2

Officer Paul Kelly sat across from Sara in the precinct. He'd wrapped up his investigation of Pat Keegan's murder and the events in her home. It was a clear self-defence situation, with the exception of the illegal possession of a handgun. However, neither Jacob nor Pat were around to worry about that.

Paul had a face of genuine sorrow and with soft words, he said, "So, Sara, your house has been cleared. You can go back home with the kids whenever you think you're able to." Paul grew silent again, struggling with this conversation. "Ahem … as far as Mr. Keegan is concerned, the coroner confirmed blunt force trauma and the murder weapon was found. It has been sent in for DNA analysis, but that's all pretty much moot now." Paul leaned over his desk to look Sara in the eye. "Look, Sara … I can't tell you how sorry I am about all of this. Jacob, Pat, just all of it. If there's anything you need from me, please … and I mean it, call me any time, day or night, okay?" Paul looked down at his desk for a moment. "I just wish Jacob…" He caught himself before going further.

At this point, Sara was like a deer in the headlights and was running on pure adrenaline and a mother's necessity to keep her children safe and well. She lifted her head and looked at Paul after his near faux pas. The look said it all.

"Okay, Paul, thanks for everything." It was an expressionless reply from Sara. She had one last event to get through before she would collapse to grief and that was to bury her husband. Jacob's best friend, Pat's funeral was just the day before.

"Sara, one last thing. Uh … the coroner completed Jacob's autopsy because of the circumstances, and well, there were no injuries. He didn't have a heart attack or aneurysm. He just, well, it was ruled undetermined death by natural causes, just so you're aware. I just don't understand what happened to him. Anyway, again Sara, don't forget I'm here if you need me, okay?" Paul rose from his chair and escorted Sara out of the precinct and into her vehicle.

The community of Clarington was shaken by the recent events. Most members of the family from Pat's side had stayed in town long enough to attend Jacob's funeral. He was like family to Pat and most of his relatives — they were best friends to the end. Irene and Sara sat side by side inside the funeral home consoling one another. Sara grabbed Irene's hand and whispered in her ear, "How can this be real? He wasn't going to shoot. We should have told him. We should have told him, Irene," Sara said, breaking out into tears again. "We wouldn't be here now if we told him."

"Please, Sara, honey. We don't know that either way. We did what we believed was right, and Jacob would have wanted us to hold on to that, and each other." Irene put her arm around Sara and held her while she cried. "If we did tell him, it might be you in that casket, and we both know with a certainty that Jacob would not want that. That man was never going to stop unless Jacob stopped him. He probably saved a lot of other people from that maniac that he would've hurt or killed." Her words helped soothe some of the pain Sara was experiencing. Irene felt a natural maternal need to be strong for the family — both families. And Sara loved Irene as her own, and she leaned on her just the same. For Irene, she would grieve at home later, alone.

Sara's parents were both having health difficulties — Joe with diabetes and heart disease, and Shannon with the onset of dementia — but they managed to attend the funeral. They sat behind Sara, her mother with her hand on Sara's shoulder. Sara turned around to them and squeezed their hands. In between gasps for air she managed to get out how much she loved and cherished them. Joe was in a wheelchair, having lost his leg from the knee down thanks to diabetes, but it didn't stop him from rising with the rest for the priest to do his service. And when the time came, he held Sara like he had when she was a child, then lost control and cried with her.

A light rain fell the day Jacob was buried, and many of the attendants had to stand outside of the funeral home due to the large turnout. It was no different with Pat's funeral. Sara read a beautiful heart-wrenching eulogy for her husband that included his best friend. She promised Pat and Jacob that together — with Heather and Melissa in the front row holding Mary and Ben — they would keep Able Hands going for everyone involved. Sara read out that both men never liked the term "working for"; they preferred "working with," and they believed they would have wanted everyone to keep going, to keep creating. This news was well-received by all who knew them, and all those who worked with them throughout the years. There couldn't be a better tribute to their memory and their talents.

James, Michael, and Kevin formed half of the pallbearers, and they carried their little brother to his grave, shaking with tears they couldn't hold back. After setting his casket down on the taught straps, they couldn't stand by and listen to the priest again. They all made the sign of the cross, kissed their forefinger and thumb, and went to stand by the hearse, with heads down and hands folded in front. The priest finished his standard farewell for the dearly departed and everyone slowly made their way back to their vehicles. Sara had Mary on one hand and Ben on the other, as they completed their slow dirge back to the car. Without any warning, Ben suddenly broke free from her grip and ran back to his father's grave. Sara knew Ben wasn't ready to grasp the reality of his father being gone. He was already back to the grave before she could catch up, so she walked slowly to give him time and see what he would do. He bent down and grabbed a handful of earth and threw it onto the casket. He was too upset or scared to do it along with everyone else there.

Sara was watching Ben go through this when suddenly, she stopped in her tracks. She could swear there was a familiar glow about Ben's little hands. Astonished, Sara put her hand to her mouth. Her expressions appeared to fluctuate, her emotions created looks of worry combined with sadness and joy. She walked over to Ben, picked him up into her arms and turned him around to look at her.

"Ben, honey, Daddy is gone to heaven to be with the angels."

"I want him to come back, Mommy." Ben stopped crying, but some tears still fell.

"I know you do. So do I, but he can't. He has to stay with the angels because they need his help. But he will always be watching over you and Mary, and me — all of us."

"He will?"

"Yes, he will. And he will be right here with you, in a special place in your heart, forever." She gently tapped Ben's chest. "Your daddy was a hero, a very brave man, and he loved you so much. He doesn't want you to be sad anymore. He wants you to be happy. Do you think you can do that, honey?"

Ben smiled through drying his tears and hugged his mother as hard as he could. He looked at her and nodded his head with vigor.

"Yes, I can, Mommy. Daddy told me I can do it."

"He did, did he? That's wonderful, honey. When did he say that?"

"Just now," Ben said, smiling, looking back to his father. And Jacob, leaning up against the tree near his casket, smiled and waved goodbye to his son. He turned around, began walking into a small grove of pines that lined the graveyard, and slowly faded into the light of day.

Forever Grateful

The list of people humbles me, but I must thank my mom, Irene, my Sister, Marie, and my friend Phil, for their love, support and constant encouragement.

About the Author

Mark J. Cannon was born and raised in Canada, a country he's travelled several times from coast to coast, with breathtaking scenes that painted the way. After over thirty years working in construction, time, at last, allowed Mark to create this story. It was the support of family and friends, with personal experiences along the way, that inspired his first foray into fictional writing. It's only the beginning.

CPSIA information can be obtained
at www.ICGtesting.com
Printed in the USA
LVHW051254130120
643337LV00016B/372/P